Also by Tony Cohan

THE FLAME
CANARY
OUTLAW VISIONS
NINE SHIPS

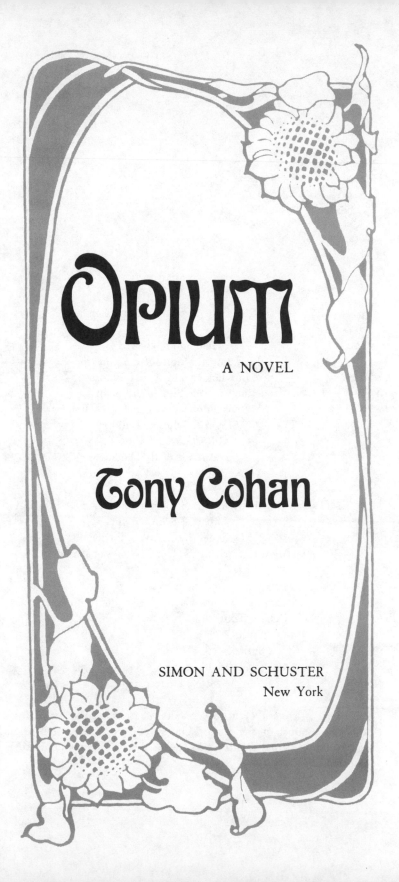

OPIUM

A NOVEL

Tony Cohan

SIMON AND SCHUSTER
New York

SIMON AND SCHUSTER and colophon are registered trademarks of
Simon & Schuster, Inc.
Designed by Levavi & Levavi
Manufactured in the United States of America

1   3   5   7   9   10   8   6   4   2
Library of Congress Cataloging in Publication Data
Cohan, Tony.
    Opium.
    I. Title.
PS3553.O41606   1984   813'.54   84-5605
            ISBN: 0-671-47327-1

The courageous and seminal work of two people deserves special acknowledgment, one for his information, the other for her art: Alfred W. McCoy, whose pioneering book *The Politics of Heroin in Southeast Asia* inspired my story from the outset; and Han Suyin, whose novels and memoirs lend feeling and vision to cold events. I am also indebted in different ways to the valuable work of Peter Ward Fay, Paolo Lionni, Dan Sherman, Gordon Beam, Gary Snyder, Richard Hughes, Fenton Bresler, Jackie Pullinger, David Halberstam, W. P. Morgan, Jean Cocteau and Arthur Waley; and to those who cannot be named.

To Maya

Prologue

The northern Thai town of Chiengmai, hot most of the year, grows fevered in April. From all over the world the opium dealers come to buy, filling the bars and hotels and teahouses.

In a cramped teak shed where Alec Potter had squeezed himself atop sacks of rice, among beer crates and barrels and casks and crawling insects, he was slowly drowning in his own sweat. The slatted wall facing him had a knothole needing no further enlargement to offer him a view, if he put his eye to it, into the dusky teahouse on the other side. He had paid good baht to the owner, a wizened Chinese-Lahu known simply as Old So, for this perch. Money alone wouldn't have gotten him here; Old So had debts to Potter's family going back to Grandpa Potter, who had come from across the sea to harvest brown and yellow souls for the Lord sixty years earlier.

Potter would later remark the date: April 10, 1963.

Through the knothole he watched Old So scuff across the reed matting and begin shooing the regulars out into the flat, dusty afternoon street. Potter knew them all: Ma, the armless betel-chewing woman who sold warm Cokes and oranges at a stall with her feet; Touby, the gaunt Meo arms trader who peddled U.S. M-16s strung across his bare chest for $250 each; the idle gray crones with eyes of celadon, smokers of the pipe. Old So's leather mouth pulled down taut in frozen grimace reminded Potter of Kurosawa films at the Brattle in Cambridge.

Two months back from Far East Studies at Harvard, Potter spoke Thai, the hill dialects, some Chiu Chao, and a little Cantonese. Jaunty, glib, good-looking, he was a candidate for a new Asia pretty boy; an American with languages and a history in the area was like found gold. Potter had allowed himself to be courted by every agency in Washington but intended to stay independent; the northern Thailand he had come home to after seven years was too rich with private opportunity. He ridiculed both his dead grandfather and his father—a sometime missionary, CIA stringer, and museum director in town—for having danced to Washington's fife and drum. A State Department evaluator had noted in Alec's folder: "Sharp. Really sharp." A scribbled addendum said: "A smartass."

Licking salty sweat raining from his eyebrows, Potter secured his spot on the rice bags, felt for the Walther semiautomatic on his hip, leveled his breathing, and watched.

Old So locked the door and closed the shutters. He dragged a large round table to the middle of the room and arrayed seven chairs around it. He made ready a pot of tea and set out five thimble cups, Chiu Chao style. Old So's lips were shaking like petals; Potter had never seen him like this.

Then the slits of light around the far door were obliterated, and a knock came. Old So scraped over and opened the door partway.

A small trim man appeared in backlit silhouette—a rich middle-aged Hong Kong Chinese, Potter surmised from the haircut, tailored slacks, and silk pongee shirt. He kept one hand in his jacket pocket; Potter couldn't see his face. Behind him were other men.

The visitor spoke in sharp Swatownese, the Chiu Chao dialect, as if addressing a domestic: "What is three times eight?"

Old So, his voice a dusty tremolo, answered: "Twenty-one."

This odd answer seemed to satisfy the man. "Haven't you died yet?" he snapped, his voice like the chop of a hand.

"I have died once."

"How did you die?"

Old So looked skyward, appealing to some rusty deity to bring him the phrase. His interrogator stood still as stone in the doorway.

"By being covered with a yellow quilt."

The visitor brushed silently past Old So into the room, followed by four others. Old So, trembling with relief, trailed them in, his sandals scraping the worn slats.

In the shed, Alec Potter's mind was running wild calculations off the quick cram of lore that boozy, decrepit Peg, the local British hand and former Hong Kong customs officer, had given him the night before in the shadows of the Bhubing Palace: "You want to look for your twenty-one in all configurations, Alec. There's your tipoff."

Three times eight is not twenty-four but twenty-one, Old So had said: the character for Hung, the Heaven on Earth Society. The "yellow quilt" would have been a reference to the Hung flag. And twenty-one is composed of four, eight, and nine, the ceremonial number of the Shan Chu, the Hill Chief. "That's the head bloke, Alec, the leader," Peg had croaked. "If they speak Chiu Chao, then it's the Sun Yee On, the biggest Triad in Asia. It's a *gong sou,* a big talk between Triads. Major doings, Alec. These chaps mean business."

Now Potter watched the man who had entered step through the dusty leaking light to the round table. Facing Old So, he placed his left hand in the center of his chest, thumb up, little finger down, the other fingers bent back into his palm.

This then was the Shan Chu, or Hill Chief, the leader of the Sun Yee On. Seeing this display of rank, Old So seemed to curl into himself. He raised his own left hand to his chest with thumb, middle, ring, and little fingers extended: the signal of the Grass Slipper, or Messenger.

Two others took seats on either side of the Hill Chief. One, Potter surmised, was the Fu Shan Chu, the Deputy, and the other the Pak Tsz Sin, the Adviser, known as White Paper Fan.

The two remaining figures, large and swarthy, stood fiercely on either side of the door, arms crossed, pockets fat with weapons. Each gave his hand signal—left hand forward with thumb raised, third and little fingers clenched—identifying him as a Hung Kwan, Red Pole, a rank-and-file fighter known by the number forty-nine.

Soon after, the other faction entered in the same numbers and rankings and each took his place opposite the Sun Yee On. These were the powerful Green Pang, originally from Shanghai, who had taken up exile in Hong Kong and abroad. Peg, who had seen them arriving at the hotels, claimed their Hill Chief had come from New York, the White Paper Fan from San Francisco, the Adviser from Singapore.

A final arrival was a chubby, pockmarked local merchant whom Potter would never have suspected of being a Heung Chu, or Incense Master, of a third Triad. He would mediate. He took the chair between the two groups.

Alec Potter, fighting for air in the stifling shed, his eye glued to the knothole, saw a pack of Lucky Strikes hop onto the center of the table, the bright red label picking up a dingy beam of light. Each Hill Chief drew one and lit up; smoke flooded the purgatorial dim of Old So's teahouse.

"Keep your eye on the table, Alec," Peg had said. "And watch the teacups."

Conversation began in Hong Kong Cantonese, the common tongue, little of which Potter caught. He kept his eye on the table, and tensed when at last the Green Pang Hill Chief reached for the pot and filled a teacup. He lined the cup up with the spout of the teapot, set it down, and stared fixedly at the Sun Yee On leader.

The Hill Chief of the Sun Yee On took the cup of tea. With impassive deliberation he poured it off into an empty cup. Then he poured out another cup for himself and drank it.

Tension flooded the room. This, Peg had said, was a monumental insult, indicating that no help would be forthcoming from the Sun Yee On. The Incense Master, situated between the two factions, paled.

The Chiu Chao Deputy now placed five empty teacups in a row facing the spout of the teapot. "Your Five Tiger formation, Alec," Peg had briefed, puffing on a *chalyo,* his Guinness breath mingling with the jasmine in the night air. "If relations are to continue, the other Hill Chief will fill all the teacups, starting with the one nearest the pot, and drink from the third."

This the head of the Green Pang did not do.

Alec Potter was growing dizzy in the dead air of the shed; the scene in the teahouse wavered. Only his fear kept him conscious. He felt for the slim comfort of the Walther. Soft laughter rose and fell in the umbrella factory in the next building. Potter cursed his own curiosity and wished he were back at Harvard Yard; the chance to spy upon this unprecedented secret meeting in the hopes of getting information to sell had clouded his perception of the danger.

He must have blanked out momentarily, for he next became aware of a shiny brown cockroach halfway up his bare forearm, its slow antennae feeling the air. Bugs spooked Potter, a childhood in Asia notwithstanding; he reached to brush it off. A cask of Tsingtao beer shifted above him, making a soft thud as it came to rest on his neck.

In the teahouse, a Green Pang Red Pole jumped forward. Sun Yee On fighters barred his way, weapons drawn. The White Paper Fans leaped to their feet. Potter's Walther slid hopelessly between his legs to the floor. Trembling, he stared wide-eyed through the knothole.

Old So stood up and addressed the moment with surprising authority, claiming that the noise came from the umbrella factory. Upon signals from their respective Hill Chiefs, the four Red Poles disengaged and retreated to their posts near the door.

But the beer cask had brought down a rain of spiders, roaches, and silverfish. Pinned painfully in place by the case of Tsingtao, the insects roaming busily over his arms and face, Potter bit his shoulder to stifle sobs; he forced himself to peer back into Old So's teahouse.

The Green Pang leader called for a final pot of tea. "Your critical act," Peg had said. "This tells whether there will be war or no."

Old So filled three teacups and placed them in a row in line with the spout of the pot.

The Hill Chief of the Sun Yee On took the first cup and drank it. When he did this with the second, the room became motionless, a frieze. The Incense Master's forehead sparkled with sweat: the drinking of the third cup, Peg had said, would be the signal for war.

In the shed Potter glanced down at his chest. A hairy black tarantula with white and orange markings inched toward his neck. With soaring panic, Potter tried to flick it off.

It clung to his hand.

Inside the teahouse, the Hill Chief took the third cup and drank it.

Sweet Jesus.

The Red Poles, the White Paper Fan, the Grass Slipper, and the Incense Master all stiffened and rose at once. Potter groped futilely for his pistol.

But it was as old Peg had prophesied: Both parties bowed to each other and left the teahouse without another word.

When they had gone, Alec Potter came utterly apart. He picked up his Walther and smashed at the tarantula with the butt of his pistol, breaking a bone in his hand. He knocked the latch on the shed door off, and rolled screaming out onto the ground. He got up and staggered wildly along the *klongs* until he got to the Erawan Hotel, where he locked himself in a room on the top floor and wouldn't come out.

He stayed there for two weeks. Food and newspapers were left outside his door.

The first seven days, nothing unusual happened in the world beyond. Then on the eighth, four Green Pang Red Poles were shot in front of the Sze Hoin Restaurant on Prinshendrikade Street in Amsterdam.

On the ninth day a Sun Yee On was found dead on the beach at Aquatic Park in San Francisco with a bullet in each eye, each ear, and the mouth. A second was found floating in Tai Tam Reservoir in the New Territories of Hong Kong. His eyes had been cut out, acid poured on his face, and all his fingers cut off so he couldn't be identified.

The following day in New York, the body of a *boo hoy dow,* a Chinese street warrior, was found in a sack on Chinatown's Doyers Street, known as the Bloody Angle, sawed in half at the third vertebra with an electric saw.

On the eleventh day Hong Kong's Royal Commissioner of Police was accused of massive corruption and fled to a newly purchased villa on the coast of Spain, where he announced his plans to write a book on the affair.

Alec Potter, mad and unshaven in his hotel room, tracked these events in the daily newspapers with all the paranoid absorption of a cabalist. He noted that on the twelfth day eight hundred Mafiosi were suddenly arrested and locked up in a Palermo prison by the Parliamentary Commission of Inquiry into the Activities of the Mafia. The next day he circled with a pen the item that the head of the U.S. Consulate in Hong Kong, the biggest in the Far East, had been dismissed and called back to Washington; his successor was to be an obscure former director of the American Cultural Center in Kuala Lumpur named Fletcher Doody.

On the fourteenth day a Corsican gang war broke out in the streets of Marseilles. In a gas station eleven bullets were pumped into one of the two Guerini brothers, who reputedly ran Marseilles' underworld. The Gaullists accused the Socialists; the charge was returned. The surviving Guerini brother accused one Bébé Spiritu, a dwarf and underworld rival, of masterminding a takeover of the Turkish heroin trade.

The same day there was a revolt in the Buddhist monasteries in South Vietnam. For the first time publicly, the U.S. Ambassador, in an interview with William Strange, Saigon *Time* correspondent, expressed reservations about Diem's policies.

Alec Potter, still quite crazed, figured each of these events ritualistically from the date of the Triad meeting in Old So's teahouse, looking for numerological patterns, drawing broader occult relationships. But the "string of firecrackers," to use Old So's Chiu Chao phrase, seemed to explode off into the borderless reaches of infinite conspiracy.

Finally Alec's father Eliot came over from the museum. Finding his son haggard, unfed, and ranting, he took him to a Chinese doctor, who set his hand in a cast. Then Eliot set out to find Peg.

Eliot Potter was a watery, bespectacled man who still had a small Methodist congregation among the Meo and a fat native second wife taken seven years earlier after Alec's mother had died of a mysterious fever. Hurt by his son's apparent atheism since his return from Harvard, not to mention his insufferable arrogance, Eliot was no less intent upon registering his displeasure to Peg for having tipped Alec off about the big *gong sou* at Old So's teahouse.

He found the hoary, decrepit former customs chief, whose real name was Perigord Trench, holding forth loquaciously on his stool in the dingy bowels of the Erawan bar.

"What in God's name did you do to my boy?" Eliot Potter's thin voice trembled in the alcoholic twilight.

"Ay," Peg said, weaving on his perch, his one bad milky eye staring into space. "Your boy Alec's just had his first glimpse into the second kingdom, Eliot, the world of the *yen*. The world just beneath the visible, where the strings are pulled that make the puppets dance. Buy us a stout, Eliot, there's a good lad."

"Damn you, Peg." Eliot Potter, his fists clenched, turned and stalked out of the Erawan bar.

In the weeks following, Eliot Potter was pleased to note the gradual abatement of his son's inexplicable psychosis and the return of at least a portion of his normal jaunty charm. Still the incident at Old So's teahouse had seared Alec, and wouldn't pass off so easily. Alec knew that what he had seen was but the beginning of a dark season to come, and that the world would change somewhat.

But since there was little he could presently do about it, Alec Potter gradually relinquished his obsession and commenced to look at it all in a manner more to his liking. He began to wonder what use he could make of it.

ONE

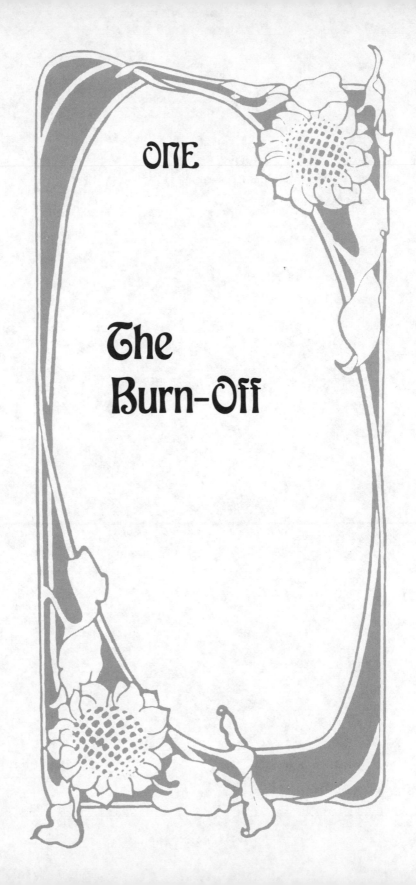

The
Burn-Off

1

Little Fook climbed out of a cream Rolls-Royce and stood in the twilight of the underground terminal of Hong Kong's Kai Tak Airport, blinking and sniffling, wiping his runny nose on the crusted sleeve of his chauffeur's jacket. A navy blue cap sat low on his tiny head, bending his ears down. Cold sweat beaded his parchment cheeks and flat, bloodless lips.

Fook walked to the curb and pushed open one of the glass doors. He scuttled through the terminal to Arrivals, and stood at the back of a crowd of other chauffeurs, Chinese families, hustlers, and American GI's awaiting the Pan Am from San Francisco via Tokyo. Plangent Cantonese pop songs drifted from a newsstand radio. A board above told Fook it was August 23, 1963, 30.5 degrees, humidity 90. A red blinking dot told him the plane was landing.

Fook's eyes began to water. He scratched his arms and the back of his hands. A mute, frantic dance began inside him; he became very uncomfortable inside his own skin.

Fook turned and spotted an eyeless Hakka woman selling cigarettes on a blanket next to a row of baggage carts, a bound sleeping baby hugging her back. Beside her wares was a tiny tray bearing a little red shrine, burning joss, and a plate of oranges.

"Ni hau?" she said as Fook approached and greeted her. How are you?

"Gei do?" Fook placed a pack of Players in her hand. How much?

His waxen fingers trembled as he handed her the money and an additional two Hong Kong dollars in coins. At this the woman rubbed the coins, then nodded toward a utility closet door a few yards away. Fook looked behind him to see that the customs exit was still deserted, then walked to the door and knocked. A voice told him to enter.

A sallow man squatted in the gloom among mops, buckets, and paper supplies. From a tiny cloth bag he shook a ridge of fine sand-colored grains onto a piece of silver tinfoil. Fook held the foil as the man heated it from below with a slow-burning screw of toilet paper. The grains dissolved into a light-brown syrup. Fook put a matchbox casing to his mouth, leaned over the tinfoil, and inhaled the mixture, moving from one end of the silver foil to the other until it was gone.

When done, he stood for a few moments as if suspended out of time. His body took on the soft, voided neutrality of a slightly stunned animal.

"M'goi," he whispered.

When Fook emerged from the broom closet the passengers were pouring out of customs. He went to the back of the crowd and stood, a spectral gnome, searching for a face he had forgotten.

The rumpled crowd, surging irritably forward, seemed to part instinctively to allow a tall young woman in a black dress to move ahead. She carried a single small suitcase and walked with a deliberation, a feline reserve that gave her grace. Her face was delicate, wide at the cheeks, with a slight flatness to the nose; the skin was light and smooth like the inside of an almond. Her shoulder-length hair was black, with bangs in front. Her eyes, large and still, looked straight ahead. To an Asian, she might have looked European; a European could have said she was Asian.

"Missee?" Fook whispered. But the shredded, ghostly word barely carried beyond his lips, and the young woman swept past him.

She was almost to the exit when she felt a tug at the sleeve of her dress. She stopped and looked down to see the tiny grinning figure peering up at her from beneath the too-large cap.

"Missee?"

She stared at him, swallowing alarm. Finally she said, "Fook?"

He nodded emphatically. Stumpy fingers emerged from his coat sleeve and reached for her suitcase.

"No," she said. "I've got it."

His clouded eyes looked up at her. "No takee bag?"

Perplexed, Fook followed her outside and rushed to open the door of the Rolls.

"I didn't recognize you, Fook," she said as he pulled the Rolls out among the taxis and jitneys and pedicabs of Kai Tak's exit. "I'm sorry."

"Long time, missee," he barked. "Ten year?"

"Yes." The Rolls surfaced and turned left, toward town. Su Lin looked out at the high roiling clouds stacked behind the concrete jigsaw of resettlement housing off in the New Territories. "Where's my brother?"

"Peter no come yet. You' faddah at New Asia."

"Does he know I've arrived?"

"Mebbe." His face split into a grin in the rearview. "No worry, missee. Big week, ya?"

Chatham Road thickened suddenly into a swarming dance of life. Dragons leered from shops along the roads, abject hungry faces from the alleys. With precise perception, Su Lin registered shoulder poles, schoolgirls in slit skirts, Shanghai jars full of fermenting soy sauce, strange yellow vegetables in the markets. Along the Kowloon waterfront double-decker buses rolled past dead neon in the bright daylight.

"Clouds," Fook said as they crossed the harbor on the vehicular ferry, "but no rain."

Su Lin stood at the rail feeling the small breeze on her face, studying the frenetic water commerce, busy boats in a tub: sampans, freighters, tugs, *walla-wallas,* high-sterned junks with square bows and lug sails. She took a black Grumbacher notebook from her purse and leafed through drawings to a blank page. She wrote with a Rapidograph in a sure hand:

"Ten years. . . . I see it all with American eyes now. . . . Life where I live is so much more chosen, deliberate, the illusion of originality or independent action pursued. . . . Here death is cheap; but here it matters less, because one comes back again."

"To New Asia?" Fook asked as they docked.

Her eyes jumped the business spires of Central to the sweating green hump behind it.

"Let's drive past the house."

As Fook pushed the Rolls up the Victoria Peak switchbacks, Su Lin sat by the window glimpsing the dizzying, tilted sunlit harbor behind until the tall trees obscured it. Near the top, Fook turned off on Plantation Road and pulled up before a pair of huge locked iron gates. He turned an electric gate opener toward them.

"No," she said, reaching forward to stop him. The sharp gesture left Fook's hand trembling violently, his tongue working soundlessly in the hole of his mouth.

She let herself out and walked across the gravel. Chinese ideographs were woven in metal into the gate's grillwork. Beyond, a hedged driveway ended at a looming green-roofed colonial house of stucco and wood, its upper windows shuttered.

"Who lives there now?" she called to Fook. A hot wind blew against her hair, rippling her dress.

Fook stood by the car twisting his hands. "Just you' faddah," he said. "And him."

A tall turbaned Sikh idly paced a horizontal command path at the foot of the driveway, a rifle crooked in his arm.

Su Lin wrapped her fingers around the bars and felt the cold iron against her cheek.

I had to see them—the gates that make the sound in my head that I hear walking down Grant Street, crossing the Bay Bridge from Berkeley. The last time I passed through these gates I was clutching a doll.

A small pagoda-shaped gazebo stood beside the house, a bougainvillea in purple bloom twined about its columns.

Her tears broke on the black iron grilling.

When she came back to the car she found Fook rocking slowly against the black fender, eyes closed, seemingly asleep on his feet.

"Fook."

Fook opened his eyes, Su Lin looked into them, and what she saw made her shudder. A cool predatory hunger lay behind the little man's dotted pupils, a display of absolute, indifferent need—distant, ageless, inert. She felt as if she had blundered into a forbidden room. Fook's bottomless inward gaze, so evanescent yet so stark and forceful, caused her own reality to quiver and register a small crack, as an imperceptible earthquake leaves its mark on an urn.

An instant later it was over. Fook seemed to recompose himself into the shaky, ravaged little family chauffeur who had picked her up at Kai Tak. Bowing and sucking air, he reached for the limousine door.

"Long time," he croaked, looking back at the gates.

"Yes," she whispered, feeling cold, already beginning to doubt what she had seen.

"Faddah not same since . . ." Fook fell mute, his crushed jowls trembling, his milky eyes filling.

Su Lin turned away. "Let's go now."

As the Rolls turned slowly on the gravel drive, Su Lin took a brush from her purse and pulled it through her hair, welcoming the rough claw of the bristles.

2

The train south from Paris crossed the Pyrenees at dawn, as it does each day, and clattered to a stop at the Port Bou border.

Jim Cross awoke and peered out the window. Guardia Civil in patent leather hats and carbines milled through the steam.

"We're in Spain," he said.

Eva opened her eyes and leaned sleepily against him. "So many police."

"Franco's clowns."

She giggled and jammed her floppy straw hat back on her head, still a little drunk from the champagne, and sat up cross-legged on the bunk; the empty bottle had rolled back and forth across the floor all the way from the Gare de Lyon. They had slept in their clothes.

Cross stared sleepily at his reflection in the window. His long jeaned legs were pulled up in the narrow small berth. His wrists stuck out of a white linen jacket. Black hair fell over a high pale forehead crossed by a pair of scars, one a youthful collision with the sprung glove compartment of a Buick Roadmaster at a shopping center stop sign, the other more nobly gained: a surfing wound. His maternal grandmother's curious green eyes burned back in the reflection.

Eva had on a light summer dress; she plumped her hair, laughing at the sight of them. Together they looked, Cross thought, like a slightly demented couple heading for a jazz festival.

Cross reached over and felt her tummy beneath the blouse. It was a small swelling, a new moon. "The visitor," she called it. She had a private way with English.

A customs official appeared at the door and beckoned them out onto the platform. He asked for their passports.

"*Esposa?*" He looked at Cross and put his forefingers beside each other.

"*Si*," Cross said, contradicting the passports—his American, hers Danish with another name.

The customs officer glowered lasciviously at Eva, taking in her breasts, her good legs. Finally, as if bestowing a favor, he stamped the passports.

"It's none of his fooking business," Eva said irritably when he'd left.

"This is Spain."

They boarded the waiting Spanish train, and lay awake on their stomachs watching it descend the mountains. A warm and flat morning light, a southern light, spread across the emerging plain and suffused the cabin. A Paris *Trib* lay on the bed. Cross noticed the date: 23 August 1963.

"I feel so excited," Eva said. "I don't know why."

"Travel," Cross said. "There's magic in each beginning."

In Barcelona they got off and walked from the station up the Ramblas. It was a weekend, the summer streets spilling color and noise. Cross watched delight dance in Eva's eyes as urchins made matador passes with red rags in front of a flower seller.

They took a room in a high, ancient pensión off the Plaza Real with mirrors on the walls and stucco angels carved in the molding, and slept all afternoon in a sagging bed beneath rough sheets.

Cross awoke at dusk to the sound of a beggar crying in the square below: "*Limosna, limosna por favor.*" Pale dusty light seeped through the lace curtains. Eva was still asleep, her hair coiling across the pillow.

Cross reached into his jacket, hung on a chair by the bed, and fished from the pocket a matchbook. He opened it and stared at the name written in pencil on the inside cover.

"Jiminez," it said.

Eva had kicked off the sheet and was lying on her side naked and warm, breathing quietly. Cross jammed the matchbook back in the jacket pocket. He watched her, his desire kindling. Her breasts were plumping already, her belly curved like a scythe. She stirred and reached for him. He moved onto her and took her from behind, warm and silent. Seeing the act sidelong in the wall mirrors, Cross surged. They finished frantically and fell exhausted together on the bed.

She rolled over and nestled into him. "You seem nervous."

"Do I? I just wonder if this is silly."

"Silly?"

"Combining an abortion and a vacation."

"Oh, I hope so," she said, laughing.

When Cross didn't laugh she said in her soft even way, "You don't want it. I don't want it. If it's not safe he'll tell us." Then she said, "I've done it before."

Cross got up and walked to the window. "It's getting late. You could get it in Denmark for free. Clean and safe. It's not the same here." He turned back to her. "There's still time to go back."

"But we couldn't swim and lie in the sun afterwards." Then she said lightly, "Don't be so American."

Cross watched the beggar out the window below, legless and blind, leaning against a lamppost, rattling his cup. A bib of lottery tickets, affixed by a clothespin, ran down his shirtfront. *"Limosna. Lotería . . ."*

They ate fish in a small restaurant on the Plaza Real. Afterwards Cross rented a Volkswagen from an agency off the Independencia and picked her up in front of the hotel. It was dark by the time they set out.

The road leading south was narrow and empty. Villages loomed suddenly in morbid, unlit stillness, then disappeared behind as they drove on through the night. Eva fished out a couple of joints of kif she had brought from the bottom of her purse.

"Coals to Newcastle," he said as she lit up and handed him one.

"What?"

He laughed. "You have to be careful down here."

"Careful, careful." She shook her head. "Always careful, Jim."

"Spain's puritanical," he muttered. "Seven years minimum. No habeas corpus . . ."

Cross felt the soft kif narcosis spread through him. Eva hummed a song in Danish.

"Can I draw in your notebook?" she asked.

"Sure." He swallowed the roach.

She was a playful gamine, bright without pretense, a poet and an orphan; Cross felt comfortable with her. She whispered soft Danish erotic words in his ear that sounded like *Freeza* and *Teezamaten* for cock and cunt. The knock-up, coming several months after they had met in Paris, had complicated their affair; whether it would survive the trip was an unspoken issue.

For the moment Cross, racing south, the headlights carving road from blackness, was content with the idea that he and Eva were joined in some romantic penetration of the irrational—which had something to do with why they had gotten together in the first place.

"I still think it's funny," Eva said as they neared Valencia, "that you can't give me the abortion."

"I know what's in there," Cross said, "but I wouldn't trust myself to get it out. It's illegal in the States, so I never . . ." He looked at her through the darkness. "Doctors aren't suppose to improvise."

"Is that why you left medical school, why you walked out on that . . . cadaver?"

Cross thought he saw the black line of the sea to his left. "Something like that."

As they pulled through Valencia and the first light of dawn spread, something exultant rose in Cross, some voiceless sense of imminent promise.

Tension gathered in his shoulders from the steady driving. Seeing him hunched over the wheel, Eva reached over and rubbed his neck.

"Would you like me to drive?"

"No. I'm enjoying it."

They passed through Valencia and plunged down the empty road. Cross switched off the headlights.

"Jiminez," the Gypsy in Paris had written in the matchbook.

Eva had found the Gypsy, a pock-cheeked guitarist who played a little like Django, in a *cave* off Rue de la Harpe.

"Jiminez. He's good, man. He's cheap," the Gypsy had said through a cloud of Gauloise.

"Where is he?"

"The Canary Islands."

"I thought you said Spain."

"The Canary Islands are part of Spain, man. Three days south of Cádiz by boat. Go deck passage. It's cheap."

"It's a long way," Cross had said, uneasy with the thought. "You sure he's a doctor?"

But Eva, who had never been further south than Paris, seemed to think it would be a lark. Cross, admiring her insouciance, had agreed; it was, after all, her body.

In a way, it had come at a good time. Tourists and diesel fumes were choking the summer streets, the Algerian fruit hawkers along the Rue de Buci were drenched in sweat. Cross, after a year abroad, was feeling beached in a desultory Left Bank milieu. The promise surrounding the *Tribune*'s acceptance of his first piece, on the Vietnamese refugee clinic in Neuilly where he worked as a volunteer, had evaporated into a job as a stringer, covering such critical local events as art shows and poetry readings at the Alliance. A suspenseful trip to the American army base at Orléans when his draft notice had arrived had climaxed in a 4-F on a heart murmur—a convenient affliction that had never affected his life—courtesy of a doctor he had known back at medical school. With this stone removed from around his neck, elated at the broad horizon the rest of his life presented, the idea of an adventure, of yielding to fate, appealed.

He had given up his hotel room at Rue Git le Coeur to a Dutch mescaline surrealist and told the paper to find someone else. Eva had told the Sorbonne professor for whom she translated she was going on holiday for a few weeks, and told the owner at the *cave* where she bartended nights to piss off. Friends had seen them off at the train.

"Look," she said.

Cross glanced away from the road at the notebook page. Eva had drawn bright, facile erotic images with a colored pen and captioned them with bilingual dirty puns. There were multiples of his penis; the two of them coupling; her belly and an empty circle inside it.

"Will you draw what's in there for me?"

"When we stop," he said.

Outside along the road, farmers and mules loomed through the morning mist, then disappeared; women in black gathered twigs under the olive trees.

Cross felt more comfortable the further south they got. Spain was like California—the language, the dry sun, the citrus. Eva became quieter; she talked of a clean, cozy childhood in Copenhagen, beating mittened hands against the cold, walking the streets in knitted cap, boots, scarf. Spain was Catholic, unconscious, messy. At lunch, waving flies off her butter in a restaurant in Torremolinos, she winced and said, "It's dirty here." For the first time Cross saw an uneasy shadow cross her face.

"Jiminez," the Gypsy had said.

They passed by Gibraltar without stopping and arrived at the port of Cádiz late that day, as they had planned. Cross turned in the VW and booked a second-class cabin for the three-day voyage to the Canaries leaving that night.

The boat was an aged three-tiered oversized passenger ferry. But the air was warm, the sea calm. A soft balmy breeze blew out from Africa and swept across the creaking deck; a radio played lilting Moorish music in someone's cabin. Cross saw Eva smile with relief. They ate fish caught by the cook served in a dining room with filthy tablecloths and oranges for dessert after each meal.

They made love often during long quiet hours in the cabin, gripped by some new tenderness forged in the journey. In Paris it had been just an affair.

Late the second night, huddled alone on the deserted foredeck, they watched silver flying fish shoot through the air. She went down on him as spume broke over the bow. He could feel her tummy swelling against his leg.

"You must be near three months along," he said afterwards.

She smiled and shrugged. "I've lost track of time."

Morning sickness hit her the next day. Cross brought food back to the cabin. By nightfall they had grown serious; something dark and new had entered the journey. That night Cross had strange dreams of running. Attempting to escape some force, he found himself instead rushing headlong toward it.

They arrived late in the day in Las Palmas—a wide curving beachfront with parrots and stucco buildings bleached by the sun. They danced that night to Grand Canary music in a cafe, and lay awake afterwards in a sandswept room upstairs overlooking the ocean. Plastic curtains blew in the breeze; everything, even the sheets, tasted of salt.

"What kind of doctor would work here?" Cross said.

"Aren't they the same everywhere?"

"I suppose I don't really know."

She looked at him. "Why did you leave California? You've never told me."

"There's nothing much to tell."

Cross lit a cigarette. Outside, a bloody moon fattened down against the sill.

"It was my last year before the internship. I was dissecting a corpse. Something snapped. I stood up and walked out."

"Just like that."

Cross nodded. "I remember thinking, this is where our science ends up. A bunch of men in lab coats in an antiseptic room cutting up a dead body."

"Or building bombs."

"Yes. Some reductio ad absurdum. I had an urge to kill that corpse. I knew then that I was in a hall of mirrors." Cross looked away toward the window. "I felt that through the dead eye of that cadaver lay the living world I sought." He turned and looked at her. "The next day I caught a Greyhound to New York and a Panamanian freighter to Hamburg."

Eva laughed. "In search of the miraculous."

"Or just anything living."

"Do you think you'll ever go back?"

Cross put out his cigarette. "I don't know."

Eva studied him. "The American thinks he has a *destiny,*" she said. "A European just . . . lives."

"Which is better?"

"I don't think I'd trade with you." She looked at him carefully. "You are not free. In sex. You are tense sometimes." She poked her finger in his stomach. "Is that the price of ambition?"

The next morning Cross took pictures of her on the beach with his German camera, smiling against the blue ocean. Her legs were smooth and long, her new bulge comical over the bikini bottom.

That afternoon they took a small ferry to the nearby island of Tenerife, where they were to find Jiminez.

"Do you feel anything about taking it out?" Cross asked as the boat neared the wharf.

"The fetus?" She shook her head. "My body is not that real to me. Ideas are more real."

The ferry docked at the port of Santa Cruz, on the leeward side of the island. As they searched the plaza for Jiminez' office, Cross studied her. She moved with all the calm absorption of a woman shopping.

"It's pretty here," she said.

They found it a few hundred yards off the main plaza—a tiny stucco building at the end of a dead-end dirt street: CLÍNICO. DR. J. JIMINEZ. They presented themselves to a woman at a desk and mentioned the Gypsy in Paris. *"Momentito,"* she said, and disappeared into the back. They sat down to wait.

The walls were yellow and stained, hung with crucifixes and plastic madonnas. A cheap curling poster of Kennedy smiled down. The rattan chairs had tiny circles of termite dust around their legs. A scrawny bird chirped weakly in a cage. Cross could smell food, cooking oil. Here there was none of the effluvium of antiseptics. What had he expected? Was this Jiminez even a doctor? There were no certificates anywhere. He looked at Eva; she had grown quiet, her hands folded over her tummy.

The nurse came back and nodded to Eva.

"Let me talk to the doctor," Cross said suddenly.

"No," Eva said. "It's all right. I'll be back soon."

"Dinero, señor."

Cross paid in pesetas. It left him just enough to get the two of them back to Paris.

Eva smiled over her shoulder as the nurse led her toward the back.

He sat back down on the sofa in the peeling office, fighting a desire to intercede, discuss the question of the anesthetic, examine the cervical tools.

"We'll need ice later," Eva called. "And towels."

He settled down to wait.

Cross began to think of his father, and what he would have thought were he to see this clinic. Doc Cross had been a gynecologist, as was his father before him; he had never approved of abortions. For three decades he had monitored the reproductive apparatus of Southern California aerospace executives' wives, the way the mechanic down the street kept the family cars running. American medicine, Doc Cross always liked to say, has come light-years from barbarism. He had honored this mystique of science and rational perfectability until the day he dropped dead of a heart seizure in the middle of a putt.

The nurse appeared. *"Espere,"* she said, and smiled. It had been half an hour.

Doc Cross's life had been a matter of plaid slacks and Wednesdays off and a house on the Palos Verdes peninsula with oleanders and a pool. His son had found it strange and empty growing up there; antiseptics somehow seeped into the very fabric of speech and demeanor, deadening existence, leaving it without aroma. It was a world faintly tinged with some mute concept of honor or altruism—but never at the expense of golf or quietude. The whole idea, it seemed to Cross, was to keep white people breeding.

"Va bien," the nurse said. Cross looked up and nodded absently.

He had grown up beneath the shadows of grand new medical plazas looming above the greenbelt, rising higher even than the banks, and the growing deification of the doctor in the community. Beneath photos of Eisenhower grinning before an American flag, he had made waiting rooms his playrooms, stethoscopes his toys. And he too had entered the way without really thinking about it, until whispers of another world, dark and fertile, swept down the sterile corridors of Langley Porter Medical School; and one day, without explanation, he had walked out.

Cross suddenly realized that over an hour had passed. Nobody had come.

"Nurse!"

He jumped up and rushed past the desk into the back.

There was a single deserted room. An empty wooden table with old stirrups stood in the twilight. There was blood in a bucket. Eva's shoes were on the floor.

"Eva!"

A back door was ajar. Cross ran outside into a narrow, deserted alley. A breeze had come up, swirling dust around his feet. A trail of dark drops of blood led away in the direction of the sea. Cross ran down the alley.

The path ended at a deserted stretch of beach; wind-swept waves thundered against the shore. A corrugated metal sewer ran across the sand to the sea. Cross followed it to the water's edge, where a solitary urchin in shorts stood scratching his belly, gazing down.

Cross ran over to look. Agony shot from him in a scream.

The body turned slowly from one side to the other in the surf. Her hair was matted, her soaked summer dress bunched up around her neck, her frozen blue mouth and eyes open. The tiny matter trailed between her legs.

The boy looked soberly up at him with large brown eyes.

Cross fell to his knees in the water, vomiting.

When he next became conscious of himself he was back on his feet. The urchin was gone, the beach deserted. Cross dragged Eva's body up on the sand, out of reach of the sea. Then he staggered, dripping wet, back up the alley.

The clinic door was still open. Inside, a thin mustachioed man in cheap slacks and a flashy short-sleeved shirt was sloshing the bucket onto the tiled floor. On the operating table next to an open wallet were stacks of paper money bound with rubber bands. He looked up at Cross with harsh, hooded eyes.

"*Ah, señor. Complicaciones.*" He looked away and coughed.

"Jiminez," Cross whispered.

"*Sí,*" the man answered. He smiled and offered his hand.

Cross grabbed him violently by the shoulders. Jiminez' eyes swelled. "*Accidente,*" Jiminez canted, trembling, gazing sidelong at the money on the operating table. "*Cosas de la vida, señor.*"

Cross threw him against the wall and hit him. Blood broke and smeared over Jiminez' nose and mouth. Cross's wet knuckles slid off the pummeled flesh as he struck him again.

Jiminez hung senselessly on the wall, burbling. Cross, swollen with rage, awoke suddenly to what he was doing. He lowered his arm and let go.

Jiminez, still on his feet, lurched away. He wheeled raggedly across the water-slicked floor toward the crude operating table, reaching for his money. As he grabbed the wad of bills and lunged for the door, his feet went out from under him. His head hit the metal edge of the stirrup with a sickening crack. He grunted and dropped like a stone. The bills scattered across the floor.

Cross ran over and stood above him. Jiminez' face was draining of blood, the breath slow and guttural. Cross dropped to his knees and felt for the pulse, then tore Jiminez' shirt off and began massaging his heart.

The room was silent, broken only by Cross's sobbing breath and the shrill scolding chatter of the bird in the cage in the waiting room. A breeze came in, strewing the money like leaves across the floor. Cross put his ear to Jiminez' mouth; there was only a faint breath.

Outside, the ferry horn blew twice from the wharf. Footsteps came up the alley.

Cross stood up, frozen with horror above Jiminez' body. The footsteps stopped outside the rear entrance.

Cross turned and walked dazedly into the waiting room. The caged bird shrieked with outrage as Cross reached down for Eva's suitcase and his own. He opened the door and stepped out into the harsh, blinding daylight. Down the dirt street, across the plaza, he could see the ferry waiting at the wharf.

Bursting with grief, he walked—then ran—toward it.

3

Kuan Yin, Goddess of
Mercy, stood in the corner of the banquet room, five feet high, her
body a frozen lacework of ivory carved from elephant tusk by the
tiny knives of the imperturbable master craftsmen off Nathan Road.
In each of her eight hands the statue held an object of faith; in her
crowned forehead sat the jeweled pineal. The full eyes of her Buddha face were cast down in an attitude that Su Lin, standing alone
in her black dress below the empty dais, saw variously as sadness,
modesty, resignation—or simply a tolerant, ironical smile. The statue
was a present to Father from the Kaifongs, the voluntary welfare organizations, in honor of the occasion.

The New Asia, the family restaurant on Hollywood Road in
Hong Kong's Central District, had been refurbished with gilded
molding and silk wallpaper, and hung with crepe, balloons, dragons.
Someone had strung Christmas lights across the ceiling, though it
was August. This festive montage of the family's Eurasian self had
engendered a baseless fear among the Chinese guests, all regulars of
the ranking Chiu Chao eatery, that Harry Lin's eclecticism would
extend to the menu itself.

A rectangular banquet table covered with red and blue bunting sat on low risers at the front of the room. The round tables on the parquet floor below were set with lacquer soup spoons, chopsticks, forks, and turtle-shaped nameplates for each guest.

HAPPY 70TH HARRY LIN. THANK YOU said a sign in gold spray lettering hung on the wall. Another, bearing the stenciled image of a high-rise building, said, LIN FAMILY ORPHANAGE. THANK YOU.

As the room filled, Su Lin headed for the safe harbor of a front table reserved for herself, her brother, and the department heads. From there she watched her father in the center of the room, greeting guests, his eyes crinkling. Her lawyer brother Peter stood beside him nervously rubbing the top of his head as if to speed along an incipient bald spot. Only this event would have brought Peter back from Boston, she supposed. It was a shock to see him losing his hair at twenty-six.

Flanking them were several unusually large and dark Chinese— one with a scar, another an earring—looking uncomfortable in suits. Their muttered Swatownese was the common dialect in the room, along with English, Cantonese, French, and Portuguese. Harry Lin's birthday, it would seem, was the big event of this drought season in the Crown Colony.

"I'm so happy you're here," Father had said to her at the door. "We must talk." But his secretary, stern in bun and mandarin dress, had hustled him off. "Afterwards," he had promised gaily over his shoulder.

But it was always that way: the press of "business." For three nights running she had had variants of the same dream, trying to reach him through obstacles. The last of his rare Stateside visits, over lasagna in North Beach, had been contentious.

"Medicine?"

"Yes."

"A midwife?"

"No. A doctor."

"Don't be ridiculous. What about your artwork? I understand you are very good."

"There are other things that are important."

"Like these protest rides? You have the blood of two races. Why champion the travails of a third? Is this part of the . . . Maoist affectation?"

She hadn't known how to answer.

"Come back and work in my new orphanage. That will exercise your idealism. And you should begin to think of marriage."

"That's not what I want."

He had reached for the bill. "We'll talk later."

The medicine phase had passed—he had been right about that—but the relationship had hung in time there. On the plane over she had rehearsed a comportment befitting the proud and dutiful daughter of a hong merchant, determined to give him this on his day. But later, dammit, they would talk.

A tiny ancient lady in a neat silk dress was standing before her. "You look so *beautiful*," she said with a kind of official adoration.

"Thank you." Su Lin couldn't remember her name, only that she had been the family bookkeeper for decades.

"What a wonderful occasion." The lady looked across the room at Father. "He looks well, doesn't he?"

Indeed Father seemed to be aging like an Oriental, like his own father—burnishing rather than cracking. He was talking to a tall Caucasian Su Lin recognized as Nigel Mason, one of the family bankers.

She suddenly had the thought that this little lady loved her father. The idea delighted her. But love? She was carrying Western baggage. Here, there was only duty—the business kind, which was tax-free, and the filial kind, which was not.

"You're graduating soon?"

Bessie, that was her name. Father liked to give his staff European nicknames.

"Two weeks ago, Bessie."

"Goodness." She clucked at time's passing. "You coming back to Hong Kong?"

"No."

"Ooooh."

The orphans paraded in, thirty strong, holding hands, dressed in maching blue schoolgirl skirts, jackets, caps, and white blouses. The plump, beaming scrub-faced lady from the Kaifong led them to the right of the risers, where they clustered giggling.

"Su Lin. You look . . . *ravishing*." The family banker Nigel Mason stood before her, drink in hand, licking his lips. He was tall and narrow, a whippet, with tiny veins in his cheeks among freckles: an unrepentant Scotch drinker. Custom forbade Chinese men to stare at her, but Mason labored under no such constraint.

"You couldn't have been more than twelve."

"Eleven."

"Ten years it's been, then. You've become a great beauty. I'm rather . . . stunned, Su."

He pronounced it "Sue," like the Americans. The Chinese put another twist on it, more melodious. She was terribly embarrassed.

"Five generations, our two families. That makes us practically cousins."

She found that an unpleasant thought. Her nylons itched.

"Your great-great-grandfather, the comprador, worked for mine, you know."

"I've heard the story."

"Aha," said Mason, yielding to her brother. "Number one son."

Peter Lin stood before her holding two drinks. "Welcome to the Charlie Chan show," he said when Mason had moved away.

"They all look so well off." She took the drink Peter handed her. "Business must be good."

"All power to teak, rattan, and Chiu Chao cooking," he said darkly as they sat down at the table. "And the Hong Kong Crown Bank."

"When did you get in?"

"Last night. Haven't seen you in a year. You look very . . . *guai.*"

"I'm working at it." The word, one of a half dozen Chinese terms they shared, was Mandarin, and meant submissive, well-behaved, passive: the ideal in a Chinese woman.

"Hope this will do until he's eighty," Peter said.

She sipped her Scotch and gazed at her brother, finding a certain fascination in how much he looked more or less Caucasian, more like Mother, or Father. She had seen him doing the same thing to her from across the room. He was tall and dressed American with his button-down blue shirt, Brooks Brothers tie, and penny loafers. But for the bald patch and his expensive gold watch, he could still have been a student. His skin was more white than yellow; but his eyes, black and rather hard, had the fold, and his nose was wide. He'd been a good tennis player; now the shadow of a paunch strained against his linen slacks. She realized how little she'd seen of him since she'd graduated from high school in Boston and gone

West to Berkeley while he, four years older, had finished at Harvard, then did law school.

"I hear you're with a good firm."

He shrugged. "Venerable. All Harvard people. I'm the resident slant lawyer. Maybe I should change the spelling of my name to Lynn. They never seem to tire of asking me to recommend good chop suey joints."

"Stop it." Peter's humor, once warm, seemed to have developed a jagged edge. Hoping to brighten him, she said, "Congratulations on your engagement."

Peter had sent a note and her picture a month earlier: Candace Gaines, all blond ringlets, tennis racquets, and WASP trappings—less a lover, perhaps, than an acquisition. But Peter seemed to aspire to these things more with each year—wrestling, it seemed to her, with demons of race.

"How is she?"

"Fine. Great." Peter gulped his drink and called for another, then lit a cigarette from the last. He seemed all nerves.

"Do you ever think of coming back?"

"Here?" He swirled the ice in the glass and laughed joylessly. "It's not to my taste."

Guests surged toward the front of the room, the important ones climbing the risers to the banquet table.

"Hear from your old boyfriend?" Peter asked abruptly.

"He joined the navy."

"I thought any boyfriend of yours would be a draft resister." Peter winked and swilled more Scotch. "That was a joke. Or supposed to be."

Su Lin forced a smile. "He was. It's a long story."

"Does he write you?"

"Yes."

"From where?"

She looked down at her drink. "Saigon."

"Shit. Let's get drunk."

The principals had taken their seats, Father at the center. Next to him was little ancient Chen Po-chi, the family adviser, trim and impassive, dressed in a dark business suit. Mason the banker was to his left. Next came the new American Consul, Fletcher Doody, a tall pasty man with horn-rimmed glasses, and his pert wife with a Doris

Day bob and dead social smile. Completing the main table was the orphan lady from the Kaifong, the Anglican bishop from St. John's, and beefy, erect Roderick Hughes, the new Royal Police Commissioner.

"Remember your old amah?" Peter nodded to the far wall where a hunched woman, her silver hair slashed across the back in widow's mode, stood with a young man in a blue suit. "She doesn't recognize you. You must speak to her afterwards. She'll go crazy."

"Is that her son?"

"Song Wei."

"He was just a little boy."

"He's a Cambridge lawyer now. Works for Mason at the Hong Kong Crown Bank. A secret Red warrior from what I hear."

Song Wei stood stiffly beside his mother, taking in the room without expression.

"I heard you got a job teaching," Peter said.

"At the Art Institute."

"Why work?"

"I want to. It pays for my flat in North Beach and my paints."

"How much do they send you from here?"

"I don't remember."

Peter stifled a laugh. "God. You're Chink that way. They don't talk about it. Maybe it's from the old days. Our Swatow ancestors. Bandits. Or maybe they're still afraid the British will take it away from them."

"I wish you wouldn't say Chink."

Su Lin's eyes drifted to the statue of Kuan Yin in the corner. Its whiteness seemed to absorb all the colors and motion in the ornate room into itself, an undisturbed nothingness. Kuan Yin was her Chinese self, her Buddhist self, she decided, her silent, private patroness.

"I can't help thinking of Mother," Peter said. "The orphanage was her idea."

"I know."

An image of an empty rowboat floating on a misty New England pond drifted by. They both fell silent, as they inevitably did on this subject. Mother was such a hurt, a mystery that hung in time, like the helium balloons clinging to the New Asia ceiling with the stenciled blue images of the high-rise Lin Orphanage she understood would soon be under construction somewhere in the New Territories. The unsettling image of Fook the chauffeur and the drive past the villa rose in her mind, then dispersed like smoke.

Suddenly the room was organized. Deferential family staff surrounded Peter and Su Lin at their table. The orphan girls stood up, shoulders pressed together. Directed by a stern young Chinese woman with a baton, they began to sing:

Oh when the saints
(when the saints)
Go marching in
(go marching in) . . .

They sang it with careful reverence, in the wispiest of round, thin tones, as if it were the Lord's Prayer, their lips forming O's at the beginning of each line, then spreading into eee's, at the end, showing their shining teeth as they mouthed the unfamiliar syllabary.

It was the sort of thing Father loved.

"I want to be in that number, When the saints go marching in."

Then, ritard: "Go . . . mar . . . ching . . . *in*."

To great applause, the orphans smiled and bowed together. They turned and clapped to Harry Lin. He stood to acknowledge.

"Father's in heaven, isn't he?" Su Lin said to Peter. He looked at her drunkenly, his reddened eyes jumping with tension.

What is it, Peter?

Nothing. It was just the way they were. Looking down, she realized she had emptied her glass. She turned back to the dais. Father in his tweed jacket and tie seemed almost jolly up there, far from the sober young man with pipe and blazer she had seen in pictures taken at Harvard, his hair slicked in a pompadour; or in Japanese drag, mugging *The Mikado* in Hasty Pudding. She really couldn't recall ever touching him. Only Mother. But here one didn't speak of Mother.

Nigel Mason the banker got to his feet and spoke of his "esteemed colleague of long standing." Then he proposed a toast to Harry Lin's health. Fletcher Doody, the new American Consul-General, was next, muttering stiffly of "the growing postwar atmosphere of co-operation between our two peoples in the face of the Communist threat."

Chen, the family mandarin and second in charge, rose to speak in quiet, careful Oxford English of ancestors, and a great Eurasian trading family of five generations, a Lucky Strike burning in the fingers of his good hand, his right sleeve held primly behind his back, hiding the pink stump that had given him the nickname Left-Hand Chen.

Peter leaned over and whispered, "He looks like Chou En-lai."

"Shhhh."

The big Swatow guards flanked the podium, hovering motionless along the walls, arms folded.

"To Harry Lin," Chen concluded, "a man whose foresight and energy have helped bring prosperity to Asia. May he live another seventy years."

Chen must be older than Father now, Su Lin thought. But he looked tight and vigorous as he raised a toast of Iron Buddha tea. Something in his little glittering eyes always seemed wily to her. The family liked to describe him as "smart as a whip."

What's smart about a whip?

When the third tiny cup of the astringent tea had been swallowed, the lady from the Kaifong rose to speak. She had a fat face and blazing red lipstick. She gave a florid tribute in Cantonese singsong, then repeated herself in English for the benefit of the *gwailo*:

"This great man has bestowed a great gift upon the great people of Hong Kong. This orphanage will carry the Lin family name forward forever and help the unfortunate orphans of our great Hong Kong. It is in the tradition of Hong Kong to do this, and we are very proud and grateful."

She swung into view a large architect's rendering of the Lin Orphanage mounted on an easel, its thin blue lines barely visible from the floor. It was twenty stories high and precariously narrow, for cross-ventilation like the TB hospitals.

Harry Lin smiled humbly, his cheeks aglow. Su Lin, happy and proud, rose with the crowd to applaud. Peter stood beside her, grim and sotted, clapping loudly.

"Peter," she said in his ear over the noise. "Do you notice? Nobody looks at anybody else."

"It's China. You've forgotten."

The ceremonies over, waiters slid bounties of steaming food onto the lacquered lazy Susans: swallow's nest soup, Chinjew chicken, pigeon topped with charred onions, sliced scallops, *shan hu,* fried eels, vegetables in black bean sauce.

"And now," barked out the Kaifong lady, "while you please enjoy your dinners, the grateful daughters of Lin Orphanage will sing for you a second and final selection."

Su Lin saw a poker-faced orphan lick her lips helplessly. Must they forever sing for their supper?

The orphans began, as a round: "Row row row your boat, Gently down the stream . . ."

Feeling giddy from the drink, Su Lin dipped her bowed ceramic spoon into the melon soup and imagined that the spoon was the oar, row, row, rowing the boat.

Bowl of tea with two hands. Eat slowly, never act hungry. Drunk means low breeding. Always finish your rice. Don't use chopsticks for soup. Imprints of her amah's wasted training. She searched the room for the old woman, but she and her son were gone.

Looking up toward the banquet table, she saw Father smiling down at her with his eyes. To her own surprise, she winked sultrily at him, then put her soup aside and wheeled the lazy Susan to her favorite dish, soy goose with garlic and vinegar sauce.

As she reached out to spoon the goose, a rattle of tiny explosions, like firecrackers, rocked the room. A fork clattered noisily to the ground in the direction of the dais. A chair scraped violently.

"Good God!" Mason called out. Someone at the banquet table shouted something in Chinese.

Su Lin looked up to see Left-Hand Chen pointing with his good arm toward the back of the room: "Stop them!"

A dark stain of Iron Buddha tea spread down the front of the white tablecloth. Ice cubes showered and skated across the parquet floor.

The Swatow bodyguards rushed among the tables, pistols drawn, as hysteria began to seep through the room. Consul Doody's wife jabbed woodenly at her face with a Kleenex, her husband cowering behind her. Left-Hand Chen shouted multilingual orders: "Catch them!"

More shots rang out. The room became an ocean of screaming, lurching bodies and upended tables as the exits swarmed. A banquet dish rolled like an errant wheel across the floor. Police Commissioner Hughes stood brandishing a pistol, looking for somewhere to aim it.

"Row row row your boat, Gently down the stream," sang the orphans, too terrified to stop.

Then Su Lin saw Nigel Mason the banker at the banquet table, his eyes bulging, clutching his blood-reddened arm, standing over her father.

Harry Lin's arm was outstretched, his wrist hanging limply over the edge of the table, his face in the Chinjew chicken.

"Father!" she called, struggling to extricate herself from the table.

"Oh, God, I knew it," Peter moaned, transfixed in his chair, his teeth drawing blood from his lip, hands gripping his head.

The singing had stopped. The shrieking orphans clung to each other, fists to mouths.

Su Lin turned in agony toward the statue. Its head was gone. A dazed orphan girl sat with the head of Kuan Yin in her lap. She began to sing, "Merrily, merrily, merrily, merrily, Life is but a dream."

As Su Lin rushed toward her father, his head suddenly swiveled as if on an invisible lazy Susan and stopped, the eyes looking directly at her. In the middle of his forehead was a small clean round black hole that reddened and began shooting blood as she watched.

Harry Lin stared at his daughter with fathomless surprise.

4

The Mediterranean port town of Tangier, having endured centuries of violation by Phoenicians, Romans, Moors, and Western juntas, has come to offer a timeless image of corruption; no indignity remains to be visited upon her. Still each day, as the sun passes over the Pillars of Hercules, Tangier, spilling down its hills to the bay like bougainvillea, offers herself to every ship that passes to or from Marseilles, Naples, Piraeus, Beirut, Alexandria, or the Red Sea.

A man stood alone at a stone parapet in the native quarter overlooking the Straits, smoking a cigarette, watching the ferry approach. The summer sun, fattening down over the Atlantic, cast a blood-red stillness on the water. In the distance lay the low mountains of Europe, close in miles but to him untouchably remote.

He wore a djellaba made of rough brown cloth, its hood up on his head. Loose canvas fisherman's shoes clung to his lank brown ankles. His face was gaunt, scalded from sun; his eyes were still and empty.

Ragged cliffs of granite fell steeply to the stone quay at water's edge. Long whistles blew as winches groaned over a Yugoslavian freighter loading sardines for Dubrovnik. To the man's right the new tourist hotels of the European section rose tall and white to the sky.

The ferry, coming toward the harbor, seemed not to be moving at all, its wake frozen like a painting.

Then the overlook where he stood dropped into shadow, and it was cool. He flicked his cigarette over the wall and turned into an alley leading back into the quarter.

Quickly the air became silent. Fear rose in the eyes of people coming toward him. The light behind him disappeared.

Three men grabbed him roughly, pinning his arms to his back. A flash of pain ripped through his shoulder.

He was wiry and struggled well. But he was also hungry. The men, Arabs dressed in cheap European clothes, dragged him off down a dank, steep-shadowed dirt path. He was pushed through a stucco entry and up a narrow stone stairwell.

The four men burst into a white room overlooking the harbor.

A corpulent man sat looking out the window through a pair of mounted binoculars. He wore pressed jeans and a silk shirt bought on the black market, his belly spilling out over a studded Western turquoise belt. His shoes were Italian. A gold Swiss watch shone in the red twilight as his wrist moved, focusing the binoculars.

The men deposited their captive in front of the desk, then stood back against the wall. The figure at the window, without turning, gestured to a chair in front of the desk. When his guest had complied, he said in English, "What are you doing in Tangier?"

He received no answer.

"Ah," the man said. "So it is true, you do not speak much." He wheeled sharply in his chair and leaned across the desk to confront his visitor. "But you must speak to me. I am El Jefe, Chief of Tangier Police."

His face was pocked and oily, his eyes swollen slits. "What are you doing here?" he repeated. "Answer, please."

The man replied in the English with which he was being addressed. "I am waiting." His voice bore contempt, and the deliberation of one unused to speaking.

"How long have you been in Tangier?"

"A few days. I don't know."

"Remove your hood, please."

He pushed back the djellaba's hood to expose a gaunt head, feverish eyes, and dark hair matted with sweat from the struggle with the men.

"You are staying at the Carlton Hotel?"

He nodded.

"A cheap and filthy place. Still, you must pay your bill. According to the *patron,* you have not."

The reply came slowly: "I am expecting money."

"From?"

"California."

"Ah, California. . . . It is in Hollywood, yes? I have heard it is beautiful. Not like New York. A vile place. I have been there. I was bodyguard to King Hassan."

El Jefe smiled, showing unpleasant teeth. He brought his large body forward and his eyes bored in upon his visitor. "You wander the alleys alone. Your demeanor is most unhappy. You go to the overlook and watch the ferry. Then back to the cafe in the Socco Chico. Today you attempted to bribe an Algerian to sail you to Gibraltar. You are in some difficulty?"

The captive became aware of the shooting pain in his shoulder where the men had grabbed him. Out the window he could see the ferry nearing the wharf, its passengers clustered on deck. It would berth here for the night, then make its return run to Algeciras in the morning. An ache of longing rose in his chest.

"No," he said, though he couldn't remember the question.

"You wear native dress. Why?"

"My clothes were stolen."

"Where?"

"In the desert."

El Jefe reached out his hand. "Your passport, please."

The man fished it out from the depths of the djellaba. El Jefe took it and opened it with interest.

"James Cross." He looked up questioningly. "Strange travels, Mr. James. A stamp for the Port Bou border into Spain six weeks ago. Then I see here Morocco. But from the south? Tell me, how did that happen?"

Cross, trying to form words, found them hollow, the vowels resonating in his head. For weeks he had barely spoken, and then only French and the few words of Arabic he had learned on the journey.

"I was in Paris. I went to Spain. I went to the Canary Islands."

"By ship?"

"From Cádiz."

"Alone?"

Cross felt his neck tighten. He was silent a long time, staring at an alabaster Virgin Mary on the wall. "Yes."

"And then?"

"Las Palmas."

"How long?"

"A week." Cross, making each word, felt how language crushes experience into a frame.

"Purpose?"

"Swimming."

El Jefe scowled. "Do not make jokes to me, Mr. James. And then?"

Cross said each word slowly, trying to order his mind around the forgotten guile of speech. "I came across the Sahara. With a camel caravan from Senegal. To Goulimine."

"And from there?"

"To Casablanca, Rabat. Then here."

Cross assumed he had already betrayed himself. But his words to El Jefe did not disclose the visions his recounting tore open. He did not tell El Jefe of standing on the deck of the Tenerife ferry, crazed with grief and guilt as it pulled away, leaving Eva behind on the beach and Jiminez on the clinic floor; nor of the fevered, howling night on the stone wharf at Las Palmas; nor of bribing an Arab fisherman the next morning to take him to Ifni. He did not tell El Jefe how the Senegalese musicians had found him wandering sick in the desert after the Spanish garrison had robbed him and driven him out; nor of the week coming north with the caravan, tied to a litter, hallucinating. He did not tell El Jefe of the night he left Eva's suitcase outside the door of the Danish Consulate in Rabat; nor of rifling through back issues of the *Tribune* in the Rabat library looking vainly for some mention of Eva, Jiminez, or himself.

He had arrived in Tangier in the back of a fruit seller's truck and sunk quickly among the human detritus. Each day he walked to the harbor overlook, imagining that if he could but get back on European soil what had happened would reveal itself to have been a dream. But he did not dare take the ferry, for he expected arrest at

Spanish customs for the murder of Jiminez. His only hope was a letter from his sister containing enough money to fly to France, though even rescue meant nothing to him; he could not imagine his own redemption, or caring to live again.

"A dangerous and unusual journey, Mr. James. Was there some reason?"

"I like to travel." He realized the flippancy only after he spoke; his words were beyond his control.

El Jefe's belly shifted over his belt. "You try my patience." He rolled a Gauloise over his lower lip until it stuck, then lit it. "What is your profession?"

"I have none. I was a medical student."

"Ah. Then I should say Dr. James!"

Watching the loathsome man before him, Cross realized he had been mad for weeks, and with this came the first relief from it. But it brought a precise and disturbing terror that left him gazing into the remorseless eye of his own culpability. Outside the sun was gone. Cross saw the ferry passengers file like shadowy pilgrims down the ramp to the wharf.

El Jefe shook his head sadly. "I am afraid I will have to place you under arrest."

Cross stared at him. "You have no cause."

"The hotel owner is irate. You are without visible means of support. There is the question of your behavior. And then . . . perhaps there are other indiscretions? Please speak freely. I am trained in these things, Mr. James. I may be able to help."

Cross shook his head.

"Of course I could turn you over to the American Consulate for repatriation. If they believe your story, they ship you home on a military plane and make you pay them back. But I have a feeling you would not welcome their questions. They despise destitute Americans. And you hold secrets, Mr. James. They would take you for a drug dealer, at the least." El Jefe leaned forward suddenly. "Is that it, Mr. James? Drugs?"

The Byzantine shape of El Jefe's mild interrogation filled Cross with confusion. He suspected El Jefe knew about Tenerife and Jiminez and was inviting a confession. He saw too that he had encountered something not uncommon in a poor land: a literate man in a cheap job, corrupted by its small powers. The police chief's image began to flicker and run, as if melted by the heat of the faded day outside.

"Let me see your money."

Cross emptied his pockets, spilling paltry dirhams—coins and paper—on the desk.

"So you are indeed desperate for this letter from Hollywood," El Jefe said.

"California," Cross corrected him meaninglessly.

El Jefe reached inside his desk drawer, pulled out an airmail envelope, and brandished it. "Would *this* be the letter you await, Mr. James?"

Cross jumped from the chair and reached for it. El Jefe grabbed his wrist and slammed it to the table.

"Please!"

Cross sat back down, breathing heavily. "You stole my mail," he whispered.

El Jefe laughed. "I saved you a trip to American Express, that is all."

El Jefe held out the letter again. As Cross reached gingerly for it he saw it was indeed the one he had been waiting for. He took it, ripped open the short end, and shook out a long letter on onionskin:

Dearest brother Jimmy. Here it is, a cashier's check. You can pay me back somehow when you return. God, I hope $500 helps. Wish it was more, but even this much was a scrape. Dental bills. Can you believe? Cavities at my age. . . .

Cross shook the envelope again. He reached up and felt inside with his fingers. Frantic, he turned the envelope over and looked at the flap. It had been opened, then clumsily resealed.

He looked hotly at El Jefe. "My check! You took it!"

El Jefe had been gazing idly out the window. He turned slowly around in his chair. "Nothing happens in Tangier without my knowledge, I assure you." He shrugged and opened his palms in the eternal gesture: "The mails are most unreliable. Instruct people in the future to wire money."

Cross lunged across the desk. As his hands found El Jefe's throat, the pain in his shoulder hit. The three Arabs were upon him, pinning him from behind and forcing his face down onto the desk. They eased him back into the chair.

"You seem to have come to life," El Jefe said, standing over him, weighing a small black Luger in his palm. "Perhaps you are not so indifferent to your fate after all, Mr. James."

El Jefe resumed his seat and placed the pistol on his desk. He took a large handkerchief from his pocket and mopped his face. "You have a temper. I must tell you that in this regard your reputation precedes you." He smiled. "But I had to see for myself."

El Jefe blew his nose loudly, then stuffed the handkerchief back in his pocket. He removed a file from his desk and produced a document. "Mr. James, let us stop playing. A Danish woman's body was washed up on the beach in Santa Cruz de Tenerife. She died during an abortion. The abortionist, a Mr. Jiminez, was questioned."

So Jiminez is alive. Relief surged through him. The light in the room seemed to expand. *I am not a murderer.*

"This Jiminez," El Jefe went on, "claims he was beaten near death by an American accompanying the woman, causing him some loss of memory or brain damage."

"No. That's not what happened."

El Jefe smiled at Cross's implicit admission, then said, "Jiminez says this beating caused the failure of the abortion and the bleeding to death of the woman. He says you dragged the woman's body to the beach."

Cross's exultation darkened into horror as he realized what El Jefe was saying. "No," he whispered. "He lies."

El Jefe handed him the police brief. There was a cheap reproduction of Eva's smiling passport picture that made his throat tighten; a recounting of Jiminez' fabrications about the incident; a physical description of himself in four languages. At the bottom of the brief were the charges against him: murder and deadly assault.

"Of course you don't wish to cross into Spain, Mr. James. Not when you are wanted for killing this Danish woman."

Cross sank down in his chair. El Jefe reached for the document. "Tell me about it. You will feel better afterwards."

"I didn't kill her," Cross said, his voice shaking with rage. "Jiminez did. I found her body on the beach. I struck him for killing her, yes. But he hit his own head trying to run away with the money."

"Ah, Mr. James. These . . . *distinctions* would be lost on Spanish police. I know. Tangier used to be a Spanish protectorate. I am half Spanish. The best you could hope for is life imprisonment. The Spanish understand . . . crimes of passion, if this is such a case. It is more likely you will receive the *garrote*. Do you know the *garrote*, Mr. James?" El Jefe curled his hands about his own throat and showed his tongue. "The iron collar. Tightened with a screw. Medieval, but the Generalissimo's tool of choice. Horrible. I have seen it."

"Jiminez must be charged and tried. He killed her." Cross felt the blind rage stir in him again.

"Then why did you not go to the police in Santa Cruz?"

"I was upset. It was a strange place. He was a vile man. Somebody was coming. He . . ."

El Jefe shrugged. He took an emery board from his desk and busied himself with his nails.

Cross looked to the window, searching for the outline of the hills across the Straits, but they were swallowed by the night. "What do you want?" he whispered.

El Jefe gazed coolly at him. "What do you have?"

Cross looked down at his hands. "Nothing," he whispered. "I have nothing."

El Jefe sighed wearily. "I will have to keep you in jail then, while I confirm the details with Spanish and Moroccan police. It could take months, you realize. There is also the question of your . . . sanity. We have an asylum here . . ."

Cross stared at El Jefe.

"What a pity. And you are such a handsome boy. Such kind, pretty green eyes." He took a bottle of Cinzano from a shelf and poured two glasses.

"But then you are not . . . like that, are you, Mr. James?"

Cross didn't reply.

El Jefe gazed thoughtfully at him through the twilight and shook his head. "You Americans. Where do you come from? Where are you going? One of you suddenly appears among us and gets into trouble. It's always the best of you, it seems. Why? What are you looking for? Life is simple. Are you never satisfied?"

Cross gazed desolately at the proffered drink.

"You know, Mr. James," El Jefe said suddenly, "I may be able to save you."

Cross felt a sickening twinge of hope as El Jefe shamelessly played him.

"There is a man who has lived here many years. An American, of Russian parentage. His name is Ilya. He needs something delivered to Paris. He is willing to pay someone to do it."

"What is it?" Cross whispered.

"How should I know? But it needn't concern you. You are hardly in a position—"

"Give me my check. Let me fly to Paris. Then this . . . *blackmail* will be unnecessary."

El Jefe reached to the wall beside him and flicked a light switch. A tiny pink Christmas bulb illuminated the Virgin Mary on the wall above him. El Jefe gazed at it and his voice grew soft.

"We are discussing *absolution,* Mr. James. A chance to cleanse yourself of whatever misfortunes have befallen you in this part of the world. Do you understand? Your fate is in my hands. I offer the gift of *charity.*" El Jefe smiled softly. "I will see to your clearance through Spanish customs. After Paris you are free. Free to live. Free once more to see . . . Hollywood."

Cross nodded bleakly.

El Jefe clapped his hands sharply. The three Arabs came forward and reached for Cross. He lashed at them with his good arm. El Jefe spoke in Arabic and they stepped back.

He turned back to Cross, his voice hardening: "You move about Tangier at my liberty. Do not expect help from your Consulate. You are outside their jurisdiction. I will keep your passport here. If you make an arrangement with Ilya it will be returned to you. You will be gone on the noon ferry tomorrow, or be jailed and held on the charges."

El Jefe brought his girth forward and stared fixedly at Cross. "Go to the cafe in the Socco Chico. Ask for Benny the Guide. He will take you to Ilya." El Jefe's eyes narrowed. "Good evening, Mr. James."

Cross gathered his money and his sister's letter from the desk and stumbled out and down the stairs.

In the darkening alley he stood rubbing his shoulder, listening to the sinuous, worried drone of Radio Maroc curling out of the shops and stalls like some oversweet incense of the ear. Then he turned and dropped into the mindless, compelling reverie of the quarter.

5

Harry Lin's funeral at the family villa on Plantation Road was one of the biggest in Hong Kong memory, Su Lin was told, a testimonial as much to the esteem in which he was seemingly held as to a power and influence she had never fully understood. Bankers, consuls, and dozens of solemn city officials along with family staff and people from as far away as Shanghai, Singapore, and Bangkok came to say goodbye. Private police in reflector sunglasses frisked guests at the gates; armed guards milled among the crowd.

Su Lin wandered through the ornate ceremony as if in a dream. Relatives she had never known spoke consolations in Swatownese. Paper objects representing houses, automobiles, money, and other luxuries for Harry Lin to enjoy in the next world were burned. Bessie the bookkeeper had installed a small shrine to To Tei in front of the entrance to the villa and kept joss sticks burning in groups of three; old Amah wept as if it had been her own father. An Anglican minister, holding up the other side of things, intoned parting praises.

Afterwards Peter, who had been drinking again, tried to get Su Lin to come inside the house, but she had refused. Instead she slipped away from the milling crowd, walked round to the porch that ran along the rear of the house, and peered through the glassed double doors into her mother's old room.

Nothing had been moved in ten years. The wicker chairs, chests, and cherrywood armoires were in place, the quilt still on the bed. A lacquered bedtable shone from Amah's daily dusting. A silk nightgown was spread over a chair. Her mother's room had become a museum display, sealed in time, as if, Su Lin thought, awaiting a ghostly successor.

She saw the remnants of a Japanese paper kite hanging from a rafter, a leering samurai dissolving into dust. For an instant she saw Peter at ten, in shorts, racing along the top of the Peak with one of the kites Father brought home from all over the world, eyes cast upward, shining bright with the promise of his dual ancestry. How she had looked up to him!

A cough brought her wheeling around. Royal Police Commissioner Hughes stood at the end of the porch rocking on his heels. "A word with you, miss?"

Peter joined them, and the three walked up to the copper-roofed gazebo on the side of the hill. They stood looking down the back side of Victoria Peak at Aberdeen and the sampan-rich blue waters of Causeway Bay. Hughes was a large, stiff man, recently arrived by way of Bulawayo to smooth over the scandal left by his predecessor. He spoke as if through a small bullhorn.

"We've been pursuing the matter of your father's killing with, ah, vigor. In the week since the banquet we've questioned hundreds. We've learned that it was a planned attack. The perpetrators were from one of the local gangs."

"The Green Pang," Peter said irritably. "Triads who fled here from Shanghai."

"Hm. So you know." Hughes looked mildly deflated.

"Left-Hand Chen told me. Have you arrested anyone?"

"Scores of the devils. But I'm afraid the gunmen may have already fled the country by now."

"Why did they do it?" Su Lin asked.

"I don't really know, dear." Hughes looked down at her. "Your father was a man of influence, what with his restaurant, the furniture export business, real estate . . ."

They waited for him to go on. But Commissioner Hughes fished a pack of Senior Service from his pocket and stared off toward the sea.

"It's all rather complicated, isn't it? Hong Kong. I'm new here, you know. Perhaps they wanted money in some manner. Perhaps"—he squinted up at the sky—"there was no reason at all."

Su Lin, seeing Peter growing livid, said quickly, "Thank you, Commissioner."

"No effort will be spared. You can be certain of that. We'll keep you informed. Miss Lin? Peter? My regrets."

He was offering his hand. Peter shook it woodenly. Commissioner Hughes, evidently soused, strode off tacking into the breeze.

"Peter, my plane leaves in an hour and a half."

"I'll take you."

"No. Fook already has the car out."

"I'll drive you in the Mercedes."

"You're drunk."

"The hell I am."

Peter ran his father's black Mercedes furiously up Chatham Road, careening past a row of cars. Su Lin clutched the door handle.

"Must you drive like this?"

"Fuck," Peter said, speeding on, looking as though his face were about to crack.

Chatham became To Kwa Wan Road, running straight toward Kai Tak. Su Lin gazed out past the reclamation projects to the water where a Russian tanker lay moored in the harbor. The sky was cloudy, the air oppressive. Soon the storms would surely hit, driving the sampans to the shelters.

What happens between eleven and twenty-one? At the funeral Su Lin had found herself peering into the unsettling shadows of a family life she had known only as a young girl, a shifting backdrop against which dolls had played and simple desires cried out behind iron gates, imagining it all designed to please or displease her. How many family secrets were there? She was afraid to wonder. Here Freud never penetrated; here one revered the secrets, guarded them with silence.

Now it was over. There was no reason for her ever to return.

"I feel like I never really knew him," she said absently as they approached the Lung Cheung flyover.

Peter reached forward to light a cigarette, his fingers shaking. Suddenly he burst into tears.

She hadn't been ready for this. "Pull over," she said.

Peter edged the car off the road and brought it to a stop. He leaned over the wheel, sobbing into his hands. "Candace broke it off."

"Oh, Peter. I'm sorry."

She put a hand on his shoulder. Out the window she saw a jetliner dropping onto the Kai Tak strip and wondered if it was the one that would take her away.

"When are you leaving?" she asked softly.

Peter raised his head and looked away. The car was damp, stuffy; for a moment she felt afraid with him. Wearily she leaned against the car door. Peter lit his cigarette.

"It was a race thing," he said. "Somebody did a little campaign on her parents. Yellow menace. Got them terrified. Brahmins. Probably worried about losing their club memberships."

"It was something you wanted, wasn't it?"

"Candace, or the legitimacy?"

"Both."

"Yeah. I suppose." Peter wiped his face on his sleeve. "They'll find her a society white."

He looked at his sister. "So what about you? On your merry way back to the States." He pulled fitfully on the cigarette. "The artist. The little liberal."

"Why are you being cruel?"

Peter rolled down his window.

"Commissioner Hughes doesn't know."

Su Lin looked at him sharply. "About what?"

The thing she feared began to force its way up. She had so wanted to make it to the plane first. Now there seemed to be nothing holding it back.

"Opium."

Su Lin looked away and took a deep breath.

Peter turned toward her.

"Tell me what you know," she said.

Peter's voice picked up certainty. "I used to go over to Boston from Cambridge on weekends and work in the Lin shipping offices. They were importing rattan into Boston and San Francisco. During law school I did some legal work for them. Import licenses, customs. I'd see the printouts. The export business has never made much money. The restaurant's successful, but still small change. The family kept getting wildly richer. It became evident. Father never said a word."

"How big is it?"

"Huge."

"Millions?"

"Billions." Peter laughed miserably, blowing out smoke. "Our father was the biggest fucking gangster in Asia."

Su Lin felt desolate, blank.

"All those politicians and officials at the funeral. You think they came to honor a man who runs a restaurant? Father had every one in his pocket. And the girls in the slinky cheongsams? Father's mistresses."

They sat in silence watching the plane taxi in on the new runway built out over the water. Then Su Lin spoke. "When Mother left Father and took us to Japan in 1953, we stayed with the American."

"Terhune. The Asia scholar."

"There was always a *smell* around his flat."

"An addict. His name is shit around here."

"I remember rather liking him. A few years ago I met someone in Berkeley who smoked opium. There was that smell again. And Fook the chauffeur—he'd aged fifty years in ten."

"He chases the dragon. One out of every forty people in Hong Kong uses."

Su Lin looked at her brother. "Two years ago Father came to San Francisco for the yearly visit. I was doing a course at Berkeley in modern Chinese history. I'd just read about the Opium Wars of 1840–42. Over dinner I asked Father about the old days, about opium and the family. I was curious. He became very upset and said I mustn't speak of it again to anyone, even in America. I thought it was strange, but didn't think much more about it." She looked back toward the harbor.

"I used to think it was something from Great-Grandfather's time," she said. "The days of the compradors and the clippers. Silk, teas, opium."

Peter spoke bitterly. "Do you know what Chiu Chao means throughout Asia? Opium, vice."

Su Lin stared at her brother.

"For five generations the Lins have run most of the Asian trade, along with the Mason family and the Hong Kong Crown Bank." Peter materialized a hip flask from under the seat and took a pull. "The principals probably never see the stuff. They run other things too, like 'Thirty-six Beasts,' the Chinese numbers racket. They fix the double quinellas at Happy Valley. Sweet, isn't it?"

Out the car window, Kai Tak seemed suddenly distant.

"Know what I'm afraid to think about? If this had anything to do with what happened with Mother." Peter's mouth was quivering.

Su Lin found his eyes. "Why was he shot?"

"I don't know. If Left-Hand Chen knows, he's not saying. And Commissioner Hughes sure as hell isn't going to come up with anything."

Peter flipped his cigarette out the window and took a deep breath. "Does it matter to you?"

"Yes. No." Su Lin rolled down the car window and fought for air. An image of a seedy Berkeley junkie who used to follow her into a laundromat on Telegraph Avenue appeared in her mind.

"The night before he died," Peter said, "Father called me in. I'd just come in from Boston. I hadn't spoken to him in three years except on the phone. He told me he wanted me to move back to Hong Kong and train up to take over the business." Peter glowered. "It wasn't a request, it was an order."

"What did you say?"

"We argued. He said that for five generations the sons have always come back."

"Did you discuss opium?"

"No. Only food and furniture and ivory. Can you believe that? But he knew I knew."

"But why now?"

"I'll tell you. Chen had a son. His English name was Sam."

"I remember. Quiet, and smart like his father."

"We were the same age. A few years ago Father adopted him. He changed his name to Lin and named him his successor."

"Were you hurt?"

"Not at the time. I was glad. I was finishing law school. Sam had worked in the business and knew it. And Left-Hand Chen is very powerful in the family. By then I'd begun to figure out what the real Lin scene was. I thought Father might have done it to protect me." Peter shook his head. "Two months ago Sam died of typhoid."

"Chen must have been crushed."

"He never shows feelings. But I know it ruined his hopes of seeing his family take over the business." Peter looked at her in pain. "I was Father's second choice."

Su Lin couldn't look at him, and turned toward the water. "What of his charities, his orphanage?"

"Guilty money. To buy family respectability. Our fancy educations were paid for by opium. Everything was." Peter ground his jaws. "Our lives are a lie."

Across the harbor she saw a U.S. Navy helicopter drop lazily down the face of Victoria Peak, then swing out to the carrier *Enterprise* moored at North Point and land.

Peter reached to start up the car. "I think you should know that he expected you to come back too one day."

"And be the next *tai tai*? I wouldn't have. And I won't."

"They're going to read the will in a month or so. When Father's estate is settled, it will make you rich beyond anything you ever dreamed."

"I have no dreams of wealth."

Peter threw the empty flask onto the backseat. "I see. So where does art fit in?"

"I don't know. I know it's not evil."

"Is that enough?"

"Maybe it . . . bears witness." She looked at him. "Peter, there are things going on where I am. New life. A chance to change. I want to be part of that."

"Things don't change. Look at the Lin history."

Peter pulled the Mercedes back onto the road and gunned it toward the airport. Su Lin stared numbly ahead.

"When are you going to leave?"

Her brother fixed his eyes on the road. "Not right away."

"If all of this is true, you mustn't stay."

"I'm on a month's leave from the firm." He glanced at her warily. "I want to find out about things here."

Su Lin sat up, stunned. "Peter, your life may be in danger."

"Someone killed my father. Do I just walk away?"

"Yes," she said urgently. "That's what you do."

His voice was remote, stony. "Go back to Boston and chase around the Bennington slopes with some new Wellesley whore who thinks it's hip to go out with a rich Eurasian?"

"Opium's not just another commodity. You've seen the junkies."

"It's our family. It's what they've built for five generations. Somebody's got to deal with it."

"Chen can settle the estate. He knows everything," she pleaded as Kai Tak loomed around the curve.

"It's easy for you to say. You're not the son." He put a trembling hand to his head. "And you fit over there."

Su Lin turned and stared at him. "Is that it? Or is it money?"

Peter's hands shook on the wheel. "I went through a thing with horses. Hialeah . . ." He looked away. "Some Italian Father knew took me down to Havana one weekend a few years ago. I have a few debts."

"Take a draw from Mason's bank and clean it off."

"I tried," he muttered. "They're putting me off."

"I'll send you what I have."

"It wouldn't be enough.' He looked at her in pain. "I'm a little under it, Su. But I promise I'll get out."

They pulled up to the terminal in silence. Peter took off his sunglasses and opened the glove compartment to put them in. A black Beretta pistol sat inside like a shiny beetle. Su Lin flinched; she stared at her brother, horrified. Peter's wounded eyes looked back.

"Stay, Su. Just for a while. I may need you."

"That didn't sound Chinese enough," she said angrily. "You're supposed to snap when you speak to women."

Peter's shoulders slumped. He locked the glove compartment without looking at her and went to the back of the car and took her suitcase from the trunk.

"What's going to happen to his orphanage?" she asked inside the terminal.

"It'll get built. I'll make sure when I get back."

"From where?"

"Southeast Asia. Chen's taking me."

Her knees went soft. "Peter . . ."

At the boarding gate he reached down and hugged her awkwardly. His eyes had begun to redden again. "What do you feel you owe the family?" he asked.

"What family is left?" She pulled away.

Peter tightened. "He was our father, whatever he was or wasn't."

"Get out, Peter."

"I loved him."

"So did I."

She was crying too as she turned and ran down the corridor to the plane.

The last things Su Lin saw as the plane shot up off the strip at Kai Tak were the walled villages back in the New Territories, the new dam being built, the sun glinting off the fish-fattening ponds. Then the rice fields and stone bridges became a diminishing mosaic, like the lines on the back of a turtle. Up above the clouds there was only empty sky.

6

Benny the Guide sat in a slatted outdoor chair in the Socco Chico, pushing crumbs around on the table with a toothpick. He was dressed in an overcoat six sizes too large, wearing cheap European shoes with no socks. His unshaven face was narrow and pitted. He gazed emptily into the dense human mosaic of the Socco Chico—merchants, hustlers, tourists—letting his eyes go soft, feeling along the blind edge of motion.

The Socco Chico was a mere widening on the path from the harbor below to the European quarter above, forming a small plaza. Sagging Spanish buildings, their rusted balconies thick with cats and dead plants, crowded in over the tiny souk in the glimmering evening. Lights came on inside the cafe, casting a soft glow out upon this neocolonial terrain Benny the Guide knew as his own, where cultures met on the vilest of terms, bartering tokens of illicit desire.

The harbor whistle sounded. A cool breeze swept the cafe tables. Benny the Guide idly registered the arrival of a gaunt European in a dirty djellaba, with green eyes and a haunted mien, whom he had observed in the cafes the last few days, taking him for just more human driftwood cast up on the shores of Tangier.

Benny watched the man take an empty table several behind his own, then returned to his predatory contemplation of the Socco Chico as the first passengers from the ferry, breathing heavily, appeared on the steep winding path leading through the square.

Behind him, Jim Cross sat down at the cafe table with his sister's letter in his hand. A waiter approached in a black jacket, dirty white apron, and a red fez on his head. *"Thé menthe?"*

In the rippling brass tray that hung at the waiter's side Cross saw himself in miniature—knuckles looming forward like monstrous boulders, his robe sweat-stained, his pupils large with terror.

"Thé menthe?" the waiter repeated.

For a moment Cross had fallen down inside his own eyes. *"Café leche."* His lips pursed the words in the metal tray.

The waiter raised the tray, breaking up the image, and began clearing dirty glasses off the tables. "So when you leave?" he asked Cross in the peculiar unplaceable accent of the city. "Tomorrow?"

When Cross didn't answer, the waiter turned away. "Tomorrow," he repeated, his speech thick with disdain.

Cross reached faintly toward the waiter's sleeve. "Benny . . ." he muttered.

"Qué?" The waiter looked at him expectantly. When Cross said nothing more, the waiter shrugged and moved off.

Cross opened the letter from his sister he had begun in El Jefe's office:

> We despair of ever seeing you again, Jimmy. It seems like years. Why are you still in Africa? If that's where you are. Mother says she's heard the Arabs capture young white girls and sell them on the slave market. Is it true?
>
> Congrats on your 4-F at Orléans. Interesting it turns out you knew the doctor. Father always used to say thank God for connections. Seems a lot of people are getting drafted lately. My assistant's boyfriend got called up and sent somewhere in Indochina. Isn't that where the refugees were from in that clinic where you worked in France?
>
> What was it Kennedy said? "Ask not what you can do for your country. Ask what your country can do for you." Oops, I've got that backwards. Anyway.
>
> Your old friends ask about you. They just don't understand. You were such a God to them.
>
> Your letters *have* changed. I hardly recognize your voice. I keep try-

ing to match it with your face. Mother says, "Has Jim become what we used to call a *bohemian?*" She met someone—a surgeon, wouldn't you know. They may tie the knot. Ugh.

The girl you mentioned. Where is she? Are you still with her? Do you love her?

The waiter arrived with coffee. Cross looked out into the Socco Chico, waiting for the knot in his chest to subside. Vendors and hawkers were descending upon the new crop of tourists with imploring, unctuous glee.

Your records sit in a pile on my rug. "Sketches of Spain" is so worn it hardly plays. It always makes me think of you. And what about your writing? That was the idea, wasn't it? Oh, I liked your orphan piece in the *Tribune.*

The Dodgers and Koufax are headed for the Series. Everybody in L.A. is trying to get tickets. Our clinic's patients come and go. The country feels uneasy somehow. . . .

A grizzled, toothless Bedouin stood directly in front of him dangling a live chicken and jabbering a hoarse, mealy Arabic-Spanish patois through cracked, sun-furrowed lips. Cross waved him away. The Bedouin muttered an imprecation, illustrating it with his fingers, and moved on.

Uncle Oscar says you're the only Phi Beta Kappa he ever knew who turned into a bum overnight. I got *furious* at him for saying that! He just can't forgive you for walking out on *his* medical school.

Hope you use the money to come home. Love, Kathy.

He folded the letter and stuck it in his pocket. As the waiter passed, Cross called him over.

"Benny the Guide," Cross said, more emphatically.

The waiter nodded toward a front table.

Benny the Guide, hearing the sound of his name, stood and drifted back to Cross's table, smiling through stained teeth.

Cross shook a Pall Mall out of its pack and offered it.

"Anything you need, man?" Benny the Guide said, sitting down.

He took the cigarette and lit it with a wooden match, then held it between his fourth and fifth fingers, drawing smoke not from the tip of the cigarette but through his cupped hand.

"You want to buy kif? *Majouun?* I got Congo, man. I got *katama.* Good cheap *gibli* too, man. Or you want boys? Hoors? Guns? What do you want, man?"

It was a comment upon the nature of Benny the Guide's clientele that he spoke nothing but hipster slang.

"I want to see Ilya."

A wary silence settled over Benny. He stared into the Socco Chico. Finally he said, "You got business with Ilya?"

"El Jefe said you'd take me to him."

Benny the Guide sat still for a while, sucking slowly on the Pall Mall. Then he leaned close to Cross and grinned. His breath was hot and sour with whiskey. "Anything you need, man."

Cross gazed into Benny's blunt face a few inches from his own, searching the harsh, reddened eyes and finding in them only the terrible dark bloom of his own despair.

"Let's go."

Cross fished a couple of dirhams out of his robe and dropped them on the table. He followed Benny the Guide into the darkening plaza, stuffing his hands in his robe to keep them from shaking.

They dropped into the hooded, unlit maze of the alleys behind a group of women from the Rif mountains dressed in red and white striped aprons and terry-cloth robes. The women carried sticks, babies, and bound portage on their backs, their legs strong and short and placed wide like men's.

By the time the Rif women turned away, Benny and Cross were deep in the airless pathways of the casbah. Crazed alleys, stitched in stone, seemed to end suddenly at blank walls, then twist improbably off down winding, urine-drenched paths so narrow they had to turn sideways, scraping their chests against the stone. Robed figures huddled on the dusty floors, open palms frozen aloft. Cross was disoriented, in a trance, all direction gone.

They came to a crack in the wall where water trickled from a broken pipe. Cross leaned down, cupped his hands, and brought his face to the water.

"Come on, man," Benny the Guide whispered. "It's dangerous here."

Cross heard the rattle of a tambourine, a drum, a bowed instrument. As he stood up, the whirling silhouette of a dancing boy appeared behind a cafe curtain, lipsticked and rouged, a tube around his hips beneath a dress, hermaphroditic and strangely alluring.

Following Benny the Guide deeper into the quarter, Cross stumbled over a beggar woman and fell to his knees. She looked up at him with frightened animal eyes, making no sound, then wrapped her tattered burnoose around her and scuttled back against the wall. Cross scrambled to his feet and lurched on.

The alley became steep steps that suddenly widened. A moon burned through clouds, spilling soft dusty light on the stone. There was a mosque at the top. He could see his own shadow, long and fragmented, running diagonally across the steps.

"We're almost there," Benny the Guide said.

Cross felt an aching lassitude. Climbing the moonlit steps, he had an urge to run back to the woman in the alley and drop his head in her lap and lose himself in the enclosure of her mute, bottomless robes.

Suddenly the moon moved behind the mosque tower, throwing its shadow over him, obliterating his own. He stood in utter darkness. A cool wind from across the water rippled through the quarter, hitting his forehead like ice.

Cross felt further from earth, from the known world, than he had ever been, blinded and bound in darkness.

He had been born in seasonless light, the unremitting California sun: an overrich, empty excellence, a nightmare of reason. Now, frozen in a labyrinth of lunar blackness, a pure lucidity gripped him. He knew now he had always sought this darkness, to understand and own it. Cross stood on the mosque steps, swollen with remorse, staring into the indifferent heart of the universe.

A sudden memory of California waters told him, If a wave casts you under, struggle and you will drown. Rather let yourself sink until, having found bottom, you may chance to spring sunwards. Edging across the black mosque steps behind Benny the Guide, like a crab on the darkest ocean floor, Cross felt true bottom. With it came a new, bittersweet hunger for light.

"Hey, man, we're here."

The moon had reappeared from behind the mosque. Benny the Guide stood before a tall wooden doorway. A tile in the stucco said 99 CASBAH. Benny knocked, then stepped back into shadow. When Cross turned he had vanished.

The door opened slowly. A dark Arab in burnoose and slippers stood in an unlit entryway. Cross stepped inside and followed him down the hall of a vast run-down villa.

They emerged into a high octagonal room lit faintly by guttering candles. There was no furniture, only a few scattered pillows. A balcony wound around an open second story, forming an interior courtyard. Spectral figures, Europeans and Arabs Cross vaguely recognized from the cafes, moved silently about the cavernous, pillared room. The smell of kif was strong. In one corner Cross saw a blond woman in a worn burnoose stirring couscous over a burner.

The center of the eight-sided floor was a motif of large black and white tiled squares arranged like a chessboard. Upon it sat a solitary man in a white robe slowly cleaning piles of kif with a knife and a tilted board, seeds rolling idly across the tiles. Dozens of books lay about him. A rifle sat at his side.

"Hippocrates," he said softly, his voice caroming off the tiles. "So you've come."

Cross peered through the candlelight, certain he had come upon a madman.

"Come. Sit." The man gestured toward a pillow beside him.

As Cross approached, he could see the books: Coleridge, *Alice in Wonderland,* De Quincey's *Confessions of an English Opium Eater,* a pharmacopoeia, various cabala studies in Hebrew.

Cross sat down opposite the man. "Who are you?"

The answer came in a voice of soft patrician irony. "Your savior, if you choose. If so, until Paris, your master."

Cross watched him work a tiny pinched red clay bowl onto the end of a *sebsi,* a wooden pipe. He filled and tamped it with fresh dark Congo kif from a pile at his feet.

"You have met trouble in the South," he said.

He lit the pipe and inhaled ruminatively. Cross watched his eyes redden and begin to water.

"How do you know of me?"

A tiny laugh issued forth. "El Jefe teases the Europeans. He is only after sex. His lust rises up off him like some terrible rank perfume. If you had had a woman or a boy for him, your difficulties . . ."

The thought hung unfinished in the motionless air.

So this was Ilya, spoken of in the cafes: a man of involute, ravaged elegance, his eyes brimming with teahead sagacity, who presided magisterially over Tangier's exiles from the chessboard floor of his villa, prince of dreams, drawing them around him like a blanket— the dealers, refugees, hoods, and bad poets who hung about the casbah, clothing their transactions in a cloud of messianism and bad art.

"I too am a lapsed doctor," Ilya said, shifting on his cushion. "My interests led me to explore certain *larger* pathologies."

Ilya called himself an alchemist, a Jungian cabalist, a biochemical exile. He lived in the world's exotic and cheap outlaw towns— Cuernavaca, Istanbul, Tangier—writing endless treatises on drug arcana, corresponding with LSD physicists in Cambridge, electro-convulsive Pavlovians in Belgrade, *yage* anthropologists in Peru—a network of mad scholars and criminals seemingly committed to an inchoate revolution in consciousness only he could see. Encountering him, Cross sensed the absolute authority Ilya's bent erudition gave him in his own surroundings, a power that would shrivel and die like some rare larval insect on contact with the light of day.

"What do you do here?" Cross asked.

"What do I *do?*"

Ilya's amusement was echoed by a dissolute ghostly chorus from the shadows of the surrounding rooms.

"I *provide,* Hippocrates." He tapped his pharmacopoeia and smiled softly.

Ilya knocked out his pipe on a tray and began to finger his rifle, his head bobbing slowly as if on a string.

"In my work I am aided by certain elements who imagine they control us, but who in fact support our . . . revolution."

Cross, knowing he hadn't the luxury of finding Ilya ridiculous, nodded. "El Jefe says you need something delivered to Paris."

Ilya, seemingly distressed by Cross's brusqueness, looked dreamily away. "The American abroad," he intoned, "bears the arrogance of Empire. He browses the Old World as if it were a museum, thinking he will not be touched by its evil."

Cross watched Ilya scratch his neck, the back of his hands, as if suddenly infested. A rash, he explained, attributable to the efforts of certain governments hostile to his researches.

He pointed to the array of substances around him. "I play them like an organ," he whispered, grinning.

Cross felt a rising hopelessness. "What is it you wish me to take to Paris?"

The query seemed to dissolve into the suffocating vastness of the room.

"The courier is not well served by knowing the contents of his delivery."

Cross spoke with sudden feeling: "I am in trouble. A girl I was with was killed. All I want is to get back to Paris. Do you understand?"

Ilya gazed quietly at Cross, nodding. "After Paris, what?"

"I have no plans."

"Desire has failed you. Now back to duty, is it, Hippocrates? Back to your medicine?" Ilya clucked paternally. "Exile is a state of grace. Why must you tamper with it?"

Cross gazed warily at his host, feeling a disembodied tension rise in the air. He knew the fitful small treacheries of the kif smoker, who countered the remorseless shifts in reality that shattered his reveries with a cruel acerbity, suddenly turning upon allies, accusing them of dark complicities. That this was to be the man with whom he must forge a blind pact for his freedom filled him with foreboding.

"The terrible *garrote*," Ilya whispered, as if reading his thoughts. "But here, smoke, Hippocrates. We will turn dross into gold." Chuckling, Ilya held out the pipe.

Cross looked past it to Ilya's pale, shimmering visage. "What is the errand?"

Ilya sighed wearily. "You think you are above the others. People like you suffer difficult fates." He withdrew the pipe. "I can find another."

"I said I'd do it," Cross whispered.

At this Ilya seemed to swell into focus and become suddenly precise. "Good. Then you will take a suitcase to a man in Paris. A Corsican friend. His name is Spiritu. You will like him. I will give you his number. Call when you arrive."

Ilya placed before Cross a pair of crisp hundred-dollar bills. "Change one at American Express here before you leave. Take the ferry across the Straits. At Algeciras take the train north to the border. Then take a train to Paris. There will be a control, someone who will travel nearby but whose identity is unknown to you. He will make sure your trip goes well, that you are not disturbed, that you do not leave the train or try to abandon your cargo. In Paris you will receive a thousand dollars. Enough to get back to California, yes?"

"You don't understand. I can't cross into Spain."

"You needn't worry. We are not fools. El Jefe has full accommodations with Spanish customs."

Ilya offered Cross the pipe again. "To celebrate your imminent release from the nightmare of the South."

Cross thought the kif smokers fools, an attitude suspect in the quarter. He attached no blithe hopes or holy attributes to using, shared none of their fantasies of social transformation. Since Tenerife he had avoided any expedient to deaden the torment of loss, wary of the contents of his own fantasies. Now, sensing that whatever he refused at this moment would adhere to him, Cross took the pipe.

He inhaled it in two puffs, then tapped the tiny residue out onto the tray. The black ash hopped weakly, glowed, then expired.

The villa recast itself into a floating ship. The distance between a question and an answer became a desert. Ilya had receded into the villa's bottomless twilight. He heard his quiet laughter.

Cross was somewhere far from his body, far from memory and pain, when Ilya appeared before him again holding out a shiny black flattened ball that looked to Cross like tar.

"Opium," Ilya crooned. "The queen of drugs. The milk of paradise." Ilya brought it close.

Cross saw that he had mixed it with the kif. He looked up at Ilya.

Ilya grinned. "A doctor should know his tools."

He lay in a tiny windowless room lit by a candle, watching the ceiling move and change. The blond woman in a burnoose he had seen when he arrived entered silently with scissors and European clothes. When she bent down and kissed his neck, Cross gently pushed her away.

She cut his hair, and left.

He lay in dark, dreaming of light.

The muezzin's cry came. Dawn spread through the villa. Cross sat up. Next to him was a black suitcase, locked. On it was his passport. His notebook lay open. On a fresh page someone had written the name Bébé Spiritu and a Paris phone number.

7

Su Lin sat by the window of the Tokkaido bullet train rocking through the outskirts of Kyoto, watching the low sun flicker on the rice fields. In the distance the mountains were still; at her feet the ground was a racing blur of monochromatic shapes. The train altered its direction, suddenly throwing up her own image before her, broken by the glint of sun through the window opposite.

Somebody in the seat across the aisle lit a match; it flared in the window, behind her eyes. Luminous, she contemplated her own head as if it were a statue. A head that belongs nowhere, she thought.

The train rushed on through the low surburbs. Su Lin looked out across the valley surrounded by hills and the spread of slate rooftops, broken only by the tips of the hundreds of temples and shrines. Gazing at herself, she made a faint effort to account for bolting the plane at Haneda, making the call, and boarding the train from Tokyo. She could not recollect ever having acted out of such pure spontaneous need.

At the station the train hovered in sleek silence, seeming to breathe. Su Lin took her purse and single leather suitcase from above the seat, stepped past a tiny, bent woman consuming an open box lunch of seaweed, fish, and rice balls, and descended to the platform.

She came out in front of the station into a clamping, sticky summer heat and found her way to the taxi stand. *"Kita-ku,"* she said to the driver, indicating the northern district.

When she showed him the paper with the address, the taxi driver brightened and chuckled. *"Terhune-san desu ka?"*

She smiled, wondering if every cabbie in this city of two million knew him. *"So desu."*

As the taxi raced up Karasuma-dori, she peered out at the city's curious war-spared beauties: Higashi-Honganji Temple, Shinshu sect headquarters, the Goshō, the Imperial Palace. She was surprised at how much she remembered after nine years. The city was modeled after Peking, with its gridded streets and palace at its center— a hymn to Chinese culture, built seven hundred years ago from the descriptions of returning monks. Indeed Japanese esthetics seemed more Chinese to her than the blind mercantile Hong Kong streets. That a city so drab from above could hold such internal splendors she found curious; but the lining of the kimono is more beautiful than what one shows on the outside.

In the northern district the taxi came to a quiet gravel street with pines and bamboo and long slatted wooden fences, and pulled up.

"Ōki ni," the taxi driver said in Kyoto dialect when she paid him.

She slid open the wooden entry, stepped inside, and found herself in the garden of a small estate with trimmed pines, several carp ponds, and bonsai. An ancient thatch-roofed teahouse sat beside the largest pond.

She stepped up the round stones laid out in a path to the entrance. A note was pinned to the shoji paper door: TEACHING AT THE Y. BE BACK AT 3. COLD TEA IN THE ICEBOX. JACK.

Su Lin stepped out of her shoes and slid open the shoji.

The teahouse consisted of three small tatami rooms, intensely austere; the only furniture was a lacquer table, bedding, and cushions. Glad to be out of shoes, she padded across the tatami in her nylons to the refrigerator and removed a pitcher of Japanese tea.

The air was hot. A cockroach rustled across the tatami, making a sound like bunching paper. There was a strange, rather pleasant, dark smell that she remembered from years ago.

Sipping tea, she began to examine the flat. On the lacquer table were three snapshots in small frames. One showed Jack Terhune, tall and bearded, dressed in tweeds, wild graying hair curling unfashionably down over his collar, standing alone before a nameless country temple gate. Large, pensive eyes stared out at the photographer from beneath bushy brows.

A second photo showed Terhune with a group of university students in the snow in front of the orange struts of the Heian Shrine. He towered above them, dark and brooding and fierce. But the tilted head and the eyes bore some hint of soft surprise, or wonder.

The third picture occupied Su Lin a long time. A younger Terhune in a three-piece suit stood with a Caucasian woman on a bridge in Arashiyama overlooking the rapids. The woman was tall, fair, well-dressed; she gazed at the camera with flushed defiance. The flowering pride of a love affair at its height shone from both faces. Su Lin didn't need to look on the back to know the date: 1953. Terhune looked intense, handsome—the dark poet-scholar. The woman looked beautiful, proud, even happy. But behind the eyes lay a nerve-jagged distraction; something had begun to erode.

Finally the rich aroma pervading the room caused her to turn away and seek its source.

Sitting in the tokonoma, the alcove, beneath a scroll were a pair of objects. The first was a gleaming Japanese short sword on a black lacquer stand.

Su Lin slid over and sat before the other object.

It was a pipe, several feet long. Its stem was cane, black from use, its mouthpiece of horn. The opposite end was encased in beautiful copper, inlaid with silver. Midway on the pipe was a round copper socket resembling a flattened turnip with a tiny pinhole on top. There was dried matter on the pipe, and dust.

On the wooden floor next to the tokonoma were notebooks bound in brocade. Beside them were piled scholarly monographs and books in English and Chinese: Lao-tzu, Pound, Wilhelm, Confucius, Waley, Fenellosa, Li Po—and Terhune's own published works.

One rainy afternoon in Berkeley her professor of Oriental history had described Jack Terhune over coffee:

"A legendary scholar, really. *The* man on northern Chinese art until his peculiar, ah, *predilections* resulted in his defrocking. A passable poet as well, I believe. And a martial arts master? Or am

I thinking of someone else? In any event, he's a certain type, a rare creature of postwar Asia who lives in the bittersweet half-lit world of the cultural or sexual exile. Some fractured descendant of Conrad's people, one could say, or Lafcadio Hearn's.

"An opium user, of course. He settled down in Kyoto some years ago after being dismissed from one university after another throughout the Far East because of his habit. Became addicted to morphine in the Spanish Civil War, I believe. American originally. Ended up at Oxford. And he's really your godfather? Amazing."

The professor had paused to light his pipe. "How long since you've seen him?"

"Five years ago he passed through Boston. I was in my last year of high school."

"Hm. Well, Kyoto's not a bad place for a fellow like that. Since the war almost all the American Chinese scholars live there. It's the closest thing to a Chinese city. None of the Americans, and few of the others, can get to the Mainland. Certainly not one with Terhune's past." The professor had shaken his head. "It sucks one in, dear, Chinese history. It's a bottomless obsession, like the bloody drug itself. I can't think of a better example than Jack Terhune. A scholar consumed by his subject. One who slipped over the line. It can happen . . ."

The professor had grimaced, fishing in his cords for coffee change. "He was allegedly cured some years back. But nobody believes it for a moment."

Su Lin reached into the alcove and took the pipe in her hands, feeling its blackened cane stem, turning its copper bowl in her hands.

"Hello!"

She looked up, startled to see the image of Jack Terhune filling his own doorway. He wore, in spite of the heat, a tweed jacket over a starched white shirt.

Su Lin replaced the pipe and scrambled to her feet, wiping her eyes. "Jack!"

Slipping his shoes off, he entered and walked across the tatami toward her.

They sat in a private restaurant room in Pontocho, the geisha quarter, overlooking the river. Sipping cold tea against the sweltering heat, she watched Terhune's hand aloft, his eyes moist, eyebrows raised in conspiratorial drama. The remains of the meal sat about them. Throughout dinner, accompanied by ravenous quantities of beer and sake, he had listened raptly to Sun Lin's sad recounting of the events in Hong Kong—her father's murder, the funeral, Peter's outburst in the car—frowning with disapproval, nodding in sympathy, as if the tale confirmed his worst suspicions.

Su Lin had picked at clams in clear soup, watched without appetite small esthetic meats and scallions grilling on a hibachi, licked dispiritedly at green tea ice cream between sentences. Now spent with speaking, she turned to the window.

The Kamogawa was a silver ribbon beneath a white moon. By day they washed silk here, she recalled. Across the river people milled about the entrance to the Gion Kabuki theater beneath huge red paper lanterns. She turned back to the room to find Terhune gazing at her, his dark eyes full of wonder.

"I always knew someday I would be here in Pontocho talking to you."

"Yes."

"God. You look so like—"

"Mother. Yes, a little." Watching emotions run through Terhune, Su Lin felt stirrings of her own.

Having embarrassed himself, Terhune began to toy with his sake cup. "And you graduated?"

"Yes. Last month."

"Brilliant, brilliant."

Young students in blue uniforms walked along the river bank beneath them, arm in arm. A waitress in kimono knelt and freshened her tea, then disappeared.

"You knew nothing of the trade before his death?" Terhune said.

"Only surmises. I'm sure it was Father's intention that I didn't. I rarely saw him after we left Hong Kong. Once a year he'd come to the States. We'd have dinner."

Terhune took out a cigarette and lit it with a wax match. He began to speak with uncharacteristic hesitation. "Let us speak . . . frankly. I know you've come to find out about certain things of which you now have an inkling, as well as for whatever little solace a man you hardly know, your mother's old lover, can offer."

He frowned and stared off into the flickering river below, lit by Gion's lanterns. His broodingness, drawn into itself, struck Su Lin as sensual.

"I first met your mother a few years after the war, at a consulate cocktail party in Hong Kong. I was teaching there, doing research. Through my . . . interests, I had some idea who your family was. Here was this beautiful, bright lady from Boston who found herself in a strange postwar Mikado world with two young children and a husband who . . ." His voice trailed off for a moment. "She was a wounded bird. My kind."

He paused to sip sake. "We began to meet. Just friends. She was glad to have someone to talk to. Not very good at keeping secrets, she told me things about the trade, the family. I encouraged it. The subject was . . . close to me."

"I know you've been a user," Su Lin said, anxious to cross the barrier. "A professor at Berkeley told me. I saw the pipe, smelled it in the flat."

Terhune's dark eyes rested upon her. She couldn't quite read his expression, unsure if he was dead serious or ironical.

"Picasso once described it as 'the least stupid smell in the world.'"

"It means nothing to me if you smoke opium."

"The new generation. Where were you when I needed you?" Terhune smiled faintly. "What do you know about drugs?"

"Four years at Berkeley. I'm not naive."

"I don't mean the silly ones. Marijuana. The psychedelics. Cocaine. They trivialize the imagination. Smoking opium empowers it."

Chastened, Su Lin sipped her tea awkwardly. "Then I suppose I don't know much."

"When I first met Winny I hid my addiction from her. It's not that hard to do—for a while. But your father knew. When he found out she was seeing me he had me banished from Hong Kong—as a degenerate. It has its amusing side. I was smoking his stuff in the dens. He lost a customer." He chuckled blackly. "Your mother fled Hong Kong to join me in Kyoto, bringing you and Peter along."

"I remember leaving the house on Victoria Peak suddenly one night and arriving here."

"Your mother and I became lovers then. During those months she told me more of the Lin history. Astonishing things. And I had pursued my own research, compiling notes, journals, as a substitute for the comfort of the drug perhaps. I wasn't smoking then." He sought her eyes. "Nor am I now. Though you needn't believe me." His eyes fell. "I have no right to ask that."

He refilled his sake cup, then leaned toward Su Lin and spoke with great intensity. "I must know more about opium and the history of the Lin family than any man, white or yellow. More even than Left-Hand Chen."

"They are inseparable, then. My family and the drug."

"That," Terhune said, almost as if asking forgiveness, "is indeed the case."

Su Lin looked down at the tatami, ashamed.

"I am the Lin family's secret scholar," Terhune said. "It is an obsession, my interest, and a dangerous one. It has come close to costing me my life, and may again. Your father feared me for what I knew and despised me for giving solace to your mother."

"What happened after we came here?"

"The three of you stayed with me in a rented house near Higashiyama. Your mother's . . . dissolution had begun. She would wake up screaming, consumed with terror. She feared poisoning. It was only later that I realized her fears were real."

"You can't be serious."

Terhune darkened. "Frankly your arrival alarms me. I don't doubt you were followed here, and that we are now being watched."

"That's ridiculous. Nobody even knew I was coming."

Terhune turned to the window; Su Lin couldn't help but follow his eyes. "He could be anywhere. Beneath the paper lanterns of Gion, milling among the crowd by the river . . ."

She had an urge to laugh. "But why would anyone follow me?"

Terhune's eyes flashed in the soft light. "The sword in my alcove next to the pipe. A remnant of days here with your mother. They came after me then. Why not now?"

She felt the heat of danger, less of being followed than of the haunted mind of the man across from her.

"Would you prefer that I leave?"

"No," Terhune said quickly. "Please stay."

"The past is over. My father is dead now."

Terhune smiled wearily. "The one-handed mandarin is not."

Su Lin flinched. His intimations were becoming her own, lacing the night with unexpected fear.

"The trade is subject to great pressures," he said. "The defection of an insider is a serious thing. In the case of a family member it is simply unacceptable, traitorous." Terhune looked at her carefully, as if debating whether to continue.

"You were telling me about my mother," she said.

"Your father always showed a kind face to the world. But with the years he grew inwardly monstrous. The trade does that. He beat her—"

"No," she whispered as new sadness entered her.

"I think it wasn't always that way. Perhaps the early years were good for them. It seems to me things worsened when Left-Hand Chen arrived from Shanghai and joined the Lin business—"

"Then we left for Boston," she said, eager to move the recounting forward.

"She was not received well by her family. The rest you know."

"Yes." Su Lin cupped her hands around the teacup. "When we got to Boston she broke down entirely. My grandparents, the Churches, had doctors come in. She was diagnosed as paranoid schizophrenic. They installed her in a wing of the Wellesley mansion. Peter and I were sent off to boarding schools. Father sent checks from Hong Kong to support us."

"And Winny?"

"Electroshock, drugs. There seemed to be no end to it. Peter went on through Harvard. I went out to Berkeley. Mother never left the mansion again."

"I came to the States in 1955 and tried to see her. Your grandparents wouldn't allow it."

"I heard. Perhaps it was just as well."

"Tell me," Terhune said earnestly. "How mad was she?"

Su Lin looked away. "Sometimes she simply wasn't there. Other times she'd be terrifyingly lucid. Then the drugs would kick in." She took a breath and looked out at the river. "One day four years ago Peter called me at boarding school. Mother had gotten out of her room and crossed the lawn to the pond. They found the rowboat just drifting. She jumped, she fell. Nobody knows which."

Terhune bolted the rest of his sake. When he looked back at her his eyes had reddened. "Peter," he muttered. "How did he take it?"

"It devastated him, I think. But things were already rough for him, a Eurasian in New England. He carries that burden."

"And you don't?"

"It's different for a girl. They find you exotic."

"Or beautiful." He gazed at her.

"Peter struggles," she said.

Terhune shook his head. "I remember him as a boy with his kites. He was like a child-king, adored by both races along the Peak. An image of hope."

"Things changed," she said.

"The first blow must have been when he was taken from Hong Kong and brought here. He became sullen. Your mother so wanted to protect you both from the effects . . ." Terhune turned the empty sake cup in his fingers.

"Tell me what you know of my family's history. The early generations."

Terhune drew back. "Volumes. I couldn't possibly—"

"Please," she said, surprised at her own urgency.

Terhune studied her in the soft light of the restaurant room. "I can get you a room at the Miyako, or . . ."—he gestured carefully—"you could have the other room in the teahouse."

"I'd like that."

"It's a warm night. We could walk home along the river."

It was an oppressively dank evening, the kind that envelops Kyoto in the summer, making sleep impossible and sending residents drifting aimlessly through the city just to be out. Su Lin strolled with Terhune northward along the river. Mosquitoes jabbed the air, a bloated moon ducked in and out of hazy clouds. Cockroaches, frozen in the light, pimpled the earthen path. Su Lin could see the soft silhouettes of Higashiyama's hills as they mirrored the line of the Kamogawa.

"For five generations, since 1832, your family has been the custodian of an ever greater share of the Asian trade in opium."

"This began with the comprador?"

"Yes. Your great-great-grandfather worked as comprador for a Scotsman named Jacob Mason, the founder of one of the biggest British trading firms in the Far East. This Lin, from Swatow originally, was a hong merchant who worked in one of the Canton godowns, the warehouses, in the zone where the British were allowed to trade.

"In 1832 Mason, with Parliament and the Queen's tacit blessing, began shipping Indian opium from Patna, Malwa, and Ghazipur to Canton in great chests aboard the old China merchantmen clippers, forcibly cultivating a Chinese market—and enslaving a nation to opium in the process."

"I thought opium was grown in China."

"A myth inserted into schoolbooks by the British. Before they began shipping it in, China had no opium problem. But Parliament considered this cultivated plague to be China's punishment for having overcharged them on tea and silk, draining the Royal Exchequer of silver. They saw in opium a way to get the silver back out. They were right."

The moon appeared from behind a cloud as they came to the Imadegawa-dori bridge. Terhune looked down at her, his lips and face suddenly large, sensual in the unexpected light.

"One spring Mason went to London to be knighted by the Queen for his work in preserving the Empire. While he was gone the comprador impregnated his daughter. When Mason got back and found out what had occurred in his absence he was enraged, of course. But his daughter swore love to this Chiu Chao man, and they married. Mason reluctantly took him into the firm."

"Fantastic," Su Lin whispered.

"Yes. Now their offspring, your great-grandfather Charles, was sent off to England to be educated. After college he stayed on and became a . . . *confidant,* if you get me, of Coleridge, Wordsworth, the Romantic poets, as Jacob Mason had once been to De Quincey in Edinburgh." Terhune chuckled. "The artists. All users. De Quincey took it with alcohol, Coleridge as camphorated tincture of laudanum."

"My great-grandfather was their connection?"

"He would have objected to the term. Opiates weren't illegal. People don't realize that ten to twenty tons entered England every year through most of the nineteenth century. Working people took it routinely, gave it to their children to cure colds. It was sold under names like Godfrey's Cordial, A Pennyworth of Peace!" Terhune laughed vehemently.

A hot, swirling breeze rose off the river and rushed past them toward the center of the city.

"Later in life your great-grandfather Charles Lin tired of being an exotic and moved back to Hong Kong with an English wife who couldn't take the climate and died in the first monsoon. Charles then married a Swatow woman who bore him a son, quite Chinese in appearance."

"Grandfather Robert?"

"Yes."

"And what happened to the Masons?"

"The Mason clan had backed two successful opium wars and grown unconscionably wealthy from opium at the expense of the Chinese. But they came under new moral pressure from a Victorian Parliament, and drifted away from opium and into banking and legitimate trading, where they are to this day. The *gwailo* no longer traffic in opium directly. That they leave to the Chinese. They merely finance it."

"The Hong Kong Crown Bank."

"Yes."

Su Lin thought of the leering Scots banker Mason at Father's banquet, and his assertion that they were all but cousins.

"You look pale." Terhune was looking down at her. "Are you tiring? We could take a taxi the rest of the way."

"No. Go on. We haven't gotten to Grandfather."

Terhune, feigning protest, resumed his recounting as they walked on. "Your grandfather Robert went to France to be educated. He fell in with the fin de siècle crowd—Rimbaud, Beardsley, Jarry, the Club des Hachischins—a little smiling man with a hookah in a bag! You see how art runs through your family in its way? No surprise you wish to be a painter."

Su Lin found a smile.

"In Robert Lin's time there was still no particular dishonor attached to the trade. In fact it was considered quite *courant*. The substance hadn't yet fallen on hard times. But history will remember Robert as the man who made the contract with the German company Bayer, securing the first real Lin fortune—not to mention Bayer's!"

"The people who make aspirin?"

Terhune nodded. "In 1874 an English research chemist had synthesized diacetylmorphine when he boiled morphine and acetic anhydride over a stove for several hours. Bayer put it on the market in 1898 and sold it openly over the counter for years—under their coined brand name Heroin!—until the Geneva Convention of 1925 outlawed it."

Wandering through the sweltering night in an Asian city not her own with this strange exiled man she hardly knew, suspended between worlds and identities, hearing tales of her family's past, Su Lin felt oddly comforted.

"Robert Lin," Terhune was saying, "eventually married a French woman, your grandmother, and returned to Hong Kong to run the trading company from there. They all seem to return, you see."

"The family was wealthy by then?"

"Well off, not wealthy. That came with Harry, your father. Robert sent his son Harry to Harvard just after World War I. A high-strung young debutante named Winona Church fell madly in love with him—Orientals having been all the rage since Rabindranath Tagore had passed through Boston a few years earlier. Your grandparents were horrified. Later when your mother fell apart I suppose they felt it only proved their point."

"Peter and I embarrass them, though they've tried to be kind," she said. "God knows what they would have thought if they'd had an inkling of Father's real business."

"But don't you see, they do! All the Boston clippers came East. The Americans had their concession in Canton too—the Astors, Cabots, Russells. And your people, the Churches. They all shipped opium a century ago."

Terhune laughed with harsh delight as Su Lin tried to embrace this unsettling idea.

"Perhaps they have guilty consciences, your grandparents. You and Peter are reminders of their own opium heritage!" Terhune paused and looked up. "My God, we're practically home."

Su Lin followed him away from the river and down the quiet graveled lanes of Kita-ku.

"I'd like to know the rest."

"The story of the present century is monstrous, a descent into base criminality. Better your brother tell you."

"But Peter knows little more than I."

"That will change soon enough. Where is he now?"

"Off to Southeast Asia, I think."

"With Chen?"

"Yes."

"To the Golden Triangle," Terhune muttered.

"He's staying on to settle the family's affairs."

Terhune smiled faintly. "Already you begin to cover for him." He shook his head emphatically. "Peter will stay longer than that. Left-Hand Chen Po-chi will see to it."

They stepped through the wooden slatted entrance and into the garden, now illuminated by moonlight. Su Lin followed him into the teahouse.

Seeing her discomfort, he said brightly, "Shall we console ourselves with a masseur? We have a neighborhood man. Blind. Very rigorous but . . . thorough."

She feared encouraging longing in him, but she had her own needs. Terhune was the one person on earth to whom she could talk just now. "Let's," she said.

Fat and wheezing, clad only in loincloth, the blind masseur came tapping up the path. They lay in futons in summer robes, separated by a partial screen. The masseur used his knuckles like drills, delivering something close to pain that Su Lin welcomed as pleasure.

Afterwards they lay quiet, tired but awake. The room was lit by moonlight diffused upon the rice-paper door.

"Tell me about your life here, Jack."

Terhune lit a Players and inhaled before speaking. "It's sufficient. I have my students, my books and monographs." He spoke with somber irony. "I am a banished scholar, published in obscure journals. An exile from opium. And my country."

In the silence Su Lin heard the whirring of cicadas, the tires on gravel of a passing car.

"I come from a big brawling Montana family. Drinkers. I ran away to San Francisco and shipped out in the merchant marine. I wanted to write, think. A fatal early dose of Jack London. In China I found an old British Orientalist who was translating the *Tao Te Ching*. He took me under his wing and later sponsored my admission to Oxford."

Terhune drew on the cigarette in the dim light. "In 1938 I ended up in Spain. I was wounded, given morphine. My habit kept me out of World War Two. Afterwards I finished up at Oxford, then came to Asia on a Messageries Maritime freighter from Marseilles to Saigon. In the forecastle everyone smoked. I smoked steadily for years after that." He nodded toward the alcove.

"You never returned to America?"

"Only once. I wanted to see your mother. There is something in

America I despise, something that offers life while killing it, some empty, self-congratulatory idiocy. In Asia, and the drug, I found a culture deep and wise, one that understands death."

Su Lin watched Terhune stub out his cigarette. The top of his kimono fell away. She saw a pair of tattoos circling his pectorals, one of a dragon, the other of an eagle.

"Tell me about opium."

"But I did."

"Tell me what it's like to smoke it."

Terhune lay still for some time.

"Why does someone smoke?" she pressed. "Why willingly court your own oblivion?"

"What is the price of ecstasy? There are certain risks, unless one wants to live insipidly."

Su Lin saw his silhouette shift in the darkness. His voice filled with weary desire: "We all carry within us something folded up like those Japanese flowers made of wood which unfold in water. Opium plays the same role as the water. None of us carries the same kind of flower. It is possible that a person who does not smoke may never know the kind of flower that opium might have unfolded within him. It was Jean Cocteau who said that."

Su Lin listened to his slow breathing.

"Everything one does in life, Su Lin, even love, occurs in an express train racing toward death. To smoke opium is to get out of the train while it is still moving."

She felt Terhune's dark opium soul rise through the night, filling the room. She felt afraid, elated.

"I exploited your mother," Terhune was saying. "An addict's world is so perfect, everyone and everything is viewed with distance, as prey. I used her to learn of opium, in the hope that I could somehow master it, control it." His voice cooled to a whisper, rich with regret. "Don't misunderstand. I loved her. But the user answers to only one mistress."

"How much did you take when you smoked?"

"Twelve pipes a day. For years. It's a myth that the dosage must increase. If he takes care of himself an addict will be fortified against flu, colds, sore throats. I know people who've smoked twelve pipes a day for forty years."

Feeling Su Lin's silence, he went on. "You mustn't be quick to condemn, even though the truth of opium brings you pain right now. Is 'normal' reality any less absurd? Is flight into opium flight at all?" He gazed at her through the shadows. "Or is it actually arrival?"

Su Lin was alarmed by his passionate defensiveness, his advocacy.

"The Chinese word for opium is *yen*. The origin of our English word for desire, yearning. It's fitting. Opium is consummate desire, the desire against which all others must be measured."

"Stronger than love, sex?"

"Much."

"What about heroin, morphine?"

"Mere derivatives. Pure opium is the mother of drugs. The others are beneath contempt. Smokers form an aristocracy of the spirit. If you understand opium you needn't concern yourself with the others."

"But you have stopped smoking."

"A matter of access, and health. And some fragile sense of reason as transparent as that paper screen door," he said, nodding toward the entrance. "Opium has expelled me for now. That's all."

His voice was cold. "Don't expect me to be a traitor to the drug. I owe it my perfect hours." Terhune shifted on his mattress, fighting her gaze. She sensed his reluctance to continue.

"There's another reason I abstain," he said finally. "I do it to deny them the victory of controlling me."

"Who are they?"

"The Chinese, the British, the Corsicans, the Sicilians. And the men who are their masters. Those who traffic in desire and seek to control it." Terhune nodded toward the alcove. "That short sword. I learned how to use it from a master at the Toho studios here who trains samurai actors. That was during your mother's time here. I needed it."

Now it was Su Lin's eyes that dropped.

"The sword goes with the pipe. The smoker sits, calm and inert, as around him evil rages. It would never occur to the opium smoker to go to war, to make bombs, to torture people for information. But in the name of the drug, wars are fought, nations toppled. It is a spoil of empire. In the last century they called these wars by name. In this one they are more indirect. But it is a fact, Su Lin, that he who controls opium controls the world."

Su Lin was up on her elbows, peering at him, fascinated. "Why do you care so much?"

"Because I want to go back to the garden. Perhaps if those who seek to control ecstasy were vanquished, the drug would be unnecessary."

Su Lin fell silent. She felt her father's ghost pass between them. Outside a car passed slowly, as if from another world.

"Do you consider yourself cured?"

"There are no cures, only respites. Opium stalks the user like a shadow. One who smokes, dies smoking. I took the cure several times. It is horrible. Once when I met your mother, because I loved her. Again after she left, when I thought I loved someone else. But if I ever returned to Hong Kong I would smoke again."

"What of your willpower?"

Terhune snorted. "Opium toys with the will. It turns stone to water. The user dances happily toward his grave, mimicking life and in doing so exceeding it. Opium equips him with a steely logic—dispassionate, brilliant—that the straight person never achieves. Don't let anyone fool you. That is the allure, and its fascination for the artist."

Su Lin reeled from Terhune's words. "What did you know of my mother's condition?"

"It was the madness of being stalked in the night by a vast criminality. In a sense, she was just being reasonable. Opium leaves no one safe. Also she suffered the madness of humiliation, of defeat. You see, Winny Lin found out a terrible truth."

"What is that?"

"During the war Hong Kong was occupied by the Japanese. Your father, Peter, and your mother, pregnant with you, hid out in southern China with Chiang Kai-shek and the Americans. Afterwards, when things became difficult in Hong Kong, Winny went to the Americans for protection. The American Consulate threw her out."

"But why?"

Terhune laughed bitterly. *"Because they are players in the game. Winny Lin fled one enemy right into the arms of another. It was the final blow. It left her no ground to stand on."*

"Why didn't she stay here with you?"

Terhune's voice was steel. "Me? An addict? I was just another part of the circle closing around her."

Su Lin lay in silence, staring at the paper screen.

"They'll call you back to Hong Kong, Su Lin. What will you do? In a family even half Asian, disloyalty is impermissible. You know that. In a daughter or sister it is unspeakable. The vise will twist."

Su Lin turned defiantly away. "It doesn't concern me."

"Yes. Try and stay away. Lead your own life. I don't know if it's possible. If there's any way I can help you, I will."

"What about my brother?"

"It may be too late for Peter. The temptation will be to risk yourself for him. Don't."

They lay for some moments without speaking. Then Terhune said suddenly, "I have a favor to ask. My journals. When I die they will come to you. They concern the family, all the way back. They expose everything about the present trade—the players, the interests. If the time is right, perhaps you could see to their publication. I once imagined I could get them into the right hands in my lifetime. But it's too soon."

She found the bearded, furrowed face through the shadows. "Of course," she said.

Su Lin awoke in the middle of the night startled by a sound. She sat up. A figure stood outside the shoji door, silhouetted by moonlight, a sword in his hand.

Terhune appeared in the doorway in his kimono. "I thought I heard someone." He looked perplexedly down at the blade in his hand. "Sorry."

Su Lin dropped back to her mat. He came and sat down next to her. She looked up at him, afraid.

"You should leave. In the morning."

"I know."

"You look so like her." His dark eyes explored her.

"I'm not her." Her voice was shaking as her hand reached up to fend off her own desire.

Terhune looked at her a moment longer, then turned and went back to his mat.

Su Lin lay awake trembling in the darkness until dawn brought mercy.

8

Dawn rose pale and cool over the Straits. Cross stood at the entrance to Tangier's European quarter, his hair shorn violently, dressed in a worn jacket and slacks given him by Tetyana. He carried Ilya's black suitcase, its blind contents locked within.

Walking up the wide paved boulevard, an initial feeling of relief washed over him. Traffic moved in straight familiar lines, boutiques and cafes rimmed the streets. Tall white apartment buildings rose to the skies like operas. But behind fenced villas, flowers languished below signs: DEFENSE D'ENTRER. NO PASE. KEEP OUT. Police patrolled square intersections. Suddenly he felt the emptiness, like a breeze through the bowels, and missed the scrambled, vital cacophony of the native quarter, with its warmth, its stink, its dangerous contact.

On Rue Mohammed V the electric glass doors of American Express opened for him. Within, the air conditioner hummed loudly in the face of cooling breezes coming in off the water—a spiteful, unnecessary demonstration, it seemed to Cross, of whiz-bang American ingenuity.

He stepped to the counter and handed the clerk his passport and one of the hundred-dollar bills Ilya had given him.

"You had a beard," the clerk lisped in his peculiar city accent, looking at Cross's passport photo. When Cross said nothing the clerk said, "Dirhams?"

"Pesetas."

Cross watched the little *maricón* in the tight tan slacks mince over to the safe. It occurred to him that he had been the dancing boy behind the cafe curtain in the casbah on the way to Ilya's the night before.

"Esperanza. Esperanza. Solo sabes bailar cha cha cha!" sang the *maricón*.

Cross idly wondered too if he was the one who had passed his letter with the check to El Jefe. Perhaps it was even he who had stolen the check. It no longer seemed to matter. But flipping through travel brochures advertising flights to the United States via Lisbon and Madrid, he wished desperately he could take a plane home.

Inside a glass display case, large black-and-white blowup photographs showed the Kennedys talking to black children in an American ghetto; in formal dress, listening to Pablo Casals; shaking hands with a robed African dignitary. Lyndon Johnson, slack-faced, played with a beagle: images of a distant, inexplicable world.

When the clerk returned with the money he gave Cross a strange look of intimacy. "You're leaving?" he queried with the pressing familiarity everyone in the city assumed.

Cross took his passport back without answering. The pesetas he put into the envelope with his sister's letter. As he walked out he could see in the reflection of the glass door the pouting face of the *maricón*.

The air was sweet and heavy, the boulevard swept by early sun. The harbor below, shimmering in the morning light, seemed to float. The first passengers were snaking their way slowly down the hill toward the ferry like a row of dark ants. A longing, mixed with regret, rose in his throat.

As he passed the Cafe de Paris, already filling at the height of the season, he saw Benny the Guide sitting near the back in his overcoat, sucking on a toothpick. Benny flashed a wide smile of conspiracy that made Cross look away.

The silver-blue harbor waters heaved, slow and viscous, like a gel. Smoke curled from the waiting ferry. As Cross climbed down the narrow path toward the port, the sun began to burn the mist off the waters. He tried to make out the low Spanish hills across the Straits, but they still lay hidden away.

At the wharf, a crowd of sullen Arab laborers smoking malodorous Spanish cigarettes waited to board. A group of pasty Britons on holiday clustered together prattling. A solitary Spanish businessman in a cheap Madrid suit and dark glasses looked off to sea. Cross stood among them, restless and tired, eager to board.

The ferry ramp came down and the whistle blew. He followed the others up the ramp, went straight to the rear deck, and dropped his suitcase.

Looking back up toward the city, his stomach clenched. High on the roof of the municipal building, his silver Western belt buckle glinting in the sun, was El Jefe, watching the ferry through his binoculars.

A sudden windy blast ripped from the ferry's horn, echoing off the cliffs below the city. The ramp came up and the rope fell and dragged in the water; the white water churned distance between the boat and the shore. Cross turned away from Africa, unwilling to give El Jefe the pleasure of looking at his face.

He sat on a hard bench facing east toward Suez as the ferry slid silently across the glassy channel, his eyes swimming with fatigue, sipping weak Spanish coffee from a leaking paper cup in the white slanting light of morning. In the stillness of the crossing, the only noise was the muted throb of the engine and the gulls circling the ferry clamoring for scraps. He turned and looked back toward Africa, but it was gone, swallowed in mist. Turning forward, Cross saw Europe's low brown hills emerge, as an image comes up on a plate in a darkroom.

Suspended between terrains, caught in the vise of passage, Cross stared up at the sky, trembling. The sun beat down, whitening into a void. Then there was nothing he could do, after weeks of holding it at the borders of vision, to stop it.

"Eva!"

She entered, silent and cold. Huddled alone on the bench, he wept.

Some terrible inversion, a mockery of desire, had left him alone beneath this pitiless sun, his past obliterated, his future a void.

He looked up into the blazing center of the sun until he felt his eyes sear and go white, his brain empty into pulsing circles of light.

A dark shadow fell over him and the air suddenly cooled. He looked up to see Gibraltar's bleak scarp looming above. He could make out the shapes of spider monkeys clinging to its barren surfaces like ghostly sailors to a black rigging, eternally drowning.

Then the ferry was out of shadow and Spain's low green hills rose ahead. The bay of Algeciras appeared from behind the point; the ferry pulled close in to the port of entry. A corrugated metal roof glinted over the low, long customs shed. On the rocks behind the town, written in whitewash, were the words MAS ARBOLES. MAS AGUA. ARRIBA ESPANA. VIVA FRANCO.

The ferry sided against the wharf with a bump. There were armed Guardia Civil milling about the port. Ancient sagging taxis waited to take passengers to the train.

Cross walked down the ramp, lost in the screaming of his own nerves. As he stepped onto the asphalt dock he reached up and felt his face; it was wooden, like a corpse's.

Then he was moving into the Algeciras customs shed with the British tourists and Arab workers. The Spanish businessman turned to look curiously up at the tall pale man beside him with dark shorn hair and burning green eyes, dressed in a black jacket too big and slacks too short.

The customs inspector was thin, snappish, with a pencil mustache. *"Equipaje. Maleta, por favor."*

Cross threw his suitcase down on the conveyor.

"Pasaporte, señor."

The inspector took it and began to examine it slowly, page by page, as if it were an illustrated book.

Cross saw he had lit a cigarette; his hands weren't shaking. He stared at the tips of his fingers with clinical interest, as if they belonged to a cadaver he had once examined in medical school.

The customs officer turned and waved at a *guardia.* The *guardia* stepped forward, his carbine couched in the crook of his arm, unsnapping his pistol holster as he came.

The customs officer looked up and searched Cross's face slowly, inviting closure, conspiracy. Cross gazed back at him with contempt.

The customs officer and the *guardia* conferred.

"Drogas?" he hissed, still smiling. *"Kif?"*

Cross matched his smile.

"No comprendo?"

"*No comprendo.*"

The officer pulled Cross out of the line and motioned for him to follow. The *guardia* moved behind him, carbine poised.

Cross entered a bare room with stained green walls and barred windows. They asked for the key to the suitcase. Cross said he didn't have one.

He complied with the officer's command and took off his coat, lowered his pants. The officer and the *guardia* laughed.

Cross stood with his arms and legs spread, his pants around his ankles, gazing through a slit of barred window at the road leading away from the customs shed into Europe, its low hillocks shining in the sun, searching for ways to deaden himself.

Then he heard the word "Jiminez." Hope, a bird, flew through the barred window and vanished.

Now a second life has been thrown away, he thought, feeling a black sense of symmetry.

A customs officer whacked him heartily across his buttocks, jerking his loins forward and snapping his head back. Warming to his task, the guard imprinted welts upon his thighs, the small of his back, his flanks. Cross stood against the stucco wall, his legs wobbling, gazing blurrily out at the dusky hills.

Two hours had passed. The suitcase remained unopened. Cross understood that the men awaited the arrival of a high official. The guards, reveling in their catch, spent the time in a rare and happy sadism, trading off with the truncheon.

With the sun's ascent Cross was able to see less of Europe beyond and more of the room behind him in the glass, forcing him to anticipate each blow of the club before it arrived. He tried to visualize the prison, rehearse a phone call to California if it were allowed, to screen the pain and so not to think of the *garrote.*

The logic that had led him to accept El Jefe's proposal was lost in unreality. The days from Eva's death to the Algeciras ferry bore all the insubstantiality of a dream. How he had been able to believe that El Jefe or Ilya had arrangements with Spanish police was unclear; he saw now they had simply hoped he would slip through customs by chance. What was he carrying? Surely any doubt about his criminality would be erased by the opening of the suitcase. A boundless culpability spilled off Cross like perfume.

In the window he saw the other officer enter, the cruel one, and his partner go out. The little man gripped his club and raised it. Cross shut his eyes.

The blow didn't arrive. When Cross opened his eyes he saw in reflection another man at the door in a rumpled suit, tie, and aviator glasses. The officer with the truncheon pulled stiff in servile attention.

A brief abusive monologue issued from the man in the suit. When it was over the officer slouched toward Cross, black with humiliation.

He tapped Cross lightly across the buttocks. *"Fuera!"*

Cross didn't understand.

"Fuera! Go!"

The guard rudely pulled Cross's pants up. Cross grabbed them, fiddled with his fly, cinched his belt with fingers that wouldn't work. As he turned around, the pain made him collapse back against the wall.

"You go now," said the man with the aviator glasses.

The other guard handed Cross the unexamined suitcase. *"Tómelo."*

Cross did as he was told and took it.

The door was opened. The guards escorted him ceremoniously out through the Quonset shed. The man in the rumpled suit watched from behind, arms folded.

The ferry wharf was deserted in the noonday sun. Water lapped against the pilings. The officer who had beaten him worst was smiling, offering him a cigarette. Cross took it and bent over the flaring match.

The officer was pointing up the road north, toward the train terminus.

Cross began to walk gingerly across the wooden quay, staring straight ahead, bathed in sweat. He set a course for the asphalt foot of the road, every inch of quay a mile. He hit the road and staggered on, a soldier in an open field, expecting at any moment to be cut down from behind.

When he had rounded a turn in the road he dropped the suitcase and looked back. The customs house, the Straits, Africa were gone.

A midday moon hung overhead behind the suppliant branches of an olive tree on the hill slope. A flock of crows clustered in an oak, cawing.

He turned and looked ahead down the deserted road. Europe lay before him, quiet and luminous, full of sunny promise.

He began to dance, wheeling and shouting, driving the crows from the tree. Songs tumbled from his mouth. Something deep in him, a bloody tumor of remorse, came rushing up and exploded into the still blue air in the form of a scream.

Spinning, he kicked the black suitcase away. It landed on its side.

He fell exhausted in the weeds. Above him the crows streamed toward the sun. The air was hot and silent, the sky pulsing blue.

Slowly he got up and walked over to the suitcase. He picked it up and headed down the road to the train north.

9

A wild-haired Corsican bush pilot in reflector glasses sat at the controls of a noisy twin-engine Beechcraft circling high in the mountains of northeastern Laos, savoring the alarm his sudden banks exercised upon the little ancient Chinese and the tall English-speaking Eurasian he ferried.

"The Phou Phacau mountains," Left-Hand Chen said directly into Peter Lin's ear over the engine noise.

Peter held on to the plane's metal ribbing and gazed biliously out at endless rows of sharp limestone ridges stacked across the landscape like Chinese scroll paintings. Stretching westward from the mountain spires was a great flat plain, running to the edge of vision.

"The Plain of Jars," Chen shouted.

The sour taste and blur of too many Scotches the night before in the Hotel Continental bar in Saigon mixed with recollected snatches of Chen's intense dinner briefing on the subject of the family trade.

"Opium," the little mandarin had said in his precise English, "is the most lucrative business in the world. The trade in the poppy *Papaver somniferum* and its derivatives—heroin, morphine, codeine, Dilaudid, and various tinctures and nostrums—generates close to two hundred billion in revenue each year."

"That's more than AT and T."

"Indeed. It is smoked, sniffed, eaten, drunk, and shot into the veins of a seemingly insatiable world clientele."

"And it's entirely illegal?"

"A tiny amount is grown legally in northern India for medicinal purposes. The rest is illegal. For a hundred and fifty years, Peter, opium has been a law and a nation to itself. It crosses national borders, supersedes alliances and loyalties, directly influences the rise and fall of nations. The backbone of the trade, as you must know, is the American user."

Chen Po-chi had sipped his tea primly with his lone hand, the stump of his right discreetly hidden by the sleeve, while Peter had worked on another Scotch.

"Opium," Chen had gone on, "rivals gold and diamonds as the most alluring substance on earth. It is certainly the most dangerous. In its name an otherwise rational man will willingly seek his own destruction, not to mention that of others."

"Where does our family fit in?" Peter had asked, growing grim at Chen's unrelenting exposition.

"Just as gold and diamonds have their great dynastic families, their Rothschilds and De Beers, so does opium. But opium's families are of necessity secret families. For several generations now yours has been the largest in Asia."

"Like the Mafia?"

"Not at all," Chen had replied curtly. "By the end of our trip you will understand better."

Peter had spent the next hour trying to call a friend of Candace's in Boston, but the operator kept getting him a noisy boys' school dormitory in Bangkok. Then he had called San Francisco, but inexplicably Su Lin's roommate said she was sure his sister was still in Asia.

The Corsican pilot banked steeply, seeming to head directly toward the Laotian mountains. Coming in over a ridge, Peter saw first smoke and then flames rising from dozens of fires scattered along the slopes. The plane dropped low, dancing among the peaks, sending Peter's stomach up in his mouth.

The Beechcraft headed straight into a cluster of flames. Peter grabbed onto a metal strut, certain they were about to crash. The Corsican, who sported a pencil mustache, brown leather jacket, and crumpled white scarf, looked back and grinned madly.

At the last minute a small dirt landing strip appeared. The pilot taxied in, bumped and skidded, and came to stop sideways a dozen yards short of the cliff face.

Rubber-legged, Peter followed Left-Hand Chen out of the plane and stood unsteadily on the dirt runway. It was oppressively hot, though Peter couldn't tell at first if from the flames or the sun. Choking clusters of smoke swirled around them.

"Look, Peter." Chen was pointing to the fiery mountain incline beside the runway.

Bare-chested young Meo men raced down the scrub jungle slopes, igniting savannah grass and virgin hardwood timber with torches as they came. Others circled the perimeter lighting stacked timber and brush on the edge of the field. Flames crackled and smoke rose toward the high clouds above the ridges, crossing the sun with a bloody orange haze.

"The burn-off," Chen shouted. "To prepare the fields for the new planting."

The Corsican pilot had disappeared around the edge of the slope into the Meo village. Peter's face stung with the heat, and sweat poured down his chest. He turned away from the flames as Chen carried on in his soft, precise English.

"Porous limestone. Very alkaline. That's why this area is so good for growing." Chen pointed up along the steep burning slopes. "The crop can survive as low as three thousand feet. But here at forty-two hundred feet is best. See that old man?" A shriveled gnome in underwear crouched at the foot of the burning fields. "He can taste good limestone soil by its sweetness. They send him out every year to find the best spot for planting."

"Why burn wood they could use for building or firewood?" Peter called.

"It leaves a layer of ash over the fields. Phosphate. Calcium. Potassium. Good for growing."

Peter followed Chen along the perimeter of the burning mountain. Chen, waving his good arm, began to describe in terms that seemed to Peter almost lyrical the cycle of the poppy.

He explained how in late summer all across the mountains of Asia, from the Anatolian plateau through northern Iran, Afghanistan, and Pakistan—the region they call the Golden Crescent—and across northern India into Burma, Laos, northern Thailand—the

Golden Triangle—through these 4,500 miles of mountains, peasant women from eight different nations bend to scatter the seeds of the poppy over the fields.

During the fall months, Chen said, the seed ripens in the ground. Late in the year a green plant appears with one main stem about four feet high and as many as a dozen smaller stems. On each is a brightly colored white or red flower bearing within it the drug *Papaver somniferum.*

Peter looked through the smoke, his eyes watering. Chen was holding up a withered plant. At the end of its thin stalk was a round bud, or capsule, about the size of a crabapple. Peter reached out and felt the skin; it was thick, hard. He took the plant and turned it in his fingers.

This put me through law school.

Chen explained how at year's end the petals drop to the ground, exposing the green pod. Within, a milky white sap forms and the outside becomes covered with a hard, transparent white coating.

"In January, Peter, the harvest begins. All over Asia the farmers come with their curved knives, speaking a hundred different languages—Kurdish, Bengali, Meo. They move backwards through the fields, cutting shallow incisions across the bulb's surface so the white sap will ooze."

"Raw opium."

"Yes."

Peter took a handkerchief and wiped sweat from his forehead. "Haven't they come up with a more modern way to do it?"

Chen drew a Lucky Strike from his pocket, deftly lit a match with his one good hand, and held it to the Lucky.

"This is the way they grew opium when the first Mason first went to Ghazipur with the Lin comprador in 1832 to buy for the Canton market. This is the way they grow it for the syndicates five generations later." Chen smiled and drew on the Lucky. "Undoubtedly it is the way they will do it long after we are gone."

Chen took Peter's arm and led him away from the fires to the other side of the landing strip and the edge of the plateau. Below them the cliffs fell thousands of feet to an ochre plain.

"Sit down," Chen said.

Peter, glad to be where it was cool, sat at the edge of the runway and let his eyes run out across the plain to where the horizon disappeared in mist.

"The Plain of Jars," Chen said, pointing, "is the center of the Golden Triangle trade. The Meo, the Yao, the Shan tribes of Burma all trade through these regions. In the spring the Chinese hill traders come through with their caravans buying opium. Nationalist Chinese soldiers, the Kuomintang, protect them. These KMT troops have been here since before World War Two."

"Where do the caravans take the opium?"

"Down to Long Tieng or Vientiane, to sell to the Chinese shopkeepers. The shopkeepers sell some to the local smokers or refine it into morphine base and resell it in Bangkok or Saigon to other Chinese. They turn it into heroin."

"Chinese right down the line," Peter said.

"Exactly. But not just Chinese. *Our* Chinese. Chiu Chao dialect people. From Swatow." Chen traced a pyramid in the air with his finger. "The Lin family at the top."

"But they don't all work for us."

"In a way, yes." Chen took a small abacus out of the jacket of his pocket and his fingers flashed across the tiles.

"The Meo receive about five hundred dollars for ten kilos of raw opium. That will yield one kilo of morphine base in Bangkok. Our chemists in Hong Kong process it into a kilo of high-grade number four worth twenty-five hundred dollars. From there, if a courier takes it to the States, he gets about twenty-five thousand dollars. Then it will be diluted with quinine or milk sugar and packed in little gelatin capsules that sell on the street for five dollars a shot. The profits will multiply perhaps fifty times. The first non-Chiu Chao to touch it is usually the courier. He buys from a Lin representative."

"How many kilos will this village produce in a season?"

"About seven hundred."

After a moment Peter said, "That's around a hundred fifty million dollars at street level."

"Very good. And before that we have made how much?"

Peter figured quickly. "A million and seven hundred fifty thousand. Unless the courier worked for us. Then it would be much more."

Chen, impressed by Peter's facility with numbers, watched him with new interest. "And this field is only one of many hundreds in Laos, Burma, Thailand . . ."

Peter looked over his shoulder. "For that field the Meo will make only thirty-five thousand."

"To them that is a lot. If they had to grow rice they would do worse."

Seeing Peter fall silent, Chen said, "Let me put it another way. Each pod contains half a gram. Ten thousand pods, an acre's worth, yield twenty pounds of raw opium—the same today as a hundred years ago. This same acre also produces two hundred pounds of poppy seeds—which are used in food or pressed for oil—and several dozen pounds of petals. The opium crop brings more money than any other crop grown on earth."

"How much of it becomes heroin?"

"Some is put aside for the Asian smoker or eater. *Chandu* is the smokable extract the Chinese prefer. For this, the opium will be boiled in water, the solution filtered, and then boiled again until it becomes rather muddy. Muslims like to smoke it as *madak,* mixed with tobacco or betel. Others will sniff it, eat it, rub it into their skin. In Hong Kong they 'chase the dragon,' 'shoot the ack-ack gun,' 'play the mouth organ.' But most will become heroin."

Peter was gazing out over the plain, frowning.

"What is it, Peter?"

"Why didn't Father tell me about the trade?" His fingers dug into his palms.

Chen followed Peter Lin's eyes into the void that hung above the Plain of Jars. "Harry Lin dreamed of respectability. He wanted you and your sister to stay in America, out of the trade. He was going to turn it over to my son Sam. When Sam died last year, Harry Lin's fortuneteller told him it was fated that the trade would stay in your family for another generation." Chen's words became ice. "If Sam had not died, he would be standing here with me right now, not you."

Peter, feeling Chen's bitterness, said, "I wish it were Sam standing here too, Chen."

Peter stood and began to pace unsteadily along the edge of the cliff. Each word of Chen's seemed to draw him further in. He had an urge to reach out and hurl the little adviser over the cliff, as if by destroying the messenger the message would be cancelled.

Peter saw the Corsican pilot back at the landing strip directing Meo men wrapping life belts around large tin crates they had dragged from the village.

"That opium, Peter, will be processed into morphine base in Saigon and Bangkok, except for what is smoked locally. Some goes overseas through the Corsican syndicates to Marseilles. There it will be refined into high-grade no. 4 heroin and sold in America. Some comes to Hong Kong, to us, to become low-grade no. 3 for local smokers. And some of that is made into no. 4 and goes on to America."

Peter recalled a dead-eyed Boston junkie outside the Howard burlesque house who pimped a girl he had taken home one miserable night. The thought that his own family might have been the pimp's supplier made him shiver.

"Most American heroin," Chen went on, "comes out of Marseilles, refined from Turkish opium. But all that is changing, Peter. In Asia. And in Europe too."

The Meo fields burned freely. The tribesmen had gathered at the bottom, chattering and singing. The Corsican pilot had loaded in his tins and waited, arms folded, by the Beechcraft's fuselage.

Chen looked up and said suddenly, "Have you ever heard of Lucky Luciano?"

"Sure."

"Luciano ran the European trade into the U.S. for sixteen years. Last year he died in Naples. Now different Corsican gangs fight for control of Marseilles. Presently it is run by a new man named Bébé Spiritu. A dwarf." Chen squinted as he drew heavily on his cigarette. "But there is a man in Florida . . ." Chen looked carefully at Peter. "I want you to remember his name. Franco Termini Jr."

"Franco Termini Jr.," Peter repeated, paling.

That's who took me to Havana gambling.

"This Mafioso wants to take over the entire European trade. To succeed Luciano." Chen flicked his Lucky into the emptiness below. "We are counting on the fact that he will make it. Do you understand?"

But Peter Lin was back in Boston five years earlier, his first semester in law school, at a cocktail party at the home of a well-known Italian politician. Peter stood alone on the lawn with a drink in his hand watching a smiling, well-dressed man approach him, hand outstretched. "So this is the son of Harry Lin," the man had said. "Hell of a man, Harry Lin. Met him in Washington after the war."

Drinks and dinner downtown afterwards. April 1958. Two weeks later an invitation came to jet down to Havana: Cuba Libres, dog races, girls, and gambling. The money ran like water. Franco Termini Jr. was a nice guy—a little crude, but fun. Peter kept winning at the casinos. Sunday on the way back they stopped at Hialeah. Peter, flush, bet loose. When his horses began to stiff, he doubled up; Franco Termini Jr. was always at his elbow with a tip, a fresh drink, a bankroll. By the time the piebald in the eighth fell six lengths back, Peter owed him $14,000. "No problem," Termini had said, patting Peter's knee in the private jet back. "Someday you pay me back."

Five fucking years he's been cultivating me, Peter thought bitterly. Laying a chip down in Asia. Betting I'd come back.

Left-Hand Chen's cool voice brought him back to the precipice over the Plain of Jars. "Already, Peter, the Americans are putting pressure on the Turks to close down their fields. A Mafia gangster named Valachi is preparing to testify in front of the U.S. Senate. It is known that he will expose the European traffic. There will be a big public outcry."

"That would mean less opium from the Mideast. Marseilles will have to come to Asia to buy."

"Very good," Chen said with his maddening didacticism. "However, there are already Corsicans all through Southeast Asia ready to supply Marseilles. They are strong." He pointed to the plane on the landing strip. "They have political power in Phnom Penh and Vientiane. And in Saigon, Diem's brother Nhu openly runs the trade. He works with the Corsicans against the Chinese. They are both Catholic."

"Then what's the use?"

"Diem and Nhu will soon be out."

"You know this for a fact?"

Chen nodded primly. "Your father arranged it with the Americans before he died."

Peter Lin, rapt, watched Chen's finger slicing the air, trying to encompass the great events of the secret world Chen described with the seeming detachment of a scientist detailing a lab experiment.

Peter pulled a silver hip flask from his pocket. He swilled, licked his lips, and replaced the cap. Chen, with a broad expression of distaste, slid away from Peter to escape the liquor's terrible perfume.

"Look at the name on the side of that plane," he ordered, pointing toward the landing strip.

Peter read the words AIR LAOS COMMERCIALE.

"Everybody calls it 'Air Opium.' Each time the Americans put a new landing strip in the mountains the Corsicans fly in behind in Beechcrafts and Cessnas to buy. They drop it in the Gulf of Siam. Thai trawlers pick it up and run it to the jungle. There it is refined into morphine base and shipped back to Marseilles." Chen nodded toward the Corsican. "That pilot picks up maybe five hundred kilos of raw opium a season from these dirt runways. Right under our noses."

Peter stared at the Corsican with new eyes. "Why don't we have our own planes and pilots?"

"No need. I will explain. You see, it was your father's wish to dismantle the Corsican network in Asia and force Marseilles to come to us to buy. Much work has been done to this end. Right now a thousand tons of opium is grown worldwide each year. Only a third comes from the Golden Triangle."

"With the Turkish supply diminished and the Corsicans gone from Asia, we could become the main supplier of product to Marseilles. Is that it?"

"Very good," said Chen. "That is why the Corsicans killed your father."

Peter's breath left him. He wheeled and looked at Left-Hand Chen. "I was sure it was the Shanghai Green Pang," he muttered.

"That is what you were supposed to assume. We think that Bébé Spiritu contracted them to kill your father. The Green Pang has been driven abroad. They are no longer our serious rivals in Asia. The Corsicans are."

"So there is war with Marseilles." Peter looked back toward the Beechcraft. "Why bother with them? Why not ship directly into America? That would make Hong Kong the world center of trade."

"There are two problems. First, our supply lines are not secure." He pointed down the mountain to the vast expanse below. "Three years ago the Pathet Lao began to overrun the Plain of Jars, driving the villagers up into the mountains. Now the Chinese caravans cross the plain protected by Kuomintang soldiers. But by next year, who knows? The cross-country opium routes may be gone. In Vietnam it's the same. Burma too."

"Then what?"

"War is coming, Peter. For sure it is coming." Chen turned back toward the hills. "All through these mountains Green Berets are working. They put the landing strips in the hamlets to connect the village up with CIA headquarters at Long Tieng. They drop in rice and arms, and take the young men off to fight the Pathet Lao. Five hundred kip for an ear, five thousand kip for a severed head. The villages go on growing their opium. And the Corsican planes come and pick it up for them."

"But when the Corsicans are gone, who will fly it out?"

"Air America."

"For us?" Peter was incredulous.

"Yes."

"So they're involved in the trade. The CIA."

Chen ran his finger across his neck and grinned. "Up to here."

Peter looked warily into Chen's bright, ancient eyes.

"The Americans and the free Chinese work together in Southeast Asia, Peter. They call it democracy. We call it business. It's the same. They can't afford to stop the trade, or they will lose the hamlets. They will support anything that keeps these countries from going Communist. Do you understand? Anything."

"Even dope that ends up in the hands of their own children."

Chen gazed into the abyss, letting Peter's comment dissolve in the air. "America has to keep its client states in business. What else do these poor countries have to export? A mere word from Washington would shut off the trade. But the word never comes. It never will. Capitalism cannot survive without the drug traffic. This is a historical truth."

Chen spoke as if explaining the most indifferent matters. "It is unofficial policy. Not just in Southeast Asia. In Turkey, Iran, Colombia, Mexico."

Peter fell dazedly in beside Chen as he began to walk slowly along the precipice above the Plain of Jars.

Chen looked up at Peter and smiled faintly. "Over a hundred years ago the *gwailo* came and enslaved China to opium. The revenues kept the British Empire alive. Now it is the *gwailo* who consume it and keep us Chinese alive."

Chen chuckled without pleasure. "The pattern is always the same. First the people of the street use it. Then the artists and intellectuals. Then the middle class become users. Now it becomes a scourge, an epidemic. But nobody can stop it, because it is inextricably bound up with the economic and political affairs of the empire. Then the country crumbles from within, easily dominated by foreign powers."

"China in 1840," Peter muttered. "Or . . ."

Chen's soft laugh drifted into the air over the Plain of Jars. "This time the shoe is on the other foot."

"But, Chen, if war comes to Southeast Asia the fields will be destroyed."

"It depends on how *much* war. There are no fields left in Vietnam. They were all in the north. Ho Chi Minh destroyed them. Saigon is a big shipping point, but Bangkok serves just as well. The fields in Burma are quite safe, and those in Thailand will be safe for years. Even these hill fields are secure for some time. The Pathet Lao can't penetrate up this high. And we have new refining technology, as you will see. We can produce enough opium to supply America for generations to come."

He stopped and looked at Peter. "So what would a war cost us really? Even if the Americans lost? As your father liked to say, a little war mightn't be so bad."

"The Americans won't lose," Peter said emphatically. "But what would we gain?"

"You asked why we can't ship directly to the U.S. instead of going through Marseilles. *Couriers,* Peter. Even if we produce that much heroin, how do we get it in?"

Peter waited for the little mandarin to answer his own question.

"What if the Americans came to get it themselves?"

Peter reeled as the answer went off in his mind. "The soldiers," he whispered.

"Yes. They will be our couriers."

Chen contemplated Peter's amazement. "In the last century two opium wars were fought in Asia. This war in Vietnam will be history's third. But nobody will call it that."

Peter looked at Chen. "Will they come?"

"The Americans? They are already here. Twelve thousand now,

and tens of thousands on the way. When they leave they will take home the purest heroin in the world."

Chen turned back toward the Beechcraft and beckoned for Peter to follow. "Tomorrow we fly up the Mekong to the tri-border area. You will see the first factory in Southeast Asia that processes ninety-nine percent pure no. 4 heroin from morphine base, staffed by one of our master chemists from Hong Kong. We will no longer have to ship morphine base to Hong Kong. We will make China White right here."

Chen spoke with visionary pride as Peter followed him along the edge of the cliff back toward the plane.

"U.S. addicts consume three to four tons of heroin annually. They would use ten times that if they could get it. We can produce and refine a thousand tons of opium a year by the end of the decade. The balance of power will shift from Marseilles to Hong Kong. The Lin family, and all free Chinese, will enter an era of unprecedented prosperity."

Chen stopped and turned around. Peter had sat back down and was gazing vacantly off toward the horizon. Chen watched him for a while without speaking.

"Are the victims nothing to you, Chen?"

"Victims? I see no victims, Peter." Chen paused, then said, "We are each of us responsible for our condition. Is this not true?"

Something in Chen's logic was diabolically miscast, but Peter was too blasted on the whiskey to challenge it.

"So you must decide what you are going to do, Peter."

But Peter Lin was riding somewhere in the shifting sky over the plain, chasing the blond ringlets of Candace darting teasingly among the clouds.

"Your grandfather had a dream of a link between Hong Kong and the Southeast Asian fields under the Lins. Your father's dream was the consolidation of the trade and the expulsion of the Corsicans. You can avenge his death by bringing this about." Chen's voice softened. "And you too, Peter, must have a dream."

"What?" Peter turned and stared at Left-Hand Chen.

"You said Asia could become the world center of the trade. Is that your dream?"

Peter glowered. "I've seen the junkies in New York and Boston. It's a bad dream."

"Bad dream, good dream. The question is, Is it yours?"

Peter sat with his arms around his knees and didn't reply, trying to pull apart Chen's cool Asian pragmatism.

"Were the Americans so kind to you?" Chen gently inserted his voice like a needle beneath Peter's skin.

For so long Peter had lived suspended among warring dreams, antithetical ideas, clashing eras and identities, with neither homeland nor home, unable to feel anything firm beneath his feet. The weariness of a life that had brought him neither love nor respect settled around him like a shroud.

He stood and looked at Left-Hand Chen, who was gazing idly out over the Plain of Jars, smoking.

One of us is evil, Peter thought.

"I'm not Chinese," Peter said.

"Pardon?"

"I said I'm not Chinese."

Chen rested his eyes upon Peter's. "All the men in your family except the first, the comprador, were Eurasian. Each was European in his youth. Each later came back to Asia."

"That was another time," Peter said.

"The history of the family is the history of the drug. You cannot separate yourself." Chen's soft eyes bore in upon Peter.

"What if I took over the business and legitimized it?"

"Restaurants and rattan? That is why the Chinese stay poor. There is no money there. But of course you are the boss now." Chen's voice spread like an oil. "Also you must consider how many thousands of people depend upon our enterprise for food, housing, education. Yes, there are those who are trampled. But we bear the future of Free China on our backs. Perhaps later you can legitimize. But now? That would be difficult."

"What happens if I don't take over the business?"

"The Asian traffic will fall temporarily into the hands of the Corsicans, the men who killed your father. Then the Communists will take over. With the Mideast supply diminished, perhaps it will be the end of the world traffic."

"Maybe that would be good."

"It's not a question of good or bad. It's a question of business."

"I don't need business. I have more money than I'll ever need coming to me."

Chen spoke sharply. "Did your father not tell you? Any money you would receive from his estate is contingent upon your coming back and taking over the business."

Peter struggled to his feet. "No!"

"It's in your father's will."

"I'll contest it!"

Chen turned toward the smoldering mountains. "I'm afraid that would be fruitless. The executor of the will is the Hong Kong Crown Bank."

"That prick Mason," he whispered. Peter felt as if he had been clubbed.

Chen waited, smoking quietly. "The condition is the same for your sister. She will come back too after the will is read next month."

"Su Lin may refuse the money."

"Surely you are joking. Besides, she is vulnerable. Unpleasant things could befall her. I shudder to think. Our enemies . . ."

Bright clouds came racing eastward over the Phou Phacau Mountains behind them, sending shadows over the plain below.

"She must come back, Peter," Chen said. "The matter is beyond discussion."

On the Meo hillside the fires had burned out. Only a fringe of low flames remained, sending wisps of smoke curling to the sky. The Meo were trudging single file up a path that ran behind the hillside to the village.

"So it's a war," Peter said, his voice thin as they walked toward the Beechcraft. The Corsican, seeing them approach, flashed his white teeth in a smile and jumped in the cockpit.

Peter saw the pilot now as an enemy, one of those who had killed his father.

"Yes," Chen said. "It is a war."

"When will we know we've won?"

Chen Po-chi smiled and kicked a small stone back in the direction of the cliff.

"When Franco Termini Jr. comes to Hong Kong to buy from us."

10

The train rocked north through Zaragoza, tossing Cross gently against the tiny rest-room wall. He stared into the clouded washbasin mirror at his torn face, newly shaved. He looked like a mad flagellant, a fugitive from a tireless enemy. He smiled, an unfamiliar exercise.

He had relived the event at customs a dozen times. His sudden release had upset some notion of fate, as if the penance for Eva he had come to expect against the customs house wall had been belittled, disallowed. This turn of events seemed to call for some ceremony or ritual whose exact steps eluded him.

He left the rest room and returned to his second-class cabin. The compartment was crowded; his suitcase sat beneath his seat. The faces in the car, those passing in the corridor, the shabby conductor who checked his ticket, filled him with paranoia, absolute threat. Somewhere on the train lurked an invisible black angel: his control, who had cleared him at Algeciras.

An old peasant woman offered him an orange. He took it, peeled it, bit into it. The sweet juice flooded his mouth and rolled down his chin.

*   *   *

As the train moved further north, the shifting relativity of Europe provided Cross with a benign embrace. After the warm chaos of the bazaars, Europe's towns beyond the window seemed formal, fashioned by some vain rectilinear mind. This very strangeness left the hallucination of the South behind, dissolving one dream into another.

Still he was haunted. What in him had sought and found that darkness whose vestige still moved with him in the suitcase beneath his seat, this evil that Ilya had warned would trail him?

At the Gerona stop before France he saw Eva there in his mind, laughing, and imagined he was rewinding time. She would be waiting for him on the Gare d'Orléans platform in her sun dress and floppy hat, talking excitedly about the Gypsy she had found.

His eyes welled with tears.

Watching the fields of southern France turn by, he wondered if he was to be a wanderer now, no longer at home in his own country, doomed to seek comfort in the strange, the distant.

At the moment of his release from the draft, life had seemed limitless. Quickly, desire had withered into death. He had failed to perceive the fragility of goodness. Evil, like a dark flower, had bloomed beneath his hand. What now? Return to the clinics and a simple altruism? Was evil a microbe, a germ, to be countered with serum?

But passing along the Loire, an absurd elation overcame him. He experienced his own resurrection as fact. He thought again of medicine, and California, and all he had left, with ridiculous affection.

He began to separate himself in thought from the suitcase. It was not his at all, but chattel belonging to yesterday.

Cross took Ilya's second hundred-dollar bill out of his pocket. Considering the issue of his right to it, he decided Ilya owed it to him for the truncheon blows at Algeciras that still made sitting an agony.

His laugh woke up the old peasant woman.

At the Gare d'Orléans Cross waited until all the passengers had left the compartment. Then he shoved Ilya's suitcase beneath the seat opposite and quickly left the train.

At the platform he walked, just short of running, through the crowds toward the station entrance, his fear revving, blood pounding in his head. He saw armies of conductors rushing after him shouting his name. Ilya's suitcase had legs and chased him up the stairs to the street. El Jefe had locked his name and home address inside the suitcase. . . .

He took the stairs to the street three at a time, lunging like a swimmer for the surface, the sunny Paris air of the youth he had lost in the South.

Above, it was midafternoon. Summer had turned; a wind picked up crisp leaves and swirled them about his feet. Cross pulled his jacket collar tight around his neck and took the brief yards from the station to the metro.

He knew he must spend little time on the streets, as he would soon be a hunted man. The Corsican named Spiritu would certainly want him. Nor did he wish to encounter anyone he had known before who might recognize him or Eva.

Europe, once his haven, was no longer safe.

He took the metro to Opéra, swaying in the warm anonymous embrace of rush-hour bodies. There he got off and stood on the platform looking for pursuers. He mounted the stairs and walked quickly across the street to American Express.

He checked downstairs first for mail, finding none. At the travel desk upstairs he asked about flights leaving for Los Angeles. The first available left at eleven that night from Orly, then connected at London to a Pan Am polar route flight that stopped once in Iceland.

"Are there seats?"

"Quite a few."

"Then I can buy a ticket at the airport?"

"It is easier here."

"Yes, yes, I know."

He went back downstairs to the telephones and told the operator to place a collect overseas call to California. The transatlantic lines were busy. Try again in fifteen minutes, she said.

He changed the second hundred-dollar bill into francs and went outside. Crossing the street in front of Café de la Paix, he was accosted by a Jamaican painter he had known from Rue Git le Coeur, dressed in a U.S. army parka, earring and goatee, flapping his arms against the chill, selling the *Herald Tribune*.

"Paris ain't what it used to be, baby," the Jamaican said.

"Yeah," Cross agreed, not quite sure what either of them meant.

"Hey, man. You seen Eva?"

He bought a paper and told the Jamaican to keep the change.

At a table inside, he read over coffee, shocked by the exotic spill of events in the months he had been gone. An Italian named Valachi was testifying before the United States Senate about Cosa Nostra and Turkish heroin. A church bombing in Birmingham had killed four black girls; Doctor King would make a statement. Defense Secretary McNamara announced that the American troop count in Vietnam was up to 16,000. It came to Cross that a small faraway war was on, and he had almost been in it.

It's not just me. The times are turning.

On the third page, a courier had been arrested on a Marseilles–New York flight with ten kilos of Chinese heroin. "An ominous new wrinkle," an Interpol official was quoted as saying. And Ray Charles and his Raylettes were packing them in at Paris's Olympia.

Cross paid for his coffee and stood up. He would call his sister; she would be there and wire the money for the ticket. The imminence of freedom, of escape to America, raised a sigh of relief from deep in his chest.

Ilya was wrong, Cross thought. I have outrun the devil.

"Excuse me, m'sieur."

A thick mustachioed man stood before him. He wore a black turtleneck sweater and navy peacoat, and his head was clean-shaven. He gazed at Cross with damp brown eyes.

He reminded Cross of pictures he'd seen of the philosopher Gurdjieff.

"Your suitcase, m'sieur. I believe you forgot it on the train."

Cross looked down, then back up, directly into the man's barrel chest, where a shoulder holster bulged beneath his jacket.

The man who looked like Gurdjieff took out a pack of Spanish cigarettes, shook one free, and offered it.

"Thank you," Cross whispered to his control.

11

It was monsoon downpour, and everything was knee-deep shifting mud in Ban Houei Sai, a small clearing of fragile stilted houses and narrow winding lanes hacked out of dense forest on the Laos side of the tri-border area.

A large lumber mill sat in the clearing. Built on a long sand embankment extending a hundred feet into the Mekong, it was separated from the surrounding forest by a lumberyard, which had become a moatlike sea of silt as well.

Chen and Peter sat on the covered porch of a long wooden building with a Chinese chemist and a local Yunnanese who spoke English. In the clearing, beneath a wood shelter, several men in loincloths were converting opium into morphine base.

A row of horses loaded down with heavy sacks and escorted by soldiers plodded through the downpour on the other bank of the river, headed for the crossing bridge a few hundred yards down that led into the village.

"A Shan caravan, from Burma," Chen said.

"Who are the soldiers?"

"Kuomintang. They and the Chinese merchants from Yunnan

control the trade around here. They used to be based in Burma. The CIA was using them to turn the Shan States into an independent bastion. But the Communists drove most of them out two years ago. They moved across the Mekong to Laos, some into Thailand."

"Near the Chiengmai railroad," said the Yunnanese. "Good for transport."

Chen pointed to a Quonset shed in the clearing where the first men of the caravan were entering. "That store is run by Yunnanese traders. The soldiers will buy supplies as their payment for escorting the delivery. The Yunnanese merchants have already bought the opium from the villages."

Peter watched the caravan wending its way single file across the swaying river bridge.

"They look to be packing about twenty tons," Chen said.

"You can get an M-16 in Chiengmai for two hundred and fifty dollars," said the Yunnanese, who seemed to be something of an expert on arms. "American sixty-millimeter mortars, fifty-caliber machine guns, seventy-five-millimeter recoilless rifles. Russian Kalashnikovs. Anything you want."

"These Chinese from Yunnan all know each other," said Chen. "They make up a silent organization. See up there on Mae Salong Mountain? That is the KMT Fifth Army headquarters. General Tun Shi-wen. He calls himself the 'watchdog at the northern gate.' He spends most of his time in Chiengmai attending to his personal fortune." Chen tittered. "But occasionally he makes a raid into China just to polish up his image."

"Who does he report to?"

"General Ouane Rattikone, here in Laos. Militarily, they ultimately report to Taiwan. But the Yunnanese merchants report to other Chinese in Chiengmai and Saigon. They have no idea who we are. But there is not an ounce of this opium we won't eventually profit from."

"Necessity knows no law. That is why we deal with opium." The Han spoke in a violent, impassioned voice, seeming to refer to some earlier point in Chen's explication. "We have to continue to fight the evil of Communism. To fight you must have an army. An army must have guns. To buy guns you must have money. In these mountains the only money is opium."

Peter was watching a man running across the clearing in a yellow slicker. He was bespectacled and looked tall to be Asian.

"Who's that, Chen?"

"An American. Eliot Potter."

A needle of shock shot through Peter as the man disappeared into the Yunnanese store.

"I knew his son at Harvard," he said tightly.

"I'm not surprised. Your father and Eliot Potter were acquainted. As I recall, he wrote you a letter of recommendation."

"Alec Potter used to tell stories about his father. And his grand-father, the missionary."

"Yes, the Lahu's White God. You'll probably run into young Potter. I hear he's back in Asia. Hs father works at the Chiengmai museum. But he's CIA. He knows the dialects and has great cur-rency here."

The rain had abated. Chen got to his feet. They slogged across the clearing to the roofed platform where men worked among oil drums.

"The morphine process, Peter."

A chemist squatted over a wood fire heating water in a drum, testing the temperature with his index finger. Peter watched an assistant dump the dark, sticky raw opium in while a third stirred with a heavy stick until it dissolved.

The chemist came over and sprinkled lime fertilizer into the solu-tion, precipitating out organic waste and leaving the morphine sus-pended in the water near the surface.

At a second tub a man in a loincloth filtered the waste through flannel cloth, then poured the solution into another oil drum.

As the solution was heated and stirred a second time, concentrated ammonia was added, causing the morphine to solidify and drop to the bottom. Once more the mixture was filtered through flannel.

Peter gazed at the chunky white morphine kernels sitting on the gauze. They looked to him like borax, or sea salt.

"Dried and packed for shipment," Chen said, "this morphine will weigh about ten percent of the raw opium from which it was ex-tracted."

"They can do this openly?"

"At present. But there may be fighting here soon between the

Chinese and the Shan in Burma. Maybe General Ouane's Laotian army too." Chen smiled. "One thing you learn about the fighting, Peter. Whoever wins, we win. Unless the Communists take over."

They plunged across the swampy clearing to the long shed where they had squatted during the downpour. Chen Po-chi paused and looked at Peter pointedly, as if to confirm that his protégé was indeed following his unfolding picture, then led him through the screen door.

There were three men inside. Chen introduced Peter to the "cook," a bucktoothed Hong Kong chemist named Yuk, and his two Yunnanese apprentices. The room itself was dusty, disheveled; but the new lab equipment gleamed.

Chen explained that the master chemist had memorized the difficult, dangerous five-stage heroin recipe after years as an assistant. The goal is to chemically bind morphine molecules with acetic acid, then process the compound to produce the powder later liquified and injected from a syringe.

Chen gestured around the shed. "You are looking at the first factory in Southeast Asia. Before the decade is out, if all goes well, there will be thirty. A hundred kilos of raw opium per day. Three and a half tons a year of pure no. 4 per lab. Enough to supply the world into the next century."

Peter studied the dim, cluttered room. The burners, flasks, and metal drums seemed crude somehow for such a "master" process. He struggled to grasp the idea that tens of millions of dollars sat in solution in this rainy shed.

Yuk, the Hong Kong "cook," began to demonstrate the process, heating equal amounts of morphine and acetic anhydride in a flask.

"After six hours at a hundred and eighty-five degrees Fahrenheit," Chen translated from Swatownese, "the morphine and acid become chemically bonded, creating an impure form of diacetylmorphine, or heroin."

Peter followed Chen and the chemist to a second area where the assistants were busy with precipitation. He watched them treat the solution with water and chloroform until the impurities precipitated out, leaving a somewhat higher grade of diacetlymorphine.

Next the heroin particles were filtered out of a sodium carbonate solution under pressure by a suction pump. These were then purified in a solution of alcohol and activated charcoal. The new mixture was heated until the alcohol began to evaporate, leaving relatively pure granules of heroin at the bottom of the flask.

Peter recalled a promotion film he'd seen in high school showing the research lab of some great American chemical company. In a sterilized ambience, crew-cut assistants in lab coats poured colored solutions from one beaker to another while a chesty voice lauded the virtues of industry and applied capital. The profits from the process Peter was watching in this jungle hut, it occurred to him, would exceed those of that chemical company by a hundred times.

Yuk was bent over a large flask, achieving the fifth and final stage.

Chen explained: "This yields the fine white powder prized by addicts. It requires considerable skill. A careless chemist could ignite the ether gas and produce an explosion that could level this laboratory."

The cook placed the heroin in a flask and dissolved it in alcohol. As he added ether and hydrochloric acid to the solution, tiny white flakes began to form.

"China White," Chen whispered almost reverentially.

When it was over the chemist took from beneath a wooden table a plastic bag of the white powder and held it up for Peter's inspection.

"Ready for GI's now," said the expansive Yunnanese, who had joined them in the lab.

Peter took the packet in his hands, feeling its weight. It could have been a sack of sugar or rice or coffee, and he a grain merchant, a commodities broker.

"Each bag contains seven-tenths of a kilo," Left-Hand Chen said.

Ink-stamped in the center of the plastic parcel were the words TIGER AND GLOBE BRAND. A tiger was stretched over an image of the earth turned to show India, China, and Southeast Asia. Chinese lettering surrounded the graphic.

Peter, gazing at the true product of his family's business, felt unaccountably giddy. Silently he handed the bag back to the master chemist.

They walked back outside, leaving the Yunnanese behind. It had begun to rain again. Peter rejoined Left-Hand Chen on the top step of the porch and watched the KMT caravan pour off the Mekong bridge into the village clearing.

"Chen," Peter said. "You ever smoked it?"

Chen turned away and looked off toward the ghostly shapes of the mountains through the mist. His face became tight, waxen. Then it seemed to warm, or change in tone, like rice paper when light shifts behind it.

"What's it like?"

"It is heaven."

Chen's voice was distant and scratchy, like an old phonograph record.

"Why don't you smoke it now?"

Left-hand Chen gazed expressionlessly off toward the mountain. "Desire," he said quietly. "One indulges. It runs well up to a point. Then it turns into its opposite. Yin becomes yang. Like an alternating current." He wiggled his hand. "Black, white. White, black. The master becomes the slave."

Chen studied the muddy river beside the clearing. "Opium was used in Europe as a curative, prescribed by doctors. Then it became a scourge, a disease. The same with alcohol. I point that out to you, as you like to drink. Today's solution is tomorrow's problem. Even sex is subject to this law. Politics. The liberator becomes the tyrant." He turned and looked at his protégé. "Opium is this way, Peter. More than anything in the world."

"Maybe it's not so bad for some people, Chen." Peter was not beyond including himself in his thoughts.

"Perhaps." Left-Hand Chen drew himself up into an image of fastidious stoicism. "But not the Han warrior."

Watching him, Peter imagined he had glimpsed the lacquer soul of the little mandarin.

"But you provide it for others, Chen."

Chen reached up and stroked his small chin. "It is a good test. To deal with fire without being burned. One is . . . privileged."

Peter heard himself sounding like a lawyer. "What's in this for you now that your son is dead?"

Chen Po-chi sat very still, like a mantis on a leaf, squinting out over the wet clearing. "When you become more Asian you won't ask such a question."

The yellow slicker of the American Eliot Potter reappeared down in the village. A rush of bitterness surged through Peter.

There had been a Cambridge evening at a folk club on Mount

Auburn. Peter had been with a Boston College girl in a gunnysack dress and black leotards, showing her radical colors; if Peter wasn't black, he was the next best thing. Su Lin, seventeen then, was visiting from high school. Alec Potter, fair and tall and bright, he of the expensive cashmere sweaters and brown loafers and yellow Corvette, was drunkenly chiding Peter across the table because he spoke no Chinese.

"Why should I?" protested Peter. "I'm less than half Chinese."

Alec was a year ahead, about to graduate—a mainstream anthropology twit, an Elliot House preppie with all the right things going, part of Candace's crowd, headed for a Far East Studies Ph.D.; Peter was a fringe character, an "ethnic." The joke was that he did laundry cheap. Peter lived in an apartment near campus, drinking alone when he wasn't studying; on weekends he was either working in the family trading firm or visiting his mad mother.

"Is this your sister, Lin? She reminds me of a girl I knew one night in Bangkok."

Su Lin had flushed and looked to her brother. But Peter, desperate for acceptance by the white upperclassman and his crowd, had sat in mute panic.

Then in the parking lot afterwards Peter had emerged from the restaurant to find Alec Potter trying to grope Su Lin up against Peter's Thunderbird.

"Peter!" she had called out.

Peter had watched in horror, unable to act. Finally he had started to move, but Su Lin had cooled Alec Potter with a knee to the groin. Alec's friends had dragged him away.

Someone from the *Advocate* had written up Potter's drunken quip and the parking lot attack in a short story; Peter Lin came off badly. He had carried the shame all the way to graduation, when his hair had begun to fall out.

The incident came back to Peter five years later in the clearing in Ban Houei Sai as vividly as if it had just happened, all its sting intact.

"Tomorrow, Peter," Chen was saying, "we go back to Hong Kong. There is much to do."

All through the Southeast Asia trip Peter had been designing escapes, struggling against his fate, reviewing legal ploys to settle the estate and get his piece and go back to Boston. Now as the yellow slicker disappeared into the Yunnanese supply store, Peter Lin's perception shifted. The idea that he might encounter Alec Potter in another arena, on more favorable terms, and perhaps redeem that humiliating Cambridge night, made Chen's offer of power seem suddenly sweet.

A bolt of lightning flashed, illuminating the clearing at Ban Houei Sai. Then rain poured down in sheets. The Shan opium caravan unloaded by the morphine refinery at the open shed. The landscape seemed plunged in a thick, dark cloud, as if the sticky essence of the opium precipitate in the oil drums had risen to tinge everything, like a dusky, damaged Chinese painting.

12

Early evening mist hung low over the scalloped lamps of the Pont Neuf. Cross paused halfway across, fighting a final urge to cast the black suitcase into the dashing waters. But the man who looked like Gurdjieff was twenty yards behind, his pate gleaming beneath the deco streetlamp, his hand by his peacoat at the chest. It was dark, there were few people on the bridge; Cross was certain he'd be dropped if he so much as raised his arm. He turned and walked on, locked in headlong flight into fear.

The darkened arcades of Rue de Rivoli gave him the drumming of four footsteps, and his own racing, fractured silhouette in the barred shopwindows. His heart jackknifed as Gurdjieff's footsteps suddenly drew close.

Gurdjieff was whistling a song.

"You like jazz?"

He was beside Cross.

Cross walked on, staring ahead, wondering if Gurdjieff had actually asked him if he liked jazz.

"You recognize the tune?"

" 'How High the Moon.' "

"Yeah." Gurdjieff shook an Ideale from a pack and offered it. "I play piano at a club on San André des Arts. The Cameleon. You know it? Five years ago I came to Paris to find Bud Powell. There is Tatum, there is Garner. But ah, Bud Powell . . ."

Cross looked at his control. "You're Corsican?"

He nodded.

Cross took the cigarette. They walked on in rhythm to the echo of their own footsteps.

"You were lucky at Algeciras, monsieur." Gurdjieff flicked his cigarette away. "I had to work very hard to save you."

Citröen headlights swept the intersection ahead.

"What's in this suitcase?" Cross asked.

Gurdjieff laughed and shrugged.

"You could have taken it from the train and delivered it yourself," Cross said.

"You wouldn't have gotten paid, monsieur. After all our work. But please, I am just, how you say, a *fonctionnaire.*"

Cross turned to him. "Why do you do this?"

"Ah. I would do anything for Bébé Spiritu."

They walked a few more yards without speaking.

"Did you find Bud Powell?"

Gurdjieff smiled angelically. "Yeah," he said.

"How was he?"

"Beautiful, man. Beautiful."

Gurdjieff receded into the complex shadows of the arcade. "Night in Tunisia," tunefully etched, whistled off the walls.

Cross turned up Rue St. Honoré. After some yards he stopped to check the address he had been given and found to his surprise it was the elegant hotel before which he stood. He had expected some Latin Quarter teahead enclave typical of Ilya.

He approached the entrance and pulled open the huge cut-glass door. A ghostly doorman appeared from within, white-gloved hand raised.

"*Monsieur?*"

Cross was suddenly aware of his filthy, ill-fitting clothes.

"*Je voudrai voir Monsieur Spiritu.*"

"*Entrez, Monsieur.*" The doorman waved Cross through with a tight glance.

Cross stepped across the mirrored corridor, disoriented by the light of chandeliers, the confusion of Moorish carpets. He stood alone before the elevator, listening to his own breathing.

The elevator mounted laboriously upward, guided by a shrunken, silent man in uniform who wheezed. It stopped at the seventh floor. Cross got out and padded alone down a thick red plush runner past Chinese brocade walls toward a gilded door at the end of the hallway.

As he approached and raised his hand to knock, he heard the elevator again behind him. Gurdjieff emerged into the hall.

The elevator closed. Gurdjieff walked silently down the carpet toward Cross, blocking the light behind him as he came.

"Stay cool," he whispered, stepping past Cross and rapping his knuckles on the door in a pattern.

A swarthy man, solidly built, opened the door. He was dressed in a light jacket, sporty tan slacks, and a wide-collared black shirt.

"You the doctor?" He spoke in a thick Lower East Side accent, motioning Cross in. "I'm Bonaventure."

He extended a hand, which Cross shook. Gurdjieff followed them in.

The room was large and ornate, part of a suite, with thick rugs and silk wallpaper. The reek of men convening—cigars, brandy, cologne—filled the air. An older Latin man with silver hair and horn-rimmed glasses sat in a rich three-piece suit on a couch, swirling brandy in a glass. A Southeast Asian, small and tense, stood by the window in military uniform.

Sitting in a large armchair was the strangest figure Cross had ever seen. He was dressed in a white suit with black pinstripes and wide lapels. A diamond stickpin held a black tie in place. A Borsalino sat on his lap. The bottoms of tiny patent-leather shoes stuck straight out from diminutive legs. His large neckless head lolled on his shoulder. A thin stiletto mustache almost touched the pointed chin. Only the eyes, large and brown and quick, seemed to be there. In his hand was a miniature silver derringer. He was a tiny dandy, a dadaist fantasy.

Cross watched the man who looked like Gurdjieff lean down and kiss the dwarf's rings. The others in the room were regarding Cross with tense, sober expectancy.

"*Cet homme, c'est le docteur?*" said Bébé Spiritu, his voice reedy and querulous.

The Asian military man turned away from the window.

"I'm not a doctor," Cross said, putting the suitcase down.

"We heard you're a doctor."

Bonaventure looked at him. Cross stood uncomfortably on the plush carpet, shifting his weight.

"Who said that?"

"Ilya."

Bonaventure spoke to the dwarf in a Latinate tongue, then turned back to Cross. "You have something for us?" Cross pointed to the suitcase. "I have a plane to catch."

The little man in the chair smiled softly and said, "A plane."

They conversed among themselves in the other language. Cross heard the word "Marseilles."

"So you're not a doctor?" Bonaventure asked.

"A medical student. *Élève.*"

Bonaventure turned and spoke to the others again. He pointed to a chair. "Sit down."

"I have to catch a plane," he repeated.

"Relax," Bonaventure said. "This is Captain Thien. From Saigon." Captain Thien bowed. "This man is Mr. Francisci." The older man barely nodded. "And this is Bébé Spiritu."

Limpid eyes regarded Cross from the depths of the chair. Gurdjieff lit the dwarf's cheroot.

"Have a seat."

Cross looked around the room, measuring his options—a brief contemplation. He sat down in an armchair from which he was able to see into the other room of the suite, where a richly dressed effete Asian stood surrounded by several Caucasian women.

"So you're a friend of Ilya's."

"No. I'm making this delivery for him. That's all."

"How much did Ilya say you'd get?"

"A thousand dollars."

Bonaventure told Bébé Spiritu in Corsican. Spiritu nodded to Francisci. Francisci took his wallet out and peeled off ten American hundreds and handed them to Bonaventure, who handed them to Cross.

"Thank you," Cross said, standing to leave.

"Wait."

Wearily, Cross hovered by the chair.

"That man is Prince Phoumi, from Laos." Bonaventure gestured toward the other room into which Cross uncomfortably peered. "This is his suite."

"What more do you want of me?" Cross asked.

Bonaventure leaned close and spoke into Cross's ear: "Look. I'm from New York, understand? Over here on a trip. These are important people. They want you to take the suitcase on to California for them."

"No," Cross said quickly. "I'm done."

"You're going anyway, right? This could be a great opportunity for you." Bonaventure patted his knee. "Just do like they tell you. They'll pay you good, much more than what you just got."

As Cross looked around him, some sense of absurd rage rose up. These men were ridiculous, comedians. They underestimated his own extremity, what he had been through. He cursed Jiminez, hating him as on that day in Tenerife. The debasement of complicity spread like a stain.

"Tell them I'm not interested," Cross said, his voice rising. "I'm not interested at all."

This announcement seemed to raise a palpable displeasure in the room. Bébé Spiritu looked personally affronted. "Twenty-five hundred extra cash, doc. Right now."

Cross moved to stand up again, but Bonaventure held his arm. He leaned close to his ear once more. "Look. You heard about Valachi? The Senate testimony? These men, they're in business. They have transportation problems. You're a doctor. This does not shock you. This is for outpatients, know what I'm saying? Non-prescription. There's a lot of sick people in the States right now. A mercy mission. No risk. Customs in L.A. has been taken care of."

Bonaventure turned exasperatedly toward the other men. "See Mr. Spiritu there? He's got the Corsican medallion. He's what they call *un vrai monsieur*. A big man. A very big little man."

Gurdjieff added, "You don't say no to *un vrai monsieur*."

"I'm out," Cross said.

"No, doc." Bonaventure walked to the suitcase, removing a key from his pocket. "You're in."

The key fit the suitcase. When Bonaventure opened it, Cross saw his cargo for the first time: neat stacked piles of clear cellophane bags holding the soft white powder. Each bore a logo of several inked circles, in the center of which was an image of a tiger over-leaping a globe. Chinese writing adorned the borders, and the legend "100%." Above the tiger was a star.

"The best smack in the world, doc. All the way from Asia. Brought by you. The guy what killed some girl in the Canaries. Or so they say." Bonaventure grinned. "Stop playing around, doc. You're our mule."

Cross looked around the room, but nobody was looking back.

"So what do you say, doc?"

Cross broke for the door.

"Hey!" he heard Bonaventure call. "Don't you care what happens to you?"

Cross heard them both coming. As he reached the door and twisted the handle, Bonaventure caught the back of his coat. Gurdjieff ripped at his shoulder. Spinning around, Cross saw Colonel Thien, Francisci, and little Bébé Spiritu watching in cold silence.

Cross reached up to protect his face but his arm flew away like a twig. Gurdjieff's blunt fist, as pink and bare as his head, popped his cheekbone. He fell against the door, his fingers clawing the jambs. He ended up crouched, holding his face, swimming in pain.

He saw the shadow of the hand again. Then Bébé Spiritu spoke sharply in Corsican and the shadow dissolved.

"Fuck," Bonaventure said wearily. He grabbed Cross by the shoulder and lifted him up. "Goddamn amateurs. What the hell does that hophead Ilya think he's doing?" He opened the door and shoved Cross out.

The suitcase came after.

"Don't make us kill you."

Cross stood in the empty hall holding his face, blood running between his fingers.

"You'll hear from us, doc" were Bonaventure's last words.

The carpets were so thick that they muted the door slamming behind him, making it sound almost soft, polite.

13

Peter Lin stepped out of Saigon's Hotel Continental near noon, stuffing freshly changed money in his wallet. He was to meet Left-Hand Chen by the flower market, then take the five o'clock jet back to Hong Kong.

By the time Peter got there, a buzz was spreading down through the alleys and past the shacks all the way to Tu Do Plaza. A line of somber, shaven-headed monks in saffron robes walked by chanting, and people began to follow them down the boulevard. Peter and Chen fell in behind.

A crowd had gathered on the sidewalk. Someone had pulled an East German car across the street, blocking off traffic. Peter heard a British reporter say it was a demonstration protesting religious persecution against Buddhists by the Diem regime. Hardly the sort of event to inflame the foreign press around the *terrasse* in these times. There had been dozens of protests in recent months; but here they came, reporters and photographers, rushing up from every side to join the swelling crowd.

The chanting monks had formed a large circle in the middle of the street. Now an old one stepped out from among them. His name was Quang Duc, Peter heard someone say, and he was seventy-three years old. Silently Quang Duc walked to the center of the circle, followed by a pair of younger monks, each carrying a two-gallon tin of gasoline.

So that's why all the press, Peter Lin thought.

Peter, being tall, could easily see over the crowd. Next to him little Chen, dressed in a nondescript business suit, his face waxen and impassive, stretched and craned to see.

Quang Duc had removed his robes and placed them on the ground. He sat cross-legged in the center of the circle, inert and calm. When the two monks began to empty the tins of gasoline over him the crowd shuddered, and the photographers strained forward.

The remaining monks dropped to their knees, their hands clasped in prayer. The younger ones among them, unable to simulate the calm of Quang Duc, closed their eyes and clutched their beads as they chanted. A young Vietnamese next to Peter was translating the chant for a reporter:

> Ignorant people miscall it death,
> While heretics hold that it is annihilation . . .
> And the various phenomena of sound and voice
> Are equally unreal, like a dream or an illusion.

The two monks lit matches and threw them. The flames shot upward, and a deep moan rose from the crowd. Quang Duc sat silent and impassive, neither moving nor emitting a sound as the fire closed around him. His robes blackened, his ears erupted in fire. His face began to sputter, bubble, and drip like meat on a spit; his hands turned black. Still he sat, indifferent to the flames, exhibiting neither pain nor discomfort. The crowd, moved by the monk's terrible demonstration of his understanding, fell silent.

He is mad, Peter Lin was thinking. But watching Quang Duc burn, Peter also felt the sting of envy. This monk had seemingly found a world beyond phenomena, impervious to pain and suffering. Peter wondered if Quang Duc's way was the only way—or if one could perhaps wall oneself deep within the stony black vault of materiality, dead to all feeling, and achieve the same result.

Peter began to imagine that the flames that freed Quang Duc's soul cauterized his own.

Quang Duc slowly toppled over backwards. The fire raged around him. As the smell of gasoline and burning flesh drifted over the crowd and curled up to a dead blue sky, Peter Lin thought, My indifference will match his.

When only the ashes of the monk Quang Duc remained, the crowd began to disperse in eerie silence, the reporters to file their copy and photos of the incident. Only the Buddhist adepts lingered, murmuring a sutra over the remains.

"The plane," said Chen softly, touching Peter's sleeve.

Peter Lin had been gazing intently at the monk's remains. Now he looked up sharply. A tremor of surprise passed through Chen as Peter's eyes, hard and distant, met his. Peter glanced at his gold watch, then turned abruptly away and started off down the boulevard.

For a moment Chen Po-chi was transfixed there on the Saigon street, his left arm clasping his useless right one. Gazing after Peter, the little adviser felt a sudden mixture of foreboding and happiness. As Quang Duc's cinders fell out of the air around them, he hurried off to follow.

"Welcome back," Left-Hand Chen muttered in Swatownese, like a minister of state whose king had just returned after an absence.

14

Cross awoke and gazed down at the silver, turning sea. His stomach rolled as the plane banked against a pile of bright early morning clouds.

He reached in his jacket pocket and found the ticket bearing his name, reassuring him that he was indeed himself and on board a Pan Am polar route flight from London to Los Angeles.

Seated near the back, he could see that there were more empty seats than passengers on the midweek flight. The gray expanse out the window he registered as the North Sea. He stood up unsteadily and felt above his seat for blankets and pillows. A surge of nausea made him grip the edge of the shelf overhead.

He took all the blankets and pillows and sat back down. Pulling his long legs up across the three seats, he stuffed the pillows behind his head, pulled the blankets over himself, and began to shiver.

Deep yawns ripped through his body. As his hand crossed his face he felt the burn of stubble, then the bruise on his cheek and the scab forming. His head felt thick, clouded.

Gazing into the shuddering innards of the plane, Cross tried to call up an image of his arrival at the airport. But sleep fell back in on him, a soft sandbank.

"Reykjavik," said the stewardess. "Thirty minutes."

He opened his eyes as the plane dropped out of the night and onto a shiny landing strip. He stared for a few moments into the sickly light of the interior cabin, then stood up and lurched toward the door.

A lunar desolation hovered about the tiny airport. The inky shapes of Iceland's frozen mountains loomed in the night behind the landing strip like the ragged edges of a crater. Shivering, Cross followed the passengers across the tarmac into a lonely neon-lit coffee shop.

He sat at a gleaming Formica table watching the plane refuel through the window. Stale pastry and coffee sat untouched before him. A New York newspaper on the table spoke of the World Series. Koufax was leading the Dodgers into the series. Valachi was back in jail. A monk had immolated himself on a street in Saigon.

Reaching in his pocket, Cross found a notebook. He opened it and saw the bright erotica Eva had drawn in colored pens that day on the road south through Spain. On the next page was Bébé Spiritu's name and the Paris telephone number.

The rest of the pages were blank.

I have written nothing. Instead, life has scrawled itself all over me, in graffiti.

As he gazed in the airport window he saw reflected in the glass not himself or the room behind him but the men in the hotel: Bonaventure, Colonel Thien, Francisci, the Laotian Ambassador, Gurdjieff—and the little "vrai monsieur," Bébé Spiritu.

He broke out in an icy sweat. He strained his memory like an injured muscle gone slack, groping for revelation.

Eva's body on the beach turning in the tide, the urchin boy soberly watching, scratching his navel. Eva, the orphan with whom he had gone South, mourned now only by him.

A vision of El Jefe, shifting his girth before the Holy Mother: "We are discussing *absolution,* Mr. James."

Ilya, squatting on the chessboard floor of the Tangier villa: "Desire has failed you. Now back to duty, is it, Hippocrates?"

Cross clenched his fists and cried out. Another passenger eyed him with alarm.

A woman's soft voice came over the PA in the Reykjavik airport calling the passengers back to the plane. The image in the glass began to fade. Cross stood and followed the crowd out of the coffee shop into the night, stumbling across the freezing tarmac toward the plane which carried in its belly the dark merchandise.

A stewardess announced their descent into Los Angeles. Cross pressed his head against the window and peered through the brown clotted air at the vast streets of his homeland.

At customs the agent's eyes met his. He thumbed a large green book, glanced at Cross's black suitcase, then waved him straight through. Cross passed into the terminal, down the long tiled corridor, and out into the bright sun.

A black skycap approached and offered to take his suitcase at the curb. His eye hooked Cross's. *Spiritu,* he whispered. Cross put the suitcase down.

"Jimmy!"

It was his mother waving from the parking lot across the road, clutching a handkerchief as she came toward him. With her was a man he didn't know. His sister came running up behind.

Cross turned back to the skycap. But he was gone, with the black suitcase.

There was a desolation of palm trees along the freeway as Cross stared out at the empty landscape from the backseat of the Chrysler taking him home.

15

John Quincy Adams Terhune sat cross-legged on a cushion at his black lacquer table, a cup of tea before him, his long arms extending from the sleeves of a summer robe. Beside a stack of corrected galley proofs in Chinese, a fresh diary page lay open. Soft light from a paper lantern suffused the teahouse. Outside, a muggy summer squall rustled the garden leaves, stirring the surface of the pond. A large moth, drawn by the light, beat futilely against the paper screen.

Carefully he opened out two newspaper clippings he had folded into his journal and smoothed them on the table. One was the sequence of photos of the burning monk Quang Duc, as reported in the *Asahi Shimbun,* an English-language Japan daily. The other was a small article in the Hong Kong *South China Morning Post,* sent by an acquaintance and informant at the British Consulate, announcing the death of restaurateur and business leader Harry Lin, chairman of Lin Trading Company Ltd., specializing in the export of furnishings. Terhune wrote in the diary:

> Two deaths this season, Winny. One of a monk, one of a monster. They bracket things, the Yin and the Yang of it, all that lies between earth and sky, between heaven and hell.

He lit a Players and wrote on in a deliberate hand.

So he is dead at last, the victim of an assassin's bullet. Great wars commence for control of the trade. Harry Lin's megalomania will, I fear, be transferred, through the diabolical agent of the Left-Hand, to his successor: your Boston lawyer boy, thrust reluctantly onstage, turning Swatow. Imagine.

Ah, Winny. In my dreams I see you rising to return to Asia now that he is gone, reclaiming your family, your home, your garden. And your Jack! In my dreams this letter reaches you. In my dreams . . .

Terhune looked up, his eyes moist, then wrote on.

She was here, Winny. Beautiful, bright. And a rebel, like us. She renounces the family trade, of which she is no longer innocent. This may cost her her fortune. They will pressure her to come back to HK, mark my words.

A card from her today brings news of another sorry death—her college boyfriend, in the Gulf of Tonkin, the hundredth U.S. casualty.

Troubling days loom, Winny.

Terhune watched the shadow of the huge moth battling repeatedly against the paper door, ever lower, exhausting itself. His eyes moved to the alcove where below a Sesshu scroll his opium pipe reclined. Sweat broke out on his brow. Involuntarily his hand reached to his neck and began to scratch. He sniffled.

Ah, opium. On soft nights like these it sweeps through me like a warm wind, calling me to other times. My sweet sticky mud. Yet here I sit at my screen in far Japan, among the dross of my life. An article to finish for the *Kansai English Review,* a guest lecture to prepare at Kyoto University. And a reissue of my book on Han by a publisher in Seoul!

I drift among dreams, like a lost ship among idols. My cells grow restless. Cicadas whir outside like the new helicopters over Cochin. Perhaps the baths are still open. Oh, Winny. Is there any greater boredom than that of the user who has been cured?

Terhune looked again at the pipe poised in the alcove in the half-light. His eyes clouded over, his skin softened; reverie enfolded him like a gauze. His hand moved across the page steadily, like a dowser's wand.

Settling upon my side on the couch, I take a drop on the point of a long needle and hold it over the spirit lamp. Under the heat of the flame it gradually turns pale, softens, swells, and begins to bubble and sputter. Before it vaporizes I carry it, still on the point of the needle, to the surface of the bowl.

I tip the bowl to the flame, put the stem of my pipe to my lips, and inhale. It passes into my lungs in the form of a heavy white smoke. Two or three puffs and I have entirely consumed the drop. I repeat this operation three times, and soon I have begun to feel the effects. Ah, opium!

Terhune wrote on evenly, as if dictated to from outside.

I feel the universe rush in to fill me, like water into an empty vessel. I am a permeable membrane, a palimpsest upon which messages from eternity scrawl themselves over and over in disappearing ink.

Flames erupt at each of my joints, and burn. I reach out and light my cigarette by them. I watch colors drain into pure black and white, then soak their pigments back in until I feel I know the essence of color.

Entire symphonies play in my head, note for note, with such clarity that they defy transcription. Poems form of such perfect symmetry that they are unutterable. Images pass by in luminous profusion, leaving "normal" reality far behind, an old gray newsreel of dead armies marching.

I hear languages in unknown tongues, images organized around perceptual principles of a different order. Dozens of crystalline mathematics, each contained in a snowflake, float before my eyes.

I experience the most pure and prolonged disembodied orgasms, lasting for hours, rushes of mounting pleasure beating like waves against the shores of my body, each greater than the last. My skin sprouts hundreds of sexual organs to accommodate them.

Ah, opium, I have raced the corridors of heaven with you, trudged each black circle of hell.

Terhune paused and looked up, his eyes emptied of physical interest or longing, as if the entire universe were no more than the expiring moth batting at his screen. He wrote on, summoning the drug, his vision turned dark, as if triggered involuntarily by the external image of the dying moth.

I have known the gray desolation of withdrawal, my cells screaming across the charred, burnt landscape of my own nerves. I have heard the profound grieving of the universe, contracted in a sob. I have heard the silence of a sanitarium room broken by the hideous shrieks of a thousand enraged monkeys.

I have heard freight trains thunder through my cortex, elephants stampede my veins, steam hammers excavate my inner ears, echoing to the ends of infinity. I have felt my skin crawl like a termitary, my temples wither and crack like dry leaves, my eyeballs burst from my head, my tongue swell to the size of a porpoise.

Ah, opium. My church, my confessor, my disease, my cure.

When God wishes to make love to me, he uses as his instrument opium.

Without opium, I merely make art. With opium, I *am* art.

The clopping of wooden sandals on the gravel outside interpenetrated Terhune's rumination. Slowly he reinhabited the present.

I return to life against my wishes, Winny, renouncing the sublime peace of opium for the drab, contentious mind wars the others call Reality.

As he put his pen down and closed the journal, Terhune's empty gaze surveyed the teahouse, drawing comfort from its estheticism, and the sensuous image of the girl who now stood in the doorway in *yukata* back from the baths, bucket and soap in hand—as if to signal Terhune's transference from the one obsession to another.

"*Ii desu-ka, Terhune-san?*"

"*Fumiko-san.*"

She came to him. Terhune reached up and touched her face, feeling the heat from the baths rising off her skin. He began to slide his hand inside her robe, then stopped and withdrew it. Fumiko looked at him quizzically, then smiled and slipped past him to the futon.

Terhune sat quietly before his journal for some moments, then turned off the light and crawled to the mat.

He lay beside the girl, staring at the paper door, lit only by the moon, where earlier the moth had enacted its frenzy.

TWO

The Planting

16

Su Lin stood at the darkening corner of Grant and Vallejo among rush hour streams of people, dressed in her job interview outfit—black dress, coat, heels, and patent-leather purse—holding a half-eaten *cha siu bao,* a pork bun she'd bought at the Chinese deli on Pacific. It was the dank, chill end of a mid-November North Beach day and her feet hurt.

She looked up Vallejo the two steep blocks to the top, her eyes running across the staggered white facades until she saw her apartment, the bay window curving out to the sidewalk. Turning back down Grant Street, weary despair gripped her.

It was her fate to be followed by men, but the two standing in the doorway of the Italian restaurant three doors back had little in common with the oglers she routinely trailed in her wake. These were Chiu Chao, and they watched her with neither desire nor hatred—the stocky one with the pocked cheeks and the tall, wiry one whose pants didn't reach his ankles.

Grant was safely busy at dinner hour, but up Vallejo it was deserted. If she waited with the crowd she knew the Chiu Chao would wait with her; if she started up the hill they would follow. For two weeks they had stalked her, silent and unremitting.

She slipped out of the crowd and began the climb up Vallejo. As traffic thinned she could hear them fall into place behind her, their heavy steps dogging her own. The city sounds drifted up the hill: cars, radios, sirens, hawkers, babies squalling out neighborhood windows. It was futile to walk faster; her stalkers always kept pace. At first it had been half a block, then ten or fifteen yards. Tonight she could all but feel their foul garlic breath on her neck.

Slowing into the brief comfort of a streetlamp's pool of light, she sensed them slow behind her. She turned and let her eyes run out across the pointillized San Francisco night. Nibbling her pork bun, she entertained a fantasy of violence that startled and relieved her: Turning, she whipped her purse across the tall one's face, rammed the high pointed heel of her shoe in the belly of the other, and sent them rolling down the hill into Grant Street and the waiting clutches of the crowd—who proceeded to cannibalize them.

A yellow Volkswagen turned around at the crest of the grade and braked slowly down. She had an impulse to run for the car as it neared. But it passed by and was gone; the street was silent again. Su Lin slid back into the darkness of the emptying hillside; the Chiu Chao resumed their tail.

Nearing the top of the hill, she could see down the other side where Vallejo plunged to the Bay. At Pier 21 a festively lit Matson Line passenger ship bound for the Orient was backing out of its berth. She thought she could hear voices. A foghorn sounded.

She rushed up the short stoop, scouring the bottom of her handbag for the keys. She had always had it in mind to go for their eyes with her keys if they came close enough.

Her two tails stopped at the foot of the stoop and watched her furiously scrape the key across the lock, fishing for the slit. In the reflection of the door window she saw the big one smile, his gold-capped teeth gleaming in the night.

"Go away," Su Lin snapped through the darkness. "Go away."

The key turned. She pushed open the door and rushed inside. Wheeling in the tiled hallway at the bottom of the stairs, she tried to slam the door; but a doorstop caused it to drag. The silhouettes of the Chiu Chao loomed and swelled in the curtained window, then pressed flat against the frame.

The door clicked shut. She fell against the wall breathing heavily, listening to the shuffling on the stoop outside, raging at Peter and Chen's game of pursuit.

When she saw the shadows diminish and heard the footsteps recede, she climbed on leaden legs to the first landing and opened the door to the flat.

Her roommate Junie sat cross-legged in a smock on the living-room floor in front of a canvas, smoking.

"You okay?" she asked, looking up.

She rose and poured a cup of tea from a china pot. They stood together looking at the new painting.

"It's strong," Su Lin said charitably of the roseate abstraction, still shaken by her stalkers.

Junie looked at her. "You sure you're okay?"

"Yeah."

"Any luck?"

"No."

"Come work with me tonight then."

Su Lin turned away. "I should paint."

"You've got to eat. Your bones are showing."

The front room of the apartment was tall and white with ornate fake Victorian molding, small inexpensive chandeliers, and Junie's canvases. The furniture was pillows and crates draped in dropcloths and madras. The windows faced downtown toward the financial district, a towering view of stacked steel and glass. From the roof upstairs the full sense of place unfolded: the Bay from Oakland to the Berkeley hills, up to the refineries at Richmond and across the brick-red Golden Gate and beyond to Sausalito and Marin County.

Su Lin and Junie had known each other at Berkeley and had come across the Bay to the Art Institute—Su Lin to teach, Junie to study—chasing the heady perfume of apocalyptic freedom hovering in the Bay Area air. Junie also worked nights as a topless dancer in North Beach to finance her noisy, bright acrylics.

Su Lin had been the most popular of the new teachers at the Institute and easily the most gifted painter. She'd had six pieces accepted in a juried show scheduled for January at the San Francisco Museum of Art. Everything had seemed to be working for her until a few weeks earlier.

Junie walked over to the coffee table.

"This came for you."

It was a letter from Japan, the stamp an old Hiroshige *ukiyo-e* print of a geisha opening an umbrella.

"Thanks."

She took it and turned toward her room.

Junie called after, "Some kid called from a naval hospital. He asked if you were coming to visit."

"Monday."

"Who is he?"

She paused and looked back. "A survivor."

Her bedroom, like the main room, faced onto the city. It was small, spare, neat, with a mattress on the floor covered in a silk brocade spread with dragons and birds. There was a cherrywood chest from the Mainland for her clothes, a thrift-shop dresser with a mirror over it and a collage of mementos. Painted canvases were stacked up against an easel. Beside a sewing machine were piles of fabric in various stages of becoming clothes. A stereo on the floor bore the weight of a stack of records. The one showing was Miles Davis' *Sketches of Spain*. A framed program from the Peking Opera hung on the wall over the bed. There were no photos of her relatives: only one of a young Caucasian man looking ill at ease in a navy uniform and an expression that seemed to belong to someone else.

Her room was a controlled fantasy, eerily private and certain, belonging neither to East nor West. Sometimes it amused her, gave her unique perceptions, fed her art. Other times, visiting American friends' homes, she perceived a Caucasian order, a solidity she was inclined to admire. But Su Lin was a physical and cultural exile, one who lived between the seams, designing her own emotional sustenance. She was comfortable with it, which was convenient, because she had no choice.

She fell back on her bed and took the letter out of its envelope. It was penned in a tight script on onionskin. Folded in among the pages was a snapshot: Terhune had reproduced the photo of himself and Winny Lin standing on the Arashiyama Bridge above the rapids ten years earlier, the blazing trees of Japanese fall behind them.

She gazed at the image of her mother's defiant beauty, then placed the picture by the one of the boy in uniform. The letter she put on the dresser to read later; then she rose and walked to the window. Through the dark she could see the silhouettes of the Chiu Chao in the entry of a building across the street.

When she had returned to San Francisco after her father's killing, the only contact with her brother had been a series of distraught phone calls from various hotels in Southeast Asia as Peter, trailing Chen through the Triangle, wrestled with his fate. Then one day while she was teaching her painting class at the Art Institute a phone call had come. She had taken it in the courtyard phone booth by the fountain, looking out through the graffiti on the glass. Lawyers had arrived from Hong Kong to read her the terms of Harry Lin's will, and awaited her presence at the Saint Francis Hotel downtown. She had made them wait until she was done with her class, then gone straight downtown in her paint clothes, acrylic still drying on her hands.

In a hotel room full of water pitchers and copper coffee mugs on white tablecloths, motes of dust swirling in the flat white afternoon light through the curtains, two Chinese, two British, and one American lawyer had informed her that she was to be the beneficiary of a series of trusts willed to her by her father, grandfather, and great-grandfather—should she meet the requirements—to mature at intervals throughout her life. The trustee would be the Hong Kong Crown Bank, the official in charge Nigel Mason himself.

The total amount of her share of the trust funds was to be five hundred million dollars.

The space in the room had dilated and flattened; the dark-suited figures had become distant, squawky. She had stared into the light streaming through the curtains as the drone of legalese continued.

The requirements were twofold: first, that she be of sound mind and body; second, that she return to Hong Kong and assist her brother in running the family business. She was to report to him in all matters.

Harry Lin's stubborn feudalism spoke from beyond the grave: Obey, or be cut off.

She had looked around the room as throats cleared and horn-rimmed glasses were pushed up, the lawyers' studied formality unraveling at the thought of such beauty combined with such staggering riches.

She could not have been prepared. Even the talk with Peter in Hong Kong on the way to Kai Tak had given her no inkling. The numbers were beyond human grasp.

She was informed that Peter had met the conditions of the will. Then the British lawyer had handed her a pen and pointed her toward a daunting pile of stapled documents.

She had refused the pen. Instead she had risen and chastised the lawyers for their complicity in opium, accusing them of helping spawn the desperate junkie landscape out the window below. Then she had left the room.

A young Chinese lawyer had followed her down the hall. In the elevator she was shocked to discover he was Song Wei, her old amah's son and a childhood friend of Peter's whose Cambridge education had been paid for by her father. Now he worked unhappily for Mason's Crown Bank. In the coffee shop downstairs he had tried to persuade her to reconsider. Song Wei was tall, fair, more like a northern Chinese, his manner gentle.

"Over and above your father's last wishes, there is the factor of your personal safety. Even if the wealth means nothing to you, there are family enemies who could exploit your . . . exposure."

"This is a ploy to make me afraid, force me to return."

"Those responsible for your father's death are at large. Left-Hand Chen is of the opinion that they are not necessarily Chinese."

"I am perfectly safe here."

"Your brother is the head of the family now. It is his wish that you return."

This very Chinese thought had dropped her into silence. She had looked at the tall young man she had known as a boy.

"What about you, Song Wei?"

"Like you I have dreams. My sympathies are with Mao. But your father paid for my education, for which I will always be in his debt."

"So opium owns you too," she had said.

"I recognize my obligation to the past, to my family and yours." His face heated, and tears worked in his eyes. "I am Chinese."

To his implied rebuke, she had answered, "The chains of the generations must be broken. Isn't that what Mao wants too?"

"So you still refuse the inheritance?"

"Song Wei, Harry Lin is dead. You owe him nothing more. Perhaps you can stop deferring your dreams and help China before the trade consumes you."

Song Wei had flushed and stood up.

"I admire you," he had blurted. "Goodbye."

Then Su Lin had realized she didn't even have money for the coffee.

"Someday in Hong Kong," Song Wei had said as he left money on the table, "you can buy me coffee." Then he had left her his business card and walked away.

That night in a North Beach bar Su Lin had gotten drunk with several of her students. When she told them she had just turned down five hundred million dollars, they had thought that a riot. It didn't occur to anyone to believe her.

It was the headiest night of her life.

The next day Peter had called from the villa in Hong Kong. "I'm staying, Su. I've taken the inheritance."

"Congratulations."

"You refused yours."

"Yes."

"You're mad. How will you live?"

She had laughed. "Very well."

"You must come back. It's not safe out there."

"Safe? And what do you mean 'out there'? Last time I visited you in Boston you were listening to Mississippi Delta blues."

"We can do things here. Legitimize."

"You're fooling yourself."

"There are enemies."

"I have no enemies."

"The ones who killed Father."

Peter had ranted about Corsican gangs, secret wars, international plots. Finally he had said, "Is it your old navy boyfriend? Is that what's keeping you from coming back?"

"No, Peter. He's dead."

A week earlier the father had called, the navy captain, and given her the news coldly—almost as if her being Eurasian made her party to it—that it had come in a night shelling in the Gulf of Tonkin. It had left her empty; all she could think of was that he had followed his family's will, not his own. They had been merely young together, he more a friend, their romance dead for over a year. It hadn't lessened the hurt.

To this news Peter had said, "Sorry. Maybe it would be a good time to come back."

"I'm teaching. I'm painting. I've had work accepted in a show. I'm okay here."

"There'll be no money at all."

Then she had said, "Peter, I saw Terhune. He says Left-Hand Chen is dangerous."

"Terhune is the dangerous one. He ruined Mother." His voice was horribly distant.

"Peter, listen . . ."

The line had snowed up and gone dead.

First the small monthly checks she had received for years had stopped coming. Then she had arrived at class one morning to find her paintings, the ones selected for the museum show, hanging in strips from their stretchers, slashed by knives.

She had rushed outside in tears to find two Chiu Chao goons standing in the street chuckling.

It was a peculiarly Chinese form of persuasion.

Devastated, unwilling to subject her students to what cruelty might come next, she had left the Art Institute and begun looking for other work. But each opportunity had been blown in some way by the silent harassment of the Chiu Chao. Now she was not beyond believing they would try and take her.

Tired and fearful, she shut the curtain and crossed the room to her dresser. She stood for a moment before the mirror, staring at the stranger who gazed back. She had grown thin, her skin waxen. Studying herself, she thought of a series of self-portraits, something to objectify her difficulties, as if to defy Peter and Chen by taking on the mantle of her isolation, making herself her subject.

Several unfinished oils leaned against a Grumbacher easel, gathering dust while she looked for work. The more she looked at them the angrier she became. She reached for the phone on the bed beside her, clenching and releasing the handle. Finally she picked it up.

"Hong Kong," she said to the overseas operator.

It was a bad, spitting connection. A woman answered.

"It's Su."

"Oh, hello, dear."

"Bessie, give me Peter please."

"Just a moment."

Left-Hand Chen came on. Hearing the soft, modulated British tones, she wanted to scream.

"Let me talk to my brother."

Chen said, "Just a moment."

After a long wait Chen came back on the line. "I'm afraid he's indisposed. He says to tell you just to come home."

"Chen! Call them off! Do you understand? It's not working! I'm not coming back!"

"Pardon?"

"Why are you doing this?"

"Doing what?"

She wondered if he were going mad. "These Chinatown hoods who follow me around."

"They're there to protect you. There is the matter of your welfare."

"They slashed my paintings! They cost me my job!"

"I'm terribly sorry. There must have been a mistake. I'll look into it."

"Chen! Are you behind this?"

"You must realize there is danger. All this could be solved if you'd just come home voluntarily."

"Voluntarily?"

"I will relay your message to Peter," Chen said obediently.

Junie's voice came from the other room. "You coming?"

Su Lin slammed the phone down.

A little after nine o'clock they came down Vallejo together. A light mist had collected in the air. Su Lin could sense the goons hovering in the shadows nearby. Just before the bottom of the hill Junie led her into a narrow street that cut through to Broadway. She stopped at the side entrance to a building facing on the boulevard.

"You are so beautiful," Junie said sadly as she opened the door.

They entered a narrow room with mirrors and dried makeup. There were other girls.

"Take off your coat," Junie said.

Su Lin's arms were shaking.

"Once you get on you'll feel better."

"Tweak your nipples," said another girl. "It perks them up."

Su Lin turned and rushed out the door.

Bare-legged she ran up Columbus. A light rain was falling, leaving slicks that reflected the neon. She crossed Broadway in mid-block, ducking traffic, and hurried down the sidewalk. The evening *Examiner* headlines shrieked of Diem and Nhu's murders; there were now 16,800 American military in Indochina. She wrapped her arms around her shoulders against the drizzle.

Behind the City Lights Bookstore a short alley ran off to the right, past the Vorpal Gallery, where erotic bronze sculpture, locked in mineral couplings, filled the window. She came out into Chinatown and hurried aimlessly among the fortunetellers and the toy-stand whirligigs and the fish store where live lobsters swam in tanks; hanging pressed ducks, the clicking of mahjongg tiles, the smell of garlic and soy: miniatures of southern China, Hong Kong, Canton.

There is the matter of your own welfare.

Were the words meant to convey real threat? Or was it only a chimera of the one-handed mandarin?

A tired, bent old-young Cantonese woman bumped her, a wrapped child clutching her back, trapped in the grinding mill of the old patriarchy. Pushing through the evening clutter and press of the transplanted Asian street, Su Lin felt the burn of the blunt upward regard directed at her, the mongrel, the impure.

Could she ever return to China, any China?

How devoted they were to each other, the Chinese! Continuing up Grant, she was carried on the river of the ancient, noisy, protective biocontinuum, enfolded in currents deeper than reason, offering the contentment of surrender.

She came back out at Columbus and Broadway and stood in the nip of early evening air, caught now in the clattery American riff: dogs, beatniks, winos, whores, and tourists mingling beneath the neon sizzle of topless signs. Sailors in twos and threes reminded her of Hong Kong: the boys of the USS *Ranger,* stationed in Alameda, back from the South China Sea for repairs.

She knew she reminded them too.

She was back in front of the City Lights Bookstore. In the window, Alan Watts stared back from book covers; a poster for the Zen

Center; Ali Akbar Khan teaching in Berkeley; Monets at the Museum.

Was this random cultural stew something to be prized, fought for? Up the block Miles Davis was appearing with Cannonball and Coltrane at the Jazz Workshop. Junie had wanted to go together; she couldn't afford it now.

I've never been without money.

An Odetta album in the window of a record shop on Upper Grant made her think of Peter. They had heard her together at a Mount Devon club in Cambridge, he with his deb Candace on his arm in a blue cashmere sweater, cool, smoking Kents. Now he was rich; he could pay off the gambling debt. But it wouldn't get him back his peaches and cream.

The rain began again. She ducked into the Coffee Gallery.

"Cappuccino?"

"I don't have any money," she said.

"For a drawing." Sacha, the bearded friend at the machine, handed her a sketchpad and charcoal.

The hand moved unerringly: an Asian odalisque, languidly draped across the bar nude.

Two guys next to her talked of an anti-draft rally at the Oakland Induction Center, making her remember the boy who had demonstrated there once, then turned about to follow his father into the navy.

Though they were no longer close, he must have needed to write the summer letters from the carrier *Turner Joy* in the South China Sea, describing the madness around him, missing her, full of questions, regrets, fear. Why had he gone? Too late he knew: His family's will had overcome his own.

Then the letters had stopped coming.

Sacha was holding up her sketch. "Good piece," he said, stroking his beard sagely. He reached up and hung it over the mirror behind the bar.

When he turned around, Su Lin was gripping the bar, rocking back and forth. Sacha couldn't tell if she was laughing or crying.

Near midnight Su Lin stood shivering in the rain, watching the Chiu Chao boys across the street beneath the dry painted eaves of the Chinese Benevolent Protective Society building.

"Come on!" she called. "Take me!"

The goons stared back at her, blinking, as if she were crazy; then they started toward her. The tall one showed his gold teeth as he stepped off the curb.

He was still grinning when he stiffened suddenly and stopped in the middle of the street, clutching his shoulder.

Su Lin saw blood gush between his fingers. She turned to the popping sound at the corner to see a thick shaven-headed mustachioed man in a navy blue pea jacket lower his arm and recede into shadows.

The Chiu Chao staggered off howling down Grant, his little companion close behind.

17

Jim Cross stayed in Los
Angeles for six weeks after his return. Dinners in the quiet, ornate
Spanish home on the Palos Verdes peninsula were filled with long,
terrible silences, the dolorous chiming of the hall clock, the clinking of the family silver as Mary Cross gazed upon her unrecog-
nizable son, the strange interloper who held his fork backwards
and seemed to have lost all sweetness and civility.

It was a cool fall in California that year. The Dodgers swept the
Series in four. Valachi's Senate testimony had left "Cosa Nostra" on
the nation's lips. The number one song was "Dominique" by the
Singing Nun, and the best-selling book Jessica Mitford's *The American Way of Death.*

Mary Cross had taken up with another gynecologist, a Dr. Flint,
bald and thin-lipped, with an inveterate gargly chuckle unleashed
at any provocation. Cross wondered what ovarian riddle his mother
was trying to solve with her doctors. Like them all, this one was
part of the aerospace establishment.

"They'll eat out of little food tubes while they're floating around the cabin," Dr. Flint explained over lamb chops, lauding the glories of impending manned space flight.

"How will they go to the bathroom?" his sister wanted to know.

"A kind of a device that fastens on," said Mom's new beau.

"That means women couldn't go up in space?"

"Well, the Russians did it in May. Don't know how. I mean you wouldn't want menses floating around the cabin, would you? Or Kotex on the moon?" He guffawed.

Like most doctors he made terrible, indelicate jokes, imagining that the use of Latin terms exempted crudity. Cross stared fixedly into his mashed potatoes. Mary Cross raised her linen napkin to her lips.

"You know, Jim," said Dr. Flint, "you can say what you want about your Europe, your other places. But in two decades you'll see Heaven on Earth in Southern California. Mark my words. Kennedy or no."

Cross was speechless before this man who spent his days looking up cunts, and this woman, his mother, who must be giving him hers. His father used to have a joke about meeting a proctologist at a convention. "We're neighbors," went the punch line.

Cross had heard this terrible banter all his life. His grandfather, for whom he was named, was an Ohio GP whose mother had been the first woman doctor in the state; she had come there in a covered wagon. The son, Maxfield Cross, was in the first generation of specialists. Max Cross had two brothers, both doctors. One still practiced in Cleveland; the second had gone East to Boston. Cross's father had come West because of his wife's lung condition and settled in Southern California.

Jim Cross had been born into a professional class busy and confidently ordering the world, people to whom expression was deviate, an atavistic gift to be smiled at in small children, stored away in art books and museums. The "permissive" environment, Cross had learned early, ruled certain things out. The body would feed, the soul starve.

By the time Cross hit Stanford he spent weekends examining Blake, Bosch, Turner, and Coltrane with the same intense care as he studied biopsies. At the University of California's Langley Porter Medical School his life had been threaded precariously along a thin line between the twin poles of art and service, duty and inspiration—until the day the sutures had snapped and he had walked out.

Now Europe still haunted him, forcing him to flash back, strewing his dreams with its figures. Ringing phones made him jump. He slept poorly, awaiting a sign from an unknown direction, wondering if he would recognize it when it came.

"You'll hear from us," the Corsican had said.

Often he entertained visions of Eva lying in his arms on the steamer pillow on the boat to the Canaries, the smell of her body, her thighs pale and downy in the bright southern Las Palmas light.

The physical fact of her death he could accept; Cross had seen death too often in the emergency wards to be uncomfortable with it. But the meaning of her death had been degraded, emptied, by Jiminez' crime, his greed and evasion. That, and his own grief, had driven Cross to the small violence that had begun his odyssey; this is how he understood what had happened.

Eva's own hand in it he felt he perceived now: an orphan, a poet, fragile in life, erasing herself. She had barely been here to begin with; danger had been her handmaiden, death her wedding.

There remained a medical guilt, that he shouldn't have let her go through with it. It pitted the old value he had fled—preserve the flesh at all costs—against a new one he thought he had found, then watched slip through his fingers.

There is no evil in the flesh, in physical corruption. Where is the honor in merely preserving the body? Evil must lie elsewhere. He had gone out to find it, and had become its slave.

The suburban landscape was tinged, like a poor Technicolor print, with muted terror. Across the road at his father's old country club Cross gazed out at duffers in plaid slacks lunging at errant Topflites as if the world were still intact. Cross felt like the advance man for some awful beast come to devour the land, a blinking pterodactyl reborn in the middle of a backyard barbecue.

One afternoon he looked up Luther Williams, an old friend from medical school now based at USC Hospital, and worked with him for a few days in a Watts clinic.

"Tell me about the drugs, Williams."

"Never seen so many. From both ends. The streets and the labs. The streets you see this new kind of heroin. From Asia, they say.

Strong as hell. Then you have the labs—Sandoz, Pfizer—mixing other stuff up in beakers and it goes right out the back door, down to Mexico, then back up here."

"Why?"

"Man, sometimes I think somebody upstairs wants it down here."

"Who?"

"You tell me. It's your kind who run the show. All I know is you can arrest all the Valachis in the world, burn down every field in Turkey, have Reverend King march in Washington, and the shit still hits the streets regular as the sun comes up. That's what I see. But the people down here don't think about that. They feel like they're making a statement by using."

"What are they saying?"

"Black? They're saying despair, man. Despair. White? They're saying look at me, I'm cute." They ate cold hamburgers someone had brought in. "Damned if I can put the head together with the feet, though. Someday somebody's going to follow the evil all the way back, from the spoon and dropper to its source in the fields. But it ain't going to be me." Williams moved his arm idly through the air. "And man, I swear that path runs through Washington, D.C." He was developing a paunch, worrying about his hairline. "So you going back and intern up, Cross?"

"Should I?"

Williams frowned, holding a syringe up against the light. "It's a gig."

The next day Cross wrote his old dean at Langley Porter requesting readmission to medical school.

He left Los Angeles on a bright fall morning in a Volkswagen he had bought for $200 on a lot. The last thing his mother said, kissing him on the veranda, was, "If you need any mental help, son, God knows we know enough psychiatrists."

A stiff breeze whipped feathers of spume off the wave crests along 101 as Cross sped north past Malibu, County Line, Rincon, old surfing spots where joyous, cynical anarchy had reigned among Southern California kids in the late fifties. Cross rolled the window up.

He drove on up a coastline bristling with defense installations and perimeter armaments, missiles like porcupine quills: Point Mugu, Vandenberg Air Force Base, Camp Roberts. America had become an armed camp; inside, a xenophobic people roamed endlessly, terrified of the barbarian beyond the gates. Cross felt he was running along the castle's western wall. As he turned inland and rolled past Atascadero through the soft hills of ironwood and olive trees, he saw it as a defiled Indian land, desolate and colonial, a temporary white stewardship. Crossing the culvert at King City he thought, The Barbarian has slipped in through the gates. It was none other than himself.

In Berkeley he found strange lodgings: a basement beneath the gymnasium of a decaying estate and onetime metaphysical institute. Clear Light College sat on a sloping hill among a grove of trees, overrun with vines and broken masonry, like a Fellini garden. Built in the twenties by a follower of Blavatsky, it survived on cottage rentals and Wednesday night lectures on such topics as "Auras: How to Read Them" and "A Cabalist Looks at Mu," bobbing hopelessly in the wake of the great agnostic citadel of learning nearby whose students readied to riot against punch-card tyranny.

His basement flat had a hatch-cover coffee table, a faded Persian rug, and atavistic wood statues left behind by the former occupant, a sculptor who had fled to Mendocino, convinced the second great San Francisco earthquake was imminent.

The next day Cross drove over to Langley Porter. Dean Whiteman, an old colleague of his father's, signed his application for return to medical school up against a green corridor wall in Neurosurgery.

"The prodigal son returns."

Dean Whiteman, a surgeon and bad poet who had always taken an interest in Cross, walked him to the elevator. "You were my best, you know. It shook me when you left."

Cross couldn't imagine Dean Whiteman being shaken by anything. He was a tall silver-haired Protestant exemplar of rational scientific humanism, seemingly born in a starched white lab coat.

"You've lost weight. Wild oats?" He stared up at the elevator lights. "I heard something about you working with orphans in Paris."

He pushed the "Down" button. "You think you can make your peace with this? Settle back down?"

"I hope so, Dean."

As the elevator door opened Dean Whiteman said, "The new ones, Jim. They're all after the private plane, the golf clubs, the Wednesdays off."

In the days that followed, Cross, with little to do until the next quarter began, wandered alone among the ruins of the Clear Light campus or hiked up in the hills among the pines where the winter light was sharp and pale. On occasions when he ventured into San Francisco, Mill Valley, or Berkeley to old haunts, he found a languid dilettantism afoot: electric folk music, Alan Watts, Zen, Dylan, and LSD-25. The drugs were everywhere, soft and hard, breaking from the fringe into the middle class, just as Ilya and his circle of hungry ghosts had prophesied.

At times the conspiratorial conjectures of Tangier still haunted him. Had Ilya been just an addled teahead aiding a Corsican heroin ring running Asian drugs for the money? *Who ran the runners?* The Thai general, the Laotian prince in the Paris hotel. *What were the politics?*

Would they come for him again?

Finally with the passage of days Cross put the thoughts behind him. As for Eva, she became a jewel of bright light affixed in the vault of the sky above the drape of the Golden Gate seen from Clear Light College, a star that came up early in the evening.

Dean Whiteman called and invited him to dinner the Sunday before Thanksgiving. They met at a Fisherman's Wharf lobster house.

"So what's it going to be? GP? Surgery? Headshrinker?" he asked over margaritas. He tapped his brow. "A big unexplored world in there, Jim."

Dean Whiteman raised his glass, licking salt off his lips, a paper bib with a lobster's image on it tucked into his neck. "I always had you pegged for the doctor-priest. The Jung."

"Not me, Dean."

Cross watched a melancholy come over Dean Whiteman, the facade crumble over the drink. It was something he had seen in doctors many times, the healer as tragedian.

"The interns, Jim. They watch me but they don't see me. Is it television, what?"

"The country's changing."

"The temple of reason, order, certitude. Crumbling. I can feel the darkness and chaos, like a wind down the corridors. 'Turning and turning in the widening gyre . . .' What was it Yeats said?" He leaned forward. "Will the old order survive, Jim?"

Cross sucked the meat from a claw. The dean looked suspiciously across the table. "Have you become a nihilist in your travels? No, that's not it. The challenge of . . . your generation. What is it? Give it a name, goddammit. I feel like I'm punching at air."

Cross toyed with the broken remains of his lobster. When he looked up to speak he was surprised at the rush of feeling.

"We cut, we paste, we disinfect, Dean. We want to colonize the body, tame or exterminate or convert the errant germ, the cell, the way we took on Africa or the New World. But we simply drive ourselves further from life. The body isn't a country to be conquered. We can't win the universe with syringes and surgery."

Dean Whiteman hunched down in his chair, gripping his drink. "Is it a spiritual crisis, then, Jim? Shit, the religious are no closer to God than we. Do you think you can get closer to God than the patient? Good works, Jim. The humble human event. Why do you find this insufficient?"

He wanted to say, We fend off life in the name of life. I wanted to go out and take life. I wanted it. I tried.

Dean Whiteman looked ruminatively into the freckled cleavage of the waitress clearing the table. "Is it love, Jim? Is that where we've gone wrong?"

Reaching in his jacket pocket for his wallet, he became almost stern. Cross was suddenly eager to get away.

"Take up your fate, Jim. Everything has prepared you for this."

Outside, the night swirled in clammy fog. On the sidewalk Dean Whiteman said, "How would you like to visit a neuropsychiatric hospital?"

"I feel fine, Dean."

"Oh, that's a good one!" Dean Whiteman thought that was funny and slapped him on the back. "Seriously, Jim. I go out to Oak Knoll on Mondays. The navy hospital. Meet me and I'll have a doctor take you around. They're doing good stuff out there. May give you some ideas while you're waiting for the new quarter to start."

Cross was unable to find a suitable reason to decline.

Back at Clear Light he lay awake until dawn, staring out through the dusty basement windows snarled with creepers, watching the light shift, feeling like a ticking bomb in destiny's mailbox.

18

Since the spring day in Chiengmai when Alec Potter had spied on the Triad *gong sou* meeting in Old So's teahouse, he had watched with rising fascination as Asia shifted around him: the swelling U.S. troop count in Saigon, the sudden descent of advisers and operatives of all descriptions in the tri-border area, the secret skirmishes along the Chinese border. He had duly noted that summer the killing of the Eurasian Harry Lin, a Hong Kong man he didn't know but whom Peg, the British hand, intimated had much to do with the Asian opium trade. It made him remember too a Eurasian girl named Lin he had met one night in Boston and never forgotten, the sister of a classmate, and he wondered fleetingly if by any chance it was the same family.

Potter read of the arrest in Europe of another courier en route to the States, causing tremors along the Marseilles docks, where the last of Bébé Spiritu's rivals were jailed on dubious murder charges. In Italy, the parliamentary investigation had further eroded Mafia influence, leaving the Corsicans ascendant in the European drug trade but increasingly dependent upon Asia for supply, as the U.S.

intensified pressure upon the Near East Golden Crescent fields in the wake of Valachi's disclosures.

Then on November 2, South Vietnamese President Ngo Dinh Diem and his brother Nhu were killed in a "coup." It was common knowledge that the Americans were behind it, but there was no mention of the greater role of the "free" Chinese nor of the burgeoning Southeast Asian opiates trade. Thieu and General Ky's air force, already in the Lin pocket, actively plied the traffic. The GI death toll passed one hundred.

The new Southeast Asia presented Alec Potter with a rich vista. Everyone, it seemed, wanted his ear, his languages, his contacts. War was on the way, had indeed arrived, and he was becoming important merely by being here.

His father had recommended him to the CIA as a confidential interpreter-translator, a "tribal expert" who spoke Meo, Lao, and Lahu, though his familiarity with the hill dialects made him no less contemptuous of the people. After gaining assurances he could still retain his freelance status, Potter began helping send Lahu and Lao teams into China to open up radio posts in the Shan States. He advised a special training camp that was graduating thirty-five agents every two months, sending hundreds of teams deep into Yunnan. He trained Christian Lahu in monitoring radio transmissions and handed them over to a local CIA operative working undercover as the American vice-consul in Vientiane.

The killing of Diem and Nhu had sent tremors all the way up the Mekong and across the Plain of Jars. Nhu had owned a substantial piece of the opium concessions as well as a share in a Corsican airline that made drop shipments of Laotian morphine base just north of Saigon. The Corsican opium dealers, in favor with the Catholic Diem clique, were plunged into uncertainty at a time when their fortunes seemed on the rise, what with the cry for more product from the new Spiritu clique in Marseilles and the apparent victory over their Chiu Chao competitors with Harry Lin's death that summer.

Alec Potter moved in and out of Saigon, Phnom Penh, Vientiane, Bangkok, passing information to the U.S. embassies and consulates, putting in a good word for a Laotian general or a Chinese merchant. He translated documents and business cables, drank and swapped tales of the Shan with crusty Green Berets, briefed eager

State Department evaluators in from Washington and new entrepreneurs from New York, Sydney, Tokyo.

On occasion he took squeeze: a fee here, a cut of the venture there, a little baksheesh for an introduction. The amounts, while not large, intimated more substantial monies to come.

Alec Potter was a hot boy in a hot spot, an emergent power broker. To all indications, Asia was about to become his oyster.

Mong Mon, on the Burma-Chinese border, was known to operatives as "little Switzerland." It was a center for cross-border operations. The KMT hung around there, and it was an opium center. A week after Diem's assassination Alec Potter hitched a ride with a Corsican pilot in a Cessna 195 out of Mong Mon.

It was a paid errand: deliver a new radio transmitter to an American semiofficial operative trying to restore contact with a couple of agents who had parachuted into Yunnan, broadcast for a while, then fallen silent—a fate common to their predecessors. Teams spent three or four months inside China, carrying lightweight four-pound radios with broadcast radii of 400 miles, transmitting to powerful receivers at Nam Yu or Air America planes flying back and forth along the Laotian-Chinese border.

Alec Potter grabbed hold as the pilot dropped down among scalloped limestone peaks onto a dirt runway at 3,500 feet, surrounded by opium fields. It was late afternoon and there was a drizzle. The American wasn't there to meet them. Potter and the leather-jacketed Corsican sat waiting beneath the plane's wing, sharing the pilot's Gitanes, watching a timeless scene.

Meo women in black dresses with colorful embroidery, fanciful cloth hats, silver and copper jewelry jangling on their wrists and necks, hoed the fields into furrows while others moved backward rhythmically in the light rain, scattering opium seed from baskets.

This scene is echoed every fall across mountainous Asia—in the Golden Triangle: Laos, Burma, Thailand, China, Mekong, Yunnan—and the Golden Crescent: Turkey, Afghanistan, Pakistan, Ghazipur, Malwa, Iran, Anatolia, the Kurdish Highlands. The seed will bloom, come the new year, into fifteen hundred tons of black opium, the most lethal, lucrative crop on earth.

"*C'est fantastique, ça, hein?*"

"*Oui.*"

Potter flicked the butt of his Gitane away and stood as the American operative appeared suddenly in the clearing dressed in bush fatigues, his face and clothes blackened and filthy, followed by four toothless Meo women who acted like his wives.

Back in the plane, after an hour of flying, it came to Potter that the pilot wasn't heading back toward Chiengmai.

"Qu'est-ce que y arrive?"

It was twilight; they crossed the Mekong at a spot Potter didn't recognize. The pilot smiled behind his reflector glasses. *"Une fête. Pour toi."*

He pulled a pistol from his leather jacket and set it in the crook of his arm at the control, pointed at Potter's heart. Potter sat back in his seat and stared ahead.

They were somewhere over the Plain of Jars when the Cessna dropped like a stone through a bank of clouds. A tiny collection of lights twinkled below in a vast darkness.

"Phong Savan," said the Corsican.

He landed on an asphalt runway where two armed, unshaven Corsicans looking like bandits waited in a dusty blue Citröen DS 21. In high spirits, they drove Potter off at gunpoint toward town.

They pulled up before a large hotel on Phong Savan's single main street. Above a broad stucco and wood entrance hung a hand-lettered sign with an ink-drawn image of a leaping beast: SNOW LEOPARD INN.

It was a legendary Plain of Jars venue Potter had heard of many times, a hotel and opium warehouse run by Corsicans, headquarters to the several hundred who had remained after France's military withdrawal in 1954: war veterans, colonists, gangsters. The Corsicans' various charter airlines, collectively known as Air Opium, were famed in the Triangle, as were the exploits of their pilots: Labenski, Roger Zoile, René Enjabal, Rock Francisci. It was said they ran some 500 tons of opium a year in and out of South Vietnam, Cambodia, Laos, often under the protection of *réquisitions militaires,* military charters, issued by Rattikone, Vang Pao, and the other Laotian high command deeply involved in the trade. The pilots picked up shipments from the Chinese shopkeepers in Sam Neua, Phong Saly, Muong Sing, Man Tha, Sayaboury, and Ban Houei Sai and stored them at the Snow Leopard Inn. Some were later dropped into the Gulf of Siam, some delivered to Paul Louis Levet's notorious Bangkok-based Corsican syndicate. Still more were smuggled into Saigon where they found their way aboard the freighters heading to Marseilles with Corsican crews.

Alec Potter stood in the lobby of the Snow Leopard Inn blinking and confused, awaiting his fate. A noisy party was in progress in an adjacent vaulted lodge room where a flickering fire had been lit against the rapidly cooling night. Local Laotians and boisterous Corsicans drank and sang and swayed to French songs on a warpy hi-fi. There was the smell of opium. The atmosphere was outlaw, the unruly noise made by soldiers of fortune, prisoners, exiles, illicit adventurers socializing in safe haven. There were women too, birdlike Laotian and Cambodian girls in silk dresses.

Potter asked one of his escorts why he was here. The man answered only that "Gérard" was flying in from Wattay and would see him in the morning. In the meanwhile, Potter was to enjoy himself at the party.

Alec Potter was soon drinking Tsingtao and cognac with pilots and gangsters whose names were renowned in the Triangle. The tireless French hit of the day, "Eh Maintenant," played over and over. Privileged prisoner that he was, Potter danced with a girl who smelled like magnolia. There was an opium pipe; he was in a deep chair, his fingers crooked around its cane stem as a robust smiling Corsican and the magnolia girl held the shiny mud on the tip of a pin over a lamp.

The nausea came, then passed.

It was a room upstairs that wavered and changed colors. Two perfumed Phnom Penh girls were bent over him, undressing him. Smart Alec Potter, far from Harvard Square, melted into his fantasies.

The next day downstairs in the lodge room there was Gérard. Coffee, rolls, and cognac sat between them.

"Ça te plait?" He nodded toward the room where the party had taken place.

"Oui."

He was a large, thick man, his faced etched with debauch. Bulbous blue eyes, thick oily black hair, a potbelly over a striped blue tee shirt, and a tobacco-stained walrus mustache emanated recklessness, physicality. Potter sat blurrily in his chair, constipated from the opium, feeling like a wimpy boy before the legendary pilot, the head of the jocularly named "Gérard Air Force." The conversation went in French.

"We need your help, Monsieur Potter."

"With what?"

"The Americans."

The purpose of his gentle abduction was sketched out: Gérard wished him to intercede with the Americans on behalf of the Corsican interest in Southeast Asia. The Chinese, according to Gérard, were trying to roll up their networks and squeeze them out. This Potter already knew. The killing of Diem and Nhu had been followed by sudden arrests and jailings of Corsican pilots almost daily in Saigon, Bangkok, Vientiane; there were actual threats of expulsion. Now, claimed Gérard, they were suffering the indignity of arriving at the mountain runways to discover that CIA Air America planes had been there first and bought their crops!

Gérard recalled sentimentally how the Americans and the Corsicans had always worked together, invoking World War II and the Allied efforts in Italy and the South of France, reminding him of the Corsican gangs who helped the CIA break up the Communist dockworker strikes in postwar Marseilles. He claimed that the overseas Chinese were plotting to embroil the Americans further in this Indochinese war to protect their fields, and couldn't be trusted.

It was a time for Caucasian solidarity, said Gérard. He went on to accuse the Chinese of putting in labs along the Mekong to manufacture heroin for sale directly to American troops, which was the first Potter had heard of this.

"But there are only seventeen thousand troops there," he said.

"So far," Gérard said. "But the Chinese don't waste their money. The *salauds* must know something."

Gérard wanted Potter to plead the Corsican case at the Embassy in Vientiane, then fly to Hong Kong, the true center of American power in the Far East, and persuade the new American Consul-General, Fletcher Doody, to rein in the Chinese bosses and the CIA so the Corsicans could survive and continue business locally and with Marseilles.

"This *homme* Doody. He's a fool in a big job. A *con*. You can deal with him. Believe me, Alec."

Gérard counted out ten thousand U.S. dollars to seal his point and shoved them across the table toward Potter.

Seeing Potter's eyes widen, Gérard said, *"Ah, oui. Pour toi. Je suis sérieux."*

Gérard went on to confide that Bébé Spiritu, the new ruler of Marseilles, was coming with his henchmen to Southeast Asia in two weeks. Gérard needed to show him that the Corsican opium network was functional and ready to pick up the slack left by the Turkish closings in the Golden Crescent and provide a steady flow of morphine base to Marseilles. If not, Gérard said with a broad operatic sweep of his arms, there would be a secret and bloody opium war with the Chinese, exceeding in magnitude the one next door in nearby Vietnam. High American heads would roll as well when the secrets came out. The Corsican rule of silence forbade him to say more. Gérard crossed himself.

Gérard also let it be known that the money and girls were spoils the Corsicans lavished regularly among themselves and their friends. Potter needed no more softening; his father had never seen a single sum this large in his entire life.

Gérard, gilding the lily, had the Phnom Penh girls take Potter upstairs again.

Back in Chiengmai that evening, Potter went to Old So and asked him for an herbal laxative for the opium. The next day he flew over to Vientiane for a long and productive lunch at the Embassy. Before returning he bought himself a Swiss Piaget watch from a Chinese merchant.

This was the fun Asia, Alec Potter thought as he stepped off the plane that night in Chiengmai. This was the rich Asia of his dreams.

19

On a soft pleasant morning, still and cloudless, Cross parked his Volkswagen outside the gates of the Oak Knoll Naval Neuropsychiatric Hospital. A high mesh fence twined with barbed wire encircled the grounds. A pair of armed sentries manned a guard box. Dean Whiteman greeted him at the gate with a firm handshake, pushing his glasses up on his nose.

"We're going to forty-nine," he said.

Cross followed him up a long sloping driveway between wide rolling lawns. At the top were freshly painted barracks. One on the left said 49 MENTAL HYGIENE. Cross followed Dean Whiteman down a linoleum-carpeted hall past swabbing orderlies. At the far end they arrived at a reception table, logged in, received ID clips, and entered an adjacent office.

A tall, chesty female colonel with a granite face rose to greet them. She took Cross's hand firmly and invited him to sit down.

When Dean Whiteman had introduced them, then left, the colonel leaned forward and put her elbows on the desk. "What can I do for you, young man?"

"What do you do here?" Cross asked.

"Stress and Motivation. 'S and M,' we call it."

Cross watched her fish a Pall Mall out of her breast pocket and light it. Her hair was cut short, her hands huge. She leaned back in a wooden swivel chair and blew smoke out.

"It's a joint army-navy project. We're dealing with the problem of the soldier who cannot shoot his gun or otherwise carry out his wartime duty. Needless to say, these men must be identified, treated, and made fit for all combat instances. In order to test such individuals, since we've had no actual combat conditions in which to observe behavior, we've had to *induce* fear by chemical means. So far we've had encouraging results. But now," she said, leaning forward again, "at last we have a situation where we can test out our work."

"The combat in Asia."

She nodded vigorously. "Frankly it's terrific for us."

It was the first time Cross had seen her smile.

She was evasive when Cross asked to see the S and M facilities but arranged to pass him on to a somber pipesmoking psychiatrist in a lab coat and officer's cap who had appeared suddenly at the door.

"This young fellow," she said by way of introduction, "is from Langley Porter."

The pipesmoker appraised him solemnly. "Like to accompany me on inspection?"

They crossed to a barracks opposite 49. Hospital beds ran down either side of a long rectangular room. "Mental" patients stood at the foot of their bunks in myriad variations of at-ease. Somebody switched off a radio. The doctor, his officer's uniform visible beneath his white coat, stopped to talk briefly and mechanically with each patient about his condition.

"How's your appetite? Stool? Take your pills?"

Behind the doctor came a Chaplain Weeks, also in full cap and uniform, whose query ran "Read your Bible last night? Did you pray?"

"Yessir," or "Nossir," mumbled each sheepish case, saluting at the same time. Following this triple whammy of God, Navy, and Medicine, came Cross. Not knowing what else to do, most of the men saluted him and said, "Sir."

"Vietnam. Vietnam. Vietnam," Chaplain Weeks whispered to Cross, nodding at patient after patient.

A white patient with tattoos pulled Cross aside and whispered, "Hey, man, score me some smack."

The door at the end of the row led back outside. As the doctor, the chaplain, and Cross were about to enter the next barracks a screaming black man came scrambling up the wide empty lawn in torn pajamas, his eyes dazed, spittle running from his mouth. The doctor, backing away distastefully, called for orderlies.

Three hulking men in pale green hospital garb appeared and quickly subdued the man.

"Get him back to the Quiet Room!" the psychiatrist snapped.

As the patient was hauled off, Cross asked, "What's the Quiet Room?"

"Violent cases," Chaplain Weeks said. He tilted his head in an attitude of piety.

"Thorazine. Straitjackets. Until they calm down." The doctor puffed on his pipe.

"Time for Therapy Session," Chaplain Weeks said, glancing at his watch as they entered the main building.

There were thirty inmates of two wards sitting in a semicircle in a large room. Across from them sat Chaplain Weeks, a few doctors, and Cross. During an "Open Discussion" patients asked questions and complained about various institutional practices. Most sat in stony rebellion and said nothing. Expressions of anger were treated as signs of mental disturbance. On the wall was a ladder representing the road back to "mental health." The reward for reaching the top was going back on duty. A fawning, spiritless Latino who talked party line was held up by the doctors as a model patient nearing the top of the ladder; the other patients regarded him with sullen hatred.

Afterwards the doctors and Chaplain Weeks held a discussion in a small private room and groused about the patients in technical jargon.

"Well what can you expect of a Passive Aggressive?" said a psychologist, waving a helpless hand.

"Anal Aggressive, I'd say," murmured the pipesmoking shrink.

The chaplain put in a pitch for more prayer.

Dean Whiteman, who had joined them at the end, turned to Cross. "What do you think, Jim?"

The room turned to him. Cross spoke slowly: "They're upset about being in the navy and confused by authority. They're trying to figure out what games you're playing and how to act in order to get out of here with the least possible damage. It seems like the logical thing to do. I didn't see any mental cases."

The air thickened perceptibly.

"Do you want them well," Cross asked, "or compliant?"

Cross gazed helplessly around. After a pained silence the others papered over his remarks with finalizing comments of their own, freezing him out. Cross figured that had he not been with Dean Whiteman he would have been ejected.

"Well," said Dean Whiteman in the hallway afterwards, fishing in his lab coat for a cigarette, "you speak right up, don't you?"

"I'm sorry if I embarrassed you."

"No, no." The dean looked about the hall, which had emptied. "I have to get back to Langley. If you want to finish your day here you go ahead. But you might, uh"—Dean Whiteman put his hand out, palm down, and wiggled it—"tone it *down* a little."

Cross thanked him and promised to leave after lunch.

"And, uh, Jim," Whiteman called after. "I think I've got something for you. A project. With some nuns. Down in the Tenderloin. Street work. *Meaningful.*"

Feeling bleak, Cross pushed through a set of double doors and entered the Prosthetics Lab. The shop foreman, a thick, ruddy man in a tee shirt, with tattoos, introduced himself among gleaming steel bars and machines. There were mechanical mirrors along the walls and an array of artificial limbs and devices. Exercising sailors in various states of dysfunction and amputation grunted under the eyes of therapists.

Cross was shown brilliantly devised artificial limbs. Arms worked from cables at the opposite shoulder, capable of lifting large weights, performing intricate tasks with hooks and spoon attachments. New synthetic foams and nylons made them light. Cross was fascinated; for the first time all day he felt he was seeing good work.

As he was being guided around the lab he saw in a mirror, among the patients and therapists and machinery, a small delicate man—a boy, rather—with terror in his eyes and thin, quivering red lips, sitting in shorts on the edge of a gurney. Two brand-new artificial legs, the chrome still shiny, unclouded, extended from his pelvis. There was an unwrapped gift on his lap. His soft, unshaven face was blank with fear.

Standing before the boy was the only other civilian Cross had seen since he entered the gates. She was hidden from direct view by a large weight machine; he could see her only in the mirror. Dressed in a black skirt, black sweater, and black shoes, she was leaning over listening to the boy on the gurney. Cross, seeing her at partial angle among the steel and the chrome and the mirrors, noticed that her black hair was cut in bangs, that she was holding a purse with a leather strap she twisted in her hand. At first he thought she was Japanese, or Chinese perhaps. From another angle he decided she was Caucasian after all. Finally he wasn't sure.

As the foreman demonstrated the wonders of an artificial arm equipped with a spoon, Cross watched the girl, the woman, in the mirror. Her face was radiant among the steel and the human waste in the drab, ugly institution.

"And here we have our Standard Navy Leg," the foreman said, holding it up for Cross to feel. "Our leg tech is finally getting a workout, let me tell you. Gook land mines."

She had looked up and now saw Cross in the mirror. She was startled but didn't drop her gaze. They looked openly at each other in the glass, as if finding among the human carnage and tragedy of the room something human and intact.

"You'll see the spoon attachment here on this arm, how it can rotate."

She was some fifteen feet away, mostly hidden by the gurney. He could see her fully only in the mirror. The mirror bounced off more mirrors, extending off behind her in smaller and smaller cameos, images rattling into infinity.

Her face was oval, opalescent, with eyes slightly slanted. Her mouth was full, her cheeks wide. There was a seeming calm or inwardness about her, Cross thought, an impression of modesty or wisdom or wit. She was tall, slender. Cross decided she was Eurasian. She was inordinately beautiful.

Later Cross would think that had it been a public place or had the mirror not been there, they would have looked away; here, neither could or would break from what they beheld back into the unrelieved cruelty of the room. It was a moment of utter surprise, an aperture in the universe.

The sad young man beside her on the gurney with his two brand-new Standard Navy Legs and the present on his lap muttered inaudibly to her, unaware that he no longer had her attention.

"How about *this?* A leg for the ladies, with a *high heel* built right in," the shop foreman said proudly.

"Ahhhh!"

The image of the boy exploded into the mirror, his arms flailing as he tumbled from his gurney. Cross rushed over, followed by the foreman. The young sailor was splayed on the linoleum floor in his robe, crying more in frustration than in pain.

The girl in black had bent down and had one of his arms. The foreman took the other, and Cross swung the boy's new, useless legs back up onto the gurney.

All attention was on the wounded sailor until, sitting back up, he smiled bravely.

The girl looked at Cross, then away. Cross started to speak but didn't.

A bell rang.

"Twelve hundred hours," the foreman said. "Time for lunch."

Cross was moving somehow among the steel and chrome. He turned back, but her image had slipped behind a large metal weight machine and was gone.

Cross passed quadriplegics lifting themselves on crossbars, wheelchairs run by armless men using their mouths, his eyes full of the girl who was no longer there.

The foreman pointed to a door at the end of the corridor. Cross walked through it, his senses on fire.

The cafeteria reeked of the soup of the day, boiled cabbage, burnt coffee. Cross stood in line among doctors, orderlies, and sailors, clutching a dry sandwich wrapped in cellophane and a soft drink. Crepe decorations had been strung along the walls for Thanksgiving.

He took a seat at a Formica table alone, facing the door.

She came in accompanied by the pipesmoking shrink and passed him on her way to the line.

"Of course, we never give up hope," he heard the doctor say. "In a spinal injury of that kind, urinary tract infection is the biggest danger."

Cross began his lunch, staring at the door.

"May I?"

Her voice was soft, careful; she stood over him with her tray. Cross, his blood pounding, stood up. She set her tray down across from him.

She bent over a straw and sipped milk. Then she looked up at him directly and said, "I bought him a harmonica. I heard he likes harmonicas." She removed a tuna sandwich from cellophane with long fingers.

"You didn't know him?"

"Not before today. He was a friend of a friend."

When Cross didn't speak she went on. "They were hit by a mine in a patrol boat in the Gulf of Tonkin. Some kind of crossed order. They weren't supposed to be there. They fished the boy out of the water."

"And your friend?"

"The boy was the only survivor."

"I'm sorry."

She looked away. "He was somebody I'd known at Berkeley. His father wanted him to go."

As she bent back over her lunch, he noticed her eyelashes.

"They don't talk much about the fighting in the papers."

"No."

Light streamed from the fluorescent banks above, making a vivid flattened space, like television.

"I couldn't stop looking at you in the mirror," she said suddenly. "You looked so nice in such a terrible place." She was embarrassed and began to fidget.

"I'm Jim Cross."

"You're a doctor?"

"No."

"I thought maybe you were."

"I was a medical student. I was away for a few years. I've just come back."

"I thought of becoming a doctor once."

"What's your name?"

"Su."

She opened a small bag of potato chips and looked around. "Seems like business is booming here." Her voice was modulated, ironical.

"They have a new war."

"I suppose it makes the officers happy." She brushed her hair back. "I don't know how people are supposed to get well in a place like this."

"This morning I saw their mental patients. I don't either."

Cross could smell her perfume, effectively wiping out the sour effluvial boil and burn of institutional food.

"You live in Berkeley?"

"San Francisco."

"What do you do?"

"I paint."

Cross sensed her closing off.

"You drove here?"

"Bus."

"Can I give you a ride home?"

She looked up and her eyes were guarded.

"No," she said. "Thank you. No."

It was a sharp denial after the intense encounter in the prosthetics room. Cross thought she looked disappointed.

"Are you with someone?"

"No." Her hands were unsteady as she crumpled the cellophane and stuffed it in the empty Styrofoam cup.

"I'd like to see you again."

"I'm afraid not."

"I don't understand."

She stood to go. "I can't explain." Gathering herself, she said, "It was nice seeing you." Then she whispered, "Thank you."

She turned and left quickly. Cross stared after her.

"Coming?" said the big lady colonel with a smile. She was standing at the door.

Cross rose woodenly and slid the remains of his lunch from the tray into a can. He followed the striding colonel into a lecture room where a tall heavy man with a basset face briefed the assembled upon the subject of "Disaster Plan—Revised," the title written out in large block letters on a green blackboard.

Cross sat in wild ferment, hearing nothing. He had spotted the back of her head several rows forward.

"When the disaster strikes, there is the question of, uh, *priority,*" the man droned on. "Priority will be given not to those most critically wounded but to those who might be expected upon recovery to contribute most to further civil or national defense efforts."

He stared at her straight shining black hair. She sat stiffly, quite aware, Cross was sure, he was watching her.

"Thank you, gentlemen and ladies."

The assembled awoke from the deadly lecture and stood to go. Cross, dodging heads, watched her leave the room with the psychiatrist.

"Well, young man," proposed the lady colonel. "How about a peek at the Quiet Room?"

"No. Thank you. Not today."

As she disappeared down the corridor, Cross fought an urge to rush after her. But the colonel had his arm and was guiding him toward the barracks entrance.

Outside 49, at the top of the hill, the colonel said, "Keep it up, young man. We need more like you." She clapped him on the side of the arm and pumped his hand. Cross took off down the wide steep driveway between the sloping lawns.

At the entrance he turned and looked back up at the barracks and the buildings. The rather tiny squat figure of the colonel stood at the top of the lawn waving a last time. A Filipino orderly came out of the Quiet Room, locking the door behind him.

Cross stood for a few minutes smoking, wishing for her to appear. Finally he stepped past the twin sentries and through the gates. They rattled shut behind him.

Starting his Volkswagen, his eyes swept the street and landed upon a car parked opposite, fifty yards ahead. His stomach went weak and blood rushed to his head.

Sitting at the wheel was a silhouette out of his dreams, a man who looked like the man who looked like Gurdjieff.

Gasping for air, Cross cranked the VW out of its space, wheeled in mid-block, and tore off.

But in the rearview he saw that the other car remained parked outside the gates of Oak Knoll Hospital.

Cross geared down, thinking of circling around. Then, angry at himself for having admitted old ghosts, he sped on toward Clear Light, full of dissonant energy, thinking again of the girl, the woman, her.

20

At a swimming pool in Miami Beach, behind high retaining walls of poured concrete, a small swarthy man with graying hairs on his chest sat in trunks in a deck chair irritably studying the poor returns from the week's *bolita* lottery. A James Bond paperback, *Dr. No,* and an iced drink sat on the metal table beside him. A portable radio chimed the week's top song, "Dominique, Dominique," by the Singing Nun.

"Mr. Chi to see you," a gruff voice announced from the lanai of the large house behind him.

The man in trunks sat up and put on dark sunglasses.

A small, trim Chinese in a silk suit stepped forward, bowed, and shook the man's hand. The burly man who had announced him shuffled back into the shade of the lanai. The man in trunks shut off the radio.

"Sit down."

The Chinese man sat delicately on the edge of a deck chair.

"Good weddah," Mr. Chi said.

"It stays warm here."

"You lucky."

"You got news?"

"Yessah."

"Let's have it."

"Diem and Nhu are dead."

Franco Termini Jr. shifted on his deck chair. "I read the papers, Mr. Chi. Tell me something I don't know. Who was behind it? The Americans?"

"Yes. With Chiu Chao help. Soon General Thieu and Air Force General Ky take ovah."

"What does that mean? Explain. I can never figure out Asia."

"It mean Golden Triangle trade grow again. Ky's air force work for Chinese. They fly opium from Mekong area to drop landing strips outside Saigon."

"And the Corsicans?"

"They got big trouble. They Catholics. Thieu no like them."

"Good," Termini said. "And what about Bébé Spiritu?"

"He king of Marseilles now. No rivals. He get mayor to arrest Francisci for murder. Secret Chinese money help, some say. But he still got trouble in Asia. He and his boys on way to Bangkok, I hear."

A Cuban maid in white uniform brought two iced teas on a sweating metal tray and left.

"The Turkish product is being shut down."

"Because of Mistah Valachi testimony."

Termini frowned. "Motherfucker."

"So Corsicans need Asian product."

"What about the Chinese?"

"Lin family have Hong Kong cooks, mastah chemists, putting in labs along Mekong. Eleven now, more coming. China White. They take Corsican business away."

"Where does it go?"

"They selling to GI boys."

"Does the CIA know?"

"Sure. They fly it out for Chinese."

Mr. Chi tittered. Termini grunted.

"And Bébé Spiritu?"

"He want to make deal with American CIA in Asia."

"What else?"

The Chinese sipped his iced tea gingerly and replaced it on the tray. "Left-Hand Chen. He have deal with British. Through Hong Kong Crown Bank. But he have other deal with secret party. Nobody know who."

"Who does this Lefty Chen work for?"

"Peter Lin. Fifth-generation son. But some say Left-Hand Chen real boss of Lin operation."

At the mention of Peter Lin, Franco Termini Jr. smiled and fell silent as memory closed over him: an afternoon in March 1958, five years before, in the garden of a small farm in Santa Martinella outside Naples.

Charlie Lucky, stirring his coffee with a small silver spoon, had said, "If you want to stay in business, young man, get to know the Chinese."

Termini had come across the Atlantic to pay him honor; the capo was getting on. He'd never been the same since prison and Dewey's eventual pardon in 1946. Termini wanted advice too, and his blessing for the decades to come. Now Charlie Lucky spoke of Asians. Termini thought, with all due respect, that the boys back home had been right: the old man was losing his touch.

"But why the Chinese?" Termini had never spoken to an Asian in his life except to order food.

"Look at the Near East people. Always fighting. They can't be depended upon. Mark my words. One day you'll have trouble getting product from Turkey."

A goat bell had clanged. A breeze had whispered through the olive trees, ruffled the napkins on the tiny wrought-iron table. Termini, himself the son of a don, had pulled his new Rome trench coat up against his neck.

"Know what else?" Charlie Lucky had said, his voice a husk. Termini had watched him take a gold pillbox out and slip a nitroglycerin pill beneath his tongue. "Somebody from the Families is going to talk. Not now. But in a few years. Don't ask me who."

"Then what, Charlie?"

"The fields will come under pressure. Cosa Nostra will decline. Corsicans of Marseilles will take over manufacture and distribution."

Termini, riding high in golden Havana, hadn't believed him; but Charlie Lucky, old and tired, hadn't seemed to care if he did or not.

"I say the Asians are the key. Find out who they are. Get to know them. Get them in your debt. But do it nice. Someday you will be glad you did. Then maybe Cosa Nostra will rise again."

Charlie Lucky had stood and shaken Termini's hand gently. He wore an old cardigan with a hole in the elbow.

"Be patient. It will come to you. And say hello to your father."

He had begun to shuffle off toward his small house to see to his sick wife Igea. Then he had turned, gazed at Franco Termini Jr., and said, "You dress too rich."

The year after his visit to Italy, Termini had crossed a wide Boston lawn, his hand outstretched toward an unhappy young Eurasian in his first year at Harvard Law School, and invited him down to Havana for some fun.

He had never known why until this moment.

Charlie Lucky was a prophet, Termini thought, turning to look at his Chinese visitor Mr. Chi, who seemed to have discovered a fly in his iced tea and was fastidiously replacing the glass on its coaster.

"Mr. Chi. Do the Chinese have a way to bring it into the States?"

"No. Only through GI's. That why they need you."

Termini examined his tan line at the belly. "Sooner or later they have to deal with me?"

"Yessah."

"So the Corsicans and the Chinese go at each other's throats. Who will win, Mr. Chi?"

"Aaaaah."

Termini thrust his right fist through the air as if to graze Mr. Chi's chin with a friendly right cross.

Mr. Chi said, "Yessah. Good times coming again. Just like Mistah Luciano's day."

Franco Termini Jr. laughed. "When will Peter Lin and this Lefty Chen be ready to see me?"

"Oh, six month maybe."

"Then I come to Hong Kong."

"Yessah."

"To divvy up the pie."

"Yessah," said Mr. Chi, opening his arms wide. "Big world pie."

"The GI's aren't enough," the man said emphatically. "If they want America they'll have to deal with me."

"They want America," said Mr. Chi.

A flock of gulls heading south from the Carolinas flew in loose formation overhead. Franco Termini Jr. spread suntan oil on his chest with the flat of his palm.

"Yes, Mr. Chi, they'll have to deal with me. Do you agree?"

"Yessah," Mr. Chi said.

A voice called from the veranda to announce a phone call from Tel Aviv. "It's the Little Man."

"Excuse me, Mr. Chi," Termini said.

Mr. Chi bowed and left. Triumphantly Termini picked up the white phone on the table beside him.

"Good news, Meyer. We're gonna be back in business."

21

Su Lin sat alone, her hands pressed tightly in her lap, as the Oakland–San Francisco bus left the Bay Bridge toll booth and headed across. An unseen sun dropped somewhere to the west, tinting the bridge and the water below a metallic orange.

She felt if she didn't hold herself in she would shatter. The man she had seen in the mirror at Oak Knoll and denied in person seemed the final condemnation to a world of fantasy, leaving the real unattainable, a sign that Hong Kong had indeed won. If this was the way she was to live, it mattered little whether she stayed or returned to Asia.

The tall struts of the bridge flashed by. The bus geared and droned. They would never meet again; her sacrifices grew. She had been there to see the boy from the *Turner Joy,* but it was neither he nor the one who was dead who had forced her to refuse him.

The gaze in the mirror had shaken her, and it shook her again now in memory as the bus dropped into the dim Treasure Island tunnel. Some blend of light and pain and desire in his eyes had echoed her own.

She would think of him again, many times. Gradually she would take apart his image until it was drained of feeling, buried, banished. She would turn her own capabilities of fantasy inward; in this, she was Asian.

She hung at the end of a frayed rope. Several unpromising job callbacks, then her checks would begin to bounce. Somewhere overhead, criminal forces contended for her. A college girlfriend had invited her to come visit back East; she would accept, and flee while there was still time.

As the bus zoomed out of the tunnel down the long slope into the city, San Francisco, its skyscrapers backlit with the silvery Pacific purple of a dying day, looked infernal.

At the Vallejo flat she found a note from Junie in the kitchen saying she was off to Reno for a few days to visit her brother who worked as a croupier. Unnerved at being alone, she locked the doors and windows and went quickly to her room.

She called her girlfriend in New York, but nobody was home.

She put the phone down and sat absorbing the eerie silence of the flat. Then wearily she took off her clothes and hung them up. She took from her closet a silk robe embroidered in dragons and flowers and wrapped it around her.

From an art file she removed a large sheet of blank paper and pinned it to a plywood mounting against the wall. She set up a small round mirror at a slight angle to herself on the bureau and sat before it on a stool.

Studying herself, she began to feel the repose that art always brought, the closing of the circle. The world outside was a shifting tapestry of relative phenomena, surreal patterns drifting by without reason, never more than now. Art made her fluent with life again, enabled her to sleep, and reawaken. She turned to it now, her remaining lover.

The image she found in the mirror was severe, unlike those early weeks at the Art Institute, tasting the free life she had sought. This was a face of renunciation.

The drawing came quickly. With pastels she laid in line and color. She ran more water in the bathroom into a glass, wetted Winsor and Newton sable brushes she had bought when she had money, and overpainted in acrylics. Molding served to tilt the drawing up onto planes, lending asymmetry, motion, and emotion. The face became masklike, a totem, impermeable, hiding the life within, staring outward with impassive will.

Exhausted but oddly elated, she ended off. In the bathroom she ran a shower and stepped out of her robe.

Hot water beat upon her neck, ran over her breasts and belly, down her thighs. She stared mindlessly past the blur of her nipples to the long strands of her pubic hairs, where her focus locked. They were jet black and straight, not bushy and brown or red or yellow like the *gwailo* girls. Looking further, she noticed how wide and splayed her feet were, her toes too flat. Her legs, foreshortened, looked stubby. But it was an old exercise—critiquing herself, fishing for flaws. Whatever there were seemed lost on the world beyond, which decreed her a target of desire.

The steam made her drowsy, languid. Unwelcome sensations rose. Her breath deepened and her legs began to tremble with renegade desire, born of tension and loneliness. Warmth spread between her thighs. She struggled toward abstraction, terrified to admit the object of fantasy hovering at the edge of her mind.

She stood shuddering beneath the stream of hot water, gripping the edge of the shower door.

Once when she was small her amah in Hong Kong had told her of a Chinese relative who had been a nun. She was called the Woman from the Country. She dressed in white, the color of death, and stood beneath cold waterfalls in the dead of winter to strengthen herself.

Su Lin turned the shower colder until it made her jump, pricking her skin, turning her nipples hard. Not until she felt like stone, or ice, inured from desire, did she turn off the water.

She dried, put her robe back on, and went to the kitchen to make food. Taking vegetables from the icebox, she began chopping with a Chinese cleaver on a butcher block in front of the window facing onto the back porch.

Stairs ran to the courtyard two stories below. Beyond, crisp November evening clouds ran behind the tip of Coit Tower. A pale yellow full moon loomed. She drew the curtain closed and began chopping again.

A human shadow grew on the curtain, elongating. The light in the window changed. The shadow fattened to the sound of footsteps. Su Lin let out a banshee scream and raised the cleaver.

The shadow became a silhouette and stopped.

For an instant she froze. Then she began to back away toward the hall.

As she reached the top of the front stairs, still wielding the cleaver, the back door rattled and sprung open. She turned and tore down the stairs. At the landing she threw open the first door and began working furiously at the double lock leading out.

She was aware of a tall shadow through the corrugated window even as she opened the front door, but it was too late to do anything but burst through, cleaver raised to strike.

"Hello."

She stopped right up against his chest, all but gutting him.

Cross stood before her on the pavement, looking quite irrelevant.

The front door swung idly shut behind her.

"You were cooking?" he asked, staring down at the wide gleaming blade pressed against his wishbone. Su Lin, her embroidered robe half off, her hair damp and matted, stared up at him. At the same time she registered a fleeting figure emerging from a gate two doors down and disappearing over the peak of the hill.

"Cooking," she whispered. "Yes, I was cooking."

22

In her room, among the brocade and the paintings, the tapestry of her solitary world, she stood facing him. The spires of the glimmering city spread away out the window. His arms enclosed and brought her close. His lips found hers, perfumed and warm. Her breasts pressed into his ribs, wisps of long black hair swirled along his cheek.

She reached up to meet him, her eyes tightly shut. Her arms slid around his back. As he drew her in she felt him collect and swell against her belly. Their lips, flushed with blood, explored each other as taste. She softened and grew wet and weak as he kissed her ears, her neck.

Still in the kiss, they dropped to her mattress, sending velvet pillows sliding off. Her fingers felt his face, the contours and junctures where their lips met. The silent kiss opened to admit tongues, electric tips of desire.

She trembled, hesitant, sensing this moment was not to be given or taken but made together. He leaned her slowly back onto the bed and slid his hand inside her robe. Her belly was silk beneath silk, rising and falling.

"Yes. Oh, yes."

They were deliberate, as if aware that some past or imminent pain was being stayed by this act. His hand circled her breast, one then the other. She buried her face in his neck, found her way beneath his loose shirt with her hand.

He slid away down her front to the floor. Lying on her back, eyes shut, she felt for an instant ashamed. Then her robe fell away and she lay open.

He looked up at the shadow form of her body, enraptured. His hands moved up along her thighs until they brushed her long soft black trembling center.

She felt his mouth move up her leg, and pressed him into her. She moaned, played fingers around his ears.

"Come," she whispered to draw him up, but too late, for the peaking gasping took over, and she held his head there hard against her, abandoning everything in motion, rising when she could rise no further, and then again, breathing through her pores.

He rose and slid up on her, their bellies and chests sweat-oiled, and entered deep and damp.

"Oh, yes. Yes!"

A fat bloody moon hung over the city outside. A trio of drunken sailors stumbled by, shouting and kicking bottles, flotsam of a ravenous world the lovers had exiled.

He felt a timeless inattention to anything but the union, running forward, guided by the sure tides of the moon.

"Yes. Yes."

But it came, the rhythm running through them rose, sounds from tongues, mouths, voices that must have been their own, a sudden rush into time, mouths locked, shuddering, clinging, straining to tear the universe apart.

"Yes yes yes."

They fell, exhausted and dazed, back to earth.

Cross lay over her, hardly conscious.

"God," Su Lin whispered.

They huddled in a blanket together on the roof of the building before dawn. It was clear, chill, and silent. The pendant lights of the Golden Gate draped away from them to the north. Below in the bay, a Japanese freighter loaded beneath floodlights at Pier 19. Su

Lin was looking into a lit window in the next building where a papier-mâché turkey hung: two days before Thanksgiving.

She searched in the dark for his eyes. "How did you find me?"

"With difficulty."

Cross lit two cigarettes and handed her one. "You didn't tell me your last name. You'd told me you painted. I called around. The Art Institute gave me your address, said you worked there until recently. Su."

"Su Lin. As if it were a double name."

"Su Lin."

The moon that had grazed the city earlier now hung over the western horizon. They sat smoking, aware of the fragility of peace.

"I'm glad you came," she said. It hardly sufficed to describe what she meant.

"When I arrived," he said carefully, "I felt I was disturbing you. Were you in some . . . difficulty?"

She saw herself rushing out the door with the cleaver, then making up a story upstairs about the open kitchen door. She didn't think she could or would lie to him.

"The back door was open," he said, "and the cleaver . . ."

She looked at him as openly as that afternoon in the hospital mirror. "I'll tell you. I promise. But not now."

Another foghorn blew its nose. Su Lin held him against the cool salty night, her body still streaming with sex, wanting above all to feel safe with him.

They kissed, tight in the blanket, her blown hair whirling around his head. She fell against his chest and clung to him. He picked up the burning cigarettes they had dropped on the graveled roofing.

"What about you?" she asked. "You left medical school, then came back."

A silence rose and enveloped Cross.

"I'll tell you later too," he said finally.

A dawn chill swept in as pale light stained the sky over Oakland.

"It's getting cold," she said.

A winter light, a glad light, whitened the morning curtains. Cross and Su Lin lay silently awake, entwined, reviewing the night's ecstasies.

Before they rose she looked at him intently and said, "Let's not dress."

Naked, they went to the kitchen and rustled eggs, cheese, onions, and old sourdough bread into breakfast by the window where the night before a shadow had sent her running. She reached up and closed the curtain; then before she sat down to eat, she raced around the flat closing them all.

As Su Lin took the dishes to the sink, Cross watched her straight black hair along her neck, the winking hairs below, her long straight legs. A pair of faintly shadowed dimpled indents dotted either side of her hips. Her arms were lean, long, graceful.

Feeling his eyes, she turned back to him flushed. Cross sat with his coffee. She walked over and stood beside him. "Let's stay here," she said. "Let's not go out."

He agreed.

Neither needed to say that the monochrome world beyond the windows, full of dull threat, couldn't possibly match them.

"And no clothes."

They laughed, full of reckless joy.

He was hard again and reached up to her breast, which was warm, and she came down to him.

"God," she whispered. "Where have you been?"

23

A taxi came to the tall gates of the Lin villa on Victoria Peak near midnight. The Sikh guard peered inside, then let it through. It pulled up to the foot of the driveway beside Peter Lin's new Lamborghini. Left-Hand Chen got out and entered the house by way of the veranda.

He found Peter alone on the floor of the vast living room, deep into a fifth of Johnnie Walker, listening to American blues records on a hi-fi turned up loud. The remnants of a box kite from his youth sat beside him, its paper sides shredded, a balsa strut broken. A jar of glue was open on the table.

"Fixing your kites, Peter?"

Peter muttered a reply that Chen didn't catch.

"I have just been informed," Chen said, taut and sober, "that your sister has taken an American lover."

Peter blinked. Then he lowered the music and turned away, not wanting Chen to see his face burning with betrayal. "Who is he?"

"A medical student."

"How do you know?"

"Our people in San Francisco."

Peter looked up. "I asked you to call them off, Chen."

"They discovered it before our order was received," Chen said, lying with firmness.

Peter stood unsteadily and paced the polished wood floor in his socks. "It used to be civil rights demonstrators. Then a sailor who's dead. Now a doctor." He tossed a pack of cigarettes in the air. "She's moving up in the world."

He stopped and glowered at Chen. "So what are we supposed to do? Cut her hands off? She wants to live her own life. It's America, not old China."

"There is a more ominous element here, Peter." Chen, ignoring Peter's reference to his own affliction, lit a Lucky Strike and blew smoke into the air. "This fellow has had contact with Corsicans in Europe."

Peter stared at Chen.

"His house was checked. A notebook was found with the name and address in Paris of the Corsican Bébé Spiritu. He may have met with him late last summer. We can only conclude . . ."

"How certain are you of this?"

"The chances of coincidence are . . . slight. Additionally, one of our people was shot by a Corsican in San Francisco several nights ago."

"Shit." Peter turned away. "How do you know they're lovers?"

"They've been in her apartment for three days. They come out only to buy food. They are . . . intensely affectionate."

Peter retreated to the table and sat before his bottle. "What do we do, Chen?"

"I suggest we simply bring her back."

"She won't come. You know that. She turned down the inheritance."

When Chen didn't reply, Peter looked suspiciously at him. "You mean forcibly?"

"It's the only way. It will be done delicately."

"What the hell does that mean?"

"Surely you must see that she cannot be reasoned with at the moment. If you let us move, I can guarantee her safety. If not, I fear what might come next. Kidnapping, perhaps worse. This endangers all our plans. The Corsicans could bring us to our knees."

Peter stared off into the shadows of the room. *Chen worries only about the business. What of Su Lin?* The thought of facing her when she returned depressed him.

"Your sister," Chen said, "is our exposed flank."

Peter looked up at him, incredulous. Left-Hand Chen, suddenly realizing his inadvertent *entendre,* broke into a titter, bringing his lone hand to his mouth.

24

It was the fourth morning. Cross and Su Lin lay together on her bed beneath the window in her room. Beyond the closed curtains a breeze curled through the cracks in the panes, cooling their flesh and stirring the papers on her bureau.

"We've stopped time," she said. She kissed him.

Cross touched her face. "I dreamed you," he said.

She smiled and sat up.

"We seem to find each other in mirrors." He was looking at her in the one beside the canvas.

"Wait." Flushed, Su Lin rose and went to her easel. She took her canvases and drawings and arrayed them about the room. Cross, examining them, saw the same deliberate grace he felt in her touch and saw when she moved. He looked at her with new pleasure.

She wetted a brush and dipped it in watercolors. She began to paint his face.

They stood before the bathroom mirror after showering.

"Do you feel Caucasian or Asian?"

"Neither."

"So your father was Chinese?"

"Part Chinese, part English."

He took a towel. "And your mother?"

"She was American."

"Did she live in Hong Kong?"

"Once. She died near Boston."

"And your brother?"

Su Lin sighed uneasily.

"You'll tell me later," he said.

She nodded.

"When's later?"

"Soon."

They dried off and went back to her room.

Dressing before her paintings, he asked, "What day is it?"

"Friday, I think."

She went to the window and opened it. *We know nothing about each other. Only what our senses have learned.*

Sound and smell burst in, shocking the silent enclosure of the apartment. *Is there any more to know?*

"What made you come back from Europe?"

Cross regarded her silently for a few moments. "It was over."

"And now?"

"I don't know. Finding you changes things."

Where does it go now?

Su Lin sought his eyes. "We mustn't lose each other."

He held her tightly.

She found him in the kitchen sitting over coffee, smoking.

"It's Thanksgiving weekend," he said. "I have a friend who has a cabin on Bixby Creek in Big Sur. There's firewood. We could cook our own food."

"Yes. Let's go."

Cross was surprised at her urgent enthusiasm.

"I'll go over to Berkeley and get my things."

"Can't we just go?" She seemed tense.

"My money's there. My clothes. It won't take me an hour."

"I could go with you."

"No need," Cross said cheerily. "I'll gas up the car."

They kissed at the top of the stairs. When the door had closed, Su Lin ran to her room and peered through a crack in the curtain down at the street. She saw Cross emerge and head down the hill to his car. Scanning the doorways across the street for signs of the Chiu Chao, she contented herself they were gone and turned back to the flat.

Humming, she pulled out her suitcase to pack, daring to believe her troubles had passed.

Cross headed down the street to his car in the morning chill. A *Chronicle* on the sidewalk reminded him he had been out of the world for three days. It was Friday, November 22, 1963. There were 18,000 troops in Asia, McNamara announced. Kennedy was in Dallas for a parade.

But he and Su Lin were the news.

He swung the car down Broadway and onto the Bay Bridge entry. Rush hour traffic streamed past him into the city. He drove on, full of fresh hope, bathed in the light that seemed to accumulate in Su Lin's eyes and pour over him.

There was that light—a quality of light I imagined in the darkness of the Medina in Tangier—that led out. It was her.

At the entrance to the basement flat at Clear Light College, Cross found the door ajar. The lock, which wasn't much of one, hung open.

Gingerly he opened the door and peered inside. The lone window was open. The bare light bulb above the improvised kitchen swung slowly from its cord. He heard no sound but the breeze from an open window.

Fighting dire images of the recent past, he stepped inside.

He checked each room. He fished for his roll of money beneath the mattress and found it intact. Nothing else seemed to be missing, nor was he able to perceive any further sign of disturbance.

He was certain he had been visited, but by whom or to what end he had no idea. Finding no better explanation, he decided to attribute it to neighborhood children.

Quickly he threw some clothes into a suitcase. On the table by his bed was the receipt for the check he had written to Langley Porter for readmission. He couldn't seem to find his notebook, which he thought he had left on the same table.

Perplexed, he rummaged around the flat without turning it up. The notebook was something he routinely misplaced; he decided to get a new one on the way down to Big Sur.

Back at the Bay Bridge toll gate, Cross thought he saw the operator weeping as he made change; but this unlikely vision, like a sudden snapshot, didn't come fully into focus until he was speeding on across the bridge, and still begged an explanation.

He came back up Vallejo, parked below the bay window, and ran through the side gate and up the back stairs. He burst through the open kitchen door.

"Su Lin!"

In the living room the television was on, the sound off. Kennedy was waving to a crowd from the back of a limousine.

He called her name again, taking the hall to her bedroom.

Her suitcase was on the bed, half packed. The pillows and the dragon brocade quilt were on the floor, the bedsheets crumpled.

A cold fear overtook him as he saw the Chinese cleaver on the carpet by the door.

"Su Lin!"

The bathroom was empty.

He went out back, circled the building, then came back through the flat again, looking for a note, a sign, a clue. In the living room the silent television was replaying the Dallas parade. Cross turned it off.

He waited all afternoon in the empty apartment, quelling strange and aimless thoughts. His imagination had little to work with; he knew almost nothing about her.

He thought of calling the police but had no reason. What would they say? Who was she? Who was Cross to her?

Who, for that matter, was he?

That night he lay awake in her bed sleepless and alert, the prospect of losing her so suddenly too forceful to admit.

Shortly after midnight he heard the back door open, and he raced down the hall. It was her roommate Junie, back from Reno. He scared her half to death.

No, she had no idea where Su Lin was. And who are you to want to know?

"Maybe she was just upset by what happened."

"What happened?"

"Where have you been? Kennedy was killed."

By the light of dawn Cross studied the room more closely, reconstructing how it had been before he had left for Berkeley. He became convinced there had been a struggle—clothes and objects in different places, a compact on the floor.

And there was the cleaver.

Rummaging along the top of her dresser, he came across Terhune's letter, postmarked a week earlier.

"Dark developments in the secret world, Su Lin. I am told the Left-Hand is determined to move. Great wars commence over the trade. Be on your guard, lotus . . ."

Cross tried calling Terhune in Kyoto. The overseas information operator had a number for him, but repeated calls got no answer. He walked to the post office on Washington Square as soon as it opened and sent a wire to the address on the envelope.

A wire came back late that day:

ASIA HAS RECLAIMED HER. LET HER GO.

25

Light hung like smoke along the railing of the *Brazil Maru* at Pier 19. It was a chill, misty night, the fifth since Lyndon Johnson had appointed the Warren Commission to investigate the assassination of John Kennedy. Japanese passengers thronged the deck, immigrants to Brazil returning to visit or on business, and a few California Nisei. Dean Whiteman, huffing, appeared from belowdecks with bourbon in a paper cup and an envelope in his outstretched hand.

"I got Langley to refund your dough."

"Thanks." Cross took the envelope.

"That's all you have?"

Cross nodded, pulling a windbreaker tight against his neck.

"Jesus. How long's the trip?"

"Twelve days."

Whiteman tried to light his meerschaum, stamping against the cold. Cross was looking back up Vallejo Hill.

"She must be some girl."

Cross had told him there was a girl, nothing more.

Whiteman gave up on the pipe and knocked it out against the

railing. "This will make it quite impossible for you to come back to Langley Porter, of course. But then I have a feeling you don't care."

Dean Whiteman followed Cross's eyes up the steep back side of Vallejo Street.

"Is it love, really? Or just running again?"

Cross didn't answer that, but he said, "In Europe, there was a time I didn't help somebody."

Dean Whiteman downed his whiskey and chucked the paper cup in the Bay. "I see," he muttered.

They shook hands.

"This ecstatic universe of yours, Jim. Write me when you find it, will you?"

Whiteman stuffed his pipe in the pocket of his tweed coat. A sudden windy blast from the horn spared Cross the obligatory Yeats quote. A Japanese steward came by and politely informed Dean Whiteman he would have to leave.

As in a dream, the ship backed slowly out of its berth, then turned and glided in quiet blackness between Alcatraz and the Embarcadero, rimmed by San Francisco Bay's garland of lights. Cross stood on the foredeck, his breath suspended. Passing beneath the dark strip of the Golden Gate, he thought how close it looked, almost as if he could reach up and touch it.

Then the ship was through, and out into the black Pacific. Shivering, Cross turned aft to see the bridge lights at land's end, like a tiara, dipping, dimming, then disappearing.

THREE

The
Bloom

26

"Momma?"

There was the click and the clacking, the shuffle and rattle of tiles from beyond the porch window where the maids played mah-jongg on midmorning break. *East wind*. Light danced inside her head behind closed eyes. Momma would come now. She reached for her panda. It was there, though her fingers didn't seem to close around it very well. When they managed, the panda was curiously small, shrunken.

"Momma?"

Flower card. The click-clacking stopped. Shadows broke the soft light. She smelled the garlic and jasmine of her amah, who was nice to her, then felt Amah's hand reach into hers. But something was wrong. Amah's hand, like the panda, was small, wrinkled.

"Amah? Momma?"

Her eyes opened thickly, the cage of lashes dissolving into Amah's face: old, withered, sad, her hair gray, greased, and shorn off straight across the back in widow's mode, her black pajama coat baggy. Stooped, shrunk, and puckered inside her clothes. A crackling crone's voice: *"Missee, missee."*

"God!"

A shriek raced around the inside of her head like a ball on a track. She clutched the little gutted panda, burrowed back into a cave of darkness.

She was an orphan being herded down the washed bare corridor of the new Lin orphanage. Smell of ammonia, echo of tile. The hall was dark; she was nobody. The Kaifong lady, her smile gone, herded them into a dorm with a bamboo switch. *North wind*. The other girls had scabs and sores on faces and hands. A long room, with made beds. A young Eurasian woman, herself, looked helplessly in through an observation window, face pressed to the glass, crying. The orphan ran to the window and began to claw silently, her nails ripping at the glass. The woman on the other side was scratching back. Their faces pressed to each other, mouths and eyes wide. Her heart was beating, a tinny alternating clacking sound. Ping, pong. She put her hand to it. Ping, pong. It tripped erratically, sped up, dribbled to a stop, picked up again.

"Su Lin."

A tall Caucasian man in a white lab coat had a key and was opening the door separating them. His face became huge, looming through the membrane of the dream picture.

"Jim?"

Her panda was gone. The clicking heart sped up into tiny furious beats, a hummingbird, its intervals diminishing, merging in hysterical clicks, deepening in sound: stopped. Her body went stiff, pushing against hands locking her own to her sides. She arched against force.

The room was somebody else's. Rattan, brocade, blackwood tables, jade chest. Dusty, decrepit by afternoon light. Momma's room. Where's Momma? Her heart began again. Click, click. Ping, pong.

Outside, shadows danced on a veranda; the ping and pong was the sound of her heart.

"Dammit!"

One shadow was tall and thin, the other short, lithe under the arc of the raised paddle.

The ball bounced through the door into her room. She felt her heart separate away from the ping and pong, hers a darker, slower thing under her hand. Someone was chasing it under her bed.

"Jim?"

"Su. You're awake." Then Peter's gasp. "God what have you done to your face?"

She saw dried blood under her nails.

"Where's Momma?"

Chen looked in from the veranda, smoking in his Chinese jacket and kung fu slippers, silhouetted by the light behind, his face invisible.

Amah rushed in.

Chen's even voice wafted in on the cooling air, the choppy tones of Swatow becoming a thousand pressure points embroidering her skin.

Amah had the needle.

"You're not Jim."

"It's me. Peter." He looked away, flushed. "Christ, Su. I'm sorry."

The ceiling was gold leaf, dragons in writhing carniverous pursuit of their own tails, a circular whirlwind thrashing into darkness.

"Still groggy."

The double veranda doors were wide open. Beyond, a cloud-spattered sunset sky.

"Missee?"

They were guiding her out in Mother's silk gown and slippers, Amah on one side, Peter on the other. Numb, she seemed to float. Beneath the green eaves of the roof, the veranda looked west and south, down the back side of the Peak and out to sea.

"Missee. Tha' bettah," said Amah in singsong croak, lowering her into a rattan chair before a wrought-iron table.

"Where's Jim?" But the words bumped against the inside of her lips.

Upon a lacquer tray sat a bowl of congee, a pork bun, tea, starfruit, toast. There was gleaming cutlery, blue and white porcelain, a plump linen napkin. A *South China Morning Post,* folded open to finance, hung from Peter's hand.

"Amah made this for you."

"But that's Mother's breakfast."

Amah nodded emphatically. "Fo' you now."

Receiving Peter's sudden glare, the amah receded into the shadows of the house.

Starfruit. Once she had looked all over San Francisco for one. She stared at the waxy yellow skin as Peter sliced it open with a silver knife: pulpy five-pointed, brownish-yellow insides. He skinned a piece and handed it to her. She ate it slowly.

Peter stood smoking, biting his lip, rattling ice in a glass.

The congee, the rice gruel, thickened her out of dream. She regarded her pale, thin wrists.

"How many days . . . ?"

But again the words hid in her mouth.

She brought her palms to her face, touching scabrous skin; horrified, she dropped them.

Peter, oblivious, was pointing. "Remember, Su, when we were kids how we used to play down there? Remember the time we ran away and hiked down Peel Rise along the mountain paths all the way to Aberdeen? A coolie found us and called Momma. Fook came and picked us up. I was teasing you for crying. God, I was a bastard."

Peter was looking sheepish, deflecting shame into their youth. As if that were the reason for anything, their youth.

"Remember all along Plantation Road where there weren't houses, now there are houses, and Father used to take us all to the Repulse Bay Hotel on Sundays all dressed up? So British? So . . . respectable?"

Along the hilltop ran a few dozen dwellings where the rich had built to escape heat and malaria, carried up from town in grander days by coolies in sedan chairs. Then the sudden scruff-green plunge to the silver-blue waters, the South China Sea, shimmering in the backglow of a sun setting somewhere the other side of the Peak, down over China. At the outcurving of Repulse Bay she could see a thousand vessels of indiscernible shape, at anchor or frozen on the water. Off to the right rose the stacks of the sewage plants on Apleichau, Duck's Tongue Island, and beneath it Aberdeen's harbor, sheltering the floating restaurants and sampan villages. Beyond, the turn to open water: Singapore, Vietnam.

The view from the childhood home is imprinted upon one's mind forever; against it all future homes are compared. Was it why she had chosen San Francisco? *Feng-shui,* the geomancers call it. The dragon current.

What twisted current rules this house? All the burning joss in the world could not help it now.

"I ordered new paints and brushes for you from London. Winsor and Newton, right? We'll fix Momma's room for you if you'd like, brighten it up."

Peter, playing the fool, paced back and forth on the edge of the veranda in new tailored colonial linens, whiskey in hand, not looking at her.

"The Colony's changed a lot, Su. More Americans, more modern. New buildings on Central. They're reclaiming whole sections of bay. They're going to extend Kai Tak further out. We'll have TV soon; you can even get a hamburger in Wanchai." It was *we* now, his laugh not really one at all. "The British school at the foot of the Peak where we went? It's still there. There's a new Hilton. You can get American records and books in Central. You'll find ways to make it your own." He downed the drink and turned brightly to her. "And of course we have access. We're big in the community, rich as sin what with Father's bucks. And I have great news about the orphanage."

The gray branchlets of a Chinese ash overhung the table, smooth-barked, with drooping whitish-pink clustered little ears for flowers, borne on slender stalks. Idly Su Lin's hand went out to them. She lifted up the blossoms and peered at the trunk.

There it was, in Mother's Palmer penmanship: *Fraxinus retusa.* Chinese ash, 1952. On a faded wooden stick, eleven years ancient. She would have been pleased at how it had grown.

"Come." Peter offered his arm. "To the pagoda."

She went with him, drained of will. The path running upward alongside the house was snarled with remnants of Mother's futile plantings. Some had been dug into the ground, others remained stunted in pine casks. A few had broken out, contorted, somehow surviving.

"Chen went off to walk his bird."

She brushed the latex leaves of a paper mulberry. A dwarf date palm, bearing clusters of tiny dark oval fruit, leaned toward the sun. A pale green Buddha bamboo, tall and limpid with its thick-notched stalks, bore Winnie Lin's dogged labeling: *Bambusa ventricas Mc-Clure,* 1951. Strains of childhood merged with dark visions of her mother's madness, her father's cruelty.

A spiny tree fern pricked her finger. Sucking the blood, she stared into a fanlike windmill palm, mad hairs twisted and twirled around its trunk: Mother, hair unribboned, racing across the mansion lawn in Massachusetts. Breathless, she followed her brother through the melancholy gallery, flora of a lost season, where Winny Lin, defying her captors, had seeded her prison.

"It's been rough, Su. I won't say it hasn't. The trip to Asia. Long hours at the Queen's Road office. Trying to settle the estate. The restaurant takes time. The new orphanage, the shipping business. I've learned things I . . ." Peter felt for his bald spot as they neared the crest of the property. "This whole thing of the drug . . ."

Women talk in a thousand ways, Su Lin thought. She read on every side Mother's messages, the benign plantings raised against the deadly one, the strangler: opium. And she saw in these desperate offspring the role estheticism plays as a woman's answer to pain.

They approached the pagoda: inlaid columns, shiny black tiled roof. A willow, bare in winter, bowed over it. A small stone deer, symbol of long life, stood covered in moss.

"We had to bring you back. There was no choice after we found out about the Corsicans."

She pulled her robe over her against the spreading cool and stepped up into the open gazebo.

"So your friend Cross didn't tell you? The bastard."

Now she could see beyond the vast winged house across the rest of the sloped estate. The tall turbaned Sikh, rifle crooked, stood at the barred black gates. In the graveled driveway, little Fook had taken the cream-yellow Rolls-Royce from the garage and was polishing it. For whom?

"Your guy, Su. This Cross. He works for Corsican mobsters. Drug racketeers, out of Marseilles."

She bent away from her brother and his hammering words. Up along the winding Peak Road, a fish lorry plied the grade from Aberdeen to Victoria.

"The Chinatown guys found a notebook in his flat in Berkeley. We've got it here."

Another great mansion stood near Jardine's Corner—a Communist millionaire's, she recalled, one of Hong Kong's smiling inscrutable contradictions.

"A Corsican was tailing you in San Francisco. He tried to kill one of our people."

Now she could just see over the other side of the mountain, where as evening spread the Peak Tram labored to a stop at Garden Road, eight hundred feet from the top. Two cars, carrying seventy-two passengers and a driver, the world's steepest ascent, they said, hauled by five-thousand-foot steel cables wound on drums. What kept the cables from snapping? Or her heart?

Peter came after her. "You were in danger. These Corsicans are contesting us. They killed Father. Anything could have happened." He was behind her, his voice going on. "Apparently your lover was from them. There was a likelihood of kidnapping. Blackmail. Chen felt . . ."

Another step took her higher, and suddenly there was the other side: the blazing flame sky over China, real China.

"We knew you wouldn't agree to leave him. So we had you . . . drugged. I'm sorry."

The Chiu Chao: a slashing recollection of the struggle on the stairs of the flat on Vallejo Street: "Jim! Jim!"

Turning, and there: Hong Kong, Fragrant Harbor—teeming, jeweled, efflorescent. Twin nests of frozen lights—Victoria, Kowloon—bisected by a wavering stream of lit harbor boats.

"It was arranged through the Consulate in San Francisco to have you brought back on a U.S. Army hospital plane."

Across the waters rose the lit clock tower of the Kowloon Ferry Building.

One of us is mad.

"Su? You're tiring."

"Jim!"

Hong Kong spun, a pinwheel. Peter caught her as she fell. She leaned against a column, chasing the rush of her heart.

"Let me help you back."

"No." Deadweight, struggling up.

"Take my arm."

"No!"

She managed the gazebo steps and headed back along the path, Peter dogging her.

"I know how it is, Su. They come at you. The gold diggers. There was a chick in Boston, a beatnik. She even said she loved me." Peter sighed. "It's always the money."

Winny Lin's plantings had become an inky jungle of inert shapes. Beyond, a black sea ran all the way to Repulse Bay, a necklace of lights now. She fell against a rough-barked tree and waited, breathing heavily.

"We can give you another shot of morphine if you like."

"Leave me alone, Peter," she hissed, walking on.

Out in that dark was Peel Rise, the path down the hill to Aberdeen. She tried to trace it in her mind.

Mounting to the veranda, she saw a light in the window of Father's old room. The curtain was open. Inside, above a low mahogany dresser hung a framed picture she remembered of Chiang Kai-shek in full military regalia. Beside it, in another, Sun Yat-sen frowned with great dignity.

"Peter. What's that?"

It was the third one she didn't recall: a color photo of Harry Lin in a long white robe, a knotted red cloth band wrapped around his head. A long red scarf hung to the floor. On one foot was a rope sandal, on the other a shoe. A long white pearl necklace hung from his neck.

"A society Father belonged to."

In one hand was a sword, in the other a three-cornered red flag with black Chinese writing.

"What kind?"

"Like the Masons, I suppose."

"What does the writing say?"

"How should I know? The group is called Sun Yee On. It means something like Righteous and Peaceful Society."

"What's the plaque? The equilateral triangle?"

"Heaven, Earth, Man. But you should ask Chen."

Soundlessly Chen emerged out of the garden onto the veranda and put his birdcage on the table. She had the feeling he'd been there all along.

"Tien Ti Hui, the Heaven and Earth Society. That was the name of the original group back in China. Also sometimes called Hung Mon, or Hung League. It goes back to 1674. 'Overthrow the Ch'ing and restore the Ming!' "

Chen became quite animated as he repeated the phrase in Cantonese. "A patriotic group. Sometimes known as a Triad. They were formed in southern China hundreds of years ago to fight the Manchu clans who had taken Peking. Your father was an officer. Heung

Chu. Incense Master. Known by the number 438. A great honor. Eurasians are rarely admitted."

"Was he the leader?" Peter asked.

"No. The first is a 489. Shan Chu. The Hill Chief."

"Who was Shan Chu?"

"Well, you see, these are secret societies." Chen smiled. "Good night." He picked up his birdcage and padded off.

Back in the room, Amah had laid out fresh bedclothes and was running a bath. Peter stood in the doorway smoking.

"I suppose it was inevitable, our coming back."

She studied the marks on her face in the dresser mirror. A window enabled her to just see the gate at the end of the driveway where a car's light on Plantation Road illuminated the Sikh guard leaning upon his rifle. How can he stand for so many hours at a stretch?

"Childhood's end, Su. Or something like that."

Amah came out of the bathroom. "You ba' readee, missee. Goo' night."

She scuffed off in black pajama pants, white socks, black slippers. "You'll get over him, Su."

Peter remained, a shadow in the doorway. She regarded him in the mirror.

"You'll stay?"

"It's not really a request, is it? Leave me alone."

Peter stubbed his cigarette out on the veranda floor. "Good night."

Su Lin closed the doors after him and stood among the silent desultory chinoiserie of her mother's room, the mausoleum where she was to be installed, the new Lin queen, Winny's infertile successor.

At the dresser she tied back her hair tight with a rubber band. She took off her robe and laid it over a porcelain hamper.

The steamy bathroom reeked of odd herbal odors reminiscent of her mother. Is that what remained of a woman, perfumes and essences? A wicker basket shredded under her fingers as she reached into it for a washcloth.

Settling into the hot bath, she felt the blood rush out of her body. A straight-edged razor folded into a black ivory sheath sat on the tile edge of the bath. A fragmented recollection of some incident near the end, before Momma's flight to Japan and Terhune, played through a child's eyes. Picking up the razor, she saw that it was rusted at its base.

It opened easily. She lay the blade edge against the narrow blue veins in her wrist and held it until she could count her own pulse through it. Her hand began to tremble.

Her lips formed his name. She slumped back in the bath, her sorrow merging with the steam and the water.

There were no tears.

27

"Yesterday Monday. Today Wednesday."

"If yesterday Monday, today *Tuesday.*"

"No." The Japanese bartender proffered Cross an Asahi and a glass. "We cross International Date Line last night. No Tuesday."

"I see," Cross said, as if he understood any better now.

He took the beer to a back table of the *Brazil Maru*'s glassed lounge. Astern, albatross that had joined up at Honolulu idly circled the wake, stabbing at garbage. Below, the head cook sat in a deck chair as he did every afternoon, trying to pick up Radio NHK from Tokyo on his shortwave.

It was midafternoon and cloudy. Cross watched the wake's churning white water feather and re-form, folding in over itself, swallowing the past with each curl. He'd spent hours of the voyage staring into the water, trying to decipher his mission and the events leading up to it. Upon reflection, the slim evidence of Terhune's telegram had seemed nothing to go on. Had he been on land, he wondered if he might have turned back. Worse, the more he tried to remember Su Lin the more her image dissolved into abstraction. He had no photo of her. She had left him a love without object. What he had were fragments: bits of conversation, the things of her room. Then she was gone again, leaving him only the disembodied hurtling motion toward her.

Stalking the decks, hands jammed in his peacoat pockets, he had gazed emptily at silverfish arching free of the waves, dolphin herds teasing the prow, night storms washing luminous starry plankton over the green-painted rivets of the deck plates—a swirling vacuum swallowing her vanished form.

He sat at a round Formica table in the lounge and poured the beer into the glass. Perhaps, he thought, as the sway of the ship brought hauntings of an earlier water crossing half a planet away, he had become the eternal passenger, sailing off to somewhere, trailing the restless consequences of a first act lost in time.

The other passengers huddled along the decks, stayed in their rooms, idled in the lounge's plastic furniture playing *go* or mahjongg, hunched at the bar. There were two hundred Japanese; Cross was one of five Caucasians. Asian music wafted steadily from the bar radio, bringing strange rhythms, a strange tongue. In the ship's library he had found a lone book in English, *The Fire Next Time* by James Baldwin, full of apocalyptic warnings.

The night before, one of the Americans, a pensioner on his way to farm a rubber plantation in Ceylon he'd bought by mail, had picked up the Armed Forces Far East Network on his shortwave. A third American, a journalist, had joined them to listen to the news report that there were now 19,000 Americans in Vietnam. When Defense Secretary McNamara reported that he had it on good information that the soldiers would be home by Christmas, the journalist laughed out loud and his mouth hardened.

An American disc jockey, a woman sergeant, had come on: "And by special request for Eddie, chasin' VC up there in Ap Bac, 'Fingertips, Part Two,' by Little Stevie Wonder! And for you Tennessee boys out there on patrol, Elvis's 'Houn' Dog'!" Cross had stayed and listened, for there was time—too much of it—to register these things: the unbroken, unwelcome reverie of shipboard. The set had closed with "Blowin' in the Wind."

Cross stared out the solarium window at a weak storm front chasing up from the south. The flag on the bow dipped from side to side, marking the horizon like a level. A little Japanese boy who had taken a fondness to him brought him a small plastic package of *sembei*, seaweed and rich crackers.

"*Arigatō Gozaimasu*," Cross muttered.

According to his Japanese primer, though the phrase was translated "thank you," it meant literally, "rarely exist," or "Such an act of kindness as you are showing me is rarely met with, hence I am grateful." But the underlying thought, the book went on, is more like "It is through the grace of Buddha that I meet with such kind treatment."

And *hana*, he read, the word for "flower," is the same as the word for "nose." A synesthetic language? Can it really be that they don't think in two?

His book went on to speak of *shibui*, that quality of spare, unassuming beauty so highly valued in Japan, sometimes translated "astringence."

"To the true connoisseur of *shibui*, a beautiful object (and what product of nature is not beautiful?) does not become less beautiful with the passing of time but rather more so. A teacup, for example, that develops minute cracks with constant use has indeed become a cup suitable for the drinking of tea."

The ship listed to starboard. His beer bottle slid across the Formica and tottered against the lip. He grabbed it before it fell.

Asia has reclaimed her. Let her go.

Terhune's telegram had seemed almost a commandment. Who was this man, Cross's only hope? Did he have her? Did he even know where she was? What could he have meant? Perhaps she was not there at all; or perhaps it was to this very Terhune and his love that she had fled, and disappearance was her manner of dropping him. But she had seemed more truthful.

He was sailing off the edge of a flat world into some lashing current, the American parvenu on his journey to the East, chasing a ghost.

The ship listed. Cross looked up. The journalist was standing above him, a glass in his hand, three beers under his arm.

"Mind?"

"Sit down."

"Strange," he said. "Billy Strange."

"Jim Cross."

Strange was a short, intense American in jeans and a ratty fatigue jacket and several days' growth of beard. He spoke in a haunted, rapid-fire delivery, with eyes that wouldn't stay still—some sort of bookish East Coast type gone awry. He was Cross's age but seemed older. Billy Strange was electroshock, a glass of cold water breaking Cross's reverie.

"First time in Asia, man?"

"Yes."

"It's different. Especially Japan. Modern, but very foreign. You'll see. What are you going for?"

"To find someone."

He looked wary. "Are you . . . official?"

"Official what?"

"Government, military, press."

"No. Where are you headed?"

He paused, then: "Saigon."

"Voluntarily?"

He smiled in a funny way, sideways. His teeth were a little yellow. "Yeah."

He poured a beer into a glass, seeming to disappear into the absorption of it. "I was *Time*'s man in Vietnam. Or rather one of them. Until a few months ago."

"That must have been—"

"It was. Up at three A.M., flying out to the Mekong Delta. Four A.M. breakfast in Tan Son Nhut airport, scared shitless. At five the sun comes up over the paddies, then suddenly they drop you out of a Huey into the war. People shooting, running, trying to find cover. You never know where the fire's coming from. That night you'd be back in Saigon having a quiet French meal. Whew."

He downed the rest of the first beer then poured the next. "When I first got there I was reasonable. I thought Diem was better than Communism. Then I got hipped. The ARVN is a total fraud. I watched them day after day, doing no fighting. Then we'd get back and the PIO's would lay it on at the briefings about the 'great victories.' It isn't working, man. We kill a hundred, they recruit a thousand. We're fighting the birth rate. So I'd write these dispatches. Everyone there knew about the bullshit and would say so, but always off the record. My editors in New York kept saying, 'Attribute.' It was a lie machine. Did you hear McNamara the other night? 'Light at the end of the tunnel.' Fuck. I saw a battle with a VC battalion cornered on three sides. American fighter-bombers, armed helicopters, armored personnel carriers everywhere. At three o'clock the ARVN deliberately allowed the VC out the fourth side. The ARVN were afraid to fight. They were shelling their own men!"

The second beer disappeared.

"Westmoreland and Alsop talk about our 'great victories.' Our American government wouldn't lie like that, right? Kennedy leaned on Luce to pull me. He did. I swear. *C'est la vie.* It had to come. If he hadn't, Johnson would have. Besides, I was tired. I couldn't get on the helicopters anymore. They said I was 'negative.' I started taking LSD-25 and taxis to the war. For 150 piastres a Saigon cab-driver would drive me to the battle area in a beat-up Chevy. And keep the fucking meter running. Whew."

Billy Strange was like broken glass. His eyes, behind rimless glasses taped on one side, were embers. Cross realized he knew nothing of the war there; it was just coming to him that there was indeed one.

"I thought if you told the truth people would listen. Camel?"

"No, thanks."

"Then I ran into the smack."

"Smack?" Cross looked at the ravaged little journalist.

"Horse, heroin. Opium. I don't mean I took it. I mean . . . well, I still can't figure out about the smack. I don't know where the hell it comes from. Joints the size of your arm too. I figured it was the black GI's. The front looks like Harlem, you know. The closer to the shooting, the blacker it is."

He laughed, a kind of gargle.

"I figured those guys were scoring it somewhere cheap. Pure China White. You never see that back home. Where did it come from? Then once up in Vientiane on a press junket I got drunk with this American guy. Young. Arrogant Harvard bastard. But he knew Asia. His dad was a missionary, his grandfather before that. He said none of us knew why the war was being fought. I said yes I do, it's about the mineral rights in the South China Sea. He laughed in my face. 'Then why?' I asked him. He said the Chinese. 'The Reds?' 'No,' he said. 'The free Chinese.' 'What's their interest?' 'Opium,' he said. 'Marginal,' I said. 'No,' he said. 'It's *all about* the opium.' 'Bullshit,' I said. Then the guy took three beer glasses. We were real swacked. 'This one's a gallon of oil', he said. 'This one is an ounce of gold. This one's an ounce of no. 4.' He tapped the oil glass. 'Worth fifty cents.' He picked up the gold glass. 'Thirty dollars. This glass,' he said, picking up the third one, 'seven thousand dollars.' Bastard was right. 'H' is worth 366 times its weight in gold at street level. 'So you tell me,' he said. 'Which wheel gets the grease?' The next day I saw him and he told me to forget what he'd said the night before."

Cross remembered the hotel room in Paris, staring into the suitcase as the Corsican lifted the shiny plastic bags toward him with the Chinese lettering: the China White he had brought from Tangier.

"So I got back to Saigon and filed copy on it. Then I told them I wanted out. You're too late, Billy, they wired back. We already sent you your ticket."

"So what now?"

"I'm working out of Sweden. A different group. Look me up if you ever get that way."

"Why are you going back to Asia?"

Billy Strange smiled. "Shit, I don't know. I'm into the war. It's my Gordian knot." He looked at Cross with suspicion. "What about you? How come you're not in? They need doctors."

"I was Four-F."

"What for?"

"A heart murmur. They said I wouldn't be able to run."

Strange laughed. "Yeah. That's what you have to do out there. Run. Run fast." He leaned forward. "And you know what? No matter how fast you run, the VC are going to run a little faster."

He pushed his glasses up off his nose and smiled a rather endearing smile. Cross felt the dull sparks from distant events.

"Okay, you're lucky you're not in. But this war will touch you, brother. One way or another. A fuse is burning." He leaned forward. "It's not that the Commies are so great. But you can't stop these people. Uncle Ho is plugged into them. Either we'll kill them all or they'll kick us out."

The ship was pitching as storm clouds rolled toward them. The water had turned a steely purple-gray. They grabbed their bottles; the conversation lurched.

"You said you were looking for someone," Strange said.

"A girl."

"You don't know where she is?"

"No. I'm going to see someone who may know."

"Where?"

"Kyoto."

Billy Strange shook his head. "Man, you're as crazy as I am. You're Orpheus, aren't you, going after Eurydice."

Outside, the cook had taken his radio and gone back in. Thick raindrops hit the window, darkening the tarpaulin on the hatch below. The dinner bell rang. Cross stood up.

Billy Strange was looking at him wildly. "Hey, Orpheus," he said. "Maybe the journey is the goal. Maybe trying to find her is her message to you. Maybe your looking is the instrument of your renewal." He downed the last beer. "Or your destruction. Just kidding."

That night the American pensioner rounded up everyone and showed them his little 8-mm home movie *Oriental Ports of Call*. A tape played Harry Owens faintly in the background to a parade of stock shots of Waikiki, Hong Kong, Manila, Yokohama, Kobe, Singapore, Bangkok. Invariably in each scene his fat wife stood in a pineapple muumuu in the foreground. Cross found himself scrutinizing the crowds in the Hong Kong sequence. The pensioner, mistaking this for intense interest in his photographic work, approached him afterwards and asked him if he wanted to play Scrabble.

"Thanks. No."

"You sure? We're terrible. You can beat us."

"No, thanks. Really."

Cross had a dream that night that stayed with him into the morning: Massive waves rose and shattered mountains, dissolving them instantly into the finest white sand. Coastlines wriggled like snakes and readjusted their promontories and coves. Earth buckled and thrust upward into new configurations. The sun suddenly swelled, turned crimson, leered, then dropped from the sky as if a string had been cut.

Late on the tenth day Yokohama appeared out of a mist. A pair of tugs came out and led them in among stationary moored barges. As the anchor dropped from the hawsehole, Cross stood near the prow, his heart beating, peering out through the dying light at the cluttered waterfront. Behind him the western sky, suddenly cleared, was afire. Ahead ran a long concrete pier backed by sheds, and a red and white striped beacon tower jutted skyward. Long low warehouses with dark green louvered doors clustered near the customs shed. Cross read, NO SMOKING.

Noisy chains lowered the gangplank. He stood alone on deck looking down through the twilight at a gaggle of weeping, laughing greeters on the dock. Neon advertising signs began to light up all along the streets facing the dock. Unable to read the characters, he tried picking out syllables of the kana alphabets he had taught himself, the ones used for foreign words.

Suddenly Billy Strange was beside him. "There it is, man. Asia. Now *we're* the minority."

As Cross reached down to pick up his bags, Strange handed him a slip of paper. "The address in Stockholm. We counsel draft dodgers, release straight information. If you're there. look us up."

They walked down the ramp together. Cross's hands were cold.

"Takushii? Takushii?" Small men were waving and calling.

"They want to know if you want a taxi," Strange said. "See you, man. I'm off to Hanoi."

"I thought you said Saigon."

Strange looked at Cross quizzically. "Did I?"

Then he reached out his hand. Cross put his bag down and shook it.

"So long, Orpheus. Hope you find her. If you do, grab her and don't look back, right? Or you'll turn into a pillar of salt. Oops, wrong myth."

Billy Strange dissolved into the night.

Cross turned away and stared blindly into the streaming Asian dark, then picked up his bag and entered it.

28

United States Consul-General Fletcher "Fletch" Doody stared out at the rain dripping off the purple liana at the entrance to the Consulate compound. He could just see the basketball netting in the driveway below, hanging gray and limp from the hoop. In the parking area his black Cadillac with its white CC emblem sat next to a khaki military supply truck. Doody took a soft imaginary jump shot, landing on his flat stockinged feet.

"Swish," he whispered.

The three-story dormlike complex rose over steep Garden Road down from the Victoria Peak tram, all white stucco and gray pillars. Black metal grillwork adorned the windows, a concession to Chinese style that disguised an elaborate security layout that fooled no one. Though it was a consulate and not an embassy—Hong Kong being not a sovereign nation but a British colony—behind its palms and greenery sat the largest U. S. Consulate-General headquarters in the world, an unabashed spy post and the heart of Washington's Asian information-gathering operations.

Stationed at the entrance were Marine guards. Closed-circuit television cameras swept the grounds. On the roof was a giant white enamel radar dish. Inside were three floors of efficient squared-off 1950s-style American offices, employing more than seventy consuls, vice-consuls, and attachés. The third floor was all CIA.

Consul Doody, still buzzed from a martini lunch at Jimmy's with his British counterpart, shook a Pez from a plastic dispenser and popped it in his mouth. He walked past his wide oak desk to the other window, facing downtown. Tall and thin, shoulders curving with the effort of pushing against forty, Doody peered between the silver taping of the burglar alarms through the smoked one-way glass at palm-lined Lower Albert Street Road. Down the block was St. John's Cathedral, Anglican bastion of the old community, then the new Hilton. Normally he could see the fabled sweep of the bay across to Kowloon, but the sleeting rain left him only shadowy impressions. He drummed his nails on the thick security glass. The rain hammered back. A great worried sigh issued from his narrow chest.

Six months earlier the posting had seemed a plum, a triumphant and unexpected step up after undistinguished Kuala Lumpur's American Cultural Center—nothing but a library, USIS press releases, English classes—a sudden, happy turn of events. Here the social scene was gay, the flow of work stimulating: trade missions, spying on China, liaisons with the British Joint Intelligence Committee, soirées on the Peak. A notch in the old gun.

But suddenly things began changing after Diem's death. Shadowy operatives from Washington and Langley had all but taken over the place, arriving unannounced at all hours of the day and night. Consul Doody had begun to suspect that his malleability lay behind the posting, the perception that he could easily be run over. "Responsibility without authority," ran his lamentory phrase in the imaginary telex to Washington he'd never send. He reached up and rubbed his soft Gillette-nicked jaw.

The intercom buzzed. Absently he reached a long arm behind him and flicked it on.

"Your wife, sir."

Doody stepped to the phone. "Hi, Joyce."

"I'm at Lane Crawford. God, this rain. Did the packages get there?"

He gazed glumly at the pile in the corner that had arrived while he was at lunch. "I wish you wouldn't send them here, Joyce."

"It was raining. They don't care. Who's the boss over there anyway, Fletch? Bring them home with you tonight, honey, wouldja, poo?"

Doody ground his jaws. "I may be late. Someone's coming in from Vientiane."

"Anybody I know?"

"Some missionary's son from Harvard. I'll tell you about it tonight." And he would, for he told his wife everything; in this, he was eminently American.

"And Joyce. Couldn't you . . . cool it a little on the buying? I mean, we don't know where the hell we'll be next year."

"Fletch, this is Hong Kong, not Kuala Lumpur," she said irritably. "It was on sale. Gee. We have to entertain. I bought you something too. A silk ascot. *Très* British."

A mounted photo next to the phone showed the nuclear quartet: he the tall, tired jump-shot whiz from Dartmouth; she the thickening cheerleader with the Doris Day bob; little Billy and Liz in the uniforms of the British school at the foot of the Peak. Somehow one musters a smile for the camera.

"Fletch. Are you there?"

"Yes, Joyce."

"I have a Chinese lesson at four, so I'll order food brought up. Okay?"

It was a deal they had. He was allergic to languages and made no effort to speak the local tongues, so she took the lessons and gave the toasts at the banquets. Here the tutor was a young Cantonese martial arts whiz. They were always young, it seemed, always muscular.

"Okay. See you at home."

His secretary entered and placed a stack of fresh telexes in front of him, then left him alone again. Consul Doody sat in his black leather high-backed chair, put on his glasses, and looked at the top one; but the purple ink on yellow was swimming, like maggots on a pond.

He took off his glasses and walked to the private bathroom provided him. Bending over the gleaming beige enamel basin, he splashed cold water on his face with long freckled fingers. He looked up at himself in the mirror under the fluorescent light, fingers spread, the water running down over his pale wrists, wetting his cuffs. "Jesus," he whispered. Purple circles hung beneath his eyes. Incipient blotches dotted his cheeks. He spat water off his lips.

Sometimes he wished they were back at the old job in Kuala Lumpur. He felt overmatched here, thrust onto the center stage of a play whose lines he could only mumble. Dread lived and grew in him like a tumor.

This was British turf. They'd never heard of Jerry West, Bill Russell, Oscar Robertson. He was in an awkward position, no Asia Hand by any means—just an isolated man called for reasons he would never understand into the service of empire, to move as a stranger among darker peoples of the world of whom he was deathly afraid.

He reached blindly for a towel and rubbed his beaked, freckled face furiously, further reddening it. "Pussy-whipped bastard," he whispered. "Wimp."

If only he'd been able to graduate on time. If only he hadn't had to go to Korea. *If only he'd been good enough at Dartmouth to go pro.*

The intercom buzzed again. "Mr. Potter called. He'll be a little late. Five, he said."

Asshole. Who does he think I am?

"Okay."

Consul Doody threw the towel on the floor and stalked back around his desk.

29

Alec Potter gazed up at the high-rise projects with their strange ornate window grillings, washing poles jutting out in the afternoon sun, jumbled lines like sprung piano wires. As his taxi wound along the Tsimshatsui waterfront, he felt the teeming comfortable press of Asian street poverty close in around him, with its noise and color he knew so well. To Potter, Asia's beggary was the white man's balm, a constant reminder that the poverty was theirs not his, a meditation on the blessedness of his own fortune. There but for the grace of God, his missionary grandfather used to say. By the time of Alec's father, the words were not spoken; with Alec, it simply *was*.

He flipped through his wallet to affirm that he had changed enough piastres into Hong Kong dollars at Kai Tak to keep himself amused for a couple of days. As the driver came out from narrow Mody Road onto Nathan Road, Potter saw a glimpse of bay to his left. Rain clouds sped overhead, dimming the profusion of color along the thronged, sign-strung street. In the privacy of the taxi's back seat Potter reached down, wincing, and scratched his genitals. Cursing his Corsican hosts on the Plain of Jars, whom he considered responsible for this new and mystifying affliction, he looked at his watch and saw he had two hours now until the meeting with Consul-General Doody.

The taxi let him off at the corner of Nathan and Carnarvon Road. He bought a *South China Morning Post,* then walked up Nathan until he found a shoeshine boy beneath a banyan tree at Kimberly Road in front of the Miramar Hotel. Potter always felt comfortable getting his brown loafers shined by a boy, though the "boy" might be, as this one, ancient of age. The shoeshine was an affirmation of privilege, a reassurance that there would always be a sustaining underside of human life to look after him, pick up his clothes, do his bidding, complain to, and bully a bit. Afterwards the flicking of the coin, the tip if it was good, and the grateful smile that followed made him feel like a *good person.*

To the few of Alec Potter's caste, it was not just the privilege of being white but being versed as well in the other person's wiles and ways and tongue that bred a condescension different from the simple chauvinist's. Since so few Americans ever bothered to acquaint themselves with the foreign culture, he was of a tiny elite. The Caucasian who overheard and understood the whispered invective as he passed was omniscient, dangerous; he knew he was hated. His grandfather, who had come to preach to the Meo tribes of the Mekong, had mistakenly thought he was loved, through Christ. His father, a less emphatic man, had made himself of transient political and social use in the Triangle. Potter, the young lion in the age of Asian Communism, took his reign for granted. Wasn't it Luce who had proclaimed this "the American century"?

After his shine, Potter walked west down Kimberly Road into the quarter's narrow spilling streets. He looked up into the orchestra of advertising signs hung overhead on the buildings, awaiting their nightly illumination, looking for the characters that matched the ones on the paper he held. Though he spoke little Chinese, he read enough; the signs were the same all over Southeast Asia—in Saigon, Bangkok, Vientiane—wherever Chinese merchants had taken root: GREAT SPRING, GOLDEN DRAGON, WHITE LOTUS.

Shiny pressed ducks hung in windows beneath bare light bulbs. Green winter crabs twitched in squat barrels. Stalls proffered gold, diamonds, jade, pewter, ivory, watches, clothing.

Past the Astor Hotel and down Hanoi Road, he paused before

the window of a shop over which hung a neon deer, symbol of long life, and the name he sought in white lettering on red: CHU KWAN KONG.

In the window, jars and plates and pans bore strange and curious substances, each identified by red Chinese writing on yellow labels. They looked to Potter like dried mushrooms, withered fruits, or things from the sea. There were mysterious parts of fishes, snakes, arcane animal organs. Some floated in liquids; others sat in glass baking plates beneath the counter. Most of the store's goods, which continued on shelves inside, were strange and incomprehensible, but Potter knew that, to a Chinese, medicine and food merge in the herbalist's shop; no part of an animal is without benefit to humans.

"Mr. Chu?"

The smooth-faced man who looked up as he entered wore glasses and Western dress. "Yah?" He was shoveling what looked like blackened pea pods into a bag for a tiny lady in a gray jacket and slippers.

When she had paid and left, Potter took a small packet from his jacket pocket. "From your friends in Vientiane," he said in English.

"Ah. Good."

Happily Mr. Chu laid the packet on the glass counter and opened it. Six small gold bars, each with Chinese writing and the number 5,000, lay clustered in paper. Potter knew Mr. Chu would invest this gold from Southeast Asian Chiu Chao relatives into the Hong Kong market for them. Mr. Chu folded the packet up and disappeared in back while Potter waited, staring at a pile of dead snakes decomposing in a tall jar, resisting the urge to scratch his crotch, which stung terribly.

When Mr. Chu reappeared, Potter managed through voice and gesture to discreetly indicate the location, if not the nature, of his condition. Mr. Chu brightened and took down from a shelf several jars containing dark, furry penile objects of different sizes.

"From Kenya," he said, pointing to the largest one. "Two thousand dollar apiece." Rhinoceros horn, he explained—the more expensive, the firmer the result. He began to scrape, hack, and trim a little off onto a paper with a small razor-sharp dagger as a present to Potter.

Mr. Chu then suggested well-ground tiger bones washed down

with ginseng. Deer antlers in a powdered tonic bore great restorative properties, he said, as does velvet fungus, shaved and pulverized. Actually, he confided, a straight shot of snake blood was better than ginseng.

Potter, realizing Mr. Chu was prescribing remedies for virility, tried again to convey that it was not impotence but a dripping and itching from which he suffered.

The herbalist nodded emphatically. In a few short moments he had produced an array of salves and herbs and liquids in bottles. He measured each out on a flat pan hung by wires to a bamboo stick with a small metal trapezoidal weight on the other end.

"Do I drink it?"

"Drinkee? No, no." He robustly grabbed his genitals through his pants and demonstrated where to rub. Adding up the price on a smooth black abacus, he further suggested Potter get an acupressure massage and have the masseuse apply the ointments. He gave him the name of a place in the quarter.

"But first, come. We go snake shop. Best for you."

Mr. Chu closed up shop and guided Potter out back and into the next street. He paused before a newly painted sign of snakes and dragons above a narrow restaurant door.

Chau fung lay, sam seh fay: Snakes get fat when the autumn wind blows. The proverb contends that one should eat them only in cold months, between mid-autumn and December's winter solstice, just before they hibernate. The bile of snake is good for rheumatism, they say, and sexual rejuvenation.

They entered the snake restaurant and sat down. Mr. Chu enthusiastically invited Potter to observe the preparation of his tonic.

The waiter removed a live cobra from a sealed cupboard lining the wall. He grabbed the snake tightly behind its outstretched hood as it tried to strike, at the same time putting his foot on its tail and stretching the cobra taut.

He ran his hand down the length of the snake's stomach, feeling for the gall bladder. Quickly he made a one-inch slit with a crochet-like needle, and with two fingers squeezed out the bile sac.

Mr. Chu explained that if the cobra were to be kept alive he would be returned to his drawer to grow another gall bladder. In this instance, the waiter took a sharp knife and made a cut in the snake's skin about an inch from the tail and quickly peeled the skin off like a long sock. The writhing denuded cobra was tossed in a bucket.

The gall bladder sat in a small teacup in front of Potter, who was feeling ill. The waiter came and broke the sac open into a small cup of Chinese wine. Mr. Chu said it took about thirty-three bile sacs from three different snakes to make one drink, and cost more than fifty Hong Kong dollars. One drop from a king cobra could cost HK $250.

Wincing, Potter downed the cup. Mr. Chu smiled and nodded approval.

"Eat plenty fresh fish too. And no fuckee for one month."

Potter stood abruptly and lurched out of the snake shop. He turned into a narrow alley and gagged against a wall, his knees trembling.

When he had recovered, he crossed back over Nathan to Lock Road and traversed a lurid alley, dark even by day, past drunken American sailors and Triad pimps. TATTOO PARLOR, ACUPUNCTURE, FORTUNE TELLING, said signs in English. He came to a building surrounded by piles of rotting food. Above the entrance a sign said BLISSFUL BUILDING.

Mah-jongg tiles rattled behind closed doors like false teeth as he mounted the narrow, urine-drenched stairs. He came to a half-open door where joss burned at his feet in a small red shrine containing oranges, lit by a bare bulb. A quiet, plain woman in cheongsam took his package and studied the labels. She asked him to remove his clothes and lie down on a table. The woman disappeared.

Uneasily Potter undressed and dropped onto his stomach. The room was warm, fetid, and smelled of garlic and camphor.

The woman returned. "Finger dancing," she said, tittering as she began to rub his shoulders and neck, applying pressure to particular points with a single finger, causing a deep drowsiness to come over him. As she worked her way down his body, he drifted into a reverie in which his grandfather's image came to him:

Matthew Potter had arrived in northern Laos in 1903, a grim, rail-thin young man in a white tropical suit, his Bible under his arm. He wore wire-rimmed spectacles and was said to have a good tenor voice for hymns. He preached and sang to the Meo tribes along the upper Mekong for thirty years. By the time he left he had established Methodist missions over a 50,000-square-mile area.

Alec's father, Eliot, was born in Laos and inherited his father's congregation. He and his American wife stayed in the Mekong region until after World War II, converting thousands more, and helping gather intelligence for the U.S. in Yunnan. When his wife contracted a fever and died suddenly, Eliot Potter, discouraged, moved to Chiengmai, where he became director of the museum. Though he had helped the Meo improve their opium-planting techniques, Eliot Potter remained puritanical about the drug, seeing it only as an unfortunate concomitant of backwardness, a transitory crop upon which his flock's livelihood had depended in lieu of more advanced agricultural techniques surely on the way from America any day.

Alec Potter, devoid of his forebears' Christian scruples, saw them as sentimentalists used by the entrepreneurs and colonialists going back to the French. He, the young White Hope, steeped in the American postwar rationale, had no illusions about his mandate. He was returning to Asia, a sympathetic independent businessman, to help secure the area for capital and freedom, by whatever means necessary.

Now as he rose back into consciousness on the massage table, it was with the memory of a warm evening a few weeks earlier, a breeze rustling the cotton curtains on the Plain of Jars, as the two lean-limbed girls bent over him. All the things his father, dry and Methodist and messianic, had never had, had been his that night in the Snow Leopard Inn—the great sexual adventure of his life.

But the intervening days had darkened that memory. Cursing the Corsican Gérard—on whose behalf he had come to Hong Kong to meet with the American Consul—for having given him the dirty girls, he opened his eyes.

"You feel bettah now?"

Potter was on his back. The plain-faced masseuse was smiling, looking down. Following her gaze, Potter saw that he was erect, his prick glossy with the balms and salves from the herbalist's jar and his recollection of the two girls on the Plain of Jars.

"Ahhh!"

The masseuse, reading his exclamation of pain as pleasure, took Potter through with her hand in quick strokes. Alec Potter, his eyes pinched shut, screamed in agony.

30

White morning
Mount Hiei floats upside down in the pond
A crow calls from a pine tree!

Cross stood at the entry, the *genkan,* of the Shiraku-so Inn on Kyoto's north side, looking out at a snowy garden: a pristine world. He could see the scalloped rooftop of Ginkaku-ji Temple, the Silver Pavilion, beyond the low wall rising above slate tiles in the foreground. Further beyond, the pine forest flank of Kyoto's western Mount Hiei disappeared into mist.

How carefully the pines in the garden are shaped, he thought, with the same attention given the pruning of the little bonsai, bending slightly under the weight of the snow. The garden had the wondrous rightness of a clearing accidentally come upon in the forest. Beyond the fence the traffic snarled; here all was order.

"English haiku," a voice said behind him, looking at the page Cross had written. "Not bad."

Ueda-san was standing in a business suit, looking toward the top of Mount Hiei. He pushed his rimless glasses up on his nose and smiled. "Kimono too short for you. I get you foreign size in town."

"Thank you, Ueda-san." He was a Fulbright applicant in cultural anthropology whose mother ran the small inn where Cross had stayed for three nights. Cross had been helping him with English.

It was the fifth day since he had stepped off the *Brazil Maru* in Yokohama. A Professor Suzuki from the ship had found him wandering along the darkened waterfront street in Yokohama and taken him by train to his house in the Shibuya district of Tokyo. Cross had stayed two nights, refusing an offer to lecture at Suzuki's school. Suzuki-san had passed him on to the Shiraku-so and Mr. Ueda.

Japan: Cross had found himself rather too tall and pale and ill-put-together, an excess of limbs and motion, moving among a compact, busy people in uniformly dark suits, purposeful and impassive. Fumbling with chopsticks over foods he didn't know, his wallet accumulating business cards he couldn't read offered by curious, polite strangers, he was being passed, in a manner he didn't understand, from person to person, being channeled to that place reserved for foreigners, a place perhaps little resembling the life of a Japanese.

"What you come to Japan for?" Ueda-san had asked Cross the first night in a curtained neighborhood bar where they drank festival sake from square unpainted wooden cups.

When Cross had mentioned Terhune's name, a great sucking of air had followed. Ueda-san let it be known that Terhune was a teacher of local renown, a *dai-sensei*. Further discourse uncovered more complex intimations: Terhune was also referred to as *hen-na gaijin*—strange or crazy foreigner. Ueda-san would not elaborate.

Cross had called Terhune from Tokyo, only to be told on the phone by a young Japanese woman in broken English that he was out of town for three days; he would contact him when he returned.

Cross had arrived by bullet train from Tokyo and spent the days since wandering the biting winter streets of Kyoto: downtown, among the department stores and the spilling clatter of pachinko parlors and coffee bars; along the stone banks of the coursing Kamogawa; out along the wooded eastern face of the Arashiyama hills; through the quiet suburbs of the northern perimeter. The temples were everywhere, it seemed: the gaudy Shinto ones with their orange gates: the staid Shin-shu Buddhist headquarters with sloping roofs; the cool astringent Zen compounds: each a river of history winding, serene and bloody, into the distant past.

At first the fabled city seemed impenetrable, hidden. The roofs were dull silver-gray tiles; the streets noisy, rude. The houses were natural wood, unpainted, seemingly drab. He sought vainly for loud beauty, something to reach out and announce itself. But by the third day the boundless, silent reverie of the ancient capital began to possess him.

> Bamboo shadows brush the stairs
> But no dust is stirred

He rarely saw foreigners—once a tourist couple at the Heian Shrine, on another occasion a missionary near Doshisa University. America's nightmare seemed far away: Johnson, Ruby, Oswald. He walked, and the walking became a penance. Occasionally he would see a woman from behind with long straight black hair and think of Su Lin. At Ryoan-ji Temple on a silent damp morning he sat before the sand garden at the foot of the ancient mud wall and let pain and loss drain from him, as if leeching a wound.

As America receded, Cross felt a weight lift off. California, for all its reclining luxuriance, masked a desperate corrosive tension—the urgency of the pleasure quest, the energy expended in too many smiles. Cross felt the relief of immersion in an old, harnessed world that aspired to nothing, in which the poles of life and death didn't strain so hard against each other—a world at ease with itself, resigned to the odds.

Finally Terhune's call had come that morning, a gruff, literate American Plains voice awakening him with the curt suggestion that they meet in a coffee bar downtown in an hour.

"Good luck," Ueda-san said when Cross had changed and stood ready to leave. "Give pleasant regards to Terhune-sensei." He bowed, pushed his glasses up on his nose, and smiled guilelessly.

Cross decided to walk; he took the path running along the Higashiyama foothills, parallel to the city and the river.

During the night the rain had turned into soft snow, muting the city, visiting an unearthly whitened morning silence upon its streets and lanes and temples. From the empty gravel lane, Cross looked up at the hills rising through mist behind the Temple of the Silver Pavilion. A woman in kimono with a paper umbrella passed, the sound of her wooden *geta* sandals crunching on the snow and gravel. He could hear the humming of his blood, the faraway sound of cars. Down either side of the path ran snow-topped wooden houses and shops. Damp gardens and smooth shiny rocks, the temple roofs and the pines, all seemed to blend for an instant, as in a painting dreamed—objective, designed, a pure crystallization of randomness, waiting to be discovered.

Walking on, Cross was overcome with a sense of age, a resonance with the earth before and after man, essentially undisturbed, as if he himself were for an instant the earth made conscious of itself—an unbroken organic tone, the pulse of the planet: slow, reflective, vegetable. It sang that knowledge for man is simplicity; and the slightest disturbance—the landing of a cherry blossom on a bed of pine needles, the ripple made by a dragonfly skimming the pond, the sudden unburdening of snow from a pine branch—punctures illusion like a blade through flesh.

Reaching Nanzen-ji, the old Zen compound, he chose a narrow lane that wound down the hill into the city. In the slim window of a teashop was a tiny scroll, white pebbles, a little bonsai—all so gray and weathered that one would hardly notice them on passing. Behind the rope screen two old men in kimono sampled teas; a woman brought fresh water and cups.

The city thickened into crowded blank streets of midday work rush. Passing a canal at Shinmonzen-dori, the antique sellers' street, Cross saw bright silks being washed in the water, rippling like carp. Turning onto Shijo-dori, the main street, he passed a shop with nothing but wooden combs, another with only colored ribbons.

A robed Zen monk, basket over his head and *shakohachi* in hand, weaved blindly across the street, treated by the crowd with no more or less deference than anyone else. Cross watched him collide with a pretty girl and drop his flute as the light changed.

Cross traversed Shijo bridge, his cheeks burning with the cold, and turned into a small tree-lined canal street, Kiyamachi-dori. Coffee bars of all descriptions ran down either side, some with signs in English: JOY STATION, TOP JAZZ, BIG SWING BAR, HAPPY BOX.

Where the street forked he found it: AZUKI ARTISTICAL TEAROOM. As he opened the door, the strains of Glenn Miller's "In the Mood" drifted out into the icy air. He ducked into a tiny low-ceilinged room with a few cramped tables and chairs, wood-paneled walls, a gas heater at full blast. A young couple lounged by the espresso machine; otherwise the place was empty. Cross jammed himself in at a tiny table and ordered coffee.

The music changed to Art Blakey's Jazz Messengers, then Roger Williams's "Autumn Leaves"; then as if to remind him of the season, "White Christmas." Cross gazed into his coffee, waiting.

"May your days be merry and bright . . ."

A sudden blast of wind made him look up. A bearded bearish shadow filled the doorway, eyes blazing like coals, blowing steam and beating mittened hands together.

"*Irrashaimase, Terhune-sensei.*" Welcome.

"*Konnichi wa.*" The door closed behind him.

Cross sat riveted as Terhune's eyes found him out.

"You came five thousand miles with no invitation, no hope." He glowered at Cross in the blue-tinged light of the coffee bar. "On a whim? You are mad."

Cross, finding no answer, gave none.

"What in hell did you expect to accomplish?"

Twenty-five years separated them. They were similar in height— one thick, dark, scarred with life; the other fair, lean. Though strangers, a recognition unexplainable by experience rose in the cramped foreign room, webbing the two Americans. Each struggled to deny it.

Terhune seemed offended by Cross's very presence. "The only reason I'm here is out of curiosity. I wanted to see a fool in the flesh."

Cross, trying to break Terhune's soft abusive patter, ventured the question whose answer he dreaded: "Where is she?"

Terhune stirred his coffee and glared. "How long did you know her?"

"Three days."

"You consider that love enough to justify this odyssey of yours?"

"She vanished suddenly. With no explanation."

Terhune spoke earnestly. "I wired you an explanation. I say it to you again. Give this up and return to where you came from. Nothing awaits you here but pain and frustration. Or worse."

"Is she here?"

Terhune stormed inwardly. Cross was new terrain the old addict labored to survey. He felt as if he were staring into a mirror of his own ancient hungers. "No," he said sharply.

"Can I believe you?"

"If you wish."

"Was she here?"

"A few months before you met her. On her way back from Hong Kong."

A Kirin came for Terhune, following upon the coffee. The waitress deferentially arranged the paper coaster.

"In your telegram you said Asia had reclaimed her. Then you must know where she is."

"That was why I advised you not to come."

Angrily Cross said, "Can't you just tell me where she is?"

"In Hong Kong, I suspect."

Terhune looked at Cross, seeing the hurt in his eyes. "There is nothing you can do, I assure you."

"Why did she leave San Francisco?"

"It may not have been her choice." Terhune studied Cross almost tenderly. No Lin affair was without meaning or consequence; this Cross was bent upon writing himself into the Lin history. This made it complicated.

How much does he know?

"What do you do back in America?"

"I was a medical student."

"And now?"

"As you see me."

"A wanderer."

"I'd hoped to be a writer once."

Terhune looked away, pained.

"I met her in a military hospital in Oakland. She was visiting a sailor, a friend of someone she had known who was killed off the coast of Vietnam."

"Yes. The one before you." Terhune watched Cross recoil. A mild sadism drove him on.

"We talked afterwards. She didn't want to see me again. Or said she didn't."

"But you couldn't get her out of your mind. Her face, her beauty."

Cross ignored the mockery. "I found out where she lived and followed her there."

"I knew she had met someone," Terhune murmured.

"Did she write you?"

He shook his head. "She was ready. It was a way to force her brother's hand."

"What do you mean?"

Terhune traced a ring with his beer bottle on the black Formica tabletop. *Then he knows nothing of the Lin business.*

"Just tell me if she's safe."

"In a manner of speaking."

"Do you have to be so damned cryptic?" Cross asked agitatedly.

"Go soft, man," Terhune rebuked. "You're in Asia. This American . . . bluntness will get you nowhere here."

Cross swallowed the rest of his coffee and looked past Terhune to the stained-glass door. "I need your help, Terhune."

"Chestnuts roasting on an open fire . . ." sang Nat King Cole. A young woman dressed in sunglasses and black leather sipped coffee and blew smoke rings at the next table.

Terhune said, "She was returned to Hong Kong by people acting on behalf of her family."

"Against her will?"

"Undoubtedly. I'm sure she was madly in love with you." He laughed.

"Then she was kidnapped."

"You could say that."

"Because of me?"

"Surely."

"Because I'm Caucasian?"

"Of course not. The family has been Eurasian for five generations. Content yourself with the idea that her love affair with you was unwelcome by her family at this time."

"She told me her father and mother are both dead."

"Her brother is quite alive and well."

Cross searched Terhune's rich, bearded face, rummaged among his dark words for hope. "You seem indifferent to this . . . crime," he said.

"In Asia, families have rights that transcend the law."

Cross felt desolate. He realized he knew nothing of her life, her circumstances, her background. All he had were three days in San Francisco, and her lingering imprint upon his senses.

"*Shikatta ga nai.*"

"What?"

"It can't be helped." Terhune nodded. "Accept the mystery."

"You're my only hope. There are a million Lins in China."

Terhune called to the waitress, fishing in his pocket for a pair of hundred-yen bills.

When she brought back change Cross tried, *Arigatō gozaimasu.*

"Execrable," Terhune said as they stood to go. "You should do something about your Japanese."

It had stopped snowing. They walked down an alley of Pontocho in the afternoon. The river below was a silver torrent glimpsed through bamboo struts and slats and cracks between the buildings. An old man in kimono and sandals, seemingly oblivious to the cold, drew slowly on a cigarette while his dachshund defecated. A *maiko,* an apprentice geisha, scuffled by in tiny steps, like a woman imitating a man imitating a woman, her neck bared.

"When you called three days ago," Terhune said, "I was here. I didn't want to see you. I was hoping you'd give up and go away."

Cross looked at him angrily.

"Asia is another world. If you wish to operate here, you must realize this."

Cross jammed his hands in his pockets against the chill and stayed with Terhune as he angled into a tiny alley full of inscrutable signs.

"How do you find Kyoto?"

"Elusive," Cross said. "Nothing stands out."

"It's internal. Shrines are built concentrically, with impenetrable centers. My landlady, Ichida-san, the silk merchant, entertains me in the outermost room, right next to the shoes and the umbrellas. And I am *daisensei,* an illustrious foreign professor who has been here ten years. But I accept that, you see. To go further is to turn in your passport."

A woman in a white apron emerged from a pale wood sliding door and sloshed a bucket of water in front of them.

"There are three hundred foreigners in this city of two million. Most are missionaries. The rest are teachers, exiles, poets. We see each other rarely. One lives entirely among Asians, day in and day out. Near here is the Chinese section, across town the Korean. Down there, below the train station, is the *eta* section."

"*Eta?*"

"Untouchables."

The day was darkening early with fresh snow clouds as they emerged abruptly on Kawaramachi, the clattering north-south boulevard. They were looking in the window of a gaudy shop full of hundreds of wooden dolls, their smooth wooden heads paintbrushed with eyes, eyebrows, button mouths.

"Kokeshi dolls. Women use them to masturbate while their men are out with geishas."

They waited at the edge of the curb for the light to change.

"How do you know she's in Hong Kong?" Cross asked.

He smiled wearily. "Asia is my domain. I'm a Chinese scholar. I have many contacts."

They crossed Kawaramachi and entered a wide pedestrian arcade.

"I've known her since she was quite young," Terhune said. "You see, I was her mother's lover."

The arcade swung left. They continued down a small crowded street fronted by two-story buildings. Cross tried to hang on to Terhune's revelations as they pushed through the expressionless crowds.

"We, so hung up on public decorum and private license, miss everything here, where people dress up *to go home.*" He laughed. "Finding Asia is like running your hand along a wall in the dark. And this is only the beginning. Beyond lie China, Tibet . . . You see, the Asian, like the Arab, is allowed to dream. So they don't fear death as we, always snapping ourselves awake with the latest urgent secular system."

They wandered into a decrepit temple, its grounds covered with garbage and rotting pools, industrial concerns of the city pressing up against the cement retaining walls on every side. The faces of the icons were eaten away beyond recognition; one old lady in black knelt before an altar. Few candles were lit, signifying the dearth of donations. A fifty-cc Suzuki was parked in front of a Buddha.

A muttering shaven-headed priest invited them inside. He carried a flashlight with an orange glow so faint that they stumbled over each other. He guided them deep inside, where dozens of gilt statues of the Japanese Kwannon, Goddess of Mercy, each with a different expression, sat unwatched in the shadows. They passed by great carved animals, oxen and carp, clouded in incense.

Before a murky altar, Terhune clapped three times, threw a coin, and bowed.

They emerged into a small courtyard where children sat at tables writing characters with brush and ink. A tiny girl in kimono made bold strokes on a large sheet of rice paper. She dipped the brush and drew the character in tall strokes. Then she crumpled the paper, threw it into a hibachi, and began again.

Terhune whispered, "You have slid off the crest of the wave of Now."

They were before a dusty glass case looking at a picture of Admiral Perry standing beneath loaded cannons on the prow of his ship, handing the Japanese representative a watch.

"There's the whole story," Terhune said. "That watch."

They followed the doddering priest across the grounds, feet crunching on gravel.

"But it really began long before that—the decline of joy, the formalization of the senses. These days, along Muromachi-dori, where thirteenth-century poets listened to incense and Genji crept by moonlight, a middle-class inscrutability prevails. But the wood and the gravel, the irregularities in the roofs, speak of lingering ghosts, of an Asia before the decline, before the advent of the *yen*."

"*Yen*," Cross whispered, thinking Terhune was referring to the Japanese currency. Terhune's eyes blazed. The wizened priest was staring open-mouthed at the unexpected monologue of the large *gaijin*, foreigner.

"Now the festivals, the *odoris*, are wind through bamboo—slow hand and arm gestures, gentle mime, protracted intonation. Jubilation is unknown here. And the sensuality, though it is real, is like a smooth stone, like the tidal insinuation of reeds in water." Terhune paused and adopted a stylized geisha pose. "Desire is a fully clothed girl, kimono appetizingly hitched back at the powdered nape of the neck, standing in sultry abandon, pulling at a brightly colored handkerchief with her teeth, choking back a sigh. Velvet shadows of repression, you see." He chuckled. "The handkerchief is held between the teeth during fucking so the woman won't make unseemly sounds. As the man is removing his cock she uses the cloth to clean it."

Cross, ensnarled in ancient visions he didn't wish to entertain, struggled to hold on to the present. They had left the temple by the rear entrance and were standing on the corner of Oike-dori, another busy cross street.

"Nestled here in the cranny of the feminine principle, like a Lilliputian in an ancient teacup, I hold up the smooth lacquered bowl of antiquity for inspection, running my hands around its worn, frictionless surface, lost in the fathomless dream of Asia . . ."

Traffic honked as Terhune stood on the curb orating.

"I am an exile," he roared. "An Asian scholar all but banned from Asia. Kyoto is my last stand." He stared at Cross. "Do you understand, American?"

Terhune moved back into the shadow of a building. His face was craggy, intense, his eyes mad. "Fool. The woman you fell in love with is the heiress to the biggest opium fortune in the world."

Cross spent the late afternoon in fitful tossing half-sleep on his futon at the Shiraku-so Inn, trying to absorb Terhune's cryptic pronouncements. Enigmas unknotted in his mind, spooling him back to Europe, Bébé Spiritu, the Corsicans—all the way to Tangier. Su Lin's behavior—her initial unwillingness to see him, her refusal to discuss her family or past, her nervousness through their days together—shaded, then reshaded, until Cross felt the icy embrace of madness. Su Lin, opium. Did it make anything different? Or everything?

A half-dream of the car outside Oak Knoll Hospital and the man who looked like Gurdjieff caused him to bolt awake.

Terhune came for him again in early evening. A shiny black taxi took them through the night to the entrance to a temple south of the train station, up against the mountain. They sat cross-legged and shoeless on the broad tatami floor of a temple room heated by a large hibachi. The painted shoji had been pulled back to reveal a rock, sand, and bonsai garden stacked against the hillside, designed with the care of a painting. A full moon rose over the mountain's rim as if on command.

A small red lacquer table and hot sake separated them. Cross sipped, gazing from the windowless room at pines pressed flat against the moon. Filtered lantern light laid calligraphic patterns on wooden pillars.

Reminscences of ginger circled slowly and settled in his head like smoke in a sealed room. Somewhere close behind him a gong sounded, exploding softly inside his stomach and pulsing outward in concentric circles. The sake burst in his nose as the steam from the hibachi seemed to brush tiny wind chimes somewhere in the garden. He looked at the woman who had bent to serve them. Behind her stiff black geisha hair and white powdered face the personality had dispersed, and Cross found himself gazing at a timeless mask of Noh rising through the steam like a genie from a lamp. An odorless, colorless hiatus—then suddenly the gong, the ginger, the wind chimes, the sake, and the full apparition of Su Lin flooded in, overwhelming him with a painful longing.

The servant was demurely adjusting the hem of her kimono. Cross desired her, but with a desire less of the genitals than of his whole being, a longing for fusion, oblivion, synesthetic annihilation—closer, he thought, to what he imagined the female sense of desire to be.

"You were seeing Su Lin?" Terhune was saying. "Or all women, perhaps? Or feeling like a woman? Yes, Asia has that effect."

She padded silently across the tatami toward them again with a plate stacked with thin slices of red meat and vegetables of many colors. She knelt and, gently stirring the coals, began to cook their meal.

"Interesting that you met in a hospital," Terhune said. "She wanted to be a doctor once, you know."

"I didn't." Pieces of meat seemed to dissolve in Cross's mouth.

"Her father wouldn't give her the money. After she went to Alabama with those freedom riders he kept her on a short leash." He laughed. "Full of ideals. All the more unfortunate for her. She is good at art, I understand. Have you seen her paintings?"

"Yes. They're extraordinary." Cross replaced his chopsticks on the table. "Tell me about her family."

"Not now."

"Then at least tell me . . ."

"What?"

"Does she smoke?"

Terhune burst out laughing. "Opium? Don't be ridiculous. She despises the drug. It's why she stayed in San Francisco. And why she was taken back."

"I hardly know her," Cross muttered.

"But you are in love with her. You needn't feel betrayed. She is . . . fabulous."

Cross stared at Terhune. "You love her too."

Terhune's eyes moved away to the garden. "Metaphorically." He looked up beneath dark eyebrows. "I loved her mother."

Braised scallions appeared on their plates and sat untouched. "Are we competitors, then? Is that why you won't help me?"

Terhune looked off into the moonlit pond. "I am not for her. I've learned to abstract many things, to reduce my desires."

Cross understood Terhune to be confessing addiction.

"Yes. I have been dismissed by opium, after many failures. One must be cured not of opium, I'm afraid, but of intelligence."

The moon had disappeared above the temple roof; the waitress had disappeared. Only the hibachi coals remained, glowing softly.

"I have only kept the works I wrote as a prisoner."

"Its influence on your art is that extreme?"

Terhune shifted, leaned back on his elbows, and lit a Japanese cigarette; its brand name was Peace.

"All children possess the magic power of being able to change themselves into what they wish. Poets, in whom childhood is prolonged, suffer a great deal when they lose this power. This is undoubtedly one of the reasons that drive the poet to use opium."

Cross gazed at Terhune, transfixed.

"You want me to help you get to Su Lin. I cannot. And even if I were foolish enough to think I could, I would have to take you to Hong Kong myself. If I did, I would smoke again, and I would die. Don't ask me to explain."

"You're my only hope."

Terhune studied Cross. "Yes, you have the mark," he said. "You could befriend the mud. I see that is so. You must watch yourself. Something in you strains against the bonds of ordinary experience. You must push yourself to extremity."

Cross tried to look away, but Terhune bore in upon him. "Can you defend yourself? Can you fight?"

"Not well."

"I would have to teach you to use my short sword. Ah, it is foolish, quixotic to even talk of it."

Cross waited, saying nothing.

"Do you have any money?"

"A few thousand yen."

"I could get you a room above the coffee shop. The Azuki Artistical Tearoom. If you can stand Glenn Miller."

Cross's heart raced with wild hope.

"I promise nothing, do you understand? I'll try and reach her brother. I'll offer my advice. It's possible he could use it now. He's in far over his head. You see, I know more about his family than anyone alive. Perhaps he needs a counterbalance, someone in whom he can confide. But I warn you, Cross, there is little hope."

"Is there some kind of work I can do here?"

"Teach English. The demand exceeds the supply. I'll get you jobs. And of course you must learn what you are up against. You may change your mind."

"What if you have no luck with her brother?"

Terhune drew himself up and shook the last drop of sake from the cup. *"Shikatta ga nai."*

"It can't be helped."

"There, you see?" Terhune said as the last coal went out. "You are becoming Asian."

31

Alec Potter, camphor still exuding faintly from his nether parts, walked down the Star Ferry terminal ramp into Central. Rickshaw drivers squatted crinkled and toothless at the entrance along Statue Square in pajamas and straw hats before their shiny red and black chariots, looking warily up at the dark clouds wreathing the Peak. Potter crossed the square to the corner of Des Voeux and Ice House Street and paused before the commanding triple edifices rising like great Monopoly pieces across the street.

In the middle stood the Hong Kong Crown Bank, the rock upon which the island colony was founded after the Opium War of 1842 had legitimized the poppy trade. *Dieu et Mon Droit,* proclaimed the leonine crest above its entrance, the royal emblem of Hong Kong. To its right stood the Standard Chartered Bank, Cecil Rhodes's nineteenth-century looting bin. The third structure on the left, slightly taller than the other two and separated from the Crown Bank by a tiny street, was the Bank of China, where Peking played its masked double game.

Potter, being American, always regarded Britain's dregs of empire with a certain ridicule; but in Hong Kong, British influence remained potent, owing in great measure to the bank before him, and Whitehall's own desperate reasons for wishing to see the Fragrant Harbour flourish again off the *yen* as in the glory days.

A narrow green double-decker trolley, bandaged in advertising graffiti and swollen with passengers, stopped in front of him, blocking his view. When it had passed, Potter crossed the street and bore left. Against a grooved marble pillar of the Bank of China squatted a beggar woman, hand outstretched in the supplicant's eternal frozen gesture, rags around her back supporting the splotched, lolling moonface of an infant. Potter passed on.

The tiny street between the two banks brought him to the rear entrance of the new Hong Kong Hilton, set into the foothill. Nodding to the Sikh in red coat and jodhpurs who greeted the automobiles, he entered through automatic doors. The escalator rise to the main lobby allowed Potter to briefly inhale the air-conditioned, odorless ambiance of the American hotel abroad—the beige decor and drab sterilized wide spaces, the monotone rugs, the flat diction his people had seeded the postwar planet with in endless augmentation. He went out the front door onto Garden Road.

It was a short upward climb along the sidewalk, the Peak rising before him in a halo of clouds and mist. He passed St. John's Cathedral on his right, dark and staid, fortress of Episcopal dreams, even more Gothic and drear in the spreading gloom as clouds descended like great parachutes from the Peak. Drops of rain speckled the pavement. Looking down wooded, winding Albert Road, he paused to marvel at a banyan tree growing horizontally out of a government building wall, its roots spread not down but along the wall face. There seemed to be no source of nourishment for the tree but the cement. Potter was thinking that the banyan was like Hong Kong: twisted life jutting from inhospitable rock.

Subtropical planting layered the steep street entrance of the U.S. Consulate. It was a cold, ungenerous structure, perched high on its built-up lot behind impenetrable charcoal-tinted windows, its closed-circuit camera mounted on the corner of the building scanning Potter as he climbed the stairs from the street, the sullen white enamel lip of a radar dish tilting on the roof.

A sign was posted in English and Chinese on the wall next to the glass and steel double-door entry: ONLY CONSULAR SECTION CLIENTS

WILL BE ADMITTED IN THE CONSULAR SECTION. ALL HANDBAGS, BRIEF-
CASES, AND PARCELS WILL BE EXAMINED. NO CAMERA OR SOUND RECORD-
ING DEVICES PERMITTED WITHOUT PRIOR PERMISSION. As Potter pushed
a door inward a thick-necked Marine on guard in a sentry box
brought his rifle up.

We rule by fear, thought Potter. Thank God I'm one of us.

"You' business, sah?"

An officious older Chinese in Western clothes blocked his way.
Potter stared into the milky striations of the smoked-glass panes
awaiting his clearance, aware again of the burning in his loins and
the effluvial Tiger's Balm wafting up. What had seemed a casual
dose, even a collegiate badge of honor, lingered, discoloring Potter's
golden recollections of the night of lust at the Snow Leopard Inn,
raising qualms about the men whose case he had come here to plead
before the American Consul-General.

Fletcher Doody strode the carpet, rehearsing comportment. The announcement of Potter's arrival made him unaccountably nervous;
the lateness added an edge of fury he must suppress. He finally settled upon a stance behind his desk as if interrupted while working,
knuckles placed resolutely on the blotter.

Alec Potter strode in smiling, a model of youth and confidence,
undaunted by the blotches of rain upon his collar, brushing back a
fetching brown curl plastered to his forehead. Fletch Doody stiffened and extended his large hand across the desk.

"Consul."

"Potter."

Alec Potter fleetingly registered his own relaxation at not having
blurted what he had feared all the way from Laos he might say at
this moment: Howdy, Doody.

"Sorry I'm late. The plane was delayed at Wattay."

They sat across from each other. Potter lit a Kent and looked beyond Doody to the tall window facing Lower Albert Street. The
rain had resumed, pelting the glass. Doody was fooling with a
humidor on his desk and a thin pipe with a perforated metal shaft
his wife Joyce had given him for Christmas.

"Well, here I am." Potter threw his palms up, all boyish pizazz.
Consul Doody considered him bleakly, pissed off anew by Potter's
tossed, insufficient apology for being late.

"It's a good thing you came. I would have called you in if you hadn't." He stuffed the pipe with Skol. "So what's cooking out there? And remember, go slow. I'm not strong on your turf."

"First off, Consul, our tri-border programs are in danger."

"Translate."

"Of course we know the trade must eventually be abolished, but it's been policy not to effect the changeover until the entire area has been secured."

Potter had begun feeding Doody his lines.

"Until the locals are propped back up."

"Exactly. And the safety of the Triangle, Consul, rests upon the loyalty of the tribesmen."

Doody took his pipe out of his mouth. "Tell me something I don't know, Potter."

Doody always tried to begin on a hard tack, a questionable stratagem, as he could seldom keep it up. It seemed to be his fate to see meetings slip away from him. Potter on his side was sticking with good form, throwing in the "Consuls," even essaying a "sir," wondering if it was laying it on too thick.

"The problem is with the Chinese, sir. They're making our intelligence and pacification programs difficult."

"Does this have something to do with the paucity of Intel-Coms from your area lately? Washington's antsy. In fact, I think they have in mind sending you back for more training."

"You must be thinking of someone else, sir. I'm not Company. I'm independent."

"A distinction lost on Washington. They consider you in-house. Your whole family, all the way back to your grandfather. But go on."

Potter shifted uncomfortably in his chair. As the months had passed and he was drawn further into American designs in the Triangle, he had become increasingly touchy on the subject of his independence; what this concept would even mean in the context of escalation bothered him. Consul Doody tamped his pipe, which had gone out, and assumed an attitude of waiting.

"Traditionally, sir," Potter began, "the trade has been divided among the national monopolies, the local entrepreneurs, the Chinese, and the Corsicans."

"Trade," Doody muttered.

"Well, opium, sir." Potter crossed his legs and balanced an ashtray on his knee. "The market has been primarily local—Southeast Asia, that is, and I'm including Hong Kong—with a bit passing from the Corsicans on to Marseilles. But recent events have destabilized the area."

"How so?"

"First off, Ngo Dinh Nhu was a silent partner in Air Laos Commerciale, a Corsican charter airline."

Glib fucker, Doody thought. "Interpol briefs, Potter." He tapped his knuckles on a pile of folders on the desk. "The new Bébé Spiritu syndicate of Marseilles. The recent interruption of the Turkish supply threatens their empire. The dwarf has a shot at becoming a big man by increasing his Asia supply lines. We have that, Potter. We have that."

Okay, Potter thought. "It seems, sir, that the Chinese are trying to force the Corsicans out of the Asian traffic once and for all. The Corsicans are upset. They feel they're being treated shabbily, being offered no protection from the Chinese. In fact they think CIA has a tacit deal with the Chinese. They think the Company owes them something from Marseilles dock days, the strikebreaking, the Allied invasions."

"That's really not our problem at this juncture, is it, Potter? I mean we've got a little war to win out here."

"There are other elements, Consul. The hill tribes are worried. If the Corsicans are forced out, they can't get their crop to market. If the tribes can't sell, they'll defect to the Pathet Lao. Same situation in northern Thailand. I imagine Washington wouldn't be happy."

"Why can't the tribes just sell to the Chinese?"

"The Corsicans have planes to go up and get it. The Chinese don't."

Potter figured Doody had to know that Civil Air Transport had plans to fill the vacuum and in fact had already begun flying opium out for the Chinese; but he wanted to hear the Consul say it.

Consul-General Doody hated talking about drugs in his office. But the subject was seldom far away in serious Asia discussions. Even he knew that one in every forty residents of Hong Kong was an addict, a problem the British Governor had alluded to that very day over lunch at Jimmy's. The whole subject was too Terry and the Pirates for Doody; he had never seen a drug in his life that didn't come in a tablet. And he resented deeply being tutored in the subject by the young Harvard hustler sitting across from him, come East with his Fairbanks and Reischauer and Edgar Snow to gall and confuse.

"Did you take this up with the embassies in Vientiane and Bangkok?"

"Yes, Consul. But it's essentially a Chinese problem, you see, and points back to here."

"How so? What Chinese are we talking about?"

"First off, the KMT, the Nationalist Chinese Fifth Army. The ones who protect the caravans. They've been there since 1949. They also help us with our penetrations into Yunnan. But the opium merchants throughout Asia are all Chinese too. Chiu Chao. The theory is that they take orders from here."

"We're not in the theory business, Potter. Do you know this for a fact?"

"Yes. Well, no, sir. I infer it heavily."

"From whom?"

"Rumor in the area. I speak the dialects, you know. Up around Long Tieng there is a lot of activity these days."

"What kind?"

"On one side you have the Laotian government forces, commanded by Rattikone. They're heavily into the trade."

"He's our man, isn't he?"

"Yes, entirely financed by us. He's trying to tax the Chinese to put pressure on the opium markets and fight the Corsicans too."

"Who else?"

"There's the Meo general Vang Pao's mercenary army in Long Tieng, also dealing in opium. We finance him too. The Geneva Agreements outlawed fighting in Laos last year, but Vang Pao's secret army is still going at the Pathet Lao. And I know of at least eight Green Beret teams operating there."

"I know."

"Then you have the Corsican gangsters around the Plain of Jars. And the Chinese putting in heroin labs along the Mekong. So everyone is pretty cozy."

"Is it true about the labs?"

"Five to date, Consul. They used to ship the morphine base to Hong Kong and process it here. Now they fly their master chemists out from Hong Kong to work the new labs. Vang Pao is jealous. Rattikone wants to tax them. There may be fighting."

"Two-bit opium wars." Consul Doody coughed. "Why are the Chinese doing this? Who do they sell to?"

"In the past it was mostly local. But the Chinese must have bigger plans. The speculation is that they want to go international, challenge Marseilles for the world trade, which is to say the U.S. market. They're highly organized and take orders from here, presumably."

"Can you name these labs? Point them out on a map?"

"Sure. I can take you there if you want."

Doody dropped his pipe in his ashtray and rubbed his long neck wearily. "So what's the implication here, Potter?"

"As I see it, the Corsicans are a counterforce. Destroy them and the trade will break out of the Triangle. First through the Triads here. Then wherever in the world there are Chinese communities. The target will be America. The Chinese will succeed Luciano. Illegal opiates will flood America. And not just Harlem."

Doody swiveled slowly in his chair, trying to decide what line to take. "So the Chinese and Corsicans are enemies," he said finally.

"It's never that simple, sir. Even now Chinese merchants in Muyong Sing and Ban Houei Sai act as brokers for the Corsican charter airlines. But the Chinese are on the move. And, Consul, there is another speculation. That they're planning to sell to our troops."

"Ridiculous. They wouldn't dare. What do you think these Nationalist Chinese are? They're our Allies. We're here for *them*. We've been here for twenty-five years for Chiang Kai-shek and the rest of them."

Potter wondered if Doody was just putting on for him. "Why else would they suddenly begin locating labs there, Consul?"

Consul Doody rose and walked to the frosted black window facing over the city. The rain laid a steady patter on the bulletproof glass.

"The Corsicans, Consul, see themselves as a lever, the antidote to this development. Also I think you have to face the fact that if the Corsicans' backs are to the wall they can cause flak in Washington. They're quite unscrupulous."

"What on earth do you mean?"

"It's common knowledge that Americans have been into the trade in the tri-border region since Burma Road days. Strictly unofficial, the usual adventurers and mercenaries. But now you have Air America planes openly shuttling the stuff. The Corsicans could give names of Green Berets, airline pilots, even Embassy people to Congress, to the press. Everybody knows each other in the Triangle, sir."

"Christ." Doody began pacing before the window. "Who are these Asian Corsicans anyway?"

"There are two main Corsican gangs here in Asia," Potter went on. "One out of Bangkok, the other out of Vientiane. They came out with the French originally. Stayed on after Dien Bien Phu. Colorful guys. Tough. Good fliers. Sometimes they fight each other. They've always maintained contact with Marseilles and supplied them with morphine base, though very little compared to the Golden Crescent fields. They had enough political power until the Diem killing."

Doody sped up his lope, measuring off the wall-to-wall carpet, hands locked behind his back. "Go on."

"General Ky is in the Chiu Chao pocket. Vang Pao and the Laotian Royal House, all the way up to Prince Sopsaisana, take opium squeeze. Same in Thailand. It's the only thing that keeps them alive. Take opium away, Consul, and you give the Golden Triangle to Ho and the Pathet Lao. There go Vietnam, Laos, Cambodia. Not in years. Months."

"What about the Reds?"

"There's no opium in Mainland China to speak of. Even our cross-border missions into Yunnan find little. It's been suppressed. To them, opium is synonymous with white imperialism."

It was growing dark outside. Doody turned and glared at Potter. "God. You make it sound as if we're in Vietnam to keep the opium flowing."

Potter looked up at the Consul. "I've heard Chinese put it that way, sir."

"Obscene, obscene," muttered Doody.

"Opium was a present to us from the British in 1945. It's in the colonial woof and warp of things. It pays for our adventures, keeps our allies afloat and Hong Kong's banks solvent. It's Asia's true currency. A hot potato, Consul, but we can't drop it now. As I see it, opium is inseparable from America's fate."

Doody took a deep breath and turned to the window. "You're sitting here in my office telling me that we should help the opium trade."

"We already do, Consul. If we can recognize that, maybe we can begin to control events and get somewhere."

"How?"

"Well, sir, by putting pressure upon the Chinese."

"Through whom?"

"Through the people who call the shots from here. That's one of the reasons I came, Consul. To find out about the Hong Kong side."

"You think the Golden Triangle networks are run from here."

"I know it, sir." Potter paused before moving on, then said, "Tell me about the Eurasian Harry Lin."

"Harry Lin was a prominent Hong Kong businessman. He was killed last summer at his seventieth birthday party. I was there."

"Who did it?"

"Some Chinese gang, apparently."

"Why?"

Consul Doody turned back from the window. "I don't think anybody really knows."

I may know, Potter thought. I could use that.

"There's another one called Chen," Potter said. "Left-Hand Chen."

"The Lin comprador." Doody was looking at him suspiciously. "What are you getting at? Why should that concern us? What's the American interest in all this?"

"Keeping Southeast Asia in our camp. Winning the war."

Consul Doody grasped his arms, shivering under the air conditioning. "Potter, don't you realize I'm under pressure from Washington to knock out the trade altogether? There was the Senate junket to Laos. Kennedy wanted it killed. Now they're rabid after the Valachi business. They're not going to burn up the Turkish fields just to have it spread here." He came back to his desk and peered down earnestly at Potter. "They've got crop conversion programs on the drawing boards. A whole package for each Southeast Asian government. Abolition of the dens and conversion to rice, or else no more arms. Washington's ready to roll it up. I'm going back next week to testify before six different committees. They'll do what I suggest. Johnson has come out for abolition. They want an end to the drug problem at home. And you're telling me we should promote it so you hustlers out there can get rich. Wise up, Potter. You're going against the tides."

As Doody turned back toward the window, Alec Potter felt uneasily exposed. He had the chilling thought that he had underestimated the Consul, that he was not the fool Gérard had suggested, merely an awkward man.

Fletcher Doody became a tall, bent silhouette pacing before his darkened windowpane, thinking.

Potter doesn't know all the implications. He's simply the smiling young worm of fate. He doesn't know that fifty thousand more troops are on their way. If the opiates are allowed to flow, what will happen when they arrive?

But what if Potter's preposterous thesis is right? America would stand to lose Asia. A shuddering thought. Would I be held responsible? What then of Big Fletch and Joyce, the kids, the new job?

He looked at the Lane Crawford packages stacked in the corner, adding up the bill.

I've read about the stuff. White powder. Anslinger's reports. First it's the reefers. Then the hard stuff. It's a damned plague, sweeping them all under. It wouldn't just be the Negroes this time.

I can end it with my testimony in Washington, put the nail in the coffin. Conversion crops for arms. Everybody will be happy, except the Potters and the other entrepreneurs.

But what about our aims here?

Steady, boy.

These young American entrepreneurs run fast. I could be walked over. Is Potter trying to bribe me? Or just educate me?

He looked at Potter's reflection in the bulletproof glass.

One must be reasonable. It's basically a matter of a few pesky senators. Soon that would blow over and they could get on with the war.

What of our troops?

Theoretical. A ways off. One bridge at a time.

Doody turned back to Potter.

This is it. The big thirty-foot jump shot at the buzzer. And I've got the ball.

"Potter," Consul Doody said suddenly. "You're backing the wrong horse."

Alec Potter felt a knot of alarm in his stomach.

"Do you get me?" Consul Doody walked the room, his fists

clenched. "When you come here it is to be in an attitude of humility, patriotism. Not pleading the Corsican interest. Who the hell are the Corsicans to us? How many are there? There are *one billion* Chinese."

He stopped and glared at Potter. "We can roll you up like a carpet. All you hustlers making fortunes out there and trading information for money, while guys like me have to get by on . . ." Consul Doody walked to the side of the room facing the Peak, his arms flapping.

Potter felt a wave of relief and relaxed in his chair. He had thought Doody was going to pull out, leave him exposed.

Is Doody asking for squeeze?

No, thought Potter. His squeeze is anti-Communism. He's a man who lives in terror of the other side. All you have to do is say "Commie." Doody takes the ultimate squeeze. He's American.

Watching Consul Doody blow steam, Potter grew more comfortable. The entrepreneur was as much a part of the neocolonial landscape as the minister, the military adviser, the diplomat. Only Communists could dream of an Asia without Alec Potter.

"What do you want out of this, Potter?" Doody asked suddenly.

"The loyalty of the tribesmen to the Americans. Not to see three generations of work go down the drain."

"Cut the bullshit. What do *you* want?"

Potter had come into the meeting seeking support for the Corsican interest against the Chinese in exchange for the $10,000 from Gérard. Now, watching Consul Doody's capitulation to realpolitik, greater vistas opened in his mind. To hell with Gérard's cheap bribes and VD. Doody was right; he was backing the wrong horse. *If I could cut a deal with the Chinese . . .*

"Consul, I want to meet the Chinese who run the operations from here. If I know the players, perhaps I can ensure that the game goes well."

"In whose interest?"

"Ours. Of course." Alec Potter gave a smug smile.

Consul Doody, recalling the assassination at the banquet, had begun to have parallel thoughts during the course of the conversation about the Lin family. An idea was forming in his head to send Potter in as a decoy.

Doody reached in his pocket and pulled out a private telephone book. With furious drama he scribbled a name and a number and handed it to Potter. "There's someone I want you to meet."

Potter stiffened as he read it. "Peter Lin," he whispered. "My God."

"The son of Harry Lin. What? You look pale."

Alec Potter looked up, stunned. "So it *is* him."

"You know him? All the better. He's becoming an important person in Asia."

Potter's mind was racing out of control. Was Doody telling him that Peter Lin was *it,* the opium taipan?

Is Doody springing some sort of trap on me?

Potter felt all his certainty ebb. Doody began to appear wily, viperish.

God, I was bad to Peter Lin at Harvard, very bad. Who would have dreamed we'd meet again in Asia, and under these circumstances?

"Undoubtedly you'll meet his comprador as well. Chen Po-chi is considered one of the most knowledgeable Chinese in Hong Kong."

Alec Potter was remembering something else now, something that made his frown dissolve. "Peter Lin has a sister, doesn't he?"

"Yes."

"Beautiful."

"Very."

"Is she here?"

"As a matter of fact I understand she returned only a few days ago."

Potter remembered her, young and fiercely bright, down for the weekend to visit her brother. Oh, he had erred that night, putting Peter Lin down, then going for Su Lin up against the Thunderbird; it was beyond hoping that he would have forgotten.

But Potter had never forgotten her. In fact his fantasies of women had shaped around her. The idea that she was nearby quickened his blood.

Damn. I will salvage something out of this unholy episode. If I can somehow get through Peter Lin.

"Report back to me after you've seen him," Consul Doody was saying. "I want to know your impressions."

Potter looked up at Doody, who was squeezing his own hands in some private agitation. Potter knew that Doody had agreed to play the opium card in Washington and would say the right things.

But what role did he have in mind for Potter?

The Consul was offering his hand. Potter rose and took it numbly.

"Remember," Fletch Doody said. "You're on my leash while you're in Hong Kong."

"Yes, sir."

When he had seen Potter out the door, Consul-General Doody turned back to his room. He went and stood by the window, shuddering.

"I can bring the trade down with a word," he whispered. "And I won't." Doody leaned his forehead against the tinted security glass.

But one day they'll thank me. One day the Doody name will make history's All-Star team.

Feeling better, he went to the closet. On the inside of the door was a tiny toy netting hanging from a wire rim basket. He picked up a little yellow foam rubber ball from the floor.

Fletch Doody, Dartmouth '47, feinted, dropped behind his desk, and sent the rubber missile on its arc through the office air.

Swish.

32

Left-Hand Chen seemed to take some peculiar delight in telling how Kowloon got its name; perhaps it pleased his anti-Manchu sentiments.

"It is said that a boy emperor and his people were driven south to this peninsula by Mongol invaders. The boy noticed there were eight hills." Chen daintily returned a crustless white triangle of ham sandwich—he ate like a bird—to its china plate. "He called them the Eight Dragons. A servant pointed out that an emperor is considered to be a dragon also. Eight hills plus boy emperor: *Gau-lung,* or Nine Dragons. The British somehow managed to work that around to Kowloon."

Su Lin could never tell if Chen liked the British or not; at the moment she didn't care. She stared into the rusty pool of her Lipton's, turning the spoon. A reflection snatched in a glass told her she must have lost ten pounds; her knuckles jutted from her hand like the Kowloon hills of which Chen spoke. On her left wrist was a trace of the scar from her mother's blade that first night in the bath before pulling back, electing defiance as her weapon.

"Though part of the mainland, Kowloon is politically British soil, ceded to them in 1860 during the time of the Opium Wars."

She gazed dolefully up at the high chandeliers, avoiding Peter's hysteria-tinged smile. Sound lazed like a cloud of smoke through the hallowed central room of the old Peninsula Hotel as Chen regaled them over lunch, on their way to the Lin Family Orphanage ground-breaking ceremony. Pale early afternoon light spilled on crystal and silver, backlighting coiffures. The four-hour daily water quota, still in effect, had brought bottles of Schweppes onto the tables; even the grand old terminus hotel, hymn to privilege, couldn't be bought on the subject of the precious water.

Su Lin took in the European shops—Gucci, Celine, Louis Vuitton—at either end of the lobby and up the stairs off the interior balcony, lightly festooned for Christmas; she had read in the *Post* that the day before Triad hoods had heisted a cool $15 million HK from a jewelry store on the mezzanine. Through massive windows Su Lin looked upon the street running up from the ferry, past the clock tower, and across the bay to Hong Kong's stacked metal columns and hunched Peak. Over the roofs of the hotel's fleet of matching dark green Rollses in the circular driveway, she could see but not hear a blind woman on a blanket in rags and brightly colored socks, her face like a melon left out too long, playing a banjo, pitching to the brisk Saturday afternoon crowd streaming along Salisbury Road.

"So Kowloon," Chen went on, "became the place where the British kept their mistresses, and this hotel where people embarked for the great train to Canton, or on to Moscow and London."

Peter nodded dully, following the moiré undulation of stocking seams on a blonde slinking up the mezzanine stairs. Buzz of conversation, driftings in the dead air. The Beatles were coming to Hong Kong, a bobbed lassie squealed at the next table to elder indifference. An Anglican priest sitting with two old birds found Macao's gambling casinos typically papist, censorious. Ill-bred American troops tearing up Wanchai, the buzz went: Doesn't it seem like there are so many more than last year?

Su Lin had come to the Peninsula when she was small, in pinafore and patent-leather shoes, with a face that didn't quite click with either team as her father dined some chunky local Swatownese with too many rings on his fingers, or buttered up some egret-eyed Englishman. Now, knowing of his affairs filled out what the child had sensed—that the Colony was a purgatorial place where people met to service each other's basest desires. She sat in silence, burning with the humiliation of re-entry and her new subjugation.

Peter grabbed a pastry from a tray, slurping a Scotch and Coke at the same time. Left-Hand Chen, who had always rebuked Harry Lin for sending his children to American rather than British schools, balefully watched his new protégé-cum-master wolf down the éclair. The light shifted outside, deepening as a sun unseen to the west clouded over, throwing up their image in the glass.

Su Lin saw herself behind black plastic sunglasses, lips flared red and unusually large against the sunken cheeks, imprisoned in the same black purse and dress she had worn to Father's seventieth: her new ghost visage. Someone had brought her a pair of red heels and a carton full of hose procured out the back door of a factory in Western district. She was a ward now, like her mother. So this is what happened to Winny. Here, a woman's dissolution wouldn't raise an eyebrow; nobody would remark a crumbling wife or be rude enough to bring it up if they did. Wives were chattel, a blot upon the family, unlucky survivors of infanticide, the trip down the well at birth.

"You can no longer count even eight dragons here, let alone nine," said Chen. "The government has ground down the mountains and pushed the earth into the sea."

Chen smiled placidly. His impassivity, a mandarin virtue Su Lin had once been inclined to admire, now seemed ominous. Perhaps America had made her suspect such reserve. Perhaps it was the "herbs" put in her food each morning at Chen's insistence to "calm" her, leaving her clotted and dim. Perhaps it was the page allegedly taken from Jim Cross's notebook in Berkeley bearing the names of two Paris Corsicans, pages Chen had insisted Peter show her when she had raged in the villa—the Chen who had taken such great pains to tutor her in their significance.

"There is a little park near Kai Tak Airport where the boy Emperor, Ping, and his Chief Minister died. They'd been driven by Mongol invaders to the edge of the land. To avoid their being captured, the Chief Minister took the young Emperor into his arms and jumped into the sea, thereby ending the Sung dynasty."

For a moment paranoia overtook her utterly; she was certain

Chen was displaying a parable full of arcane signals she was supposed to understand but couldn't. The sky brightened, erasing her image in the glass. She dropped her head and looked down into her lap, terrified.

"Ping was the first and last Chinese emperor ever to come here. There is a rock inscribed *Sung Wong Toi,* which means the 'Sung Emperor's Terrace.'"

She believed nothing Chen said. She was cultivating, like a flower in her mother's garden, a perfect indifference. She sat as in the villa, hands limply folded together, weaving escapes. But Hong Kong—sparkling, money-drenched—was a perfect prison.

"What time is the ceremony?" she asked carefully, her voice small, unused.

Peter looked at his Piaget. "Two hours. We could stay here—"

"Let's drive through the New Territories," she said, affecting gaiety.

Peter turned to Chen. "It *is* a nice day."

Su Lin watched Peter's strained smile. Left-Hand Chen bent slightly toward her. "You would like that? A drive in the country?"

She nodded, ready to dash herself into the tall Peninsula mirrors if he said no.

"All right then." Chen flagged the waiter with the wag of a burnished, tobacco-stained forefinger.

They stood and walked among the lunchers, Peter on one side of her, Chen on the other, and out through the tall doors.

Fook the chauffeur stood at attention in the circular driveway, smiling and sucking air, his face a lacquer mask of effort, holding open the rear door of the Rolls.

"Missee, ah, ah . . ."

As the Rolls headed up Nathan Road, Su Lin became giddy; nothing could keep her heart from soaring at the sight of the warm, spilling Saturday swarm, trading with rude cheeriness, the colony's clever and merciless pragmatism unleashed. Green double-decker buses and red taxis with white roofs paced the Rolls slowly up the Golden Mile, orgasmic shoppers' paradise. Foreigners rich and poor, sailors and hustlers, sellers and spies, bobbed on the surging Chinese human tide. From elegant shops to street vendors, a mesmeric celebration of commerce spewed watches, off-brand Levi's, jade, pewter, gold, rugs, diamonds. Decked eateries beckoned with trays of *yum cha;* outdoor stands offered sesame buns and oily noodle sweets. The tension between the Western concept of itself and of the East, and the East's insistence upon its own fecund wisdom and self-contain-ment and coherence, stirred the bubbling caldron of trade. Su Lin, sitting directly behind little Fook, felt a delicious exaggerated vivid-ness, her senses unchained. For the moment she didn't care what made the city run, only that it did.

Passengers crammed in the bottom deck of a bus peered into the Rolls's windows with bland unblinking interest, perhaps wondering if she were a chop-socky heroine from the studios at Clearwater Bay. Su Lin saw less resentment in the faces than the dogged hope that someday this might, with joss, be theirs or their descendants'. She began to roll the window down but Peter stopped her. Kow-loon Park's dreary banyans, elevated above a stone retaining wall, drifted by.

At Jordan Road there was a detour. A lorry had overturned, spill-ing bamboo cages of geese across both sides of the road. Baby-faced police waved futile white gloves at traffic. Fook turned the Rolls left and inched down Jordan Road for a few blocks, allowing a glimpse of the harbor at the foot of the road, the bobbing tips of Yaumatei's typhoon shelter, the sparkle of the water.

They turned right on Temple Street and inched into the fantasti-cal human density, like a gloom at first. Soaring tenement buildings cut out the light. The project streets, cheerily ignoring the imposed Western rectangular grid, the boxed formality of the supermarket, the door through which one passed, spilled across the pavement in sellers' stands, food stalls, and furniture. Every service was available, all the food obsessively fresh: duck, geese, and pigeons in cages; tanks full of shrimp, crayfish, eel, lobster. A skinny undershirted cook on a raised metal platform in the street manned a chopping board, steaming pots, and woks on either side like an orchestra leader, dishing to a slurping clientele squatting along the canopied, gang-infested sidewalk whose curbs had been erased. The sounds of bicycle bells and honking lorries blended with the chatter of Can-tonese and the din of human compression beneath buildings with latticed windows, bird cages, and bamboo laundry poles.

Su Lin rolled down her window in defiance, taking in the smell of duck and soy, limestone and joss, urine and offal. Orange boxes, tins, crates, and piles of plastic bottles provided platforms, beds, receptacles. A man in pajamas snoozed in a chair in the center of the street; Fook steered the Rolls around him. Clusters of joss were everywhere, the geomancer's *fung shui* mirrors set in little red and gold-leaf shrines at the foot of each enterprise, lit by red and white Christmas tree bulbs.

A charred, meaty aroma swept through the car.

"*Heung yok,*" Left-Hand Chen said cheerily. "Dog's flesh."

Su Lin saw piled wooden cages with black squalling fur bundles and turned away.

"Hot dogs, Su," Peter said.

But his eyes softened a little, making her remember him as he once was: a radiant boy at the end of a kite string. *He becomes slowly monstrous. What happens to young men called to power?*

The car had paused for traffic. An old woman in black, almost hairless, sat on a crate against a building, preoccupied with a piece of silver tinfoil covered with small sand-colored grains of powder. She heated the foil with a slow-burning taper of wadded toilet paper. As the powder melted into a dark brown goo, Su Lin watched her put a hollow matchbox cover into her mouth as a funnel. She bent her head over and inhaled, keeping the burning pool of treacle moving from one end of the silver foil to the other, following it with her mouth until it was gone.

She looked up and grinned, displaying two gold teeth in a mottled, shrunken face. Seeing the Rolls, the smile soured. She turned as if to scuttle off into the black hole of the tenement doorway behind her, but the effort was beyond her. She looked emptily back at the Rolls instead, then down at her leathered toes peeking through torn black sandals.

"Chasing the dragon," Chen said to Peter. "No. 3. Very poor quality. You can tell by her skin."

Left-Hand Chen sat at the other window, waxen and still, smoking, looking silently out. Peter sat between them, intense and miserable. She hated Chen at that moment, and fought to exclude Peter from the feeling.

"My dear," Chen said abruptly, addressing her as if in response to her thoughts. "You really must accept life as people live it. It does no good to do otherwise." Chen gestured out the window. "Human frailty runs deep. Neither you nor I are going to change that."

"So we service it," she said.

Chen didn't answer.

Temple Street ended at the gates of Tin Hau, where old fishermen drooped on the benches of the compound grounds. Fook wheeled them back on wide Nathan Road and up through Mongkok, the most populous human settlement in the world, where one person lives in every nine square feet of space.

"Look," said Chen. "They survive somehow. That is the message of Hong Kong." He turned and looked pointedly at her. "It has nothing to do with . . . *justice.*"

Chen had raised his right hand, exposing the bleached stump, grown in upon itself, sitting in the hollow of the sleeve.

They crossed Boundary Street, where the New Territories officially begins.

Chen nodded toward their right. "Over there is the Walled City. A sunken slum behind the airport, officially still under China's control. But it is lawless, a no-man's-land. Hong Kong police won't enter it. You must never go there."

"Why not?"

"You would never emerge. Cantonese Triads. They would like to have your fortune, Peter. And your neck."

The road broke free of the city. Fook, uncannily facile behind the wheel, steered a steady course up rural Castle Peak Road toward Tuen Mon. Su Lin noted all that passed, measuring spaces and distances the way a prisoner marks off the cell. To their left rose Stonecutters Island, then misty Lantau, low and scrub-covered. A trio of junks rode high in the silvery water. Su Lin, savoring her airing, thought, I've gained the privilege of one of Chen's birds.

Terraced green paddies hugged the hilly terrain. A woman watered a field with cans suspended from a bamboo pole balanced on her shoulders, a baby on her back. A man stooped behind a bullock-driven wooden plow.

"Look," Peter said, nudging her.

A turn in the road brought them around facing the water. She saw the rusted hulk of a huge upended Liberian freighter.

"Typhoon Wanda," Chen said. "Nobody can control them. Korean divers will cut it up so it will sink."

Shantytowns, squatter villages, and tin-roofed settlements flashed by. She saw a tiny boy clad only in a red tee shirt standing in an empty washbasin in a field fingering his navel. Hakka matriarchs in their black curtain coolie hats and *samfoo* pajama suits labored at men's jobs.

As they sped on, Su Lin recalled her peasant amah once telling her how it was on the Mainland during the times of warlords and opium, before she fled.

Each fall in the south the winds stirred the fields of the pink and white flowers; in spring the harvesters came with their knives, making the slitted incisions. In the villages and the towns and on the roads, the drug ruled, in the glazed yellow skins, the bleared hooded eyes, the set of the gaunt bodies.

The wealthy smoked, but they had food; opium destroyed the toilers, the load carriers, the pullers of junks, those who relied on it for strength. It was smoked in the brothels and opium divans and teahouses, from fine Yunnan quality to the *hakuan* bearers' dross. The greedier the warlords, the deeper opium enchained the people. Amah's father had been a manure coolie for the retreating armies before the missionaries made his daughter a Christian; he had fallen to the "fatal passion."

In Shanghai the Western interests fueled the oppression, as they had from the days of the first British incursions. The European export firms—Jardine Matheson, the "Princely House"; the Hong Kong Jewish Sassoons—supplied the warlords with guns, and opium.

There were wars for provinces, villages, fields, even sections of single villages; wars against the Japanese, against the Communists, among the feudal warlords themselves. The wars were paid for by opium, and by taxes that reached insane proportions. Every object and function in life had a tax to it. There were taxes on hair, teeth, blood, even feces. There was a "happy" tax imposed in order to promote a cheerful countenance, and a "laziness" tax on those who did *not* grow opium.

And always it was the peasants, small craftsmen, and petty shopkeepers who paid. The rich in the cities had no window tax to pay, since they surrounded their houses with windowless walls; and no lamp tax, since no light showed outside their heavy black lacquer gates. By 1935, taxes had been collected thirty-nine years in advance.

Su Lin looked out at a funeral in progress on a hillside before a ceremonial fire, mourners dressed in white, the pale wooden casket ready to be lowered into the giant gravesite, chosen at great cost and angled according to the laws of *fung shui*. Nearby stood six huge pickle jars with wooden lids containing the bones of the Chinese dead: "Grandfather's Bones" jars. In a few months the descendants would come and lay the bones out on a white sheet, wash and sandpaper them, and rebury them in earthenware urns.

They passed a small nursery, branches of peach trees trussed with pink ribbons for the New Year, destined to bring good fortune.

Su Lin wondered if Amah knew the family business to this day. She guessed not, and now she was old. Her husband hadn't gotten out of China. She had heard he had been cured, re-educated, done his self-criticism in the early 1950s. Amah despised Fook the chauffeur because he smoked; her heart was on the Mainland, in Szechuan.

They passed the Gurkha barracks, Hong Kong's paper army of small dark Nepalese executing dreary maneuvers in the pale sun, wearing hats with chinstraps like organ grinders' monkeys, or bellboys, comedic puppets of empire.

The Castle Peak Road ran along the coastline, past lettuce, cabbage, and carrot fields, above bobbing sampans and beaches strewn with fishbones, ever closer to China.

Where did this surge of Chinese feeling come from? What lay beneath the modern part of herself? It must have begun with Amah's tales of vast and silent burdens, of toiling men, women lying on their backs through laboring nights, pushing out new life, straining toward the billion.

"Tsuen Wan," Chen said. "All built on reclaimed land."

She saw tight rows of aluminum container terminals running down to the sea. A small industrial harbor town loomed ahead.

"Do we have time to drive to the border?" she asked timidly.

Peter, as always, turned to Chen.

If I see China I'll be all right, Su Lin thought.

33

At Chen's insistence they stopped at Ching Chuen Koong, a temple near Castle Peak for old people who had no relatives or means of support. It housed art treasures and a Taoist library of 4,000 books. Chen padded off to place a photograph of a dead relative in the hall reserved for such offerings. Su Lin went inside the temple.

Peter Lin lingered outside, hands jammed in the pockets of his slacks, gazing at the quilted rice terraces running down the mountain. On the flats, the glistening gridded fish farms sparkled in the sun, reflecting clouds, echoing the sea beyond. In the bay, the mossy islands dreamed.

Over his shoulder he saw his sister beneath the inner eaves, graceful but sallow now, a dark nun.

Where was her gwailo?

Cross had disappeared, the Chinatown people said. Abandoned his flat in Berkeley. Back to Paris to meet with Spiritu? Or his contacts? Snatched by Mafia? Had he hit the road again? They had checked airports and trains and found nothing. But Peter was uneasy. Anyone who fell in love with Su Lin mightn't give up that easily.

Cross was tall, he had heard, a would-be doctor. A Saturday writer, Chen called him. How had the Corsicans gotten their claws into him? Was he a junkie like so many doctors?

As Su Lin had come out of her stupor they had argued over him. When he had shown her Cross's stolen notebook she had fallen into stubborn silence; when she did speak, it was to entreat Peter to flee with her back to the States.

But events were distancing Peter from his American past. At the end of his month's leave of absence he had wired his law firm tendering his resignation because of "urgent family matters." It had been a bitter moment, the end of something he had labored with sweat and blood to gain: a position in a *gwailo* firm and an identity separate from his father's. As for Candace, she had never returned his calls from Asia or answered his letters. An old college roommate in the firm, the one who had gotten him the job, wrote Peter that she was dating another lawyer in the office—tall, fair, old money. Then, as if to seal his fate, a pointedly formal letter had come from the senior partner expressing his seemingly mild regret at Peter's departure. Peter had met the august, starchy old man only once. He could tell that his secretary had signed the letter for him.

Peter had now lost all face in Boston, and with it his drive toward assimilation. Su Lin's urgings to leave Hong Kong only raised in him drab visions of joining some low-grade Stateside law firm on the edge of a Chinatown, marrying some quiet Asian girl, while the Lin fortune stayed here to be frozen in trusts or maneuvered into the hands of Nigel Mason's bank, or signed over to Left-Hand Chen, or scrabbled for by greedy Chiu Chao successors to be plowed back into the trade.

In Hong Kong, at least Peter was *something;* even if what that was seemed vague, and at times up to Left-Hand Chen's discretion.

Would Hong Kong even let him go if he tried to leave? Would he, like she, be tailed and trailed by interests here? Or worse?

Peter knew things about America that Su Lin didn't: the grinding crescendo of racism, the introversion that poisons the non-white in America as the years spool on and the terms become clearer. She still dreamed of making it, and of *gwailo* love.

Let her dream; they would both stay here.

He needed to divert her attention to something, or someone, else.

A breeze came up, rippling his silk shirt. Rubbing his arms, Peter turned back toward the Ching Chuen Koong Temple. At the entrance he passed between a huge cast bell, rung at daybreak to waken the monks and nuns to eat and go out to the rice fields, and an evening drum thumped to call them back. The temple interior was ornate, the baroque southern flowering of Taoism. The roof rose above the tops of the walls, the space between filled with lattices of red and yellow carved wood. Old supplicants in pajamas shuffled dimly past, mixing with a few tourists gaudy with shirts and cameras.

Peter reached the central shrine and the statue of Lui Tung Bun, one of the Eight Taoist Immortals, who became a missionary twelve hundred years ago after having had a legendary Rice Wine Dream of enlightenment. He carried a scepter, given him after resisting temptations, which enabled him to become invisible and hide himself in heaven.

A thousand-year-old jade seal sat in a glass case protected by two statues carved from white stone three hundred years ago for a temple in Peking. Clusters of incense sticks burning in holders made Peter dizzy. He leaned against a pillar decorated in writings of Taoist history.

He saw Su Lin, framed by a vast open doorway, standing in a garden of lily ponds surrounded by willows and rocks. She turned away as he approached.

"How long are you going to keep this up?"

She walked slowly back toward the temple.

"Can't you get him out of your mind?" He stalked her into a hall where thousands of ancestor tablets hung on the wall. They stepped around prostrate black forms, their whispered prayers like hisses of vipers. Peter drew even with her.

"Listen," he whispered. "Do you remember one weekend you came to Boston after high school? We went to a club. There was a white guy who spoke a little Chinese."

She slowed, turned, and looked at him. "I remember."

"Alec Potter."

"From an 'Asia hand' family. A racist."

"He's in Hong Kong. I'm meeting with him tomorrow. He's coming to the New Asia."

Su Lin studied Peter through the shadows. "He humiliated you. And me."

"It's Asia now. The terms are ours." Peter's voice modulated. "He may know what happened with Father."

She spoke with disbelief. "What has happened to you, Peter? You'll deal with anyone." Her eyes were feverish in the weak temple light. "You still think of revenge, don't you?"

"Why must you consider it that way? There is the matter of honor, in any culture."

"Alec Potter has no honor." She turned away.

They passed into a room whose walls were covered with murals depicting Taoist deities—Wong Mo, the Mother of the Jade Emperor. Thick joss seemed to bury sound.

"Does your Chinese side feel nothing, Su?"

"It feels too much." She turned to him. "Look at these people. Look where feudal rivalries get you. That woman in the alley in Yaumatei snorting opium. She could have been a Lin customer." She looked up, her eyes full of appeal.

"Soon this phase will be over. Then we can think about legitimizing."

"You don't really believe that."

Peter gloomily watched her turn away. The incense had become a clotting mist between them.

He followed her into a second ancestral hall where each shrine bore an inset photo in a special number slot of a relative who had died. Peter saw Left-Hand Chen at the far end, lighting a joss stick in front of a photograph of his mother.

Something was tugging at the hem of Peter's jacket. He looked down and saw a tiny crone in raggy black pajamas. In her free hand she held an oily plastic shopping bag from a Wanchai store. Threads of silver hair shot from her scalp like frizzed ribbon.

"*Aiyaah!*" She unleashed Cantonese babble, pulling Peter behind a tall inscribed pillar. She peered out and pointed a quivering finger down the corridor at the lone small figure bent into a kowtow ball before a shrine.

"Sun Yee On," she cackled. Her squashed face worked, eyes rolling back in their sockets. "Sun Yee On." Her voice was like the spitting of a distant radio.

She set down her plastic bag and pulled them both by the hand across the corridor to one of the numbered slots. At its base was a small plate of dried fish, two eggs, a wrinkled orange, three sticks of burning joss.

The photo was of a young man. The chemicals were dissolving, the image silvering out into inscrutability, giving a haloed, numinous glow to the street tough in the photo.

The crone looked up at Peter and ran her hand across her throat, then pointed surreptitiously down the hall where Chen was slowly rising before his altar.

She wept and shook and tugged at their arms as if they were bell ropes. Peter watched Chen, his devotions over, waiting at the foot of the corridor. He wrested his arm away from the woman and reached for Su Lin.

"Let's get out of here."

As they headed for the entrance Su Lin said, "Left-Hand Chen possesses you."

By the time they got to Lok Ma Chau lookout, the clouds were thickening and a breeze had raised a chill.

But there was China.

Su Lin stood on the hill, her heart beating hard, and let her eyes run out across the landscape to the misty horizon. The Shum Chun River lazed across the rice plains, demarcating the border. Beyond lay the China side of the valley, rising up to the softly stacked blue hills: Middle Kingdom, repository of vastness and splendor, squalor and mystery, the dream of her true ancestry.

Amah used to tell her at bedtime of a monastery in Szechuan among gingko trees where the sound of water from the torrents was like music as it danced through natural rock hollows. In guest rooms stood large caged beds with mosquito nets, and painted scrolls on the walls. The temple was a thousand years old, built according to the laws of the geomancers. Above, cool azure air swirled to the rocks beyond, and the first peaks of the great ranges.

China . . .

Chen, his left arm upraised, was pointing out across the Shum Chun River from the overlook. "They let sixty thousand illegals across last year."

Why would they leave China? For the slums, the oily feel of currency, the blessings of crime? Or was it the lure of the poppy?

She followed a curl of smoke in the valley below through binoculars. She could just make out the green sides and red lettering of the Canton train.

"Do people ride from Kowloon into China?" she asked Chen quietly.

"Not anymore. The Canton train stops and starts at the Lo Wu border. Nobody is allowed across except the peasants who live in the area."

She watched the train until it vanished behind an endless grove of willows, then put the binoculars down.

The small market town of Tai Po, facing out to Mirs Bay, seemed a good site for an orphanage. The river ran nearby, as did the train into Kowloon. The fishing fleet's daily outings provided a stable gaiety, interrupted only by each morning's discovery of the shark-rended bodies of illegals washed up during the night. But the British "touch base" policy was still in effect, meaning anyone who made it across could stay—incentive enough for hungry boys with dreams of leather jackets, cheongsam girls, stereos, and White Dragon Pearl No. 4 to make the run. The wealthier illegals paid racketeers graft prices to be run in by cover of night in motor launches.

Plans were under way for Tai Po to become a "new town," with more project buildings like these to get the immigrants out of the festering tin-roofed squatter villages. The Lin Family Orphanage was the flagship, a gift of unarguable beneficence. Unfinished in time for the ceremony, bamboo scaffolding, like toothpicks, still girded sections of wall. It rose to the sky, twelve stories of lath and stucco, sterile white planes and cheap black grilling on the windows, a hymn to the same industrial optimism that had fostered similar developments half a world away.

There were balloons, lemonade, tea. The orphans and their strict Kaifong keeper charmed old beribboned dignitaries with jump-rope. Consul Doody had sent a vice-consul, a young man with acne. Nigel Mason of the Hong Kong Crown Bank blessed the proceedings with his tall, freckled presence. Commissioner Roderick Hughes, undaunted by his failure to turn up a single suspect in the killing of Harry Lin, stood rigidly beside his Chinese assistant, hands behind his back.

Opium talks, Su Lin thought as the squealing pinafore-clad girls rushed up to surround her.

"See? Shit into roses," Peter said jocularly, putting the issue in another light as they walked through the open glass doors at the entrance.

The laughter of the orphans was a balm. Two of them took Su Lin in hand and led her down the booming tile corridors into a model room. Brightly colored bunks were arranged eight in a room, with tiny study tables facing out on low scrub land behind which a wing would one day be built.

Chen Po-chi came up behind her. "There's much work to be done here."

Charity, good works: the woman's role in the imperial scheme. So Chen was inviting—or commanding?—her to take it on.

Outside, the wind had risen again, rustling skirts and whirling dirt across the razed field. Peter cut a pink ribbon. The orphans shouldered into place to do "Saints Go Marching In." Nigel Mason loomed above her, sloshing Scotch in a plastic cup, his eyes feeling her up.

"We must see more of each other, dear. Mustn't we?"

There was a tray of cookies, and the clattering sound of construction somewhere behind. Left-Hand Chen stood quietly to the side, Lucky Strike in his good hand, his cobra eyes snapping details.

A great red running flag with black lettering fluttered up into place across the entrance: LIN FAMILY ORPHANAGE. A cheer went up.

"Fantastic, eh?" Peter said. He turned to his sister, drink in his hand. "Su?"

Peter wheeled full circle. "Su!"

Chen's left arm thrust in front of Peter's eyes. "Get her," he commanded.

At first all Peter saw was the cloud of dust by the road. Then the cream Rolls emerged like a chariot, little Fook hunched over the wheel, the darting vision of his sister in back, urging him on.

Run, run.

"Missee okay?"

Fook's face contorted in the rearview, awaiting instructions, becoming aware that this was not simply a hurried exit but flight of some sort. The little chauffeur's eyes widened, his misgivings alternating with dim loyalty toward her, the family daughter.

"Star Ferry!"

The road was a carnage of cars, buses, bullocks, bicycles, farmers, and taxis. Fook, possessed now, roared on, following the line of Tolo Harbor, riding the majestic Rolls's double horn like a cabbie.

Run, run. But where?

Kai Tak Airport was a trap. It was the first call they'd make. She had no visa, no passport, no money. China? Impossible. She was a ball on a track, doomed to circle.

The tall awkward image of Consul Doody rose up. If she sought asylum at the American Consulate, could they refuse her? After all, she was a citizen.

What does that mean?

The Rolls roared past Sha Tin racetrack toward the harbor. She looked out back. If there were pursuers, they'd lost them.

At Boundary Street, green whitened into cement, estates, thickening neighborhoods. Then Waterloo Road slowed them in traffic. Waiting at Jordan Road, Su Lin saw that Fook had nodded off, his head against the steering wheel.

"Fook!"

In a single motion the tiny junkie chauffeur awoke, sat up, and hit the accelerator. He took the last bit of Nathan Road like a jockey, hunched up on the wheel, his hand on the horn. The chauffeurs at the Peninsula Hotel stood by their fleet of green Rollses, staring unbelieving as Fook screamed the last yards to the Star Ferry terminal and skidded in broadside.

He turned to Su Lin, bathed in sweat, his mouth open. As the wonder at his accomplishment began to turn into a dim sense of its consequences, his expression became horrific. "Missee!"

But she was out the door and gone, rushing with the crowd toward the ferry gate, dropping the three coins in the turnstile, hurrying up the long terminal ramp to the ferry.

As she neared the top, the passenger light turned red. She dodged the arms of a policeman and pounded across the ramp just as it drew up.

Looking back across the white water as the Star Ferry pulled away, she saw the policeman staring through the glass of the terminal at her, straightening his beret, smiling. Fook, his chauffeur's cap in his hand, was waving from the dock.

The old creaking ferry pitched into the current for the ten-minute crossing. She found a seat facing forward.

A green harbor patrol boat ran up alongside, flying a British flag, a Colony flag, and a third flag of a dragon. Two holster-clad police in blue uniforms with white socks stood at the prow. Su Lin picked up a Chinese newspaper from the seat and held it in front of her face until the patrol boat sped away.

Red neon reflections shimmered in the early evening water as the ferry bumped against the rubber-tire fenders of Victoria wharf. She stayed tight among the exiting passengers all the way into Statue Square.

Surveying the wide plaza and seeing no hostile figures, she slowed to a walk. In the sunny late afternoon, Philippine housemaids were out for the Saturday airing; only the comforting sight of a pair of uniformed police ahead stood between her and Des Voeux Road, then Garden Road and the Consulate.

The Consulate can't refuse me.

As she neared the policemen, they parted and smiled. She smiled back. They were young, Chinese, dressed smartly.

They closed around her, grabbed her arms.

"No!"

She struggled, but they knew how to hold. The strongest gripped her with his right hand.

Then with his left he did something odd. He raised it and held it against his chest, thumb up, the third and little fingers open.

At this, two scarred Chiu Chao hoods approached. One raised his left hand in answer to the policeman: thumb upraised, forefinger and little finger bent.

With eyes that held no emotion, the police relinquished her to the hoods, who dragged her, screaming and kicking, to a Lin car waiting at the curb.

34

The dream was of her in the snow, long black hair over white robes. A hut with reed matting, windows and doors open to the bright snow. An opium pipe dissolved into a sword, then back to a pipe again. She knelt before the mat trying to tell him something, but there was no sound. Her brows furrowed. She was pointing to a wound he couldn't see. He lay on his back on the reed in silent agony, wrapped in her beauty. His arms reached for her, but his body was heavy, immobile. The more he tried the more she receded.

He crawled outside into the snow. Drops of blood led to a group of black crows walking round and round the carcass of a tiny animal. The silent emptiness of the trees, the snow, was like the cracking of a whip.

Things are not what they seem.

He awoke sobbing, curled beneath blankets. Still in the spell of the dream, he looked out at the early morning street below: Kiyamachi-dori, the canal, the bare willow branches. Lilting music of strings drifted up from the coffee shop: the theme from *A Summer Place*.

The sandals and shoes of sparse walkers crunched on the snow. An old man was doing slow exercises in a beige kimono, chest bared as if it were a summer's day. A bleary pimp in a peacoat ducked into the slatted entrance of a bathhouse. The white-gloved driver of a black taxi leaned against the hood sucking on a cigarette. Daimon-ji rose behind the town, a hill of ice. Cross smelled coffee from below, in the Azuki Artistical Tearoom.

He rose and padded shivering across the tiny four-mat room, grazing his head against a beam. He pulled pants and sweater on over his long johns, then a jacket. From beside his bed he grabbed a book by Lafcadio Hearn, a gift from Terhune, and jammed it in a shoulder bag. Making himself small, he edged down the tiny circular stairway.

"Konnichi-wa, Kurossu-san."

Fumiko was warming herself at a ceramic *kotatsu,* waiting for the espresso machine to finish its routine. It was an hour before opening.

"Meri kurisumasu."

"Nani? What?"

She pointed to a paper cutout of a Christmas tree taped on the cash register.

"Ah. Christmas."

She nodded gaily. *"Kōhii kurimu?* Coffee?"

"Hai."

She poured it into an antique cup, placed the tiny metal cream pitcher on the saucer, and brought it to a table. Cross, still gripped by the dream, watched the lump of cream submerge, then reappear in tiny flower explosions on the surface of the coffee.

"You teach Engurish today, Kurossu-san?"

"Yes, Fumiko. New class, maybe. Tonight I teach you and your mother. Okay?"

His appointment, in what he took to be the usual manner, was either at nine, after nine, ten, or any time thereafter. He would choose the second of these times, leaving him room to prepare a résumé and walk the snowy streets unhurried.

"Terhune-san call?" he asked Fumiko as he did each day.

She smiled with sweet reserve. "No call. Today maybe, *né?"*

Cross fell blue and hunched over the coffee. Still no word from Hong Kong. *You must go soft, you must learn to sleep in order to awaken*. He had fallen into the abject state of waiting, his quest lost in Terhune's Taoist conundrums. He feared he was not, as Terhune had advised, becoming Asian at all; he was unable to let her go—Su Lin, his opium heiress—*as you must if you wish to find her*.

He took a notebook and the Lafcadio Hearn essays from his bag. Terhune had chuckled with dark wisdom at the plight of Hearn, the pioneer writer who had come East at the end of the last century. Hearn had learned Japanese and become its foremost explicator to the West. Honored by no less than the Meiji Emperor himself, he had become Buddhist. Then, Terhune had explained with relish, Lafcadio Hearn had made one fatal mistake: he took Japanese citizenship and married a Japanese. Abruptly his salary was slashed, his honors stripped, his lavish quarters reduced to a dingy room. He had made the error of crossing over, becoming merely an abject citizen, hence an object of scorn, a man who didn't know his place. *Shikatta ga nai*. It can't be helped.

You must become Asian. Without becoming Asian.

Cross began to draft an imaginary résumé, stating his extensive experience as an English consultant, fishing for the old language: "I would be most gratified if you should find, upon perusal of my résumé, that my qualifications suit me for the post you have in mind and that I may prove to be of assistance to you in the development of your department store's burgeoning export department through the proper training of young men in the use of International Business English." It sounded more like something they would say. An empty formality, Terhune had said, but de rigueur. Like the business cards people hand out in Japan like raffle tickets. "In truth, Cross, any English speaker whose breath steams a mirror can work here."

The first job had been at the Kyoto YMCA, a dreary building tucked behind the main drag, enclave for a dozen or so foreigners from the far reaches of empire—scholars, drifters, Zen students, artists—who delivered serviceable English for tiny wages, using oral methods not dependent upon knowing Japanese. At night Cross taught Fumiko, her giggling friends, and her mother, an ex-geisha who owned the Azuki Artistical Tearoom, each vying coquettishly for his attentions.

Cross paid Fumiko for the coffee and slipped outside. It was a blustery, hard day, a hellish wind whipping down Shijo Street. He bucked the expressionless bundled morning crowds hurrying through tamped slush toward Daimaru, the department store where he hoped to teach.

The dream kept drifting back, tracing itself on the snow. Had Su Lin been abducted from the Vallejo Street flat? Or had she simply fled? Was she someone entirely different from what his eyes and his flesh told him? Was she a Snow Queen, a phantom, leading him into illusion?

Turning into the downtown arcade for warmth, he passed a huge lurid handpainted image of Sean Connery as James Bond, clutching a titted blonde, pistol blazing, contesting Dr. No. Next to the movie theater was a tiny eroding street temple where an ancient woman pulled a bell rope and clapped three times as joss curled up. Serenity, and violent obsession: the strange Japanese bloom.

Cross had been dropped onto the other side of the world, into a culture complete without him or his people. He, like Hearn, was a presumption. On an unfamiliar continent, among different people, he sought a woman he hardly knew, whose visage he could barely recall, whose nature was a mystery to him. He had fallen off the face of the known earth, lost in the Antipodes, stumbling through pulsing Asian streets, drifting deeper into dream, losing her.

At the entrance to the Daimaru department store he was met by his man, a Mr. Ocdaira, who handed him his card even as Cross reached out a mittened hand in greeting. Ocdaira spelled his name with a c, though the natural romanization would render it "Oku-daira"; it was a Western pretension. He also had a middle initial, which was odd, since there are no middle names in Japanese. Ocdaira had a sunny middle-aged face behind thick glasses, the lone affectation of a beret branding him a self-declared eccentric, *un type*. He was telling Cross, as they passed through the glass doors into the warmth of the main floor a half hour before opening, that he was a "Christian, of the liberal sort," leaving Cross to infer something from that.

Terhune had described Ocdaira as a broker of various goods and services for the foreigner, a species of native who, thanks to some locally considered defect in character or constitution, was allowed to traffic with the foreigner—inhabiting the twilight world where cultures mime and pose in the attempt to meet and service each other, sparing the rest of the population the ignominy. Calls himself a poet, Terhune had said. Likes to rub up against the *gaijin*. Sensitive. Very strange.

Cross followed Mr. Ocdaira up the empty escalator, floor after floor, past poised mannequins in the empty store, mustered uniformed employees singing the company song, the vast deadness of goods awaiting their consumers.

In a spare upstairs executive lounge, surrounded by a display of *raku* pottery, Mr. Ocdaira studied Cross's bogus résumé.

"Impressive, Mr. Cross." He spoke good Kobe English, learned at missionary school.

A uniformed girl poured green tea into cups. "Thank you," Cross muttered.

"Your predecessor was a writer, Mr. Cross. An American. Quite a romantic. Came to study our great poet Basho. Lived in a little farmhouse. Carried his feces out to the fields in a bucket. He was in love with our seventeenth century, you see. Despised us as we are today, though he would never admit it. Attempted to study Zen at Daitoku-ji. But of course he couldn't sit properly. He became very unhappy. He left."

Cross cupped his hand around the hot mug, waiting for the end of preliminaries, wondering if he had erred already in some imperceptible way.

Suddenly Ocdaira sobered, became hushed, leaned closer. "I have a small proposition."

Taken off guard, Cross looked back into Ocdaira's polished face.

Mr. Ocdaira smiled, then tapped Cross's knee under the table. He reached down and put a small scroll in Cross's hand. Cross unrolled it in his lap. Three women and two men, kimonos in disarray, performed an acrobatic sex quintet, with exaggerated, florid genitals, faces frozen in Kabuki leer, eyebrows cocked. *Shunga*.

Cross looked up. Ocdaira was smiling.

"An ancient series of famous Japanese pornographic scrolls, Mr. Cross, along with the text, 'Memoirs of an Amorous Queen.'"

It had "fallen into his hands." Ocdaira had in mind a deluxe English edition, and proposed they collaborate. Surely the West is ready for this, no?

Before Cross could respond, a young man approached the table, blushing and bowing repeatedly. *"Sensei,"* teacher, he whispered, not looking at Cross but speaking to him.

Ocdaira introduced him as Mr. Konichi, who would show him about the store. As they rose to leave, Ocdaira looked at Cross with great significance. "We will speak later about the . . . small business?"

Cross nodded blankly, then turned and followed Mr. Konichi out onto the floor.

Mr. Konichi had recently graduated from a Japanese university, "specializing in Shakespeare Eugene O'Neill." He was the "Engurishu expaato" at Daimaru. Cross couldn't understand anything he said.

There had been an attempt on each floor to render the Japanese signs into English. Mr. Konichi pointed them out.

"That should be 'umbrella,' Mr. Konichi, not 'unblerra.' And that 'garoshes' is wrong."

Mr. Konichi contorted, sucking air.

"Don't worry, Mr. Konichi. I'll help you fix them."

As they stepped off the escalator, a tiny girl in blue stewardess uniform and white gloves bowed with supreme reserve and said in a voice of wind chimes, "Welcome to our humble floor, honorable ladies and gentlemen." Bowing, she brought gloved hands together.

I abase them. I bring the language of the conqueror.

The store had begun to fill with customers. On the sixth floor, Mr. Konichi suddenly brightened, drew very close, and said, "You like paal?"

"Paal?"

"Paal."

"You mean pearls, Mr. Konichi?"

"You like paal?"

"Pearls? Yes."

"I take you to paal farm."

"I would like that, Mr. Konichi."

"We talk about Shakespeare Eugene O'Neill. Now, crassroom."

A door opened before him. Cross found himself in a narrow room with a long table. Twelve expectant men bowed ceremoniously to the *gaijin,* the hairy barbarian, he who no amount of breeding could possibly redeem.

35

On the second after-
noon after his sister's attempted escape, Peter Lin waited alone in
the back office of the New Asia restaurant for Alec Potter. Sipping
Scotch, he sat in his father's old swivel chair behind a desk covered
with documents, many in Chinese script he didn't read. The wall
behind him bore odd historic Lin memorabilia from three con-
tinents, and photos of the restaurant's past.

The New Asia had begun fifty years earlier as an outdoor noodle
stand off Hollywood Road, where Central merges into Western,
where Hong Kong in fact becomes less Western, where the boutiques and colony banks dissolve into the clutter of old Chinese
Hong Kong. The New Asia's was a metaphorical location that de-
fined the clientele it would later come to serve—a mix of suited Europeans and earthy Chinese at lunch hour, at dinner a cacophonous
mix from both sides of the harbor, from the top of the Peak to waterfront flat, from great-grandmother to swaddling newborn—a democracy of the palate.

The original noodle stand, owned by a succession of nameless
hustling Swatownese people through the early part of the century,

gradually moved, with the street's changing character, indoors, as did most of that stretch of street, while the alleys adjacent remained teeming stepladder lanes of open-air stalls and shifting, ingenious merchantry. It was Arthur, the third Lin and Harry's father, who bought out the noodle stand for next to nothing, having been charmed repeatedly by its juicy noodle and cooperative vendor—who kept his ear to the ground for the effete opium merchant recently returned from France.

After the First World War, Arthur Lin decided to go after the British bob more vigorously, and broadened the fare from noodles to basic Chiu Chao cooking; the daily responsibility for the eatery was turned over to his new Chinese wife. It was dubbed the Colony Kitchen, a name which satisfied neither race on a number of counts. That fiasco was quickly corrected and it became for two decades the Lucky Dragon, an inoffensive modish name of the day.

It grew with Hong Kong, buying out adjacent businesses and adding wings and new banquet rooms, setting its entrance in off the street, incorporating madras carpets, carved posts and pillars, and scalloped mythological beasts in celebration of its new affluence—and enriching its culinary display.

But the Lucky Dragon was a name that reminded Harry Lin of cheap Cantonese chow mein houses Stateside; so after his father died it became in 1948 the New Asia, a prophetic stroke that served him well with the Revolution, a nod toward the motherland, but also full of vibrant meaning to the Taiwanese and other staunch anti-Communists. It read either way; the idea was that nobody was to be left out of the food.

The entrance was broad and colorful, set below street level, with fat red lacquered pillars swarming with bas relief dragons. A jewel-eyed phoenix rose to embrace the two Chinese characters of the name, then were repeated in raised gold leaf twice, on either side of the electric sliding door entrance: NEW ASIA. Joss burned steadily in two shrines at either side of the entrance, small mirrors set just so by geomancer's edict.

Just inside, on marble floors covered with madras, the visitor encountered a stern hostess in mandarin cheongsam and heels, menus in hand. If you had a reservation, or if you were known, you would be led into the great main room where the eating took place—and where Harry Lin had met his end the summer before. If you were part of a private party you would be led behind one of the painted silk flower screens that served as partitions. If you were here on Lin business you would be directed through the restaurant to the offices in back.

Otherwise, visitors sat or stood until a table came free, or tippled in the adjacent bar.

Tables were round and large, as Chinese generally eat in groups, festively. But there were also a few square lonely tables for the hapless *gwailo* who had circled it in the guidebook, or had private business to conduct. They were pampered according to their kind, their pouring of soy sauce on the rice, their calling for the sweet-and-sour, asking for fortune cookies or chow mein or chop suey—dishes unheard of in China—indulged by cheerfully rude waiters.

Confucius, who is said to have institutionalized the use of chopsticks because of a fear of knives, also laid down the rules of cuisine that have served China well: rice carefully polished, finely cleaned meat cut small, wine but not to the point of drunkenness. Food is serious business among a people whose most common greeting is: *Sik tso fan mei?* "Have you eaten?" and whose greatest insult is *Wu ky pu fen,* "You can't distinguish the five grains" of wheat, sesame, barley, beans, rice.

On an island where people live and breathe food, where the scrimmages of competing restaurants are affairs of state, where possibly the most varied and best cuisine in the world holds forth (only a Taiwanese would argue), Chiu Chao cuisine stands tall.

A typical meal at the New Asia began, as it ended, with three tiny cups of concentrated *tieh Kuan Yin,* often translated incorrectly as "Iron Buddha Tea." The meal proceeded in glorious array. As a southeast coastal people, the Chiu Chao put emphasis on fish and sauces. Blended dips and mixes prepared for each dish were placed on the table in small saucers into which the food was dipped. The salivating diner chose among baked rice birds, a seasonal fowl dish stuffed with chicken liver and served by the dozen; minced pigeon with water chestnuts, eaten wrapped in crisp lettuce leaves with plum sauce; clams served in a spicy sauce of black beans and chilis; freshwater eel stewed in brown sauce. Or if one preferred, oysters fried in egg batter; gray mullet served cold; pomfret smoked over tea leaves; steamed and shelled giant crab claws in light ginger and leek sauce—at a killing price. Soya goose was a cold specialty, served sliced on chunks of fried goose blood with a dip of white vinegar and garlic. Giant conch, minced and braised, rivaled Beluga caviar in price.

Somewhere during the proceedings a soup appeared, either shark's fin or swallow's nest. Harry Lin's pride was a long glass case, unrivaled in Hong Kong, of swallows' nests of numerous sizes, colors, and consistencies, to eat on the premises or to take home. Prices ran from a few dollars to over a hundred.

The nest itself is virtually tasteless, but its nourishing dried-saliva lining is believed to rejuvenate, and provides the soup base. Mountain climbers go to great lengths to bring these back from remote aeries where the swallows breed. Harry Lin's name would always be legend in Hong Kong, not for opium but in restaurant circles because of the mountain in Thailand, said to harbor the finest collection of sea swallow nests in Southeast Asia, he reputedly bought for the exclusive use of his restaurant.

Dinner often concluded with dessert, which might be the swallow's nest soup flavored with coconut milk or almonds.

If at first it was the Chiu Chao specialties that brought in the hungry, the catholicity that Hong Kong reality enforces upon all its citizens crept inevitably into the Lin menu: Peking duck, cooked five ways; Szechuanese beggar's chicken, baked in lotus leaves and mud; and in late fall, fresh Shanghai lake crab, its oil-braised meat and pink roe served on pea leaves.

Twice a night at the New Asia a virtuoso noodle conjurer performed. Gaunt and preoccupied, he stood at a cart before the assembled, twirling a fat wad of dough in the air, doubling it, stretching and doubling again until it divided into ribbons, and finally, magically, into tiny threadlike noodle strands, to applause and the squeals of children.

Behind this festive exterior, the kitchen was a tiled noisy hive full of caldrons, lacquer containers, chopping boards, and foodstuffs. A master chef presided over a staff of thirty who baked, boiled, braised, chopped, and fried from dawn until midnight. Three times a day the New Asia cook's helpers padded off to Central Market to return with the raw materials for this great factory. It was a place both Peter and his sister remembered well from childhood, a tiered castle of great steam clouds, white-outfitted chefs, ancient ornate bronze cooking caldrons, offal skidding across the floor. Hidden among the provisions for the advertised fare were other exotica, some illegal, provided on request: monkey's brain (eaten directly from the skull of a freshly killed monkey), bear's paw, snake, dog (outlawed but spirited in from China), pigeon, frogs, sparrows, live baby mice (good for ulcers), and lizards.

Behind the kitchen, and accessible only through it, was a narrow hallway with several doors guarded by Lin strongmen, each door opening into the same long complex of offices.

A secondary Lin operation during its early years, the New Asia had gradually become, like Chinese restaurants the world over, a social center, mah-jongg parlor, clubhouse, and contact point. The Lin shipping front, with its more businesslike main office on Queen's Road and lading offices scattered from Western to Causeway Bay, had suited Harry Lin less than the restaurant's back room-boardroom atmosphere. While his growing girth had attested to his savory interests, the rear of the restaurant became his personal Asian spy post, comparing favorably with the American radar-equipped one up the street, but running on food, messengers, cryptic and odd packages, old alliances, and debts. Its commodity was food, but its currency, always, was opium.

In some respects the back offices resembled a clubroom, with wooden drawered tables for mah-jongg, magazines lying about, a small bar—a Eurasian montage. There were mahogany tables with textile samples spread across them from another Lin enterprise, telephones, and several secretaries during regular business hours.

Not an ounce of opium had ever passed through these doors. The trade had, by the time it reached Harry Lin's desk, abstracted into a series of signals, expressed primarily in discreet envelopes full of Hong Kong dollars.

A second entrance fed out the back onto a steep, crammed adjoining alley, affording the Lins and their immediate associates access without having to pass through the restaurant. It also tailed into a branch of the Hong Kong Crown Bank, which accepted massive, steady cash deposits with no questions asked for forwarding directly to Nigel Mason at the main branch.

During the early years, Winny Lin had made occasional appearances at the New Asia—one of her few excuses to come down off the Peak. The children too would remember most, after the villa, the whirligig mosaic of the restaurant—where Chinese men of influence brought their families from all over the island to eat; keeping on the good side of Harry Lin was in the interest of everyone's health. For the Europeans in Central it was within walking distance, and the jovial host—though seldom available to any but the starchiest tai-pans—spoke Ivy League English to boot. Through it all, even the spies and spooks and embassy heads seldom had an inkling of his true business. Cocktails at the Mandarin Hotel, followed by dinner at the New Asia, became a familiar circuit among the three-piece-suit crowd; while illicit Asia was being run by Harry Lin out of the back room, legitimate Asia was being carved up by white men of power in the front. The restaurant became a metaphor of power itself, a microcosm of vaster events affecting all of Asia.

In the early fifties Harry Lin started raiding Kowloon restaurants, stealing away their master chefs, the *ta shih fu*. There is a robust traffic in prize chefs in food-crazed Hong Kong, where food comes before sex and, arguably, before gambling. When Harry Lin died, rumor was rife that the legendary Chef Wen would bolt for greener pastures, compelling Left-Hand Chen—without telling Peter, who wouldn't have understood—to quickly raise the salary of the *ta shih fu* and increase the size of his name out front until it rivaled the red poster bearing the name of Tsao Wang—god of culinary activities—himself.

Then Chen set about trying to quarantine the ill effects of the assassination with reassurances that this was an isolated incident, the random act of bad elements. Gradually the public returned, partly because staying away was a dangerous affront to the Lins, but more because of Chef Wen, the renowned *ta shih fu*. In Hong Kong, good food is worth any risk.

With Peter's return to Asia, the Lin offices had become an uneasy stronghold run by an interim leader, trying to maintain a multi-billion-dollar business that for a hundred and twenty years had never disclosed its nature even to most of its own staff. Only the head Lin, Chen, and the banker Mason opened the money envelopes; the word "opium" was never uttered. Peter Lin, even as a figurehead, provided a symbol of continuity, though his future role was not clear; none had graver doubts about this than Peter.

It was by design that he would meet Potter here in the Lin lair, to symbolize the turning of the tables. The incident between Su Lin, Potter, and himself at Harvard years ago still burned. Peter hadn't seen Alec since then.

Peter opened a desk drawer and pulled out his black Beretta automatic. He held it in his lap and wheeled to the back wall. The room was silent, the scrambled alley murmur canceled of meaning by the thick walls. The staff had been sent away; only the two guards lurked in the hallway, their animal shufflings and struck matches echoing off tile. Left-Hand Chen was due back from a trip to the bank.

Peter gazed up at a daguerreotype of Robert Lin, his grandfather, young and thin and esthetic in a silk robe on a hotel divan on Ile Saint Louis with Baudelaire and the Club des Haschischins, slinkily Eurasian; another in later years showed him chubby and Sinofied, beside the Jardine Noonday Gun at Causeway Bay.

Above him, Robert's father Charles sat at Oxford, a plaid blanket over his lap, a bound volume of Coleridge open—signed, no doubt. A second showed him in stovepipe hat with Nigel Mason's bony Scots grandfather in front of the old godown, looking less Asian than any of them.

Above that was blank wall. There was no image of the first, the comprador, except what the imagination provided: clippers at full sail from Calcutta loaded down with the sap; the lighters sliding up the Pearl River to Whampoa to offload for the wizened mainland "cloud eaters" in defiance of the Peking Mandarin's edicts; the pig-tailed Chinese agent making the beast with two backs with the wan golden-haired Mason daughter; the shock when Jacob Mason, newly knighted, gazed upon the squalling teak-colored product of the illicit seed for the first time; the clapboard colony rising on the barren rock as silver specie poured out of China to pay for its fatal passion, pink British palms rubbing together in mercenary glee.

Here, below on the wall, was one of Harry Lin around 1942, standing somewhere in Yunnan with Claire Chennault, the American Flying Tiger. One of Chiang's well-fed generals stood on the other side, the silver oxide slowly eating his face away.

Peter thought, Father was not much older than I, beginning to bald then too. And look at his little paunch, ready to swell with the decades like fattened force-fed soya goose. Peter looked down at his own new moon: the relentless dictatorship of the genes. And the little round limned picture above that one—Father the student, in woman's clothes and makeup after a Hasty Pudding satire of *The Mikado*.

Where was Alec Potter? And why wasn't Chen back from the bank?

Peter put the Beretta back in the drawer. He rang the bar for more ice; it arrived, a silver bucket in the huge hands of one of the guards. He uncapped Johnnie Walker and sloshed some over the rocks.

Peter contemplated his silhouette before a black lacquer cabinet, pulled down the vest of his three-piece suit, flattened his vanishing hair.

How ridiculous it was to be Eurasian.

The internal phone rang. An American college friend was at the entrance asking for him.

"Tell him to wait."

Peter Lin put the phone down, sipped his drink, and stared at the desk drawer where the Beretta lay, cursing Chen for being late.

Fuck the round-eyed Crimson asshole.

Chen Po-Chi, the Left-Hand, culminating a brisk round of errands downtown, entered the narrow corridor of the old Supreme Court building off Statue Square. He saw the portly, pink-faced judge several steps ahead of him, late from lunch, slipping off his jacket even as he entered his chambers. The smell of whisky lingered in the corridor.

Chen passed him and came to the tall oaken double doors. After reading the docket to confirm he had the right chamber, he entered.

It was a small courtroom, one of four, with a public gallery of seven wooden rows. Chen took a seat near the front. There was a lone Chinese woman in the row behind him, kneading a plastic shopping bag in her lap with her fists, producing an audible squeak.

On the wall behind the judge's bench was a large wooden plaque displaying the British lion and the Chinese dragon locked over the Crown, and the words "Dieu et Mon Droit."

To the left, in a dock flanked by a pair of policemen, sat five young manacled hoods in cheap suits, tousled and sleepless. One bore a welt on his temple. With Chen's entry, their demeanor had changed from sullen resistance to naked fear; none would look in his direction. The cops too shifted their weight.

Across from the accused sat the plaintiffs—a small nervous shop-keeper and his wife—hiding behind newspapers.

Below the judge's bench sat three bewigged, robed barristers—two Chinese, one white—arranging their papers. A Chinese court stenographer in spectacles and threadbare suit sat with his machine on his lap, reading a paperback.

The judge swept in from a side door, his wig slightly askew, holding his robes up over his polished wing-tipped shoes. The bailiff announced this event. Chen stood with the others, expressionlessly observing the archaism.

Florid and out of breath, the judge sat down and signaled for the trial to proceed. As boredom settled over him like a gloom, the judge looked up in response to an almost imperceptible cough from the back of the room.

Chen had leaned forward, his left arm resting on the polished wooden back of the seat in front of him. His lone hand was extended, thumb upraised, forefinger and little finger bent.

The judge's eyes jumped back and forth from Chen to the dock. His lips tightened; he pulled uneasily on his wig and looked down at his gavel, pouting. The hoods turned toward Chen; so did the police. The plaintiff and his wife looked confused. Then the curious invisible hiatus was over, leaving everyone aware that an inscrutable event had just passed them by, but unsure as to its nature.

The trial resumed with the judge's irritable request that the Chinese woman reread the testimony given before lunch.

Left-Hand Chen, looking gratified, slipped out the door and back into Statue Square.

A wind had blown away clouds. Balls of paper hopped across the grooved cement. Chen turned left and walked at a moderate pace across the western end of the Hong Kong Cricket Club's former pitch toward the Bank of China.

His delay in returning to meet Peter at the New Asia—his promptitude was an obsession—was calculated. He knew why Alec Potter was coming and had rehearsed Peter's moves with him. Consul Doody had telephoned the gist of his earlier meeting, and the conclusions had been hammered out behind Peter's back. It was important at this time, Chen had decided, to appear to give Peter rope.

The Bank of China rose before him, a staid gray-bricked forties-style building next door to the wider but shorter Crown Bank. Begun by Chiang Kai-shek's Nationalists, the Bank of China was completed by the Communists. It served as diplomatic headquarters for the Mainland and, in its offices upstairs, a host of fraternal nations. Most of its public business was in foreign exchange: a million pounds sterling passed each day from the capitalist world into China, forty percent of China's foreign exchange income, a mixture of direct trade and remittances from overseas Chinese to families and friends living inside. Inexplicably, the bank was run by a Communist millionaire with extensive landholdings in Canada and a house on the Peak. Though not a spy post—that was at the radar-mounted New China News Agency in Causeway Bay—its affairs remained vague.

Chen walked up the marble steps between great white stone lions. Inside, subdued employees in gray workers' uniforms and Mao jackets quietly conducted business beneath the yellow-star flag. There were few customers. Color photographs of Chinese abundance—workers and great Mainland temples and bridges and mountains—adorned the walls, interspersed with massive photos of Mao and teeming rallies in Red Square. The typewriters were old, the abacuses worn. Unarmed guards in frayed blue cloth suits scrutinized visitors closely. Chen nodded and was acknowledged in return as he set across the tiled floor, skirting rosewood desks and marble columns.

From an office the unlikely figure of Nigel Mason, head of the great establishment next door, emerged. They greeted each other cordially, then took an elevator upstairs together.

Ten minutes later Left-Hand Chen reappeared on the banking floor. Following him out of the elevator, holding a piece of yellow paper, was a young woman clerk. Chen walked quickly out the back door onto Queens Road.

The clerk let herself through a partition into a telex pool. She had some difficulty getting the English across to the operator, a sallow man with hair chopped up above his ears. Finally she spelled out the last part of the address in large block letters for him on a piece of scratch paper: FLORIDA. A second wire, to Kyoto, Japan, was easy to convey in Chinese characters.

Outside, Chen had turned right, in the direction of the New Asia. As he passed the alley separating the two great adversary banks, he looked down toward the harbor. In the cool, blustery breeze, he saw the five young men who had been on trial striding unmanacled across Statue Square, laughing. Chen expressionlessly turned and walked on.

"Super great to see you, Lin."

Peter waited until the pumping ceased, then extracted his hand from Alec Potter's.

"Amazing setup here." Potter looked around, full of unctuous admiration. "A long way from Frazier's Econ Two."

"I hated that class."

Potter slumped into a chair opposite. "Sure could do with a San Mig."

Peter pointed toward the small bar. Alec leapt up, a splay of arms and legs, and snapped the top off a bottle of beer. He filled the glass at an angle.

"Who would have believed we'd run into each other out here? I always figured you for Boston. Weren't you with a firm for a few years? I seem to have a vision of you buzzing around the Common in your Thunderbird. What brought you back?"

"Family affairs."

"Man, I remember your Leadbelly collection! And that blonde you used to date. What was her name? Candace?" Potter smiled. "Remember one night I saw you at *West Side Story?* And skiing at Bennington. God! How far is snow from here? Hokkaido? Or a good chowder? Cheers, Lin." He grinned and chugged his San Miguel.

Peter Lin nodded edgily, cautious of a blunder, intimidated just as years before by Potter's glib ease.

Finally it was Potter who filled the growing silence. "So I was up at our consulate."

"*Your* consulate, not mine."

"Really?"

"I had dual citizenship. You have to choose when you're eighteen. I'm British."

The silence descended. Potter was wondering too where the one-armed adviser was. *God, is that a bald spot on Lin?*

"So what can I do for you, Potter?"

Peter Lin reached into his father's old humidor and took out a cigar. He removed the cellophane and clipped the tip. Lighting it, he eased, as if the cigar had been soaked in the forceful essence of Harry Lin himself.

This is going to be tough, Potter thought. The poisonous Cambridge incident of long ago hung in the air like a shroud. Potter had been too drunk to remember the words, only the fumbling attempt to grab Su Lin's breasts up against Peter Lin's Thunderbird.

Potter leaned earnestly forward. "Lin. I'm awfully sorry about what happened that time. I was an ass. I've grown up." His face was rich with contrition. "Insecure. We all were, weren't we?"

Suck my dick, thought Peter.

"Asia's another place, Lin. Another time. We're Harvard. We have common interests here. We have to start fresh."

"Do we, Potter?"

Lin. Potter. Always the last names. Peter Lin, for reasons of color, had been barred from that collegiate male mixture of friendship and hostility, the hail-fellow crowd, the backslapping and cynical barbs and sex jokes. Anything to prevent the terror of intimacy. He puffed on the cigar, warming to the moment, watching Alec Potter shrivel a bit.

"Christ, we're all twilight characters out here, aren't we, Lin? Interim weirdos. You're what, three-quarters Caucasian? And me, my family's been out here practically as long as yours."

Peter Lin made a silver-blue smoke ring with his father's Havana Tampa and looked toward the ceiling, no longer worrying about the absence of Left-Hand Chen, paddling on his own.

Potter cursed silently. Lin, once propitiative to the American way, was going to play wily Asian lawyer here in Cathay. Asians are like onions, you go in one layer at a time. He'd always thought of Lin as American. Now here in Hong Kong, Alec Potter felt the terms of reality shift unpleasantly. Sensing the failure of his personal appeal for forgiveness, he decided to get some information on the table.

"I came about the cooks, Lin."

"Cooks?"

"Ban Houei Sai. The labs. The Hong Kong chemists. Yuk the Cook. You know. You were there."

Peter flinched inwardly.

"Look, Lin," Alec said. "You probably heard from Consul Doody. I've been approached by the Corsicans in the Triangle. They're in a snit. They think your father—sorry to hear about what happened—

that your dad had the line on the Chiu Chao enterprises throughout the Triangle, that they were under direction from here. They say the cooks come from here."

"I don't know what you're talking about."

"Then let me lay it out a little further. The Corsicans asked me to intercede with the Americans, the Consulate out here and then the Company guys, to let them keep their plane routes. You know better than I what they're talking about, Lin. I mean I'm just an American guy helping out my family with the tribes."

"Who contacted you?"

"Local guys. Headquartered out on the Plain of Jars. They've been there since Dien Bien Phu. They're awaiting the arrival of a big cheese from Marseilles. Spiritu, I think his name is. A dwarf. He arrived in Bangkok today, I heard."

So he's come to Asia, Peter thought. As Chen said he would.

"What do the Corsicans want?"

"Number quatro, old boy." Alec Potter smiled, all polish and cool. "They can't get enough morphine base from Turkey any more. They want the Mekong product."

"Did they say anything about my father's killing?"

Potter shrugged and left it there. He surreptitiously scratched his stinging genitals.

"So they've pressured you to talk them up to the Americans, Potter?"

Good, Alec Potter thought. I draw the half-breed in.

"I'm listened to out there, Lin. You know how the Americans are. I get proposals all the time. I just wanted you to know."

"I'll bet you're a real big shot in the Mekong."

Potter's smile was breaking. "Well, Lin. The point is . . ."

Peter Lin's voice rose. He stood up, gesturing with his cigar. "You want us to do something nice to bring you over into the Chinese camp. See if you can get more money on this side than you can on the other."

Peter Lin glared down at Alec Potter. "Know what, Potter? You're an asshole. A consummate asshole."

This was the great moment of Peter Lin's life. As his left hand waved the Havana, his right remained by the drawer with the Beretta.

Potter stood as if to go.

"Wait. Sit down."

Peter Lin, swollen with the moment, strode back and forth behind his father's desk.

"I know who you were at Harvard. We're in Asia now. Out here you're just a maverick with no power base. A hustler. Your grandfather is dead and your father runs a fucking museum in Chiengmai. I can turn you in to the Americans. We've got stuff on you, your involvement in the trade. You've been places you shouldn't have been." He played Chen's rehearsal ploy hurriedly, but got it all out. "I can ruin you." He paused and smiled oddly. "I don't need to tell you that nothing would give me greater pleasure."

"Yes, Lin. I realize that." Potter cast soft brown eyes of humility down at his Bass Weejuns. "Your problem, though, is that it's more than the Corsicans. You have the Americans who want to move against the trade. You also have the Burmese army pointing at the labs along the Mekong, and you have the Laotian generals who want some of the action. And General Ky would like to move the Chinese aside. Diem's death has shifted everything out there. Next week Consul Doody is flying back to Washington to testify at the hearings. He's going to be grilled, barbecued. There's heat back there because of the situation. They had a senatorial junket to Laos. It could go either way. They want to close down the fields."

"I know. But they won't."

"Can you be sure?" Alec Potter stood and faced Peter. "Look, Lin. I know we hate each other. But we have to work together."

"So you'll plead our interest with the Americans? That's not enough."

"There's another matter." Potter paused to finish the last of his beer.

"What, Potter?"

"I may be able to get some information about who killed your father."

Peter glowered. "What do you know?"

"Bet I could find out." Alec Potter smiled slightly. "You don't really think it was just the Green Pang, do you?"

Peter Lin turned away, his fists clenched. When he turned back, Potter's hands were up.

"Okay, I admit it. I'm on a cross. They've threatened me. The Corsicans. I need protection."

"You want us to pay you to betray them."

"More. I can turn Consul Doody your way. And the Vientiane Embassy. I can tell you where the Corsicans are, who they are, where Bébé Spiritu is, when and where he's leaving back for Marseilles. I can lead them a bit. But that's all. Any actions would have to be yours."

Potter looked up at the photos of the Lin generations hanging on the wall behind Peter. "I don't know your affairs, Lin. But I *know* that's what you want. I was born out here, just like you. I grew up in the fields. I've swung the three-pronged knife, ridden with the caravans. Though of course I wouldn't smoke it. Peasant stuff." He held up his glass. *"This* is for me."

"What about Doody?"

"A Dartmouth prick. In way over his head. Dangerous, too. He's flying back to Washington to testify before the committees. One word and he could ring out two hundred years of poppy. Between the Turkish rollup and the fuss in Washington over the Triangle, they're ready. Even the tribes would bite. And their GI's are coming."

"You're saying you can stop him."

"That's what I'm saying."

Peter Lin put his cigar in the ashtray, recollecting Chen's briefing that day on the Meo hillside. Now here was Potter, an American, offering up the same rationale of complicity.

"Doody hasn't the gumption, Lin. I'll talk to the right people. Lodge and Rockefeller would have his ass. Because if the opium goes, Southeast Asia goes with it."

Alec Potter sat back, flushed. In spite of his bravado, he couldn't get over the idea that the new head of the Asian syndicate was Peter Lin, the slant shylock from school.

"Lin, I took a big chance coming here. It's only because of Harvard and all that . . ." His voice trailed off.

"What do you know about my father's killing?"

"I can find out for you. I can talk to the Corsicans."

Peter was looking at him with dull caution. "What do you want? Money?"

What the fuck, Potter thought. Here goes.

"Lin. That . . . embarrassing, *terrible* night in Boston."

Peter stiffened.

"You were with a girl. Your sister, I believe?" Potter stood up and began to pace, his tweeded arms flapping in slow agitation. "Whiskey sours, and I tend to . . . head in different directions. And I was absolutely unhinged by the . . . apparition of your sister. She must have been still in high school. But God, so beautiful. All these years I couldn't stop thinking about her. It's like an obsession."

Peter twisted the dead cigar in the ashtray. "I don't believe you, Potter."

"If perhaps we met for a drink? She must be, what, twenty-one?"

"And a half."

"What's she up to?"

Peter tightened. "She's a little ill right now. She's about to start work in our family orphanage."

"Ah. A sister of mercy." Alec smiled. "The girls out here. They're whores, servants, slaves. Your sister's in a whole different class. If we're going to be working together, it might just fit in, harmonize . . ."

Peter's swelling rage was deflected toward the door, where Chen had made a quiet entrance.

"Gentlemen."

Peter coldly introduced them.

Chen extended his left hand. Delicately, Potter wagged it. "My pleasure."

"Did I hear Su Lin's name mentioned?" Chen said, full of gentle interest. "She's absolutely lovely. Gifted, full of wit." Chen looked lightly at Peter. "But lonely out here, I'm afraid. Her tastes are American. There's so little here for her to do."

Chen reached inside his jacket and took out a pack of Lucky Strikes. He removed one, in his manner, then dropped the pack on the desk.

Alec Potter's eyes widened. *Where have I seen those Luckies?*

The room wavered, then resolved itself into a slightly different shape in Potter's eyes.

"Of course it would be up to her," Chen said circumspectly.

Peter Lin sank back in his chair, his fitful performance exhausted.

"Great," Alec Potter said cheerily. "I'll be in Hong Kong a few more days. We'll talk. Okay?" He extended his hand. "Peter."

Peter stood woodenly and took Alec Potter's hand. *He called me by my first name.*

"I'll show you out through the front," Chen said. "Have you seen the restaurant? The swallow's nest display?"

Chen led Alec Potter out. Peter listened to the voices fade. Then he turned and peered out through the slatted blinds. In the alley, day was deepening into night; crowds crushed the sidewalk.

Just when he had been about to pin Potter, Left-Hand Chen had entered and turned things around. Had Chen been listening all along? *I will have to rebuke him.* Peter began to rehearse the words.

Then he suddenly turned back toward the room, his eyes wide with horror. He was trying to get it right: *Did I just agree to pimp my sister to Alec Potter?*

36

On an icy mid-January day, Cross pushed through the afternoon rush on Shijo Bridge, clutching the message Fumiko had given him at the Azuki Artistical Tearoom. Reaching the far bank, he stopped in front of the Kabuki theater and excitedly read it again: "Meet me at the Dai-Ichi Baths. News."

Following a map Terhune had drawn on the back, Cross dropped into an alley of Gion's entertainment quarter. A light snow fell. He passed a tearoom, a ribbon maker's, a comb shop. A narrow pebbled lane brought him to a bathhouse entrance between a nightclub and a pachinko parlor. In the biting cold he matched the characters on the bathhouse curtain with Terhune's: Dai-Ichi Baths. The glass doors of the pachinko hall opened and closed, emitting the clatter of thousands of tiny metal balls, and glazed somnambulists carrying cheap prizes: boxes of Ritz crackers, cans of shaving cream, deodorant.

It was an unlit stone entrance; a dozen pair of shoes faced inward. After removing his own, Cross padded into the dimness, following the steam. In the changing room a wizened man in a loincloth took a hundred yen and handed him a small towel, a folded fresh kimono, a piece of soap, and a blue plastic bucket. Cross disrobed and folded his clothes. Naked, holding the tiny towel before him, he passed through another door into the *ofuro*.

The room had tile floors and wooden walls and roof; it was surprisingly large, thick with mist. Cross could just make out several men squatting, testicles swaying like lanterns, lathering themselves or rinsing from buckets. In the center of the room was a large shallow circular pool, the *ofuro,* emanating purgatorial steam. Ghostly heads loomed on the surface of the water as if detached from their bodies.

Cross squatted and scrubbed. From a tap he filled his bucket with warm water and doused himself. The man next to him nodded, his eyes veiling curiosity at the pale one, the *gaijin,* hairy devil.

Cross gingerly traversed the wet tiles to the *ofuro,* planting his heels so as not to slip. The water was cruelly hot. As he slid in, blood shot to his head, the steam sucked his breath away. He tried to stay still.

Whimpering, he settled. Heat flooded his nostrils, burned his fingers and toes. He closed his eyes and went blank, enfolded in reverie. Time passed.

"*Sensei.*" Teacher.

Ever so slowly Cross turned. Terhune's great pale body and bushy bearded head came abeam. Settling in against the side, he placed his small towel on the lip of the bath.

"So are you Daimaru's man, Cross?"

"Ocdaira seemed more interested in dirty scrolls."

"I told you he was strange."

Cross noticed that something was concealed under Terhune's towel.

"My short sword," Terhune said simply. "This is a gangster bath. But it has the virtue of privacy."

They fell silent, drained by the heat. Finally Cross could wait no longer and turned to him, dizzy with hope.

"I got your note. You have news?"

But Terhune was watching two heavily muscled men laving themselves on the tiles. Their heads were shaved, their arms and torsos covered with lurid writhing tattoos.

"*Yakuza,*" Terhune whispered. "Gangsters."

The tattoos ran from an imaginary tee-shirt line to mid-thigh, and down the arms to the elbows, a blue swirling pointillist field with red and green highlights, rich with impossible detail, in the manner of old ukiyoye prints. Cross saw squirming dragons and snakes, a skull, a bare-breasted woman. Scalloped red peonies flared from the nipples. As one *yakuza* turned, a carp surged up a waterfall along his buttocks; a peacock flared across his back.

"They're from the same gang," Terhune said. "You can tell by the work. *Bokashi,* it's called. Yokohama style."

The sumptuous demonology rippled as the *yakuza* went through the motions of washing. The two hoods stood and came to the bath, twisting their towels. The tattoos became a vague inkiness beneath the water. The *yakuza* sighed and closed their eyes.

Terhune spoke: "I have heard from Hong Kong. The answer is yes. And no."

His head, streaming with perspiration, disappeared as he brought a second small towel over it. When it emerged he said, "She's in Hong Kong. And well, according to her brother."

Elation flared in Cross.

"However they don't wish to see or hear from me. I am to have no further contact."

Cross's spirits plunged into the steam.

"This, I'm afraid, marks the end of your quest. It was foolish of me to attempt to involve either of us."

"But she's there against her will."

"That changes nothing." Terhune rose slightly, causing the water to shift, and sting. Cross saw now that his full chest bore a pair of tattoos—one of a dragon, the other of an eagle.

"You're certain she's there, Terhune?"

"Quite." Terhune sank until only his head remained above the water. "Is she happy? No, I don't believe that for a moment. She was abducted in San Francisco by people from her family. She didn't want to return to Hong Kong."

Though it was late in the day the lights had not been turned on; the bathhouse was shrouded in gloom. Terhune seemed to be receding into a cocoon of detachment.

"Did he say anything else?"

Terhune was silent for some time. Then he turned to Cross, leveling him with a furious gaze. "Why in hell didn't you tell me?"

"Tell you what?"

"You bleeding innocent fool," Terhune rasped. "You're here to tear down my sanctuary, to draw me back into opium. You, American, with your ridiculous dreams of love."

Cross reeled from Terhune's rage.

"Bastard. You'd had contact with the trade before you met her. They found your notebook."

Cross fell back, dazed. Realization spread like a dye in the murky bath waters.

"She was taken back to Hong Kong because you are an agent of their enemy, the Corsicans," Terhune said.

"No. They don't understand. There's no connection. Bébé Spiritu was forced upon me. In another place and time. It had nothing to do with Su Lin."

"So you've met with the dwarf himself. That makes it worse." Terhune's voice was a knife. "Tell me about it, Cross. Not that it will matter now. Your odyssey is over."

In the stillness of the bath, as Cross told Terhune what had happened in Europe, his mind followed a snarled skein of doubt that went all the way back to medical school, his 4-F at the Orléans draft physical, early days in Paris. He told Terhune of the killing of Eva by the abortionist Jiminez in the Canaries, the incident in Tangier with El Jefe and Ilya, and the heroin at Algeciras. He told him about Bébé Spiritu and the men in Paris, of the final plane trip home, and of meeting Su Lin at Oak Knoll Hospital, the missing notebook, her disappearance.

"As far as you knew your involvement with Spiritu was over when the skycap took your suitcase at the curb in Los Angeles."

Cross nodded. The bath had become a tepid chamber, a confessional, the steam a drowsing narcotic. Terhune wiped sweat from his dark brows, his chest heaving in the heat. He stared maniacally at the object of his wrath. "You don't know who they were, do you? The people in Tangier."

"No."

"Ilya," Terhune said blackly, "is an old agent of the lowest order. A silly hashhead who used to sail the Messageries line. He would never smoke in the forecastle with us. He works for whoever keeps him stoned—CIA, Interpol, Marseilles." He glared at Cross. "Left-Hand Chen may be right. Your meeting Su Lin could have been engineered by Bébé Spiritu. You were a lure to bring her to the Corsicans. They may have planned to kidnap her."

A sickening image came to Cross of the Gurdjieff figure waiting in the car outside Oak Knoll Hospital the day he had met Su Lin. Had he carried the brutality of Europe to Su Lin's door? Had he been in their service all along?

"It's a lie," he said emphatically, "to keep Su Lin from me. I found her by chance. I pursued her by choice. They used the coincidence of Spiritu's name in my notebook to justify taking her."

"*Shikatta ga nai,* eh? It can't be helped. They have told her, of course. How could she ever trust you again? You've lost her." He gazed at him without pity. "In truth, Cross, you never had her." Terhune's laughter rumbled like an avalanche.

Cross spoke weakly: "You loved her mother once."

"Opiated infatuation. Not love. Love is just more opium."

Glumly Cross fell silent. Terhune turned away. His eyes fell on a small older Japanese, shorn of hair, entering the room, the clop of his *getas* loud on the tiles. The man rinsed quickly, then approached the side of the bath where the two tattooed *yakuza* sat.

"You, American," Terhune said. "You are the bait to draw the players together. The itinerant idealist. The eternal mark. You should have stayed at your orphan clinic in France." His arm eddied the greenish waters. "Every scheme needs someone like you. In your attempts to avoid evil you drag it in your wake like an afterbirth." Terhune brought his large face close, his great brows like clumps of moss. "You are the worst kind of agent, Cross. Because you don't even know you are one."

"I'm going to Hong Kong," Cross said.

"You'd never get out of Kai Tak. They'd kill you on sight. Go home, Cross. I was your hope. Now not even the Corsicans can help you. Events have outstripped you. Don't you see? An East wind blows."

Cross lifted his cupped hands from the bath, watching the water run through them.

"There is war," Terhune said. "The Corsicans will lose. The trade will shift East." He scowled with pain. "You've reached the end of the New Frontier, Cross. Just in time to watch a new generation of American junkies come back from Asia with opium in syringes, suckled at the Hong Kong tit. Su Lin will be absorbed back into the family by ancient forces, like ink into a blotter. In your profession, you would say that the graft will take."

Cross started to speak, but Terhune touched his arm abruptly. "Be still," he whispered. He was gazing at the older Japanese who had slid into the water next to the two *yakuza*. Only the five of them remained in the dimming bathhouse.

"Look," Terhune muttered.

As the man settled into the bath, Cross saw his unmarked skin begin to mottle and shape into patterns.

"Oshiroi-bori," Terhune said. "A white tattoo. Invisible except in hot water. I've heard of it but never seen it. Only the worst kind of *yakuza* have it."

Cross saw swirling Hokusai waves emerge along the man's chest. The huge white eye of a demon glowered from one shoulder.

The older man stood, revealing an inscription etched from sternum to navel.

"What does it say?" Cross asked.

" 'Save Us Merciful Buddha.' "

The three *yakuza* regarded Cross and Terhune intently. Cross felt Terhune's hand move slowly toward the towel behind him hiding the short sword.

There was a space, a partition of breath. Then a violent motion slammed Cross back against the tile. It was Terhune's arm as he struggled forward to meet the force, like two lightning sharks, hurtling toward them.

In a blinding thrash of water and bodies, they met. Cross felt an arm encircle his neck and tighten. He reached back, feeling for the wiry chin with the heel of his hand. Water rose up over him.

The man was small but skilled. They contended in a slowing downward arc until Cross's breath began to go, his eyes unfocusing before the blue blur of the attacker's forearm. A wave of unconsciousness enfolded him.

Suddenly the pressure broke. Squinting, Cross saw blood rise and curl in the water among the tattoos. He exploded to the surface, his scream for air merging with the *yakuza*'s, who was gripping Terhune's short sword, trying to remove it from his side. With both hands he brought the blade out.

It spun away. The *yakuza,* in agony, fell back in the water.

Terhune, his great back turning, struggled fitfully to throw off the large man choking him. Cross saw the silver dagger's gleam as it settled on the bottom of the bath. He shot down and reached for it, his fingers scraping the tiles. But it drifted off toward the *ofuro*'s muddied center. Then Terhune's foot stayed it, kicking it close enough for Cross to grab.

Terhune had gone limp in the water, eyes closed, curling away toward unconsciousness. Cross gripped the sword's woven hilt. Pushing off the bottom, he shot toward the *yakuza,* bringing the blade up from below hard up into his belly, impaling a blue goddess.

Spitting water, Terhune surfaced, roaring. He looked madly at Cross, then at the two tattooed assailants groaning in the bloodied water.

They turned toward the older man, the white tattoo. He sat impassively across the bath, waiting to die.

"Don't give him the pleasure," Terhune said, gasping. "Let's go. There'll be others outside."

They clambered out of the bloody water.

In the changing room they grabbed their kimonos. Still tying his, Cross rushed out behind Terhune.

They burst across the stone *genkan* without stopping for their shoes. The iced street hit Cross's bare feet like fire. Two lookout hoods lounging against the fence opposite straightened at the sight of them and reached into their coats.

"Come on!"

Terhune opened the door to the pachinko parlor. Cross rushed in behind.

Long narrow rows of people of no age or sex, eyes emptily fixed, hands on knobs, watched thousands of tiny silver balls jump up and fall back among the futile nails. The din was like a metal waterfall.

Steam rose off them as they ran madly up parallel aisles, kimonos flying. The long room smelled of sweat, old newspapers, tobacco. A tiny grandma, cigarette hung from her mouth, looked up from her encampment in horror as a bullet shattered the glass of her machine, showering her in silver balls. The *yakuza*, in pursuit, pushed players headlong into their machines.

Cross caromed off a washbasin for cleaning dirty metal from hands and banged into a truant robed monk carrying a plastic tray of balls, sending them splattering. Bullets shattered glass, strewing thousands of balls across the floor.

Cross ran crazily, as in a maze. Reaching the back, he fell into the prize counter. Cigarettes, shampoo, rice crackers, razor blades, cans of fruit, and Mickey Mouse watches cascaded about him.

"Cross!"

Terhune had found the back door. Cross followed him into the freezing alley.

It was the end of afternoon, the streets washed with pale winter light as they cut into a narrow north-south street past gaping pedestrians.

"Goddamn you, American," Terhune wheezed. "Hong Kong knows you're here."

Ahead at Shijo-dori, a great shouting arose. Terhune pulled up short as they reached the sidewalk. Chanting hordes surged down the boulevard. Young men with inscribed headbands snake-danced rhythmically past, answering to bullhorns. Cross turned and saw the *yakuza* entering the street behind them.

"Let's go."

They plunged in. Cross was swept forward by the surprising momentum. Above him placards depicted U.S. Marines bayoneting Vietnamese children. Fearfully he turned and looked into the eyes of a chanter. There was a moment of surprise; then the boy laughed. Cross tried to mimic the words: "America! *Byetu-namu!*" Beside him, Terhune sang the slogan, arms joined with students who seemed to know him. A marcher, apparently moved by Cross's solidarity, tied a headband around his forehead as they trotted on amid violent gaiety. As they approached the cordon of helmeted, batoned police girding at the Kawaramachi intersection, Cross and Terhune edged toward the curb.

Police and marchers collided. Bodies fell, blood burst from heads. Cross couldn't find Terhune. Then he saw him rise from among the crowd and leap to the sidewalk. Cross followed him down a tiny alley full of noodle shops to the shadowed overhang of a tiny Shinto temple.

When his breath had returned, Terhune turned back to the tumul-tuous streets. He stood barefoot, hoary, and frost-torn, his kimono whipping in the icy wind.

"The peace is broken."

He glared at Cross with fathomless anger, and a distant fear that seemed to shake the very temple walls.

37

A cloudy early morning along deserted Ginza-dori in Tokyo threatened snow. Bicycles, carts, an errant taxi presaged the swarm of traffic to come. A vagrant contested garbage with noisy crows from Hibiya Park. Cross, waiting for the Japan Travel Bureau office to open, walked back and forth beating his hands to keep warm, gazing up at clusters of indecipherable signs in dead neon. Squat worker women wearing white gauze masks raked the street trash into bags.

Cross and Terhune had split up wordlessly; nothing had remained to be said. Cross had given up his room at the Azuki Artistical Tearoom, said goodbye to Fumiko and her mother, and taken the bullet train to Tokyo that night.

Now he watched through the glass as the JTB employees mustered, sang the company song, then appeared at their desks; moments later the door opened. Cross requested a shipping schedule. While the uniformed clerk went for it he disconsolately counted out his yen. A cheap freighter from Yokohama to San Pedro harbor would just get him back.

"You buy ticket?"

"In a minute."

Cross was staring at a morning copy of the *Japan Times*. The front-page photo displayed the remnants of a Mercedes limousine that had exploded on the landing strip of Wattay Airport in Vientiane, killing its occupants. In the background was a waiting Pan Am jet. Inset were stock police head shots of the victims: Boniface Bébé Spiritu, a dwarf and reputed Marseilles gangland leader; Gérard Levet, a well-known Corsican bush pilot and proprietor of the Snow Leopard Inn on the Plain of Jars; and a third unidentified man whom Cross knew only as Gurdjieff. Police were rounding up local racketeers in search of suspects.

Cross stood up and walked back outside onto the Ginza. He crossed beneath the overhead tram tracks and walked on until he reached the edge of the Imperial Palace grounds. He looked up at the winter sky as he walked through the park, his feet crunching on the gravel.

"I lied to you."

Cross wheeled at the voice. A shaking, bundled Terhune stood before him.

"How . . ."

"I followed you from the JTB office."

Cross stared at him.

"Peter's letter," Terhune stammered. "He asked me to come to Hong Kong."

"What? Why didn't you tell me?"

Terhune's dark eyes were contrite, his beard melting frost. He was wearing an old black Stetson.

"Couldn't tell you. Didn't have the guts."

They walked to the Imperial Hotel coffee shop without speaking. Inside Terhune said, "Su Lin is in rebellion. Or she was when Peter wrote." He stirred cream in his coffee, his large fingers inflamed by the cold. "I couldn't face going. I fear for my own life. Hers, yours. I was sure they'd use me. Peter, or Left-Hand Chen. You see, there's the difficulty with . . . the drug."

Cross, still angry, said nothing.

"Perhaps Peter wants me to come because he thinks I can convince Su Lin to bend. Or it may be that he has begun to realize he cannot trust Chen, and needs what I know."

"That means she doesn't believe what Chen and Peter have told her about me."

"Not necessarily. Don't get your hopes up."

"They know I'm here."

"Yes. But I wrote them I'd sent you home."

Terhune reached into the pocket of his overcoat, brought his hand up and flipped something across the table.

It was an American passport, current.

"A present from Ocdaira. It's good enough to get you through Kai Tak. He used your Daimaru ID photo. You're a Lutheran minister." Terhune looked away. "That is, if you still want to go."

Cross's wild smile answered the question.

Terhune laboriously cut a piece of pastry into small pieces.

"I tried to cast you off in the bath. Even then I knew I'd lost. You've come to call me back to battle."

Cross laughed.

"God, I loved Winny Lin. We had something." Terhune shook his head. "When I see Su Lin it starts all over again." He waved his spoon. "The *yakuza* were a message from Left-Hand Chen. We are ancient antagonists, Chen and I. We battle for souls."

He blew on his hands, then issued a dark laugh. "When you get to Hong Kong go directly to the Ascot Hotel. Kowloon side. A taxi will know. Stay there. Don't stray more than a block away. Just wait for me. I'll try and contact you after I've seen Peter and Chen. I'll talk to Su Lin if I can."

Terhune's hands were shaking violently. His voice had become a husk. Cross looked away.

"Listen, American. I want you to take something with you."

Terhune removed from an old leather valise a half dozen hand-bound notebooks. Each was labeled with a date, in a small, neat calligraphic hand.

"My journals. They tell of the trade. Everything, the secrets. They must be saved. I've promised them to Su Lin. If you should get to her, give her the journals. If you don't, they're yours. Do what you wish with them."

Cross set them down gingerly beside him.

"The jewels of the Orient," Terhune said wearily. "Who runs the world, my boy."

Cross smiled. "I'll take care of them."

Terhune said with a trace of wonder, "You see, Cross? That day in Paris when you got out of the draft, your war was just beginning. Soon you'll be only a few hundred miles from Saigon."

Cross, considering this irony, finished his coffee and put the cup down. Outside, intermittent snow flurries fell.

"You are like me. You dream of a lyric life, free from all this." Terhune shook his head. "Perhaps in our next life, Cross."

"Perhaps."

"We Americans are rootless, without connection. We don't have a people, a history. So we meddle in the lives and histories of those who do. We are a plague upon the earth. We don't understand the past, and obligation."

Cross looked at the bearded poet. "Why are you doing this?"

"Same reason as you."

"For love."

Terhune nodded.

"A very Western concept," Cross said.

Terhune heaved his large shoulders. "Consistency," he said, "is not among my laudable traits."

Cross fell silent. Terhune stared at him, his heavy eyebrows knotting.

"What is it you want, Cross? Art? Glory? I suppose you find in the image of Su Lin the esthetic irrationality you seek, escape from the tyranny of reason. And Su Lin sees in you the escape *to* reason, away from the blind, tainted reverie of opium. So in a sense you might complete each other. Or you might be doomed as now always to chase each other's shadow, snatched from each other's embrace by the fleeting and the real, destroying each other's vision of the other's virtues. She needs Europe, and you. You need Asia, and her."

FOUR

The
Harvest

38

Faint wind: on the broad water,
wrinkles like creases in a shoe;
Broken clouds: over half the sky,
a red the color of fish tails.

Terhune stood at the Star Ferry railing, elbows on the worn teak, a shabby bearded man in a stained, rumpled white Panama suit, a stranger among fresh Asian crowds. He wore a Stetson hat and carried an old valise, licking salt spray off his lips as the ferry engine rumbled beneath the Kowloon clock tower and dipped forward into the harbor swell. In his crinkled bag was the volume of Su Shih's 900-year-old poems, Wilhelm's *I Ching* and yarrow sticks, and his short sword. He stood staring out, history's orphan, suspended between terrains, between cultures that mimic each other, hate each other, dream of each other, lust for each other's women, and try each other's drugs—a ghost landscape, stranded between alternatives and eras. He was a creature of it, a shaper of it and shaped by it, pioneer and parasite, in love with a culture he could never have, lost to a culture he never wanted.

Behind him, fittingly, lay China. Terhune seemed doomed to face always away from her, when China was all he had ever dreamed of. He was a dweller on the threshold, a barbarian petitioner at the ageless worn gates of the Middle Kingdom, barred first by war, now by the lingering edicts of Harry Truman and John Foster Dulles. After two hundred years and two opium wars the foreign devil had never conquered more than the quarantined hong sheds of Canton Harbor and Shanghai. Now even those concessions were gone, leaving only Hong Kong, for a few more years, in the colonial portfolio.

Still, John Quincy Adams Terhune, banished scholar, poet and opiaste, was no less a man of Asia. As his hairy pale hands gripped the teak railing, returning full of foreboding to the scene of his love and his ruin, he dreamed of China.

He looked across and up at Victoria Peak, the "Jade Lady Among Clouds," the yin, looming in the silvery morning, trees hiding the house where Winny Lin had long ago escaped her melancholy prison of plantings and cuttings to flee with him. Now he saw Su Lin in his mind, and thought of the young man who came after her.

The breeze rippled the water, rocking the ferry. Along the varnished wooden benches sat quiet Chinese businessmen, old black-pajamaed Hakka women, coveys of girls in cheongsams or jeans, solitary stiff Britons. Terhune envied them all the simple meanings of their journeys, points from which they had come and to which they were going. To him the present was always just the illusion thrown up by the past, as transparent as glass.

It had never been Chiang Kai-shek's China or Mao's China of which Terhune dreamed. In his soul he was a citizen of the walled southern city of Hang-Chou in the Sung Dynasty of the eleventh century, where Su Shih had seen a sky like this one and written of it, where later Marco Polo had come upon a civilization of contentment and riches.

Hang-Chou: the great walled settlement broken by towers rising through the mist fronting the river and the lake, or mirrored in the half-flooded fields. Hang-Chou: Persian, Turkish, and Arab traders came to her walls with sycee silver and faraway goods to trade for richer ones, the jewels of Cathay: satins, levantines, sarcenets, lustrings, pongees, jade. "The Polar star and the celestial meridian writ small" became the royal palace and the main north-south streets 450 feet wide. Within the walls, as without, were vegetable gardens and pastures. The citizens had no need or knowledge of arms. On one side ran the shallow West Lake, on the other the surging river. Hang-Chou: convivial and peaceful, a world of scholars, maidens, boating, poetry; later Japanese cities were pale imitations.

It was in Hang-Chou where one found exquisite turbans, books at the stalls under the big trees near the summerhouse of the Orange Tree Garden, wicker cages, ivory combs, folding fans.

They never understand the Mongol threat to the north, the ferocious resolve of the young Temujin, soon to be Jenghiz Khan, Great Leader. "Heaven is weary of the inordinate luxury of China," he had warned the Buddhist monk Li Chih-ch'ang. His grandson Kublai Khan would finish the Mongol conquest of China and found the Yuan dynasty: seven hundred years of Mongol rule.

It was this foreign domination that would incite the patriotic rebellion at the Siu Lam monastery, and the founding of the secret Hung League, its symbol the Triad: Heaven, Earth, Man.

"Overthrow the Ch'ing, restore the Ming!"

The Triads would serve as a populist counterforce to Peking and the local warlords for centuries, until the Ch'ing was ousted by Sun Yat-sen, himself a Triad member. Then they turned, like the Sicilian Mafia, upon the people they had once championed and became instruments of the new warlords, serving Chiang Kai-shek's rapine oppressions. These were the same Triads whose descendants, run out of puritanical China to become cheap Hong Kong opium hoods, Red Pole 49 fighters, now stood, two fore and two aft on the Star Ferry, watching Terhune, indifferent to the glares of this *gwailo,* this Barbarian Eye who knew their tongue.

Aiyaah. A seven-hundred-year descent into opium, Terhune thought, gazing down the mouth of the harbor past North Point, where a pair of sampans turned away from each other, their twin lacquered sails like the spreading wings of a great moth.

The skyscrapers and sprawling settlements ahead were ghosts to him. He knew precisely at what point lay the old godowns in what was now Causeway Bay, where the Scotsman William Jardine—the Ironheaded Old Rat, the Chinese called him—and Matheson had run the trade, along with Lancelot Dent, the Bombay merchant Jamsetjee Jeejeebhoy, and the Jewish Sassoons. In his mind he could trace the comings and goings of the old ships, the huge India merchantmen from Calcutta, the clippers anchored offshore while the speedy lighters, the "chop" boats with barrel hulls and mat sails, relieved them of their illicit cargo. He could see the *Ann,* Jardine's coastal opium brig, anchored at the foot of the Pearl River.

Papaver somniferum: it came from Patna, Malwa, Ghazipur, brought in as cakes wrapped in petal or poppy trash, to get the tea and silver and silks out. At the peak of the trade, 80,000 chests a year at $600 a chest poured into the Celestial Empire under the eyes of a weakened Ch'ing regime. Terhune could see in his mind the warehouses at Whampoa, up the Pearl River, just short of Canton seventy-five miles inland, where the first great hong merchant Howqua, robed and corrupt, thin-faced and venal, kept a wily eye on the foreigners. He saw Lin, the upright Chinese high commissioner sent from Peking, who tried vainly to stamp out opium use in 1840, precipitating the first opium war. The British had no intention of relinquishing the bulwark of colonial India's tax base, and the economic pivot around which the whole China trade revolved.

The China trade. From October through February the ships would come in from Calcutta and sail up the Bogue, the foot of the elaborate delta beyond Hong Kong where China really begins. The quarantined round-eye factories were there, lined up in a row: Dutch, English, Swedish, American, French, Spanish, Danish. They drank coffee and tea, ate white bread, smoked Manila cheroots cut square at both ends, and fingered unearthly profits as the gaunt parade of users passed by across the river, some with their lips slit by the authorities so they couldn't smoke the pipe.

As the Star Ferry neared the Hong Kong pier, Terhune contemplated this inhospitable malarial rock that opium built, China's joke on the British that backfired. There had never been any other reason for its existence, really. Now it was returning to the mother drug with a vengeance, with America as its new target of export, to swell the coffers of the tall banks rising in a row behind the ferry terminal and the reclamation, the Big Three—Hong Kong Crown Bank, Bank of China, Chartered Bank—gorging upon new money rolling out of the Golden Triangle.

There are no cures, only respites. Hong Kong had never kicked its habit; now, driven by terror of Communism and nationalist revolution, it turned once again to opium.

Terhune glanced around the ferry. With the uncanny vision of the old user, he picked out the addicts: a pair of nodding American GI's with Chinese hookers beside them slumped on the long varnished seats; an old Chinese smoker, his nostrils rotted from "shooting the ack-ack gun," standing like a mummy by the railing; two of the Red Poles, the sleeves of their jackets stiff with dried mucus from wiping runny noses, watching him with dead eyes.

The ferry thudded against the rubber fenders. The two GI's, awakened by their whores, stood up slowly. As Terhune followed them toward the ramp, an incident of long ago, just after the war, came to him.

It was a night in the forecastle of the Messageries Maritime ship somewhere in the Red Sea, hunched over the pipe. There was Cocteau himself, reclining on the bunk as a boy fixed his pipe, his unforgettable gaunt esthete fingers and wrist waving from the dirty white sleeve and black jacket in the glimmer of the lamp. "The grandchildren of the East shall take alcohol," he croaked. "The grandchildren of the West shall take opium."

American addicts will consume ten tons of heroin this year, Terhune thought. Just the merry beginning. The dragon's tail twists. Mao Tse-tung is trying to sew up the Forked Tongue of Europe. Needles in the pressure points. No anesthetic.

But even China's craving, Terhune knew well, would not subside that easily.

A wind rippled the silver water, rocking the gangplank. He looked up in the sky and saw the formation the Taoists call "Rising Dragon Vortex": fire and cloud. It portended a typhoon.

Surveying the Hong Kong skyline, Terhune knew his world was over. It was economics now. Mao Tse-tung didn't care about Hang-Chou; nor did Hong Kong's merchants, fashioning the gentle pipe into the syringe.

Terhune stepped onto the pier, waved off a rickshaw driver, and walked into Central. Two more Red Poles converged from either side. He was being given an escort, courtesy of Left-Hand Chen. He could smell them, the Sun Yee On hoods, like bad fish. An older one he recognized from years ago—he too a smoker, grown gray and spindly; another he recalled had worked for the Japanese during the war.

And you, Red Poles who chase the dragon, will feel the lash of

*the tail soon enough, as the Arrangement of the Inner World be-
comes manifest in the splay of the yarrow sticks. And the Grass
Slippers, and the Incense Masters too. Not even the Hill Chiefs will
be spared.*

Crossing Des Voeux Road between two green clackety trolleys
plastered with advertising, Terhune became momentarily confused
by the surface changes in the ten years since his banishment: the
new Hilton, the shops, the American soldiers—the vocabulary of
vast capital wealth and those who trafficked in it. Climbing Ice
House Street made him tired; he paused at the corner, holding his
chest. The Red Poles waited with him.

A few more winding blocks along Hollywood Road brought him
to the New Asia. He surveyed the new ornate entrance. Perhaps, he
thought, it was all very simple. The war in Asia was dead Harry
Lin's way of keeping the swallows' nests coming from the Laotian
hill aeries.

Terhune contemplated his situation with some satisfaction. He
was all theirs now, a fish in the tank awaiting the hungry customer.
He smiled as he walked inside. For a moment he felt he had fully
mastered resignation, the yin.

Good. For I will never leave Hong Kong alive.

Just inside the entrance stood a small red amber statue. Seeing it,
Terhune wavered and went weak. It had been a gift to the restaurant from Winny Lin—a Kuan Yin, she who postponed her Bud-
dhahood to help the people.

As Terhune walked past the Sikh guard, across the Moorish carpets, among the lobster tanks and the gilded red columns, his heart
was pounding. At the entrance to the main room he stopped.

In the shadows of the cavernous empty midday restaurant room
he saw the compact, asymmetrical silhouette of Chen. Behind him,
considerably taller, stood Peter Lin, loosely flanked by guards.

Yes, Terhune thought, drawing himself up. Even you, Chen Po-
chi, hollow-sleeved mandarin, will discover your nature this spring
in Hong Kong.

"*Huan ying.* Welcome to Hong Kong, Terhune."

"*Hsieh hsieh,*" he replied. "Thank you."

The door closed behind him.

"I've come to see Su Lin."

Peter began to speak, but Chen silenced him with his lone hand.

"Su Lin will not be seeing you," Chen said.

"Peter requested I come and speak with her."

"She has had a change of heart. She is quite content working in our orphanage."

Terhune looked past Chen to Peter Lin, who averted his eyes.

Chen directed Terhune's attention toward a small table. An ancient elegant opium rig sat there—pipe and spirit lamp—with a fat, sticky black ball beside it. Patna Fine: the best opium in the world.

Terhune's forehead broke out in sweat. Left-Hand Chen was smiling. "You are home, Terhune," he said quietly. "Your respite is over."

Terhune turned in panic. The Red Poles had bolted the doors behind him.

39

Cross sat cross-legged and shirtless, raining sweat on the sunken spring bed of the Ascot Hotel. Intently he watched a shiny cockroach frozen over a piece of tangerine skin beneath the rusted washbasin, its antennae waving as if in blessing. On a table with a fake wood laminate top curling up off it, a prewar radio gave out pinched, lilting Cantonese love songs. A Hong Kong phone book and a dead potted plant sat in an open closet. Out the window across Carnarvon Road a matching building full of seamstresses faced back; jangling street noise drifted up between. It was late afternoon, and Cross's nerves were streaming with the dislocation of a new environment.

This was where Terhune had specified he should wait. After clearing customs at Kai Tak with the false passport, Cross had taken a taxi straight to this crumbling one-elevator establishment at a narrow, honking intersection in the Tsimshatsui district of downtown Kowloon. He had crossed the linoleum lobby floor and paid a small round Cantonese at the desk whose impassivity seemed to waver at the mention of Terhune.

Terhune had instructed him to stay in and around the hotel,

where he would blend in with other foreigners, and not venture onto Nathan Road; under no circumstances was he to cross on the ferry to Hong Kong side. Terhune had offered no time for his return from the meeting with Peter Lin.

Cross planned to occupy himself with Terhune's journals, which sat next to him on the bed, but the restlessness of arrival wouldn't pass. He got up and stepped out into the narrow hallway. A white-jacketed floorboy rose from his stool, his hair close-cropped and oily: "Yessah," he said, nodding repeatedly. Next to the groaning elevator, a window opened onto a rooftop. The floorboy seemed to have no objection to Cross climbing outside among the tangle of wires, plants, crockery, plastic refuse, and cats.

He squatted on his haunches and gazed across the tops of the buildings to the bay and beyond. Hong Kong was another border town, full of refuse and exploitation, crime and opportunity, poverty and wealth—exciting, rapacious—though this one had a faint British patina.

Sunset spread a dirty peach light. Cross watched a plane drop out of the sky and taxi onto the Kai Tak runway, then disappear behind buildings. He could hear the din of human traffic below. The glimpses of water reminded him of San Francisco; but this was southern, subtropical, Asian. He saw a slit of harbor, the buildings beyond; at the sight of Victoria Peak his breath left him. Was she really out there somewhere?

As the dark settled, the lights rose on all sides, and Cross was inside a jeweled pendant. The tall curtainless resettlement buildings became rows and rows of dark movies, each window containing the spectacle of an entire family's life: tiny rooms, tiny stoves, women in black pajamas, naked children, men in underwear lying on bunks like berths on a train. The harbor beyond was a play of moving and stationary lights. Cross imagined Su Lin out there watching the same scene.

Then the aloneness became oppressive. Back in his room, he tried to tune in Armed Forces Radio just to hear English or music with a beat, but it kept fading out. Each time the elevator door opened he tracked the footsteps, awaiting Terhune's knock; but it didn't come. Finally there was nothing keeping him from the journals.

There were six of them, bound in brocade, divided into threes. On the cover of each Terhune had inscribed a Chinese character. Inside, in the small developed hand of one who knew calligraphy, entries had been made by date and place, some going as far back as 1939.

The first set of journals bore the Chinese inscription *Yen,* which Cross was surprised to read meant "opium," the source of the same English word: "to yearn, to long or desire." On the first page Terhune had also written in English the pejorative Mandarin term *Ni,* "The Mud." These journals were diaristic, containing Terhune's personal odyssey with the drug, occasional entries in Chinese or Japanese, and poems and drawings.

The hours sped by. Cross, rapt, traced both the history of a personal struggle and a narrative of the secret esthetic world of the smoker.

It began in Spain, with Terhune arriving in Barcelona by way of Asia, Orwell in his knapsack, and ending up in a hospital in Murcia, a bullet lodged in his chest, taking morphine from the nuns. By the time he arrived at Oxford to do Chinese studies he brought with him the craving. He remained there during the war, translating Chinese and Japanese dispatches and studying. Names of the great Sinologues paraded past: Waley, Wilhelm, Karlgren; the Buddhist scholar Christmas Humphreys; the Zen writers Herriegel and Suzuki— seminal men among whom Terhune seemed destined to be included. There were recountings of strange parties: smoking on Hampstead Heath with old Victorian women who had taken it up in India; Russian informants passing in and out of the scene; strange nights wandering the East End looking for a chemist who stocked laudanum; train rides to chop suey houses in outlying towns where one could procure the smoke.

Cross was surprised to find that Terhune seemed to see himself then as an American plainsman—slow, primitive, hairy, thick of head—lost in facile, refined Europe but released into poetic lucidity through the drug. He attributed much of his growing success in China studies to his smoking, and intimated that it imbued him with a superior, mystical affinity for his subject.

There was the first trip back to Asia after the war, on the ship from Marseilles, and the brush with Cocteau in the forecastle, smoking with the Annamite boys. A stopoff in Istanbul included a trek to the Anatolian plateau, and a description of the January harvest, the men moving backward through the fields with their three-pronged knives, slitting the capsule, then returning in the morning to scrape off the congealed sap.

Cross was riveted by Terhune's account of a visit to the Heng Lak Hung opium den in Bangkok, where 5,000 boarders, devotees of the pipe, lived permanently, going to work, then coming back at night to their ten pipes.

Heng Lak Hung had a collection of 10,000 opium pipes of mountain mandarin wood or bamboo, some fitted with pink ivory mouthpieces whose color had deepened with smoking over the years. The sweet, heavy smell of the drug was everywhere. Terhune described how in each of some fifty cubicles, thirty-five smokers held long gleaming pipes over the yellow flame of the oil lamps. Attendants kneeled over trays of smoking paraphernalia, holding the tips of needles covered with the sizzling black Patna opium over the lamps. Wiping the ivory mouthpieces clean with a cloth, the smokers held the doorknob-shaped pipe bowl close to the flame, pressed the mouthpiece gently against their lips. Their deep, rhythmic inhaling produced a loud hissing noise as they took the soft smoke into their lungs.

Kneeling women came to massage the smokers. Others not smoking conversed lazily or played mah-jongg to lose: this is the logic of opium, that an inferior man can win, only a superior one lose. Some ate from food brought in by hawkers, or drank tea, as smoking makes one thirsty, but for hot tea, never alcohol.

Few were elderly, undernourished, ravaged. Most seemed content just to be, their tiny pupils lying unfocused upon inner or outer trivia—the texture of one's hand, a drifting figment of the mind. Everything was pleasant, life was quite complete without any sort of compulsive action. Each pipe went down more easily than the last. For the smoker, the hours rushed by; he desired no pastime, no entertainment beyond the radiant joy of being, content to drink of the Milk of Paradise.

Always smoke in agreeable company, Terhune advised. One needn't become an addict. The constipation was a small price; one never caught colds. Opium makes one forget contention and troubles, become gentler, kinder, happier. When the opium ban comes they will turn to heroin, the killer.

Cross read on, enraptured by Terhune's pleasant portrait of an

Asia of opium. But with Terhune's first arrival in Hong Kong, it began to change.

He read of Terhune's teaching there, of writing and early publication: a portion of the *Neh Ching,* the 5,000-year-old Chinese treatise on acupuncture; the poems of Su Shih. Through all this his habit increased; he attempted his first withdrawal and failed.

"Opium is perhaps the most private of all human preoccupations," he wrote, "as intimate as one's own head, an experience of infinite allure. Cocteau has said it is 'the only vegetable which, when ingested, communicates the vegetable state to us.' To some, opium is the dream of oblivion, and the end of pain and suffering; to others it is the visionary quest for the grail of Art. But there is another side to opium," he warned. "To fail to recognize this is to miss everything. Finally, opium is descent into the Abyss."

Now the entries became more strident, the drawings blacker, apocalyptic; shining sunlit cathedrals became dark hollow mausoleums. Leisurely dream became agitated nightmare, a frenzy in slow motion. The drug had begun to win. He smoked less in the good dens, illegal but ubiquitous, and began to cross into the degraded Walled City, beyond the law, where it is dangerous but where one can get it more cheaply. He tried sniffing, eating, smoking. Once in desperation he shot up the enemy: White Dragon Pearl No. 4. The purity of the rush terrified him.

At a diplomat's party Terhune met Su Lin's mother and befriended her. Harry Lin, upset with their growing intimacy, followed the curiously insistent urgings of Left-Hand Chen and used his influence to have Terhune expelled from Hong Kong as a degenerate.

At the same time, or perhaps because of this, Terhune had begun to realize the nature and extent of the new trade, its political dimension. This, coincident with his expulsion from Hong Kong and what later befell Winny, became the focus of his journals from Japan, where he successfully kicked for the first time.

Here Cross read of the peculiar dissolution of Winny Lin, pursued by ghosts that became real, who had fled to Kyoto with the children to be with Terhune; of Terhune's secret, guilty return to the drug in the Chinese quarter of Osaka; of Su Lin at eleven, shy and willowy, already beautiful, different. Cross's awareness of her invisible proximity in Hong Kong sharpened, and with it the uneasy fact that Terhune had still not arrived.

He read of Terhune's second withdrawal attempt in Japan, after Winny left; his growing suspicion and hatred for Chen; his fitful and unsuccessful attempts to rescue his foundering scholarly and poetic career. No longer a user, his obsession with the drug had become nonetheless total, his elaborate chronicling of the trade a substitute, perhaps, for the solace of the drug, for the China he couldn't see, for the love he had lost. From correspondents and acquaintances, pimps and old hands, writers and spies and street vendors all over Asia and beyond—Peking, Bangkok, Hong Kong, Amsterdam, New York—he began to assemble the second set of notebooks now sitting beside Cross, the dossier he had entitled *Hsi*, "The Play," the drama, or game.

It seemed to Cross that Terhune had imagined some sort of revenge upon Harry Lin, Chen Po-chi, and the predators of the trade in the only way a scholar could, with an assault of information. But Terhune's pessimism grew in direct proportion to his knowledge; he prophesied at one point in the late 1950s his own return to Hong Kong. Here, Cross began to see himself as much an instrument of Terhune's destiny as Terhune was of his.

A heartbreaking trip to Boston in an attempt to see Winny had failed; her parents, the Churches, wouldn't let him near. Shaken by America, out of place, he hurried back to Kyoto. The sudden arrival of Su Lin the summer before, after her father's assassination, had added new feelings to old; the journals seemed to suggest what Cross already suspected: Terhune had begun to transfer his love in some manner from Winny Lin to her daughter.

The first set of journals concluded with notes on Cross's arrival. They began with rage and jealousy, then settled into a bizarre hope or fantasy that Cross might somehow prove to be his surrogate, his descendant, he to whom knowledge could be passed, who might even someday go after the trade. Cross realized that Terhune had known he would read these words in Hong Kong.

It was near nine in the evening when he finished; still Terhune had not arrived. Cross lay on the bed, fearful and anxious, his eyes burning. He thought he understood Terhune's behavior in Japan better now, and why he had finally decided to help Cross get to

Hong Kong. He still didn't know upon whose order they were attacked in the baths, nor did he feel he yet understood the relationship of the opium trade to Su Lin.

Finding sleep impossible, he dressed and took the tremulous elevator downstairs to the empty lobby.

The streets were warm, sourly fragrant, moody—so different in feeling by night it could have been another city. Most stores were closed, but there were people out, stalls open, bar customers mixing with peasant women and idle undershirted walkers in the droning heat. A hawker sold cheap blouses from a cart at the corner of Hanoi Road, though it was well after midnight. Beneath a bare light bulb a pockmarked candy seller fished change from a red bucket hanging by a string from a metal awning. Beggars huddled like clumps of refuse against buildings. A fortuneteller threw sticks by candlelight.

Cross, walking the small streets near the hotel—Mody Road, Hanoi Road—felt for the first time how Asia had changed him. Here there was no distance; life was continuous, a cellular sea of time he had first sensed in Morocco, not so much a straight line—his father, aerospace, progressive society—as a circle. He had begun to experience himself as part of this synchronous web of events: an agent of forces, not separate from them.

Nothing could have been more different to him. Before Asia he had struggled to extricate himself from danger; now he was moving inexorably to its center, its heart, the yin. He knew he was nearing that seamless continuity with life he had sought on the day two years earlier when he had walked out on the cadaver at Langley Porter.

He thought of Billy Strange, the fragmented journalist on board ship. He wanted to say to him, Billy I found it; it's the same war, yours and mine. He saw that all he had sought to avoid he was in fact rushing headlong toward. The release from the draft physical had been an induction after all, and Eva's death his first combat.

"All is clouded by desire: as fire by smoke, as a mirror by dust. . . . Through these it blinds the soul," says the *Gita*.

Reading Terhune's journals, some silent transference had occurred, leaving Cross more dangerous to himself, bunching the strands of his own life into a single fiber, sharpening into risk.

"Hey boy. You come. Good time. Cheap drinkee."

Wandering the flickering, dreamlike quarter, he thought of the new hip American users with their acid, weed, mescaline, and horse: children of Ilya. Soon everybody will get high, Ilya had prophesied. How American: as if desire had been discovered for the first time to be packaged and sold. Cross's own history of cravings and desire flashed past: first joint, first drink, first cigarette, first sexual desire, urges for foods, travel—even freedom, knowledge.

As war legitimizes killing, science legitimizes drugs. He saw the indebtedness of the overt, legitimate world to the covert, illegitimate one, and the indistinct line between them. Perhaps sin was merely unacceptable desire, politics its regulation, business its agentry. He saw the equality of all poisons.

"Hey, so'jah. You wan' gir'? Dope? Chase dragon?"

He had wandered into a narrow, angled street. The questions came from boys of perhaps twelve, dressed like hoods, smoking Luckies, jaundiced in the fugitive light. Cross passed between them.

The old countries, he thought, were condemned for now to act out ordained destinies, living on the edge of survival. He had thought he was here to rescue Su Lin from the blind world back into an American world of choice. Now he wasn't sure; perhaps it was she rescuing him from the illusion of choice, weaving him into the continuous world, the world of realization, the world of himself.

"Hey, man. Come in see show. Suzie Wong girls."

The idea that she was so close yet unattainable had filled him with fevered impatience. The ritualized behavior of Asia, which Terhune seemed to have adopted, had driven him mad; he had scorned the scholar's refusal to acknowledge the ticking clock. Now the polarity reversed: the yin flowed through him. The ego had come to the end of its run. He had to yield, to go soft, if he were to act. Finding Su Lin had come to mean something different. No longer a knight in armor, he was a beggar at the gates.

For a moment he thought that she knew all this; that the boy she had met in San Francisco would have to change if he were to have her; that she knew he was out here and was smiling at him compassionately; that it was her gift to him that he would have to lose himself in order to find her, the way the smoker plays mah-jongg to lose; that this is what the East would call "love."

Shadowy figures importuned him out of the night. Cheap neon blinked names: CRAZY HORSE, RED LIPS, BAR TEXAS. He had unwittingly crossed Nathan Road into the nightclub district. He thought of turning back, but the sound of American music drew him on.

Johnny Cash's "I Walk the Line" thumped, bassy and Gothic, from a basement doorway. The sign above, in neon, said BAR SAIGON. Photos of bare-breasted women—white, black, Asian—lined the wall.

A crude, riotous din of music and shouting in English rose up the stairway. Along the street, thick-necked U.S. sailors lurched noisily by with petite made-up Chinese girls hanging on their arms. Crude danger threaded the air, a kind of hair-trigger violence Cross knew from home.

The Chinese hustler in dirty dark pinstriped suit and stamped smile held out a lighter to him. As Cross lit his cigarette he saw a pair of Shore Patrol with white armbands and clubs eye him. It was the first time he had been around Americans since San Francisco, and it unnerved him. USS *Ranger,* he read on a sleeve.

"Hey, boy. You come down, yeah?"

A tiny rouged stick-legged girl in cheongsam was leading him down the stairs toward the noise. The jukebox played Brenda Lee's "I'm Sorry."

He paused at the door, smelling beer, sweat, and smoke. As his eyes adjusted he saw a bar and a jukebox. On a small raised stage in front of a red velvet curtain a squat Chinese girl in a yellow wig and a fluorescent bikini danced alone above a surging throng of American sailors and prostitutes. Feeling uncomfortable, he turned to leave, but the way was blocked by a swarm of sailors. The little girl's hand, still in his, drew him further in.

"You like somesing, baby?"

At the bar, a pair of San Miguels and a glass with ice were thrust before him. The bartender's hand swallowed his money and the change. Cross drank to inure himself from what surrounded him, and from his own thoughts.

"You army, man?"

The accent was Southern rural. He was big, blond, pimpled, and his ears stood out like doorknobs.

"No."

"Hey. Don't get smartass with me."

Cross looked up into the close-set, porcine eyes, the white sailor hat down over the forehead.

"No shit. I'll kick your ass."

He spilled his beer on Cross's shoes. The jukebox was playing Ray Charles: "I got a woman / way over town / she's crazy about me."

"What are you, in fucking civvies? A journalist or what?"

"A tourist," Cross said, turning away.

He felt the thick hand grab his shoulder.

"Hey, fucker. I'm talkin' to *you*."

Cross turned, his fists knotting, but a buddy hauled the sailor off in the direction of the stage.

Cross, watching a small contingent of black sailors enter, ordered another beer. The jukebox played "Louie Louie."

An ice-throwing war broke out at a table. Whores shrieked and shielded their faces with their purses as sailors leaped onto the tables and began lobbing ice cubes, then glasses, across the room. Waitresses cowered against the walls, glass shattering around them; the music was drowned out by rising obscene screams. Cross saw that it was between white and black soldiers.

At the entrance, the owner, an impassive Chinese in dark glasses, whispered to an aide; the man rushed out. Feeling drunk, Cross began to edge toward the lavatory, skirting the melee.

Inside the foul-smelling washroom, a tiny hunchbacked Chinese sold cigarettes, provided towels, mopped the floor. Cross stepped to the urinal. In the toilet next to him a sailor vomited. Another sailor entered behind him and began to bait the hunchback.

"How much money you make, shrimp? You know how much I make in my country? Ten times what you make. Can't you talk, gook? Can't you speak English?"

Cross turned and saw the same sailor who had accosted him swaying over the tiny attendant. Wordlessly the little man shook his head, his soft, wounded eyes clicking in fear as he pushed his mop and bucket frantically about.

"They didn't give you no fuckin' vitamins, I bet, did they, Chink? Your kids go around in rags. You got no fuckin' cars. Man, you're an animal. You're a shitwiper for us."

The sailor poked the man's hump. The hunchback cowered against one of the urinals, looking desperately about for escape. As the sailor raised his arm to give the little man a shove Cross caught it, wheeled the sailor around and cocked his fist. Then, shaken by a recollection of another tiled room, another fist he failed to stay, Cross simply shoved the drunken sailor away, grabbed the hunchback, and went back out into the barroom. The little attendant scurried behind the bar.

The fighting had turned into a riot. Shore Patrol poured down the stairs, nightsticks flying. A black sailor, his forehead slit open, staggered past. Cross pressed himself flat against the wall and edged for the exit.

"Man, you can't *deal* with people this way. Don't you realize what you're *doing?*"

Cross looked up startled, certain he had heard the reedy, contentious voice of Billy Strange, the little mind-blasted *Time* man from shipboard. He cast about the surging room.

"Billy!"

Groups of sailors were being hustled out; sirens wailed from the street.

Billy's voice came again: "Can't you *see?* This is *it,* man. The kink in the *process.*"

Cross called Billy's name again, but a pair of Shore Patrol had him up against the wall asking for ID. His passport produced brief, strange stares.

"Better clear out of here, Reverend."

He staggered up the stairs of the emptying Bar Saigon. Along the narrow streets back to the Ascot Hotel he looked for Billy Strange but only found a drifting reverie of banyans and bars, more like an echo than a sound, enfolding him back into visions of Su Lin.

40

It had been earlier that evening, before sunset. The shantytowns of North Point drifted laterally through the circle of vision. Su Lin saw baskets, paper bags, crumpled tins, rags, poles of sparse laundry. A filthy rivulet clogged with plastic bottles and broken wood wound between moss-shadowed boulders—a city of refuse, a permanent typhoon wreckage. A boy clad only in white undershirt stood on an upturned can, back swayed, belly large, fingering his penis, watching a hunched cat devour a rodent. A bent skinny man in shorts and undershirt carried a precious bucket of water on a pole to a tarpaper lean-to.

Shifting the crosshairs, she followed a brown cur to the next cluster of shacks beside a drainage pipe emitting a thread of water the color of steel. An old woman in raggy black pajamas shouted at something invisible, her arms raised. These images burned in her mind as with less interest she moved the seeing circle leftward across the long sweep of the waterfront—Causeway Bay, Wanchai, Central—then tilted up above the harbor directly into the center of a dying orange Chinese sun behind Kowloon.

Pulling back from Consul-General Doody's mounted high-powered telescope, Su Lin turned around and squinted, gripping the low redwood veranda railing until like an image on a plate in a darkroom, the clean fifties-style Peak home, alive with scrubbed Caucasian faces pinked by the sunset, emerged.

Consul Doody stood over his barbecue in a chef's hat and apron that said "Big Fletch," a spatula in one hand and a Scotch in the other, looking befuddled at the progress of his hamburgers. His recent Washington trip had given Joyce Doody a chance to hit Hawaii with a girlfriend; she fussed about, fake wood and bone jewelry clanking up and down her tanned, papery arm, wearing a pineappled muumuu, a fake orchid stuck in her short, neat, silvering coiffure, trying to explain to the wife of another consular official the difficulties of getting Hong Kong carpenters to do California-style redwood deck flooring. As she spoke she managed to load up a Kodak with one hand and brush the blond hair off the foreheads of two sullen boys who sat, legs waving, in directors' chairs with their names on them.

It was a Little America. The veranda had been done like a cheap tiki bar in San Francisco or Waikiki, with nets strung overhead couching glass balls and pieces of cork. A white-jacketed Chinese servant lit metal torches at each corner of the veranda, though it was still light, threading the heavy air with kerosene. Small plastic bowls on metal patio tables contained macadamia nuts and Fritos. Joyce Doody was asking the other woman to tell her whether or not the decor was "Asian enough" for the occasion.

"You'll like him," Doody was saying to another consular official in bright green slacks, checkered jacket, and a crewcut. "Speaks good English."

He referred to the guest of honor whose barbecue reception this was, whose imminent arrival the growing assembly awaited: the young new commander of the South Vietnamese Air Force, on his way home from Washington.

"General Khanh won't last," Doody said. "This may be our new guy. Young Turk."

Two older Chinese mixed drinks behind a portable bar.

Su Lin looked down between the veranda slats and saw the turquoise waters of a swimming pool on the level below, a wild extravagance in the thirsting town. She looked back at the crowd, then away through the sliding plate glass windows into the carpeted living room. Peter stood talking to a young American who in silhouette looked vaguely familiar.

Left-Hand Chen entered, alone as always, prim and gracious, and bowed to his hostess; he was one of a few non-servant Chinese present. The blond daughter of an attaché trotted out of the bathroom and hooked her arm in Peter's. Su Lin thought how in a way her brother finally had his America—what of it he had been able to buy. She kept waiting for Peter to wake up from his bad dream.

She knew few of these Americans and British who inhabited the ghostly, privileged domain of the Peak. She stood stiffly in the pressed black silk pongee blouse and black pajama slacks she had found in her mother's drawer, still smelling faintly of mothballs. The heat was like a compress, unremitting and dank even as daylight faded. In keeping with a new posture of seeming cooperation since her aborted escape, she had agreed to Peter's request that she come; he had someone he wanted her to meet, he said.

Ageless Chen, cigarette and Tsingtao in his single hand, stepped onto the veranda, nodded circumspectly to Su Lin, then turned to Doody. "Washington was good, Consul?"

"Excellent," Doody said buoyantly.

Chen seemed uncharacteristically intent with his question, and satisfied with the answer. Doody, in spite of his words, paused from his cooking and uneasily bolted his Scotch. Su Lin had come to learn that in Hong Kong things said were often code for something else; nothing was what it seemed.

"Do you think he'll know what a macadamia nut *is*, Fletch?" Joyce Doody asked. "It *is* Asian. I mean, sort of."

"Ah, shit!" One of his hamburgers had broken apart and fallen onto the charcoal below. Angrily Consul Doody grabbed another patty and slapped it on the grill. The aroma of cremating beef rose and hung in the air.

"Fletch, reeeally . . ." Joyce Doody's voice fell like a siren at the end of its arc.

Su Lin walked back to the railing and looked out across the harbor. The light was a chalk blue, the clouds above the Kowloon peaks pink and silvered, like little thoughts. The channel looked like an oil painting, the boats far enough away to appear still. In the foreground a clumpy banyan rose to frame the redwood veranda. The grinding Peak tram braked at Barker Road just below.

Suddenly all of it—the boat traffic, the clotted city, the endless futile comings and goings of the port, buildings going up, planes, junks, and sampans moving like insects on a pond—filled Su Lin with a desperate longing. Life being life, mindless, like a garden, life growing itself, a culture, content with its own motion; it just wasn't enough.

As the night wrapped round her like a creeper, she thought of her American now, dreaming him, invoking him. He was the soft breeze that wouldn't come. He was the locus of her dreams of freedom from the generations of opium. He was the choice she no longer had.

The details of her time with him had begun to fade, but something was imprinted in the flesh that wouldn't die so easily: a collection of sensations that added up to desire, and thought, which circled back into desire. She wondered what it would be like if he were here, or she there. She wondered if the spell would break, wondered how much she was remembering, how much she was creating.

Where was he? Back in medical school, no doubt, befuddled by her disappearance but getting over it by now. She hadn't known him well enough to care about the small things of his life, whether he was eating or sleeping well, whether he was happy. She could understand their three days better as an electrical phenomenon, a transfer of potentialities—or esthetically, as a fundamental exchange of knowledge.

The things she remembered of him were as remote as childhood, hugely distant. She recalled him as beautiful and fair and kind, though she knew this was silly. He also, in memory, was innocent, which was perhaps even stupider.

The discolorations of Chen and Peter's insinuations seemed very Chinese, guilt by innuendo. But why hadn't Cross mentioned it, the contact with the Corsicans? But she hadn't mentioned opium either. Could circumstances have delivered such a coincidence? Or had both given off their clouded histories like an attar that day at Oak Knoll Hospital, each drawn to the other with the inexorability of fate?

She was being asked by Peter and Chen to doubt the first thing in her life of which she had been unreservedly certain: what she felt for Cross.

Sometimes when she saw the American soldiers in town she thought of him, he who didn't come to this war. Most of all he served as an image of struggle against resignation, against the idea that Peter and Chen, and the trade, had won. Cross was abstracting into an image of an untainted, apolitical world.

As darkness descended and the torchlights flickered on the veranda, she allowed herself to imagine that by some elaborate path they would meet again. But knowing as she did what was coming, she imagined it would take her even further from him. Peter had told her that afternoon that Franco Termini Jr. was on his way to Hong Kong.

"You cut your lovely hair, lassie. You look like a nun."

She turned sharply.

"Makes you more Chinese." It was the banker Mason, grinning. "A bit like a boy. Of course nothing could spoil your beauty, dear."

Never remote from any public event involving the Lins, Nigel Mason seemed always to gravitate toward her. Since her father's killing, his lecherous jollity seemed to have taken on a hysterical tinge. This tall, freckled scion was among the most important figures in Asia, exercising vast control as fifth-generation head of the Hong Kong Crown Bank; he was also the co-executor with Peter of the Lin fortune, knitting him inextricably to their affairs. Nowadays around Su Lin he gave off a huge discomfort he seemed at moments about to unburden; but inevitably he slipped back into the shabby humor she took as his rendition of sex appeal.

She tilted the telescope toward him.

"Cheers." The tall Scot bent over and squinted. "I can see right into the window of my office. God, with reclamation, pretty soon the whole bloody bay will be filled in."

Su Lin turned around. Inside, people were collecting around a small, trim mustachioed man in khakis and dark sunglasses and carrying a riding crop.

"Those Yank soldiers up to no good in the Wanch," Mason was saying. "Two murders last night. Scandalous. Tense down there. If it weren't for the money they bring us . . ." He pushed the telescope away and turned to her. "I don't mind saying it to you, lassie, as I don't think of you as one of them. It's humiliating sharing the Colony with the Yanks." He reddened and shook his head. "And I hear there may be more coming."

"Don't sweat it," said Consul Doody, who had overheard. "Just a mop-up. Our boys will be home by Christmas."

"I say, is this the little bugger?"

Joyce Doody led the new Vietnamese Air Vice-Marshal onto the veranda, introducing him, his tall French brunette wife, and polyglot entourage. The little man stood in pressed pants and shiny shoes, white-scarved, one foot up on the low redwood retaining wall, cigarette in a holder, talking in brusque English of "my people."

Su Lin wondered what he actually knew of his people. Peter had said that his air force had achieved its prominence, and he quick wealth, by running hundreds of tons of morphine base from the tri-border area along the Mekong to air drops north of Saigon.

She took advantage of the fuss to step back into the empty living room. Heading for the door, the American Peter had been talking to blocked her way.

"Hello."

He was tall, brown-haired, and wore a pressed blue seersucker suit. He had a pair of drinks in his hand, one of which he thrust forward. He smiled down at her. Recognizing him now, scorn welled in her.

"You may not remember me," he said.

"I do," she said. "Excuse me." She brushed past him to the front door.

"You've been working at an orphanage, I hear," he called after. "And you paint?"

Outside she turned to make sure he wasn't following, then stepped into the driveway. The quiet was broken only by the shrill chattering of cicadas up on the hill and the distant sound of a car.

"Su Lin," came a whisper.

She wheeled. A man stepped out of the shadows into the driveway—tall, Chinese, his round eyes set wide, his skin fair.

"Song Wei?"

She found herself looking into the clear, intense eyes she had seen that day in the coffee shop of the Saint Francis Hotel, when he had come to San Francisco as a Crown Bank lawyer to try and convince her to take her fortune—and she had naively imagined that by renouncing it she would be free.

"You see?" he said. "I did listen to you that day."

As he came closer she saw that he wore not a suit but a dark blue quilted Chinese peasant jacket, poor cotton pants, sandals. He met her smile with his own.

"You went with Mao."

"I left the Crown Bank. Rather abruptly."

"You're a Red Guard."

"Yes."

"Nobody told me."

"I'm not to be spoken of in Lin circles."

"So your dream worked." She turned away. "Mine didn't."

"Su Lin, I'm sorry about the manner in which you were . . ."

She touched his hand.

"I want to help you," he said.

"Forgive me, but I can't imagine how."

He drew close. "I may know who ordered the killing of your father."

She turned away. "Does it matter?"

"Perhaps not. Harry Lin was a criminal. But you might be able to use it to bargain for your freedom."

She turned back toward the house, fearful someone would appear.

"I'll take you to a place," Song Wei said. "You'll see for yourself."

She looked back at him in agitation.

"Meet me at Jardine's Cannon in Causeway Bay a week from tonight, at eight o'clock."

"Must I decide now?"

"No. I'll be there. If you come, dress like a boy."

She reached her hand up to her shorn head.

"Amah will leave boy's clothes out for you."

Su Lin felt a heaviness descend, like the drug itself.

"I promise if you come you'll learn who and what lies behind the *yen*. And your father's killing."

Song Wei's eyes searched for hers in the shadows. "We are on different sides now," he said.

"Are we?"

His eyes wavered. Su Lin looked at him tenderly, then turned to go.

He spoke sharply behind her.

"Be resolute, fear no sacrifice, and surmount every difficulty to win victory."

She turned at the surprising utterance. Song Wei was looking at her almost fiercely, his tiny red missal open in his hand.

A mixture of feelings assailed her as she muttered, *"Jou tau."* Good night.

"*Mgoi.*" Thank you.

"*Hou wah.*" Not at all.

In the doorway she turned again. Song Wei had cocked his head rather comically. "Good night," he said in English, and grinned.

Her brother appeared in the hall, blocking her way. "You were rude to Alec Potter," he said.

"Is that his name?"

"You said you'd help. I told you he's important to us."

"If I'd known that's who you wanted me to meet I wouldn't have come."

She could see out to the torchlit veranda where the South Vietnamese was talking with Joyce Doody.

"Potter apologized for what happened in Cambridge. Can't you forgive him?"

She turned away. "Terhune was right. You're becoming like Father."

Peter sighed. "Why did you cut your hair? You look like a . . . beatnik."

"Is that part of *guai?* You tell me how to dress?"

Behind him on the veranda, flames leaped from the barbecue.

"Alec Potter's an American entrepreneur out here to make money at the expense of Asians. Enough, Peter."

"No, not enough." Peter looked at her furiously. "Terhune came."

"What?"

"You act surprised." He glared at his sister. "You read his wire to me and answered it in my name."

She stared defiantly back at him.

"It didn't work. He came to the New Asia. He said mad things, ranted about opium and Triads. He accused Chen of destroying Mother." Peter turned away. "He's a crazy poet, full of conspiracies, still bitter at losing Mother."

"Why did he say he'd come?"

"He thought we needed his help."

"We do. What did you tell him?"

"That we were content here."

She looked angrily away. "Where is he now?"

"Finished. I left him to Chen."

She gripped his arm. "No."

Out the open driveway gate she saw the silhouette of Song Wei disappear up Plantation Road.

"What will Chen do?"

"Offer him opium. He'll take it."

"No," she whispered. "He won't."

Recalling the steaming night in Kyoto with Terhune and his secrets, she felt now she had betrayed him by calling him to Hong Kong. Furious at the failure of her plan, she glared at her brother.

"I have something else to tell you." Peter looked away toward the top of the Peak. "Cross came to Japan."

She clutched the door to steady herself.

"He came looking for you. You must have really gotten your hooks in that bastard."

He came.

"Where is he?" she murmured.

"Terhune sent him back to San Francisco."

Her heart plummeted; her legs began to give way. She clung to the door.

"Terhune found out about Cross's involvement with the Corsicans."

"From whom?"

"Chen."

She broke away toward the hall, but Peter seized her arm.

"Su. Listen. Doody's trip to Washington went our way. The war with the Corsicans is over. Bébé Spiritu is dead. Franco Termini will be in Saigon in a few days. Then he comes here."

She looked up at him incredulously, tears tracking her cheeks. "He's the Mafia who took you to Cuba."

"It doesn't matter now. When he leaves it will be all over. Father's plans will be realized."

She pried her brother's fist from her arm. "You've cut us off from everyone who could help us."

Peter went on with horrible earnestness. "Just stay with me a little longer. We owe this to Father. Then we can begin to think about other things. Good works . . ."

Hearing the pain in his voice, she knew that Peter realized he was trapped too.

"You doubt him," she said feverishly.

"Who?"

"Chen."

Peter frowned. "I can't get him off my ass," he moaned. "He interprets Father to me. I don't know what to believe. It's almost as if he represents some invisible interest."

A choppy harbor wind swept in from the veranda.

She said, "If I could tell you who ordered Father killed, would you be willing to listen to me?"

He looked at her blankly.

"Answer."

He nodded gloomily.

"Give me a week."

He let her arm go. As they turned back toward the living room a breeze came up, carrying an almost sickly richness of jasmine through the air.

"It was different when we were young," Peter said. "It was better."

Feeling his misery, she didn't know what to say. They walked through the door.

"Look at the life Mother had here," Peter whispered. "She didn't fall. She jumped out of that rowboat and into the pond."

Peter walked on toward the rear veranda, where the Saigon general's discussion was growing into muted shouts. Alec Potter appeared from the kitchen and approached Su Lin again.

Aflame with news of Cross, she contemplated Potter with new scorn. "Get away," she snapped. Potter paled.

Beyond, the posturing general was striding back and forth; the voices had grown louder. Su Lin saw a small ill-shaven man in jeans and glasses gesticulating and shouting at the Air Vice-Marshal.

"Don't tell me that, man. I just got *back* from Hanoi. You're running opium, that's what, from Ban Houei Sai to the airdrops north of Saigon. You and the Chiu Chao and General Vang Pao in Laos are in business together. And turning on American soldiers to ninety-nine percent pure horse, you bastard."

The assembled had fallen silent. The two men faced each other in silhouette across the dying barbecue.

"I am outraged," the Air-Vice Marshal pronounced, drawing himself up and slapping his riding crop against his knee. He turned to his host for rescue. "Who is this bounder, Consul?"

"My name is Billy Strange," his adversary announced. "I'm a reporter."

Consul Doody, spatula upraised against the dying sun, appeared to be immobilized by this untoward situation. But finally in a single long step he reached Billy Strange, grabbed his arm, and wrenched the little American away from the Vietnamese. He led him through the living room past Su Lin to the front door.

"Your ass is mud back home, Strange," Doody said. "This is your last Asia assignment, I promise you."

"Too late, Consul," Billy Strange said gleefully. *"Time* fired me six months ago. I'm freelance. I've been liberated."

Watching Consul Doody pass red-faced in his barbecue outfit, Su Lin recalled Terhune's words from the summer night in Kyoto. *They are players in the game. Don't you see?*

A pair of security men came from outside the gates to facilitate Billy Strange's bouncing. As his butt hit the pavement he yelled back, his voice resonating through Consul Doody's airy ranch-style home, "I give you five years! Then you'll fall! The whole fuckin' lot of you! You'll bring the virus home! Your own children will condemn you! Blood will run through your streets!"

Billy Strange's parting words shrouded the uneasy night, leaving white faces gazing forlornly into drinks.

41

It was midday when Cross awoke, sweating and nauseous. Still Terhune had not come. Clouds had moved in, and the weather was pressed to the quarter like a damp cloth. The floorboy brought coffee. Entertaining the thought that he might not see Terhune again, Cross was not yet ready to think about why, or what he would do about it.

When his head was clear enough he turned to the second set of Terhune's journals: *Hsi*, "The Play." In these Terhune spoke of the business and politics of the trade in opiates from its beginnings.

It was known to ancient Arabs as *madak*, mixed with tobacco. Their traders brought it East as a medicine in the seventh or eighth century A.D., to become the Bengali *akbari*, the Chinese *chandu*. It had a quiet history for centuries, simply one of thousands of plants, herbs, and spices strewn along the Silk Route. Early Dutch in Formosa smoked opium and tobacco against malaria, and some Chinese acquired the habit as well—for the rich a luxury, for the poor an escape.

The British were to change everything. In search of a source of tax revenue, in 1772 they adopted the earlier Mogul custom of taxing Indian opium from Bengal, Benares, Patna, and Malwa for export. Later it became a government monopoly, providing one-seventh of British India's revenue, the moral objections outweighed by the profits.

The American traders in opium were the great New England shipping families—Astor, Bingham, Girard, Perkins, Lodge, Cabot—and some smaller ones like Winny Lin's parents, the Church family. They monopolized Turkish shipments of opium at considerable profit, part of an interlocking maritime network that included slaves and cotton; but though they had warehouses at Canton they were unable to compete with England in Asia.

The British wanted to trade textiles for Chinese tea and silk, but China neither needed nor wanted British goods. So the British, to meet the craze for Chinese silk and tea at home, paid in silver bullion. The silver flowed from London to Peking at an alarming rate.

The Chinese had no serious addiction problem then, only some in southern China who were partial to the pipe. It was the British who hit upon the idea of importing illegal opium from northern India into China to get their silver back out. The scheme was a great success, initially unchallenged by the irresolute and corrupt Ch'ing dynasty.

Opium poured in; silver poured out. Several thousand tons a year entered by way of Canton throughout the 1830s. After the British displayed their resolution to continue the traffic in the Opium War of 1840–42, the volume of trade grew to 6,500 tons a year. By 1880 China had begun growing its own in the southern provinces; in 1905 imports represented only half the figure. Over 22,000 tons were grown by the early twentieth century. The local was inferior to Indian but had the advantage that its dross could be resmoked.

The poppy, selling for two to four times the price of wheat, devastated China. Families were thrown into ruin as the men fell under the spell of the drug. Warlords used it as currency, to control whole provinces. Szechuan and Yunnan, more than a thousand miles from Peking, lived almost entirely off the revenue from the drug. By the early 1900s Britain's opium ploy was still running; there were five million addicts in China.

Overdosing on opium was a popular method of suicide. The missionaries protested, but to the Chinese the men of the cloth had simply come in with the "foreign mud." They knew that the British Royal Commission on Opium had decided in 1894 that it would do no good to stop cultivation of the poppy.

In the 1880s the missionaries introduced a morphine "cure" for addiction known as "Jesus opium." Chinese addicts were delighted; it was legal, and cost one-ninth the price of a smoke.

The Japanese followed the trend and began shipping morphine into China in such great quantities that by 1920 there was enough to supply everyone in China with four doses. Among the upper classes, smoking was the thing to do; men taught their daughters how to smoke lest they be thought poor. From 1918 on, the warlords, needing money, made it compulsory in their provinces to grow opium.

In the 1920s French heroin from Turkish product came into China. Again, as with morphine, it was thought this heroin, in the form of "anti-opium pills," would combat opium addiction. The formula read: "2 oz. heroin, ½ oz. strychnine, 1 oz. quinine, 5 ounces caffeine, 48 ounces sugar of milk, 10 ounces refined sugar. Mix well."

During the 1930s much American illicit heroin came from Shanghai, in large part because of the efforts of a man named Tu Yueh-sheng, a protégé of the equally infamous Pockmarked Cheng, chief of detectives in the French concession and a major Green Pang leader. American merchant ships plied the Pacific shipping lanes hauling opiates with little harassment from U.S. customs.

Nanking under Japanese occupation had 50,000 opium and heroin addicts: eating, smoking, sniffing, shooting, rubbing it into the skin. The needle, supplanting the pipe, had raised the worldwide impact of opium a thousandfold and turned it into the greatest criminal enterprise ever known to man: White Gold No. 4, No. 5; White Dragon Pearl No. 4; Brown Sugar No. 3: morphine, codeine, laudanum, paregoric.

Cross, reading Terhune's journal in the Kowloon hotel room, found the range of information astonishing, the mark of the obsessive; as if Terhune, by examining the cancer microscopically, could somehow rid himself of it.

As Terhune went on to describe the patriotic secret societies that gathered around Canton, the history of the Lin family began to weave itself through the tale. It commenced with the first comprador in the 1830s and came forward, spreading into Europe and back. There were the Five Dragons, the five Hong Kong Chiu Chao societies, the biggest being the Sun Yee On; Terhune inferred a connection between them and the Lin family through Left-Hand Chen. Chiu Chao composed eight percent of Hong Kong's population; one in six was a Triad member and most of the rest paid them tribute in some form. There was a description of the sudden rise of Harry Lin through his fortuitous alliance with Chiang Kai-shek and the Americans before and during World War II.

Terhune's journal concluded with a description of the modern trade, its political alliances, and what he called the "vast criminality" of opium. The British interest was sketched, from the old opium hongs forward: Mason's family history alongside those of Britain's best families—the Inchcapes and Keswicks, the Swires, the Russells—companies of vast global holdings, Rio Tinto Zinc, links to South African diamond and gold fortunes, Cecil Rhodes's successor companies; dire intimations of the Most Venerable Order of the Knights of St. John of Jerusalem; and the British monarchy itself, still enjoying revenue from the modern U.S. junkie as they once had from the Chinese smoker.

The role of the Mafia in the Golden Crescent traffic from early Harlem days forward was displayed, along with their rivals the Corsicans. Terhune, drawing upon a steady stream of information from his worldwide cabal of correspondents and informants, mentioned the role of Luciano, and Meyer Lansky and his companies: Permindex, Resorts International. Cross read that thousands of tons of opium were stockpiled all over the U.S. as a painkiller in the event of nuclear war.

There were mentions of Washington's tacit complicity and quietly sanctioned American opium flights in the Golden Triangle: Civil Air Transport, Sea Supply Corporation, Air America.

Terhune concluded with forceful warnings of war, claiming that American global policy hung in the balance—crystallized, from his perspective, around the issue of the drug. He prophesied an alliance between a resurrected Mafia as distributors for the new leaders of the world traffic, and the Hong Kong Chinese, headed by the Lin family and Chen Po-chi. The outcome, he asserted, would permanently stain U.S. foreign policy, and institutionalize massive drug use in the decades to come. Terhune alluded to the earlier Chinese experience to illustrate what the Americans had in store: As the dragon's tail twists, yin to yang, supplier becomes user. He foresaw an era of vast corporate control of human desire, the *soma* of Huxley's vision.

Still, he refused to entirely condemn the smoke but struck the attitude of a spiritual elitist, glorifying the artist's dialogue with it. He felt opium to be the Everest of the soul, the encounter in which a man's, and now mankind's, mettle would be tested. He held little more hope for mankind than he did for himself. At one point he said, "Cross needs opium," and predicted that Cross would smoke and become wise through it.

As Cross neared the last page of the journals, he considered getting them to a newspaper or an official. It was then that he realized how different the inner world was from the outer, how desperately dependent the visible world was upon the one it pretended not to see. Terhune's vision was utterly implausible to the "normal" mind. It wasn't only that the information was censurable, but that it so challenged what generally passes as "reality" as to be unabsorbable. Cross himself had already begun to doubt the reality of what he had just read.

He thought of Ilya and his "hungry ghosts" in Tangier who dreamed of a stoned America and were aiding its coming about; of the academics in Cambridge and Berkeley happily funneling laboratory drugs provided by CIA experiments to students and their colleagues; of the hundreds of billions of dollars involved in the illicit trade. It almost seemed as if a vast secret economy to shore up the Free World was being designed, with Americans targeted as the consumer, in the guise of the pleasure principle: *recreational drugs.*

Was the solution to legalize it? Terhune's ideas were more anarchistic, and a conundrum. Only through individual enlightenment could the scourge be erased, and this in all but a few people he considered impossible in this era, ascribing to the Hindu/Buddhist idea that this was a degraded *yuga,* or era, low on the spiral of man's descent from earlier high states.

There was a final cryptic fragment of a letter begun to Winny Lin, in which Terhune, addressing her as a temporary ward of death and soon to be released, encouraged her to take heart.

The last journal entry had been made on the Tokkaido train just before Terhune met Cross in Tokyo. It was a quote from the *Tao Te Ching* of Lao-tzu:

> On the day the emperor is crowned
> Or the three officers of state installed
> Do not send a gift of jade and a team of four horses,
> But remain still and offer the Tao.

Cross wondered, Who is the emperor? Who are the three officers of state?

Reading the last line of Lao-tzu, he knew that Terhune would not come to the hotel for him; in the next instant it came to him where he would find him.

Closing the journal, Cross rose and quickly began to gather his things.

42

Some call it Hak Nam, City of Darkness. Thirty thousand people live crammed in a six-acre subterranean labyrinth daubed with its own filth. There is no water, light, or sanitation. Though the walls once separating it from the rest of Kowloon were torn down by the Japanese during the war, the life within the sunken enclave bears no resemblance to life beyond. When you enter the Walled City of Kowloon you have left all light behind.

It is the most squalid and abject of places, a border town within a border town, unpoliced, officially damned, claimed neither by Hong Kong nor by China. Every day twenty thousand addicts come there to buy, smoke, shoot. Many live within the Walled City; others live close by.

Everywhere there are watchers, called *tin man toi*. Even as you approach, a lookout system on the streets above reports your appearance. The lookouts, through a system of relays, strings, and bells, pass the word within; thus goods shift constantly from place to place.

You may enter from Tung Tau Chuen Road on the eastern edge, an inclined street lined with illegal dentists' parlors where amateurs from Red China practice, the windows filled with gold and silver teeth in bottles on velvet cushions, teeth decorating the tips of whirring fans. Behind you the decaying high-rise housing projects of the Mei Tung Estates loom; ahead lie the sunken shanty roofs.

Or you may approach from the Kowloon City side, off Carpenter Road, where crumbling vendors' stands, *daih peih dong,* front the road, sooted and filthy. Here you may come to the intersection known as Hoklo Tsuen, just off Lok Sin Road, where the users come each day to score their opiates. An injection will cost you fifty dollars, a cigarette twenty.

As you pass down the central alley where the gates used to be, you see people crouched in stone holes, crates, tin sidings. You smell urine, shit, opium. There is no running water or electricity, no urinals. Faces you don't see watch you and pass the word inward.

Your ears ring with the sound of jets that take off from Kai Tak and fly low over the Walled City every few minutes, spilling fumes.

You turn into an alley no wider than your shoulders, overhung with hovel roofs blotting out all light. The stench is suffocating; there is no defense against it. Your feet sink into the softness of urine or stool slime. Moving through passageways, you duck to avoid the spray of piss from a hovel above. Human creatures, wraiths, appear, their eyes full of craziness and despair. Barefoot children play in the ooze with lolling infants strapped to their backs. Most of those you see chase the dragon, play the mouth organ, shoot the ack-ack gun, smoke, or mainline.

Buckets of water are carried in from taps outside. Huge rats, spiders, and roaches crawl out of ditches full of foul water and race through the fetid subterranean gloom, making an incessant scratching patter as they move. A pitiful few artisans—tin pounders, makers of plastic flowers, sequin sewers—toil in squalid shanties.

Something is pulling at you from below. You look down. Her name is Pearl, like the river that flows from Canton to the sea; she is thirteen years old, a junkie in the womb. She wears mauve nail varnish and lipstick. Pearl is retarded, and her eyes go in different directions. She squats over a broken sewer, a half-eaten bowl of rice next to her. Her mama-san, a black crone, lurks nearby, score marks on her scabrous arms from mainlining, her teeth gone from playing the mouth organ, her eyes yellow in heroin haze. Pearl is visited three or four times an hour, day and night. Now Mama-san scuttles over, her hand like a petrified branch outstretched for the coin. Pearl bends over against the wall; Mama-san lifts up the back of her dress for you, then goes back to eat rice while you perform.

You walk on, your feet scraping tin and wood scraps, old plastic bottles and containers. You have lost all bearing. You hear the yelping of dogs being beaten to death for food, *heung yok.*

You pass through a low iron gate and find yourself behind a sooty curtain looking at an ancient striated eight-millimeter film of sex acts. A sallow young man in battered plastic sandals grins at you.

Back in the alley, a gray junkie in an undershirt, his teeth brown and broken, rough prison crewcut, brushes softly against you like a foul wind, unseeing. He spits a brown-black substance and drifts on, insubstantial, like an insect, a mantis. A year ago he was a tough Red Pole for the 14K Cantonese Triad that controls the Walled City.

Sik yu. White Powder.

The police get "tea money" from the 14K vice-den lords. In return the gangs get protection and heroin at police stations. There are a hundred thousand 14K Triad members worldwide, sixty thousand in Hong Kong. They control the entire West Side, and the Walled City. Their main rivals are the Chiu Chao gangs, especially the Sun Yee On.

Exposed electrical wires, illegally tapped from above, ensnare you. A young girl passes by with shit slopping from a leaky wooden bucket; at street level there are two toilets for the Walled City's thirty thousand residents.

"You wan' Miss White? White Dragon Pearl? Number 4? Number 3 Brown Sugar? Chase dragon? Play mouth organ? Smokee?"

The *pahng-jue,* host of a heroin den, takes your fifty cents in exchange for the screw of toilet paper, tinfoil, and cardboard funnel. You squat against the offal-smeared wall, chasing the dragon.

You forget.

Some will tell you that each government made maps of Kowloon and they didn't match, leaving this seam in reality that became the Walled City. As it belongs to neither side, people commit crimes in Kowloon and "escape" into it. Peking considered it part of Mainland China, but the Chinese magistrate died and nobody took his place. During the Japanese occupation it was emptied and became a ghost town. The walls were torn down, the stone used to extend the runway of Kai Tak Airport into the harbor. After the war squatters and refugees from Mao returned in greater numbers to these lower depths to resume their place, the dross of the world.

Cross mounted a crumbling stone staircase covered with slippery green-black mold. He turned momentarily away, hand over his face, unable to bear the odor of feces and rot, and gagged against the wall.

The waxen boy opened his mouth, showing his few teeth. He called himself Wing Ding. He said he was fourteen but he looked like an old man. He had picked Cross up at Hoklo Tsuen and offered to be his guide.

Cross felt something on his hand, shouted, and jumped back. A gray rat dropped to the ground and began crawling up his shoe. Cross banged his foot against the wall, bursting the rat and smearing it into the wall's history. Wing Ding smiled his soft ghost smile and opened his mouth as if to laugh, but no sound emerged. Softly he pushed at Cross, urging him toward the entrance.

Behind a soiled curtain a woman lay on her back on a blackened straw matting. Coming closer, Cross saw that her hair was a dirty red, her skin pale, freckled. The whites of her eyes were a pure yellow, the pupils so tiny they were all but gone. Her miniskirt and blouse were far too big for her. She weighed about eighty pounds.

She lifted her dress and spread her legs.

"She?" Wing Ding asked, grinning.

Cross shook his head no.

The girl whispered in a Cockney voice devoid of earthly life, " 'Ello, sailor."

When Cross didn't reply she fell still. Then she began to idly finger herself. Cross turned away.

"She needee money, boy," Wing Ding said. "She good."

"No," Cross said. "Big *gwailo*." He sketched the large outline with his hands.

He looked back again at the girl. She had curled up fetally on the mat and begun to whimper.

Cross followed Wing Ding back into the labyrinth. Urine from an overhang splashed on his shoulder. He jumped aside and stumbled on, hearing the familiar clack of mah-jongg tiles, like the rattling of old bones.

At a turn in the alley he caught a slit of hard blue sky. It seemed distant, delicious; he wanted to lunge for it. Then a huge jetliner roared overhead. Its silver belly seemed only yards above as it blotted out the light and shook soot and insects down around him.

Cross fell to his knees in panic. His hand tangled in the carcass of an old bicycle frame.

"Come on, boy," Wing Ding said.

A fat, muddy pig, broken from its rope, came suddenly out of a darkened hovel at Cross, grunting. Immobilized, Cross stared at the little pink eyes even with his own.

Wing Ding kicked the pig, grabbed Cross's arm, and hauled him up. They wandered deeper into darkness until Wing Ding paused at last before a low, skewed wooden door.

Wing Ding called. The door opened. Cross ducked and went inside.

His eyes slowly adjusted to the sight of a long narrow hut. There were fifty-odd bodies on benches around a low rough table running the length of the room.

He saw the lamps, the pellets cooking, the bamboo pipes from which they inhaled. It was an opium den of the lowest quality, a tawdry parody of the elegant ones described in Terhune's notebooks. The heavy, haunting, sweetish smell hung like a pall.

Cross began to wander down the length of the table. Some were smoking, others had their heads in their hands on the table, others had stretched out lengthwise on the bench. Some lay inert on the filthy stone floor.

Finally, he came upon the wild, large head, resting on the table, pipe crooked between his beefy fingers, his eyes open but unseeing. There were purple bruises on his cheek and neck.

Cross bent and gazed into the colorless face. "Terhune."

Cross whispered it three times. Finally Terhune's eyes rotated slowly upward. After long hesitation, as if obeying a different set of physical laws, Terhune raised himself to a sitting position. He regarded Cross with absent deliberation.

"*Yauh,*" he said in Cantonese. I'm here. His voice was dry, distant.

"It's me. Cross."

Terhune's large, mapped face spread in a slow, ghostly smile. "Welcome, Corsican, to Hang-Chou."

Cross trembled, not from the threat of violence—the room was lazily pacific—but the sudden encounter with the arcane, unsettling opium consciousness.

Terhune whispered, "Hang-Chou, lad. The great Walled City, where life is sensible and sweet, where treasures of all descriptions . . ."

His voice, like an old recording, trailed off.

"I read the journals," Cross said. "When you didn't come back I thought you might be here."

Terhune sat, hands folded in his lap, gazing down with stolid indifference. Then he turned slightly, and Cross saw the welts on his neck, his arms.

"They beat you, didn't they?" Cross whispered. "To give you pain and draw you back into opium."

Terhune nodded.

"Who? Peter Lin?"

"The sinister one. The ancient foe." Terhune's words fell slowly, like drops of water. "Chen gave me the killer in the arm. Until I cried out for the Patna Fine."

"Why?"

"The Left-Hand schemes. He fears the journals."

"Did you tell them where they were?"

"No," he whispered. "I told them I'd destroyed them." He became still, waxen. After some time he said softly, " 'Shall I tell you the way to become a god in this humdrum world? Burn some incense and sit listening to the rain.' " He laughed an unearthly laugh. "Lu Yu. A great poet."

"Where's Su Lin? Did you see her?"

"You see, Corsican?" Terhune whispered. "These people. They hurt no one. They are kind, gentle, happy."

"Why do you call me Corsican?"

"Betrayer," Terhune said. It was spoken with flat resignation, not anger. "Why did you come? We have no more use for each other." His head dropped slowly onto his chest.

Terhune giggled soundlessly. " 'On the day the emperor is crowned / Or the three officers of state installed / Do not send a gift of jade and a team of four horses—' "

" 'But remain still and offer the Tao,' " Cross completed the verse.

Terhune looked up, surprised. "So you read the journals. Where are they?"

"Behind the desk of the Ascot Hotel. In my bag."

Terhune smiled distantly.

"Who is the emperor, Terhune? Who are the three officers of state?"

But Terhune turned away, forcing Cross to lean over to catch the whispered words: "It is over, Corsican. You have lost her."

"No."

Terhune turned and gazed down the table to the glimmering candle and the pipe a withered addict held over it.

"Cease to resist. Opium doesn't judge."

"You've given in to the drug," Cross muttered.

"I have returned to my lover," Terhune replied. "Unlike you."

Cross shrank, feeling the Walled City close in around him. He spoke with waning force: "Come out, Terhune. Save yourself. Help me get to Su Lin. We can do something about the trade."

Terhune looked at him, his old-young face recomposed into an inscrutable persona.

> See, all things howsoever they flourish
> Return to the root from which they grew.
> This return to the root is called Quietness;
> Quietness is called submission to Fate.

He turned and fingered his crooked pipe as Lao-tzu's verse dissolved in the air. The attendant was coming toward his lamp to cook a pellet.

"Here," Terhune said, holding the pipe before the lamp and offering the mouthpiece to Cross. "Find out what you are, American."

"No." Cross wavered, feeling the allure, the sly importuning pull, the user's instinct for seduction, always at the moment of the mark's greatest despair and vulnerability.

"Cross will smoke," Terhune had written in the journal.

He heard Terhune mutter:

> To remain whole, be twisted.
> To become straight, let yourself be bent.
> To become full, be hollow.
> Be tattered, that you may be renewed.

Terhune put his lips against the mouthpiece, tilted the bowl over the flame and inhaled. There was a loud hissing, a dense cloud of smoke. It sounded to Cross like breathing magnified through a stethoscope, or the sound in surgery of the opened heart. Something in medicine was echoed in the smoker's ritual. "After all these advances," Dean Whiteman had told him once, "our best painkiller is still the damned opiate. When push comes to shove, what do we give the dying patient? The labs have never produced anything to beat it."

Science reaches the edge of its own folly, then turns in on itself, drifts home to the ancient. Terhune only offered him, in an infinitely more pleasant form, what the doctor daily offers the patient against pain.

"You've lost her. Here, smoke."

Cross's pain of heart swept toward the eternal antidote.

When Terhune had finished he put his pipe back down on the table, a gesture occupying minutes. Then he slowly sank down into himself, an organic stillness, his head touching the table.

Cross leaned down and gripped Terhune's arm. The musculature seemed to have dissolved; it was soft, like a baby's, as if through the regressive instrument of the drug he was sliding silently back toward the womb.

"Terhune. Come."

After a time Terhune looked up. "Outside the Walled City Manchu bandits await us. We will die if we leave here. There is no hope for us, Corsican. Smoke. Remain with me here in Hang-Chou."

As the attendant came back around, Cross took the pipe and bent over the lamp.

It went softly into the lungs, without pain. It was not as strong as a cigar, but fleetingly, delicately stimulating. A moment later he was dizzy, then nauseous.

"It passes," Terhune whispered.

There were no visions.

Then he was thirsty.

Gradually time emptied.

At some point Cross said, "I understand now."

The planes roared by overhead.

"Welcome to paradise, Corsican."

By the end of the third day he had grown comfortable with the drug.

43

An old barefoot toothless Tanka woman, legs planted wide, poled her barge back and forth from shore to the sampans as darkness turned the Causeway Bay typhoon shelter into shadowy, bobbing forms. She wore tattered black pajamas, lantern swaying, a cat beside her on a steel drum, splitting the oily undulating swatch of water separating the great scrubbed launches of the Royal Hong Kong Yacht Club from the dark cluster of Chinese floating homes.

Su Lin stood beside Jardine's Cannon, herself becoming a shadow in the lit bowl of the harbor, dressed in boy's dungarees and loose worker's jacket and hat down over her eyes, watching the slow approach of the barge.

Jardine's Cannon loomed like a great dark penis. A shot had been fired every day from her for over a hundred years: the Noonday Gun, commemorating a day in the mid-1800s when an illicit Jardine and Matheson opium clipper had sailed into the harbor from Calcutta and mistakenly received a twenty-one-gun salute reserved for high officials. The Governor, enraged at this overt celebration of the illicit mud, ordered the gun fired every day as penance. It was a story Hong Kong children knew like Americans know Lincoln, a joke on the old order; the true joke, that the old order lived on, unfortunately escaped most of the citizenry.

"Su Lin."

Song Wei's voice came from the other side of the cannon, where he stood dressed like a peasant too.

"You came."

"Did you think I wouldn't?"

He walked across and stood next to her. "Did anyone follow?"

"No. My brother was out. I took the Peak Tram down, then a Queen's Road trolley."

"My old work clothes fit you."

"Amah left them in my room."

"Good. You will pass."

They turned and looked back into the Causeway Bay district. Workmen clung to bamboo scaffoldings rising like webs to the sky, laboring beneath night lights. The radar antenna of the New China News Agency on Sharp Street, Peking's unofficial embassy and spy outpost, cocked eastward like a great silver ear. Several blocks further was the street called Yee Woo, Jardine's name in Cantonese; beyond that was Jardine's Bazaar and Jardine's Crescent: Hong Kong's past, scored with opium.

A damp breeze that had played the city all day swept in off the channel, ruffling the canvas sampan hoods. The old poling lady neared the shore in her barge.

A cluster of American sailors from Wanchai passed, drunk and swearing. Like water insects, a coven of sampan ladies appeared on the water and poled next to shore, paralleling the sailors.

"Fuckee fuckee?" they called up to the sailors.

"You wan' pa'tee?"

Song Wei glowered. "You can get anything on the boats."

A live fiddle-and-trumpet band struck up a raggy "Yellow Rose of Texas" somewhere out in the shelter. Two sailors gave a Confederate whoop and jumped in a sampan.

"Let's go," Song Wei said.

The strong-faced barefoot women took a coin as they climbed down the ladder into her boat. A young bespectacled girl, dressed Western, schoolbooks under her arm, joined them. The old Tanka woman poled into the harbor, steering a course between the spacious berths of the Royal Hong Kong Yacht Club and the tangled floating slum.

The shelter boats were small and dark, made of wood, the best of them some twenty feet of varnished teak, with blue or green canvas ribbed over all but the front, propped up by sticks. The worst were no better than rowboats. All had bumpers of old tires against the jostling of traffic and storms. Even by dark, sounds of industry rose from the sampans, while on the British side, isolated gin-and-tonic laughter wafted weakly. In the sampan city, service boats passed water, food, and supplies in blue plastic buckets to women cooking within by butane. Joss burned at the back of each sampan.

"They live and die there," Song Wei said. "Some never come to land."

"Perhaps it's not such a bad place to live. In Sausalito they'd call this fashionable."

"These people live there because they're poor." Song Wei nodded toward the Yacht Club. "In Hong Kong the rich have everything."

Familiar British laughter pealed across the water. Su Lin saw Nigel Mason in white linen slacks, shirt, and silk scarf standing on the deck of his yacht *Victoria,* drink in hand, chatting with an embassy girl. At the sight of him, Song Wei tightened.

"Your old boss," she whispered.

"He mustn't see us."

They faced away, toward the shelter.

"Does Mason know why you left the bank?"

"Mason knows everything," he whispered hotly.

Feeling Song Wei's hatred toward the banker whose distant peals of laughter laced the night, she said, "He seems like a fool to me. A harmless rich man. Why do you despise him so?"

"Ask me again later tonight. If you still need to."

As they poled deep among canopied floating shanties, Su Lin saw exposed vignettes of lives: large families sharing single rooms beneath the canvas roofs, carpeted varnished floors populated with dogs, refuse, chickens, potted plants, and buckets and barrels, casks and tins and planting. They stopped at a houseboat to let off the schoolgirl; fifteen of her chattering family greeted her, living in the ancient way, sending the daughter off as their experiment, their wary tribute to the new gods.

They drew toward the darkening outer edge of the shelter.

"What you will see tonight usually takes place Kowloon side. This is unusual."

They approached a cluster of sampans from which no light seemed to emanate. Song Wei turned his back to the old woman.

"Do you remember what I showed you?"

She nodded.

"What is the hand signal for an ordinary member?"

She put her left hand against her chest, fingers straight out, thumb in palm.

"What is the hand signal for 'correctly paid'?"

Su Lin locked her second and third fingers over her first and second and held them against her chest.

"Good. My friend will greet you. He will ask you a question. Do you remember the answer?"

"Yes."

The sampan bumped against a large junk, its varnished sails like great shadowy wings in the night. A lantern glowed beneath the deserted deck.

"Stay near the back. The one who greets you will let you out when the time comes. If someone else addresses you just indicate your rank with your hand. Don't speak. Remember, you are a visitor from another branch."

Su Lin climbed a wooden ladder to the rear of the high-riding junk. She stood alone on the teak deck, taut with fear, listening to the pulse of her blood. Water slapped against the hull. Song Wei and the old woman poled away into the dark. Storm clouds rose on the horizon, blotting out the moon.

A Chinese boy with pockmarks appeared from the source of the glow, a curtained entrance to the hold, and beckoned to her. She crossed the deck and stood before him. He looked at her with stiff impassivity.

"Why is your face so pale?" he asked in English.

"My face is pale but my heart is red." She put her hand across her chest.

"Bare your left shoulder."

She opened the top buttons of her loose jacket. The boy looked away. This ritual of entrance, Song Wei had said, once a rejection of the Manchu dynasty, today represented defiance of all government authority.

He opened the curtain and nodded toward the ground. She dropped to her knees and crawled through the opening. A pair of guards held upraised swords over her.

She got to her feet and took her place at the back of a group of Chinese recruits, all men, dressed in plain gray workers' jackets and pants. It was a dim, joss-choked rectangular room whose contours she couldn't yet discern. Two sticks of joss were held out to her. Properly, she took one in each hand. Now she saw several robed figures near the front, dressed according to ranks Song Wei had described. She began to make out the order in this ceremonial teak room below decks called the City of Willows.

At the front was an altar, behind which hung scrollwork written in black ink on red paper. The altar itself bore a myriad of objects placed ritually: incense, five small flags, brass lamps, a pot of wine and five bowls, a pot of tea and three tea bowls. There were dishes of fresh fruit, ground nuts, flowers, red dates, vegetables, Chinese tobacco and betel nuts, water and pomelo leaves. She saw a book, a silver needle with red thread, and dozens of burning joss sticks.

At the foot of the altar was a large wooden tub painted red, filled with rice. On the floor were flags of different colors bearing calligraphic inscriptions.

To one side was an array of weapons: swords, clubs, chains. She noted numerous other ritual objects: a grass sandal, a white paper fan, an abacus, scales, a mirror, bundles of silk, candles. A blood-stained white robe she knew was in memory of the monks who had died at Siu Lam monastery, the origin of the Hung League, the Triad cult. She saw a rosary, a coconut bowl, a large bamboo hoop wrapped with sprigs of pine and cedar: the heaven and earth circle through which the recruits would kneel and pass.

On the right of the altar sat a stern old man dressed in white. A white rosary hung around his neck, a red silk scarf about his shoulders draping almost to the floor. On one of his feet was a grass sandal. He wore a knotted headband of red cloth. This was the Heung Chu, Incense Master in charge of ceremonies, his symbolic number 438.

On the left side of the altar there was a chair for the Shan Chu or Hill Chief, the leader; it was empty.

Other officials in ceremonial robes flanked the altar, facing each other: the Fu Shan Chu, who assisted the leader; the Sin Fung, or

Vanguard, who recruited new members and established branch societies. Beside them were the Hung Kwan, 426; the Fighting Leader, the Pak Tsz Sin; the Adviser, 415; the Cho Hai, or Messenger or Grass Slipper, 432; and the ordinary members, the Red Poles, the fighters, who bore the number 49.

As the recruits were led forward to undertake the ceremony of initiation, Su Lin was left exposed at the back. At this point the pockmarked boy who had admitted her gave a quick series of three hand signals to the officials to explain her presence. As their eyes turned to her she raised her hand and gave the two signals Song Wei had taught her: "Correctly paid," followed by "ordinary member," indicating her identity as a Red Pole 49 from a visiting branch. The officials accepted her display and moved on to other matters. She stood against the rear wall, shaking inside Song Wei's baggy clothes.

The new recruits, after being registered at a table, were given white cloth bands to tie around their waists. Then all eyes turned to the empty leader's chair.

Su Lin saw a small door open behind the altar. The Hill Chief emerged.

He was dressed in a red robe. On either shoulder were black insignia in a circle of white. A red scarf draped over his shoulders. One of his feet was bound in a straw sandal. A yin-yang enclosed in hexagrams adorned the front of his robe just below the chest. The red knotted headband matched the robe. In his left hand, crossed over, was a long sword. Emerging from his right sleeve was a small yellow flag on a stick with black lettering.

Su Lin was seized with terror. If she bolted out the back, as every cell in her body urged her to do, it would assure her discovery.

The Hill Chief looked up and began scanning the room from left to right. The pockmarked boy moved in front of Su Lin, partially blocking her face. His survey complete, the Hill Chief nodded to the other officials, then sat down.

He placed his left arm in his lap and his right on the arm of the chair, the tip of the sleeve closing over the place where the right hand, had he one, would normally emerge.

Though Song Wei hadn't spoken the name aloud, Su Lin had heard him in a hundred ways confirming her worst imagining: Chen Po-chi, the Left Hand, was the Hill Chief of the Sun Yee On.

The sacred part of the ceremony began. Su Lin watched from behind the shoulder of the boy who was her guide. It filled her with a dread without focus, for she could not grasp all its meanings.

The recruits kneeled, holding joss sticks pointing down; the Vanguard tapped each on the back of the neck with a sword. Oaths and poems were recited, questions posed, answers muttered. There were vows to avenge the Five Ancestors and restore the Ming dynasty to the throne.

An official raised a live cockerel into the air by the neck. Carrying a china bowl in his other hand, he walked down the line of recruits. Each recruit touched the cockerel and the bowl with his right hand. Then the official gave the bowl to the Vanguard, who carried a sword. An oath was intoned.

Suddenly the Vanguard threw the bowl into the air and smashed it with his sword. The shards exploded and fell to the ground.

The Vanguard kneeled and cut off the cockerel's head with one blow from his sword. Reciting a poem, he opened the body of the cockerel with his sword and drained the blood into a bowl.

The Incense Master stepped forward and spoke the Thirty-Six Oaths, in which the initiates promised to be slain by myriad swords should they betray secrets.

The recruits stood up. The Incense Master pricked the middle finger of each one's left hand with a silver needle threaded with red until blood appeared. Each recruit dipped his finger into a bowl of wine and licked it. Su Lin recognized the Chiu Chao: "It is sweet."

As the Incense Master showed them the hand signal of their rank, Su Lin felt the hand of her sponsor, the pockmarked boy, on her arm, edging her toward the rear entrance.

The recruits stood up, bowed to the Leader, Incense Master, Vanguard, and officials. They then formed into two ranks and bowed to each other.

As they did, Su Lin saw that one of them was her brother.

Peter's hair was shorn close to the head. His face was blank, his eyes dull as he stood among men whose language he didn't understand, swearing loyalty to a society whose values and intents were little known to him.

Her fist rose to her mouth. The pockmarked boy was steering her behind the curtain to the door. Left-Hand Chen was obscured by the recruits mustering before their new Hill Chief.

Alone outside, Su Lin staggered across the slippery deck. A soft rain had begun. The small boat was there waiting.

Song Wei extended his hand. She climbed over the side into the sampan.

All the way to shore she sat on an oil drum, her hands around herself, feeling the drops of the rain, unable to speak. To their right, in the Yacht Club, Mason's boat was still alive with guests and jollity.

Song Wei asked her for a coin for the old woman. They paid her and climbed up the ramp to the road running beside the Causeway Bay typhoon shelter. The old woman and her cat poled off into the inky night.

"Do you want to walk?" Song Wei asked.

"No. Let's just sit here for a while."

"It's raining."

As he said it the rain abated. He put his hand out and smiled. They sat down looking out at the darkened shelter. Tears ran down her face.

"I'm sorry, Su Lin."

He lit a cigarette and handed her one.

"You know, Sun Yat-sen was a member of the Triads. In 1912 he went to the Ming Tombs at Nanking and announced to the deceased emperors that the Manchus, the Ch'ing, had finally been overthrown after all these centuries."

A warm squall wind whipped through the harbor. Song Wei looked out toward the shelter.

"That was the high point of Triad history, I think. They had reached their patriotic objective. Since then they have degenerated into *pin mun,* illegal dealings—opium, gangsterism, prostitution. They have become tools of capitalist oppression."

Su Lin looked out at the harbor, shivering.

"The Sun Yee On is the biggest Chiu Chao Triad in Southeast Asia." He looked at her. "Your father was Heung Chu, Incense Master of the Triad whose ceremony you saw."

"How did my father gain entrance? He was only half Swatow."

"He was sponsored by the Hill Chief."

"Chen."

Song Wei nodded.

"The present Sun Yee On began in Shanghai, before the Revolution. In those days the biggest Triad was the Green Pang. They were strongarms for Chiang Kai-shek, along with the Sun Yee On and the other big Chiu Chao society, the Fuk Yee Hing. The leader of the Green Pang, Tu Yueh-sheng, became such a political asset that Chiang made him a major-general."

The rain had ceased. Su Lin dried her tears on her sleeve and let the smoke from the cigarette curl into her face.

"After the revolution," Song Wei said, "the gangs fled to Hong Kong. But the Sun Yee On was already established here and throughout Southeast Asia because of earlier migrations. They had people on the police force. So the Green Pang couldn't dominate them as in Shanghai."

"Is that when my father rose to power?"

"Yes. There were bloody wars all over Hong Kong between the gangs for control of the drug, prostitution, and gambling concessions. It didn't resolve until last year in the spring. A big meeting took place in Chiengmai, Thailand. Leaders of the Sun Yee On and the Green Pang came from all over the world, wherever they have branches. War was declared. Many killings followed. Not just Chinese, but diplomats and others. The Sun Yee On won. The Green Pang were expelled and have taken up residence abroad. But the Sun Yee On paid a price."

"The death of my father."

Song Wei nodded.

"The Green Pang killed him?"

"Yes. But they were contracted by Corsican gangsters."

Su Lin stood up and ground out her cigarette with the heel of her shoe. "So my brother was right. It was the Corsicans."

Song Wei drew close. "Yes. And no. The Corsicans were set up by someone within the Lin organization."

Su Lin found his eyes in the harbor darkness. "Chen," she said emphatically. "It was Chen."

A sampan appeared out of the night, poling toward shore, carrying several men from the Triad ceremony.

"But why?" she cried. "Why did Chen want my father killed?"

"Come on," Song Wei whispered. "Start walking."

44

They had walked westward into Wanchai's bar district. Intermittent rain drove them in and out of doorways. The sailors had dispersed with the wetness.

"I have to get home before Peter does."

"You have time. The new Triad members go to a big dinner now. They'll be out several more hours."

Neon blinked in puddles. The walking made her feel better. They passed the dreary clubs, custom tailors, and tattoo parlors on Lockhart Road.

"I need to tell you something about the politics." Song Wei cupped a match to her cigarette. They stepped out from a doorway and continued walking.

"After the Revolution the overseas Chinese used to send money to families back home through the Hong Kong banks."

"The Bank of Peking."

"Not so much. They used the Hong Kong Crown Bank and the old colonial Chartered Bank. You see, the British had arrangements with Peking. After the war Mao and Chou En-lai met with them. It was never the same as before, but the British managed to maintain many of their old economic interests out here through Hong Kong, especially their financing of the opium trade outside of China. Then a few years ago Peking changed its policy. It instructed the overseas Chinese to put their money in banks out of the country, and people back home were given equivalent Mainland money to spend."

"Why?"

"Peking wants to co-invest with the overseas Chinese abroad alongside the British in order to make money, and also to encourage the opium trade. They feel they can turn the dragon's tail, send opium to the West as a blow against America while making profits themselves that used to go to the British. It may or may not be a wise policy, but that's what they are doing.

"Egypt's General Nasser came to visit Chou En-lai last month. Do you know what Chou said to him?" Song Wei took from his pocket a folded Chinese newspaper clipping. Standing beneath the neon light of the Lucky Man Bar, he read aloud:

" 'Some of the U.S. troops in Vietnam are trying opium. And we are helping them. Do you remember when the West imposed opium on us? They fought us with opium. And we are going to fight them with their own weapons. The effect this demoralization is going to have on the United States will be far greater than anyone realizes.' "

Su Lin, drawn by the sound of a jukebox, glanced into the bleak interior of the Pussycat Bar and saw the ghostly lurching forms of U.S. sailors and their whores.

"This new policy," Song Wei went on, "has upset relations with the British. There had been a certain economic collusion between Britain, Peking, and the overseas Chinese, especially the Chiu Chao who control the drug trade. Now this is falling apart. Peking wants profits too, for political reasons."

"What does that have to do with my family?"

"Chen was educated in Britain. He is close to the Crown Bank's Nigel Mason. He also does business at the Bank of China next door. Your father by contrast was educated in America. During the war he worked with the Americans in China. He recruited for the OSS in Burma and Singapore. Later he aided the CIA. Chen felt he had become too American."

"Father worked for the CIA?"

"In effect. He was a lackey."

They passed the Luk Kwok Hotel, home of Suzy Wong. Song Wei's Maoist adjective describing her father saddened her.

"You see, the Triads co-invest with Peking overseas and send dope money home. As for Chiang Kai-shek, he is an American client. He has brought the Americans in too far."

"You mean it's the U.S. and Chiang Kai-shek, and the Mafia versus Britain, the Triads, and Peking?"

"More or less. The overseas Chinese network is basically under control of London. You could say it's a battle between London and Peking for control of this network, which translates into who controls opium."

"And my father and Left-Hand Chen had a split?"

"Not openly. Chen had assumed it would resolve naturally, with his legitimate son taking over the business when Harry Lin died. Also, don't forget that in the Sun Yee On, Chen was your father's superior. Harry Lin was only an Incense Master. But of course when Chen's legitimate son died the year before last it ruined his plans."

"Why do you say legitimate son?"

"Because Chen has an illegitimate son."

"Who?"

They were nearing Central. Song Wei frowned. "I will tell you shortly."

"But what about my father's killing? You say Left-Hand Chen set it up and allowed it to happen, presumably to take over the business."

"Yes. He brought in the Green Pang." Song Wei stopped and looked at her carefully, then spoke: "Chen did this at the behest of another."

She peered back at Song Wei through the drizzle, fearing to ask who.

"I will tell you something about your father. Near the end of his life he was penitent. He wanted to get out of the trade. That is why he didn't bring Peter back to Hong Kong. He regretted what had happened to your mother and wanted to legitimize the family. His seventieth birthday and the dedication of the orphanage was the announcement of that dream, of his change of ways. Perhaps it was your influence during his yearly visits to see you in the States. Perhaps it was just disgust with his own criminality. Your father had influential discussions with the Americans. They were ready to burn down the fields and substitute cash crops too. Perhaps unrealistically, he wanted to hand you and Peter an honest heritage." Song Wei turned and looked at her. "That does not excuse his earlier evils."

Fat drops of rain fell. Song Wei and Su Lin reached Queen's Road at the edge of Central and kept walking. She crowded thoughts of her father and mother from her head, hungering for more information.

"What about Chen?"

"Well, he doesn't want this, of course. He may have even doctored Harry Lin's wills."

"But why didn't you tell Peter this?"

"Chen won't let me near him. I'm a Red."

Su Lin shivered in the cooling night. "What happens next?"

Song Wei stepped beneath a canvas overhang as the rain grew, and spoke hurriedly. "There is a dissident faction in China. They don't agree with Mao. They think the new policy of overseas investment actually favors the Americans. They're willing to deal with the British."

"Who exactly is this faction?"

"I am not at liberty to tell you. But it reaches very high up. All the way to Mao's successor."

"That would be Lin Biao."

Song Wei wouldn't elaborate. "Let's just call them the Shanghai faction."

"So Chen is involved with these dissidents?"

"Yes. They have both British and Russian backing against Mao. If the Shanghai faction won, they would set up a military dictatorship in China. Chen and the Triad interests want to return Hong Kong and Southeast Asian interests to China, under certain terms. The opium money would help bring this about. But Mao knows about them, and will triumph."

"Isn't the Shanghai faction afraid of British domination?"

"No. They would rather have the British card to play against the Soviets."

"And my father's death had to do with this?"

"Harry Lin was killed because he didn't want to get involved in this intrigue but only wanted to make money. Because he was Americanized, and half Chinese. And because he chose an unfortunate time to become repentant about his criminality. Chen didn't want to give up the trade to the American syndicates. He felt the family should move out and take over the world trade."

"This is what Chen told Peter my father wanted."

"This is a lie. This was not your father's wish at all. Peter is under Chen's control."

The pathetic image of her brother at the Triad ceremony drifted by; she wondered what she would say next time she saw him.

"I had planned to gather evidence about my father's killing, then present it to Peter. But after tonight I see he's lost."

"Chen probably got him to the initiation by telling him your father was a member. The Triads are so corrupted now that the vows mean little. Peter may come around."

And if he doesn't? I will have to make a choice.

So this is what Terhune knew, or intimated. And where is he? Alive? I've got to find Terhune.

"Song Wei. You seem to know so much. And care so much. Why? Why do you believe in Mao?"

He stepped out into the night rain and turned to her, his eyes burning with shame. "Chen Po-chi is my father."

All she could do was stare back at him; then she couldn't even do that, and looked down at the rain-slicked pavement.

"I am the illegitimate son."

Painfully, he tried to laugh.

"You could say I am his missing left hand."

"Is this really true?" she whispered.

"Chen raped my mother, your amah, when she first came from China."

"He never acknowledged his fatherhood?"

"Oh, he bragged of it. But he always treated me with scorn."

"Does he know you are a Maoist?"

"Yes."

"And he allows that?"

"I think he imagines it might serve his interests one day. After all, we are all Chinese."

The rain softened. She followed Song Wei across the tram tracks to Garden Road.

"So my father and the Americans and Mao were reaching a new

political equilibrium. And your father and Britain and Moscow opposed it."

He nodded. "Since the War the British interest has never been the American interest here. It is the Americans who come and fight, the Americans who use the drugs, and the British who get rich. Your father believed China and America could get along. Chen wanted to nip any possible rapprochement between Washington and Peking in the bud. He still dreams of a mandarin China."

Su Lin saw the Peak Tram terminus up ahead, glowing in the rain among the trees.

"But if Chen was not the final person who ordered my father killed, who was?"

Song Wei said. "You know the answer. If Hong Kong lost the trade, who would stand to lose most?"

She pictured the Yacht Club, the clinking glasses, the storklike, smiling lecher with his dry laugh. She remembered the night of the banquet, and Nigel Mason standing over her father, holding his arm, as the assassins fled.

"Mason," she said quietly.

The storm reared, whipping sheets of rain across the pavement.

"He could no longer deal with your father," Song Wei said. "He feared that Harry Lin, who was making trips to Peking, would convince Chou En-lai to side with the Americans against the British interest. Mason conspired with Chen to have the Green Pang eliminate him at the behest of the Corsicans. It was an elaborate, unlikely plot, difficult to trace."

"How did you find out?"

"I'm a lawyer." He stopped across from St. John's Cathedral. "And I hate my father."

She turned and looked through the darkness up toward the mist-shrouded Peak.

"It doesn't quite end there. Mason was under pressure from the Shanghai faction to bring this about as well. You could also lay it at their feet. So it's like a circle, isn't it?"

"Is this just a theory of yours?"

"No. Peking has this information."

"Then Chen works for Mason?"

"It's more complex than that. In fact you could even say the opposite is true."

As they passed the U.S. Consulate on their left, she asked, "What about the Americans?"

"Everyone knows Consul Doody is a fool. He seems to be run by the entrepreneurs and CIA mercenaries who want to keep up their exploitation of the Asian peoples."

"Alec Potter," she whispered.

"Who?"

"Nobody."

They were at the foot of the Peak Tram stop. The cables ground through their agony as the last tram came to the bottom and its doors opened.

"So you've become a Red Guard."

"I've seen enough of the world of capital. It spawns men like my father."

"No more law?"

"British law is an imperialist structure used to legitimize this kind of crime. It's not for me. I will go underground soon if I am not arrested first."

"Then this may be the last time I see you." She reached out and took his hand.

"I'll tell you about somebody else named Lin," he said. "He was a very courageous man in Chinese history, Special High Commissioner Lin Tse-hsu, the mandarin who came from Peking to Canton to stamp out the opium plague in 1839. He failed, of course, and the first Opium War followed. But he is a hero in China today."

A wind swirled the wisps of rain. The night was dark. Song Wei squinted toward the harbor. "A typhoon coming, maybe," he said. "No. It's too early in the season." He looked at Su Lin. "Events are rushing forward. Chen Po-chi wins this round perhaps. I wouldn't advise trying to stop him."

The tram buzzer rang. Song Wei looked at her with sudden feeling. "You had somebody. A friend in San Francisco. My mother told me."

She looked down. "Yes."

"You must have been fond of him."

The rain put her cigarette out. "I think so."

Song Wei sagged slightly, then pulled himself up. "I hope you see him again."

"Perhaps not."

Silence fell over them.

"Maybe I can help you get out, Su Lin."

"Through China?" Her heart began to speed.

"Forgive me. I shouldn't have said that. I can promise nothing. Not yet." He gripped her hand urgently. "Be careful."

Then he was gone.

The tram door closed automatically; there was nobody else on it. As it plied the slope, Su Lin looked back toward Hong Kong harbor, but it was lost in mist.

"Father," she said aloud. Then she called softly, "Cross."

For an instant she imagined both of them out there in the night somewhere. A curious sense of hope, or light, entered her. Then rain beat violently against the windows, and everything darkened as the tram grunted upward into the enclosure of the Peak trees.

45

The visions began the third day. From then on Cross lived at the silent, cold heart of opium. The fetid cubicle walls above his rotted reed matting were billowing liquid scrims of changing color and shape. The cheap parlor beyond the door lay across an ocean.

He inhabited a timeless twilight, sunk down in himself, staring at his legs for hours as if they were struts of wood. His coat was full of holes where cigarettes had burned down unnoticed. Time had folded in upon itself, minutes and years of equal weight. Human shuffling and movement, the suckings and burblings in the smokers' room beyond, the scratching of insects, the regular shuddering passes of the planes overhead were contemplative occurrences, as divorced from action as movies. The only awareness causing movement was the rhythmic desire for more of the drug, sending Cross back into the den.

An abstracted sense of Su Lin drifted in at times, a trembling, diaphanous shadow, but dispersed before it became pain. A particular place on his wrist bore sores where he had observed a hand, evidently his own, scratching. He had eaten little, and what he had he had not excreted; he grew thick. Day and night merged.

Beside him, Terhune lay like a great beached sea mammal, arising only to go to the table for more of the pipe. At times he sat up, his head down on his chest, muttering Chinese verse. Halfway between doses he would talk briefly with Cross, who would answer or he wouldn't. The conversations were desultory, oblique, and hung in the air like the smoke itself. Cheap opium was everywhere, sweet and pungent.

Days passed. Cross's body seemed to have merged with the landscape and become an object. The only time he was aware of it was when some hallucination swept through, a sudden swelling of the void into sensory fantasy. Once he looked down and his skin was full of holes, like cheesecloth, tiny geysers of steam shooting from each hole. Another time flames erupted from the tips of his fingers. The visions fell through each other, like colored silk in water.

Esthetic ideas arose, ineffably brilliant; he regarded them with sublime disinterest, no longer a player but an instrument upon which a ghostly musician played. He had become pure effect, inert, a null, dead.

"You see?" Terhune whispered. He was lying still, his face in arrested pain. "Is this not superior to life?"

Cross was listening to thousands of women in simultaneous orgasm. His tongue was swarming with insects. Rainbow cathedrals dissolved like crystal sand through air.

Murmuring, Terhune roused himself and crawled to the den for more drug.

Cross observed that he was on his feet, the gesture of rising already forgotten. An impulse guided him toward the entrance to the den.

In the alley it was night.

Wing Ding was leaning against the wall in an undershirt and jeans and clop-clops, a cigarette hanging from his mouth. Harsh light leaked from a bare bulb over a mah-jongg game next to the den.

"You wan' so'thing?"

Wing Ding waited out the distance between question and answer, smoking, gazing sideways at the *mei li chien,* American, who stood weaving like a sapling, making the long journey to words. He judged Cross to be burning a good neophyte's habit after a week in the den.

Cross watched his lips and tongue shape air he squeezed from his chest into a column.

"Hong Kong side."

"You gah mo' money?"

Cross moved his head. The earth tilted.

"You ge' killed. Bad gang wai' for you ou'side. Chiu Chao boys. Chop chop. Sun Yee On. You beddah die hea wi' *yen*. Chase dragon."

Cross shaped more air. "What gang are you?"

"Sap Sie Kie. Fourteen K. Best. We boss Kowloon."

"I need . . ." Cross raised his fist.

Wing Ding took him a turn in the stench-filled alley. He hauled a box out from beneath a cart. "Triad knife," Wing Ding said, flourishing a flat piece of steel about three feet in length and honed to a razor's edge.

"Three hundred Hong Kong dolla'."

Wing Ding showed him a *mi tung,* a sharpened steel pipe. Cross took it and held it, feeling no contact between the object and his hand.

"You put in trousah leg."

There was a triangular steel file attached to a wooden handle, the end sharpened to a needle point. Wing Ding demonstrated driving it into a man's stomach, twisting.

"Blee' to death, ya?" He grinned through bad teeth.

Cross gripped the Triad knife.

"American!"

Cross shifted the dimensions of his dream to the left to encompass the figure looming in the alley. Reflecting some monumental effort, Terhune had roused himself and exited the den.

He soberly held his Kyoto short sword out, hilt toward Cross. His voice thundered through the clammy air of the Walled City. "The Mongol hordes will be defeated!"

Cross gave Wing Ding back the Triad knife. He lessened the space between himself and Terhune and reached for the sword.

"Come out with me, Terhune," he either said or thought.

Terhune stared fiercely. *"No."*

The syllable broadened and echoed into something emphatic, final. Cross knew Terhune had decided to die here in his tawdry surrogate dead-end Hang-Chou.

"I'll come back for you."

Terhune faced back toward the den. Cross watched his broad ambling back fill the alley.

At the entrance Terhune paused. He turned and opened his mouth to speak but no sound emerged. Cross filled it in, words from Terhune's journal: *There are no cures, only respites.*

As the gloom enveloped him, Terhune became his own shadow and disappeared back in the den.

Kowloon City was a melting candle. Color, odor, and sound ran together as six 14K boys spirited Cross through the night in a pedicab, knives and pistols drawn, lunging at shadows. Somewhere Cross nodded out. When he awoke he was in a *pak pai,* an illegal taxi, with four new 14K warriors, careening down Prince Edward Road.

The cab pulled up to the Yaumatei typhoon shelter. Cross had begun to sniffle, twitch. A young *yen* was upon him, bringing the soft incipient panic, the revolt of the nerves.

The 14K Cantonese hoods would go no further. They loaded him into a small skiff with an Evinrude. A kid who couldn't have been more than twelve smiled and started it up.

Intermittent showers and gusts of wind set the boat pitching. Sitting in the rear of the outlaw lighter skimming among freighters and junks across Hong Kong Harbor, Cross felt no sickness, only an ache for the drug that came and went in shorter intervals. The world outside was a hot beast, a dragon—fanged, leering. He fell over and lay in the bottom of the skiff, his eyes open, unable to command his body.

Then the boy was holding a foil and a pocket lighter in front of his nose.

"Chase dragon. Numbah three."

Cross sniffed hungrily. His nerves lit up, then cooled. He gazed emptily through watering eyes at the spinning harbor.

There was a bump, then the boy had his arm. Cross stumbled up onto a wooden jetty. An electric sign said MACAU FERRY PIER.

The boy was pointing to the left. "Dow'tow'."

"Downtown," Cross murmured.

The twinkling buildings of Central rose like irradiated megaliths through the darkness. Cross wandered off toward them.

46

It was dark along the Peak, wet with rain. The Sikh spread open the high double gates. Passing the wrought-iron Chinese lettering, Su Lin recalled the day the summer before when she had come in from San Francisco and Fook had driven her up here.

This is my last time through these gates, she thought.

The Rolls was gone; Peter wasn't back from the Sun Yee On ceremony. She pictured little Fook waiting for him at some all-night noodle dive or cheap *yen* den in Causeway Bay.

She took the path past Winny Lin's flower garden. Spring jasmine flooded her with rich melancholy; leaves, weighed down by the rain showers, bent toward her as if in greeting. Next to the gazebo, scented magnolia were in bloom, large tremulous white flowers against wide green leaves.

A vision came of Mother, the last visit: a spring day, Easter Sunday, 1958. Su Lin had arrived in dress and bonnet and flower bouquet at the high, drear Church mansion doors in Wellesley where Winny Lin had remained "under private care" since the return from Kyoto. Grandpa Church, stern and distant and endlessly embarrassed by her and Peter, the tilted eyes and tinted skin—though she was pretty, he Harvard—shook his head darkly at the door; Mother was having an "off day." Su Lin had come all the way from boarding school to see her. Grandma Church, lace hankie clutched to her nose at the foot of the spiral stairs, wept as Su Lin, not to be denied, rushed by, heading for the silent, dark wing.

She ran down the musty hall, past portraits of ancestor Churches, tintypes of the early factories, watercolors of the great ocean clippers.

Mother's room was empty. There was only the hospital bed with the straps, vials of pills on the table, tangled plantings in pots by the window labeled in scrawled, incoherent black ink. Then through the screen doors Su Lin saw her mother out on the wide lawn, long hair and colored ribbons trailing behind, eyes frantic, outrunning ghosts in a white gown: mad, beautiful. Beyond lay the pond, the rowboat. A stocky nurse in a white uniform chased along behind, hypodermic syringe upraised: the two figures, mother and nurse, both in white, frozen in time.

"Mother!"

A breeze swirled up from Aberdeen. She pulled the jacket tight to her neck, thinking of the opium poppy ripening to harvest now across the mountains of southern Asia: hard, green little pods, fat with milk, awaiting the slit knives.

Opium; Mother. Slowly, they twined.

From the back porch, looking down at Repulse Bay, she could tell where land ended and water began by the point where the stationary lights became moving ones. Turning, she saw into Father's old study, and the picture of him in ceremonial costume: Harry Lin, the Eurasian Heung Chu, Incense Master. *Who had he been? Do we know the parents? Do we just think we know?* The image filled her with pain, for she knew now its signification.

She passed the wicker porch chairs, the mah-jongg table, and opened the screen door to her room. Inside, Amah had lit a small lamp and turned down her bed.

She went to the mirror to undress, toying with mechanics of escape. She would leave at dawn, before they awoke. Where? Wherever. To the sea, perhaps.

Removing her blouse before the mirror, she registered the prominence of her bones, the outline of her clavicle in the dim light. Apparitions of paintings unpainted, self-portraits begun in San Francisco, hovered; as if swatting at smoke, she chased them away.

Then in the glass she saw a shadow loom, felt the press of a strange body. She froze as hot hands clutched her.

She screamed, struggled to break away. He, tall, bent her against the dressing table. Their twined images rocked in the mirror, his right hand fumbling for her mouth, his left locked over her breast.

There were scissors in an old sewing basket of Mother's on the dresser. She fumbled, grasped, had them in her right hand, slashing at his left.

"Ahhh!" He backed across the room, bent over, holding his hand.

"Get out!" she screamed.

Groaning, Alec Potter slumped in a wicker chair and raised his wound aloft. Blood poured down his arm. Su Lin covered herself with a robe and leaned against the dressing table gasping, still wielding the scissors.

"Out, or I'll call the Sikh!"

Fresh drops of blood dripped on Potter's white linen pants. She had severed the skin of his hand.

"What are you doing here?"

He winced. "Feeling stupid at the moment. Got a Band-Aid?"

She threw him a towel. Glancing out the tiny window above the dressing table, she saw that the Sikh was gone for the night.

"So what *am* I doing here?" He looked up at her with sly contrition. "I dream of your Perfume River. Isn't that the term hereabouts?"

"I despise you, Potter. Don't you have any pride?"

"I heard you. But you see, I just might have something you want."

"My brother and Chen are coming home any minute. Save yourself and go. They'll kill you."

"Oh, cut it. They won't make trouble for me. Who do you think defends them to the Americans?"

She readied the scissors as he stood and took a step toward her. He stopped and grinned, holding his hand up to stanch the blood.

"What if I told you your father was alive?"

"You're insane."

"If I could produce evidence?"

She looked at him icily. "I saw him shot. I was there."

Potter took a photo from his pocket and tossed it at her.

"He's in Peking. Mao sees to his well-being."

She bent down and picked it up: a Kodak showing Harry Lin in snow, bundled, smiling before the massive wooden struts of the Forbidden City.

"My father had been going to Peking for ten years. This could have been taken any time. Get out. You have nothing on us."

She tried to throw the picture back. It fluttered to the floor at her feet.

"He's alive. He was seen there last week."

"You're desperate."

"Do you know how much money you stand to lose if the Golden Triangle shuts down?"

"It's you who will go down, Potter."

He stopped patting the towel around his hand.

"Look. I really like you. Why can't we work something out? You're the greatest girl in Asia. We're both . . . Eurasian culturally. I mean . . . why not?"

She brandished the scissors again.

He wasn't strong but tall, agile. Su Lin backed up against the dresser with the scissors as he came. She screamed again, but he was on her. This time his other hand wrenched the scissors away.

He jammed the towel he had been using to stop the blood into her mouth and grappled her onto the bed. She fought the crude fumble of clothes, the smell of camphor and alcohol, the scratchy press of his face upon hers.

A sudden blow came. For a moment she went under. Potter's body dropped heavily onto hers.

Then it rolled limply off.

There was someone else.

"Peter?"

She raised herself up to look.

Her mouth opened. But the name she had uttered a thousand times would not pass her lips. His semblance stood above her, eyes milky and ill-focused like Fook's, pupils tiny, holding Terhune's short sword, its tip bloodied.

"Jim! *Jim!*" It came, with everything behind it.

Now her body followed the cry: mussed, bruised, up and in his arms, finding his face, obliterating the months of stark, lonely dreaming with furious kisses.

Alec Potter sat on the floor below them, clutching his stomach, blood leaking through his fingers, an expression of wonder upon his face.

Headlights swept the room. The sound of the Rolls roared through the open window.

Su Lin looked at Cross once.

"Come on!"

She grabbed his hand and led him out back, into the protective dark.

47

It was with a mixture of triumph and humiliation that Franco Termini Jr. stepped off a Pan Am plane onto the sweltering Saigon runway, commencing the first leg of his epochal Asia visit. There was a certain tooth to the moment. He had the pleasure of knowing he was climbing over the bodies of Bébé Spiritu and the Corsicans of Marseilles, blown up at the Vientiane airport after several unpleasant years of ascendancy over the Mafia; now the old order had righted itself. But thanks to Valachi and the pressure on the Golden Crescent fields, Termini also came hat in hand to make a deal with Chinese, a race whom he would scarcely deign to tip after dinner in New York City. In this sense his visit boded ill, and was a capitulation to a sudden alarming global power shift threatening to institutionalize Eastern domination of the world's most lucrative enterprise. Cosa Nostra would be asked to accept runner's status, edged out of manufacture into distribution. Meyer, the Little Man, had laid it out: If Termini couldn't come to some decent arrangement with the Lin syndicate, he'd have to take the Families out of the trade altogether.

It was enough to offend one's honor, Termini thought as he crossed the runway, the subtropical heat hitting him like a steam bath.

The American Embassy aide who met him with the limousine outside was dressed in an open-collar Hong Kong silk shirt, while Termini boiled in his Rome suit. Driving through town he recognized the familiar hieroglyphs of corruption, though its Asian guise disconcerted. GI Joe was there in swelling numbers, just like southern Europe after the war, where Termini had cut his teeth in the black market with his father.

The Continental didn't have yogurt—his doctor had told him to eat a lot on his trip—or pasta, only a lot of nosy journalists. After lunch his Chinese guide took him to buy some silk sport shirts. Termini gave him a twenty and a box of Havana Tampas. The Chinese didn't seem to appreciate the rarity of this gift.

He ended up in the back of a jeep being driven around town by a couple of MP's, thinking about the fact that in three days he would meet with Peter Lin, the half-Chink shylock he had taken horse racing once and put in his debt; Termini crossed himself and invoked Charlie Lucky's name in a whisper. He worried more about "Lefty" Chen, whom Mr. Chi had said was an operator; better to be prepared with the Chinks.

Termini had a concept of the deal: a steady supply of morphine base into the labs in Marseilles and Palermo, plus a limited amount of pure No. 4 delivered into their hands on the West Coast. Chinese poppy, co-manufacture East and West, and exclusive Mafia distribution in the Western world.

One sticky point: The Chinese would have to stop selling direct to the GI's in Vietnam. Washington had let him know personally that Johnson was sending more troops over. Termini liked the Chinese concept; it was imaginative: No. 4 direct to the soldiers. But that was infringement on Family clientele. He could already hear the Chinese argument: "We get them started here, you service them when they get back home." No deal. You get them loaded here on that 99 percent No. 4 of yours, most of them will never get back home.

They were driving fast in the exposed jeep on the outskirts of town. When he saw khaki choppers in the sky and heard the sound of machine gun fire coming from two sides, and the kid MP driving started talking about "Hueys" and "Charlie in the bush," Termini said, "Turn around. Let's get the hell out of here." He hated fighting.

The next morning early some old CIA guys he'd known from Havana and Miami flew him up to Chiengmai in a Cessna for lunch. Chiengmai reminded him a little of Havana in the good days: pretty girls, colorful flowers and decor, high dealings in the lobbies and restaurants of the hotels. He made a mental note to tell the guys back home: Chiengmai.

After lunch they flew him out to see the fields.

There were the CIA guys; a smiling, polite Chinese flunky who seemed to be a Lin man; and a gummy old one-eyed British ex-customs officer from Hong Kong called Peg, who seemed to know everything about opium.

It was harvest time, and the fields were a sight. They stood on the windy plateau watching the men prepare. Termini recognized it as basically the same technique as in the Crescent; he had seen the harvest in Anatolia, in the villages around Afyon. Except here the women didn't wear veils.

The Meo moved backwards through the fields, cutting shallow, parallel semicircular incisions in the round pods with a small sharp knife. The white opium gum oozed out, one drop at a time. If the incision was too deep, too much sap would come out and be smeared by the wind; if too shallow, it wouldn't exude.

That night Termini and the others stayed in a small inn on the edge of the village, and ate with the tribesmen. In Turkey it had been wine and yogurt and goat cheese and opium seed bread with gaunt, swarthy men with rifles. Here it was rice and pork with small swarthy Asian men with rifles.

The next morning the farmers, men and women, went back out to collect the gum. They moved forward this time so as not to brush against the capsules. Grabbing the pod in one hand, they scraped it with an iron scoop held in the other and emptied it into an earthenware pot. Two days later, Termini was told, the capsules would be incised again at a different place. Four to eight times this was done, until the plant had been completely leeched.

A rich harvest, old Peg said on the way back. He claimed there was enough opium and morphine base stashed away in the Mekong hills to supply the world for another seventy-five years. Bullshit, said the CIA guys. Don't tell our senators that.

On the way back Peg and the CIA crewcuts began to describe the scene in the Triangle: the trade routes, the politics; the Mainland Chinese, the free Chinese, the hill tribes, the British, the Americans; a thousand tons a year by the end of the decade, and the twenty-one heroin labs. The numbers they kicked around made Turkey sound penny-ante. Termini's head began to hurt, and to change the subject he asked about the local girls. He was wearing one of his new Chinese silk shirts, and his arms had gotten sunburned in the fields and were itching.

Asian girls turned out to be just as complicated a subject.

Back in Saigon, Termini saw a few more people that evening—a Corsican informant he'd known in Marseilles, a Sicilian restaurateur, and a certain Vietnamese lady—then decided to wind it up and get on to Hong Kong a day early. He figured the food had to be better there.

And they had horses. Happy Valley. Oh, baby. Every mama's boy had heard of Happy Valley. There was a tout at Hialeah who used to go on and on.

48

A shrill gang of jays brought Su Lin awake. Opening her eyes, she followed the smooth bark of a Chinese ash to the noisy branches dancing against the pale dawn blue. She rubbed her sore neck, struggling for a consciousness of time and place.

"Amah?"

"*Yauh.*" Amah appeared out of the clearing of Buddha bamboo in her worker's pajamas. Her withered hands clutched wild Java apples, red and white, bell-shaped.

"We go soon, ya'?"

Amah placed the fruit on the ground at her feet and left to forage for more.

Su Lin turned and looked. There he was, beside her, breathing heavily, his head lolling on spider ferns. She had abstracted him for so long that his real presence, and in this condition, unnerved her terribly.

She contemplated his face, scratched from the tree-lashed night rush down the mountain. His feet and legs twitched. His skin was damp and mousy in color, his breathing faintly guttural.

Feeling her gaze, his eyes opened. They were sticky with fluid.

"You're a sight," she said, and kissed him.

He looked at her with an alien expression like Fook's that made her turn away. "Is it really you, Su Lin?" he whispered. He reached up and touched her cheek. His hand was cold, damp.

She handed him a Java apple, but he didn't do much with it. He looked at her with puzzlement. "You cut your hair."

"You just noticed?"

He blinked and struggled up on his elbows. "I don't remember last night. Did you come and find me?"

"No. You found me. And almost killed someone."

He nodded dully. "I remember. Who was he?"

"You're sick," she said. His teeth were clattering.

"No." But he lay back down. "Where are we?"

"Halfway to Aberdeen."

"Aberdeen." He closed his eyes again.

Standing, she could see the tips of the factory stacks, the sparkle of the channel, a corner of Apleichau Island beyond. She guessed they were an hour away from the typhoon shelter, and Amah's promised haven among its 20,000 Chinese.

Behind them up the mountain, the green bronze tip of Winny Lin's gazebo broke the trees near the top. Su Lin had negotiated them in the dark down the old escape route by memory, past the sedate villas, crossing Bluff Path and then finding Peel Rise, overgrown but serviceable, just as when she and Peter had been children.

Her fear was that Peter would remember too.

"Up. We have to go."

Cross stood, all legs, like a foal. His nose ran, and she could almost see his nerves sending cross-hatched electrical information beneath the surface of his skin. There was some kind of gap between his thought and his motion.

"Who was that guy last night?"

"An American." She touched his face.

"What was going on?"

"My hero," she said, and smiled.

He has encountered the drug. With Terhune?

Amah, peasant-wise, appeared in the clearing, her pockets bulging with brown mountain litchi and more Java apples.

Cross gave Su Lin his hand. In his other, comically, he brandished Terhune's blade.

It was a narrow twisting downward path, strewn with refuse. Cross picked her a white-pink magnolia. The dew spilled down her wrist.

"God, how I've thought of you."

They followed Amah along a brushy creek bed, empty with dust in the drought, past the reservoir and into a cat-infested shantytown on Aberdeen's flank.

Su Lin guided Cross down the brief, empty dawn streets, before the markets opened. The smell of early fish catch hung in the air. When Amah saw Cross fading she took an alley to a rickety balconied building, knocked on a door, and relieved Aberdeen's pharmacist of three bottles of paregoric. Su Lin admired Amah's resourcefulness, noted her opium savvy.

The waterfront faced the surging clot of Tanka and Hoklo sampans, already busy. While Cross sat on a piling with the paregoric, Amah hailed a sampan. In minutes they had floated free of land toward the bobbing cluster of the typhoon shelter. Su Lin watched uneasy dark-light clouds roll in eastward off the South China Sea.

The floating city absorbed them like a sponge. While Su Lin and Cross clung together in the back of the sampan, Amah negotiated in noisy screech and haggle with boatmen. There was a temporary transfer to a junk, then down a ladder to a small launch with chubby twin Chris-Crafts run by an old man in an undershirt and shorts, a rolled Chinese cigarette hanging from his mouth. Su Lin paid him fifty Hong Kong dollars.

"*Pin mun,*" Amah snorted, illegal dealings, and turned away when Su Lin asked her what was occurring. The Hoklo boatman called her *kai ma,* godmother, and seemed to fear her.

Su Lin had thought they could take a boat to an outlying island, or even to Taiwan. But Amah was certain Chiu Chao people would be alerted everywhere in Southeast Asia; with the *gwailo* Cross, they would be caught quickly. Amah proposed the orphanage; they adored Su Lin, and might hide them until Cross felt better. Su Lin had no better idea.

They sped out across the glassy harbor, past the great floating restaurant palaces strung with lights by night, dead gilt caverns in the bright morning. The Hoklo bore them left past Apleichau, where wizened boatbuilders fashioned ferries, sloops, cruisers, speedboats, yachts, steel lighters, sampans, junks.

East Lamma Channel took them north and into open water. Here it was choppy, and the fat clouds racing in from Manila were sudden, the kind that come with the monsoon to send the sailors lashing their sampans in Aberdeen, Causeway, Yaumatei, Aberdeen.

Streaking past Repulse Bay on their left, Cross hung over the side as if to be sick. But he only shivered and made noises, soothed by the timely paregoric. Su Lin, salt spray pricking her face, reached out and held him, trusting to something she couldn't yet see.

"Where's Terhune?" she asked when she thought he could answer.

"Still there."

"Where?"

A great yawn racked Cross's body. "Walled City."

"God, no," she whispered, her heart sinking. She remembered the scholar's dark recitation in Kyoto and knew what this meant. "Did he take himself there?"

"No. Chen forced him back to the smoke." Cross weaved, his hands gripping the slats beneath him. "He had him beaten. When that didn't work he injected him with number four."

She shivered, watching Cross fish in his jacket for the bottle of paregoric. Was Peter innocent of this when he spoke to her on the veranda at Consul Doody's?

"Why?" she murmured.

"Chen wanted his journals. He fears them."

"Did he get them?"

"No. Terhune left them with me."

The motorboat rocked on. Watching Cross uncap the paregoric and swill it, Su Lin tasted her own despair. Her struggle had reached a precise juncture of failure: Terhune back in the dens; Cross beside her drinking opium. And it was because of her that both had come to Hong Kong.

Chen rises, looms, swells beyond control.

The enemy surrounded her; she didn't know what to do.

Cross drained the bottle, then leaned over and kissed her. His lips were sticky, unpleasantly sweet.

She searched for his eyes. The shrunken pupils made the green of the iris seem inordinately large, insectlike, cold.

"I waited for Terhune at a hotel," Cross said, suddenly lucid. "He was supposed to come back with news of you. When he didn't I went to the Walled City. I'd read his journals. I thought I'd find him there."

"He got you to smoke."

"He convinced me there was no hope."

"Of what?"

"Getting to you." Cross tossed the bottle overboard. They watched it bob behind.

"That was the last one," she said.

Cross frowned.

"Was that it?"

"That was it," he murmured.

"Sure?"

Cross clutched his shoulders and watched the bottle disappear. She watched fear jump like a spark in his dented eyes as her own ran with tears.

"Where are the journals?"

But Cross had sunk somewhere deep inside, his eyes seeming to film over, his fingers scratching invisible vermin. He slumped against her shoulder. She held him as they flew around the point at Shek O and out past the Clear Water Bay cove. The Hoklo bucked them across the wake of a departing Russian freighter at the west end of Kowloon peninsula; Cross nodded off.

Amah came back and stood next to her, her short legs wide and solid, her thin silver hair stirred in the wind. "You' boy?" She nodded toward Cross.

"Yes, Amah."

"You likee?" She smiled, all silver teeth.

"Yes."

She made the gesture of the pipe. "Lap sap." Rubbish.

"No, Amah. He's not . . ." Su Lin looked off toward the water. Opium, violence: closing over, sucking her under.

"Su Lin. You see Song Wei?"

"Yes, Amah."

"He tell you—"

"Everything."

Her old wrinkled eyes wetted up.

"He's your son by Chen." She didn't know the Chinese word for rape.

Amah's face puckered in anger.

"He took me to a Sun Yee On meeting. I know now. Chen is the Hill Chief. He betrayed my father."

Amah nodded grimly.

"And my brother is Sun Yee On now."

"Ya'. Sorry."

"So sorry."

The Chris-Crafts churned on; Cross slept. Amah asked Su Lin if she knew how Chen Po-chi lost his hand.

"In a boating accident."

"Ha," Amah screeched. "That what he say."

"How?"

Amah told her that when Chen Po-chi was a young man in Shanghai, the old Hill Chief of the Sun Yee On there saw he was smart and wanted to train him up to succeed him. But during the war with the Japanese, Chen was smoking the pipe when he was supposed to be out collecting for Thirty-Six Beasts. The Hill Chief became enraged, and told four Red Poles to find Chen Po-chi in the den and cut off the hand he used to smoke the pipe. When they found Chen and told him the Hill Chief's edict, Chen insisted upon doing it himself.

"He cut off his own hand?"

Amah illustrated with a gesture and laughed. "Chen Po-chi no smoke again!"

Su Lin fell silent, trying to visualize the act, imagine Chen's state of mind. It made Chen more terrifying to her, more formidable, extreme.

"But he became Hill Chief," she said.

"Not in Shanghai. In Hong Kong. By cheating." She glowered. "Bad for everybody."

The sun was up and they were racing across Mirs Bay. They passed the floating remains of a night swimmer, an "illegal" who had raced sharks to flee Mao and lost. Between two tiny islands they bore left. The boatman roared down Tolo Channel to Tolo Harbor itself. Ahead Su Lin saw the wharf at Tai Po, and the bamboo scaffolding of the orphanage rising behind.

Amah said, "A *tin man toi,* watchman, know we come."

But as they drew near to the rickety Tai Po wharf, there was no *tin man toi.*

Amah got out first. She found him a dozen yards away in the bushes on his back. His throat had been slit, his nose and ears removed, his eyes stabbed into pulps.

Amah scuttled back to the launch. "We get outta heah."

But the orphans were running toward them from the building, shrieking. The dark holes of their mouths and their wide eyes told of terror.

As Su Lin stepped onto the wharf they grabbed her hands. Cross and Amah came along behind.

In the lobby of the building, a large ivory figurine of Kuan Yin had been shattered with a hammer. Chinese graffiti covered the dedication plaque to Harry Lin.

"Sun Yee On," Amah whispered, her voice shaking as she read the characters aloud.

Following the orphans into the Director's room, they found the Kaifong lady hanging upside down from a rafter, passed out. The orphans were too short to reach her. Cross climbed on a desk, untied her, and let her down. Su Lin looked madly at Amah.

"Harry Lin days ovah," Amah whispered, her lips trembling. "Peter work for Chen now. Everybody work for Chen. Unnastand?"

As the orphans wailed and circled, Cross stretched the Kaifong lady out on the floor. He massaged her until she came to her senses, then told the orphans to give her tea.

"You go now," Amah said. "Red Pole boys come back. Or police come."

Su Lin looked crazily at Cross, wondering where they could go. Cross, glazed but erect, came and took her hand. He pointed out the rear window, his head cocked. Su Lin heard the faint chugging crescendo, saw the steam winding above the trees in the distance.

"Amah. Where does that train go?" Cross asked.

Amah was crying. Su Lin knew she was worried about Song Wei now.

"From China border back into Kowloon."

"Come on." Cross, eerily composed, was pulling at Su Lin.

"No. We'll be trapped in Kowloon."

She looked at him; he looked back. There was a hiatus in time; and for the first moment since they'd rescued each other, or doomed each other, or whatever destiny or risk it was they jointly carved, they were alone. The space around them dimmed—the room, the orphans, Amah—and into this dark flared the recollection of who they were, who each had seen and felt first in mirrors, later in flesh, in another land; the rich, unreasoned desire that had engendered a search across half a world, the warm center they'd glimpsed then lost. This illumination passed between them in the space of a breath, slipped behind the dots of his green eyes, beneath the wounds on her heart. She watched Cross concentrate furiously upon her, his last moments of ease before the nerves' desperate dance began, willing this tinder to heat. It caught, sparked, shone.

"Terhune," he said. "We've got to get him out."

Amah ran up to them, shaking a trembling finger. "You no go back Walled City. They kill you bo'."

"He'll die in there."

"I find somebody go get *gwailo* fo' you."

They heard the sound of a car approaching. Before Su Lin could answer Cross was guiding her out the back door of the orphanage.

"The journals," Cross muttered. "I've got to get them."

"You know where they are?"

"Where I left them."

She stared at him.

"The Ascot Hotel," he said. "Kowloon."

"Missee carefu'," Amah wheezed, wiping her eyes.

The orphans cried out after them as they broke through the bamboo grove. Car tires squealed in the dust behind them, but they didn't look back.

They hopped along the trestle ties the few dozen yards to the Tai Po station, just ahead of the train.

On the platform she said, "Do we know what we're doing?"

He embraced her weakly; she felt him about to collapse.

As the dusty green train pulled up, he said, "Last time we tried to hide."

"And lost each other."

"It doesn't work. It never works."

Elation flooded her. She saw the one who had come to her door one night, whom she had invoked against madness and made the theme of her vigil, who came to her now in pain. She allowed herself the wild comfort of imagining he was still her dream: Cross.

They climbed aboard the Kowloon train. The monsoon rain began, breaking the months of drought. They held each other like refugees all the way into Kowloon.

49

If, as Terhune had once said, those who desire control seek to control desire, Chen Po-chi was a pure example of such a man. Having ruthlessly tamed his own desires, by early 1964 he was nearing absolute control of the most powerful agent of desire on earth.

Climbing the steep steps to the small veranda of his austere bachelor home, a birdcage in his lone hand, Chen turned to study the uneasy clouds over the harbor. Sniffing the warm dank spring gusts, he sensed an early southwest monsoon.

This was inappropriate. It would interfere with the Lantern Festival. Worse, it could ground the planes at Kai Tak when he was expecting a most important arrival.

Chen's home was Mid-Levels, low on the Peak behind the Chinese Western district rather than the adjacent Central favored by Hong Kong's princes of power; here he could conduct other affairs and maintain his life as leader of the Sun Yee On Triad free from *gwailo* scrutiny.

His songbird, back from an outing at Hang Wen bird teahouse on Queen's Road, warbled sweetly as Chen replaced the metal cage on its hook among others and covered it partially with white cloth.

Chen stood imperturbably in his pajama pants and mandarin jacket in the small pruned garden, smoking a Lucky Strike; then he turned and stepped through the double wooden doors into his dwelling.

The living room was a melange of dated Western armchairs and Chinese blackwood and lacquer chests. Neat, almost monastic, it exuded the resolved asceticism of a simple pensioner. Nobody could accuse Chen Po-chi of personal greed.

A small desk at which he worked was backed by a gallery of photos, the largest and most recent of his dead son Sam, who was to have taken over the Lin business. No corresponding picture of his bastard son Song Wei was in evidence, nor any image of his Triad affiliations.

In a small gold frame was a browned photo of a grinning urchin in shorts at the turn of the century, proudly holding an abacus awarded by the English missionary school in Shanghai for his precocious skills on the instrument.

Cambridge in the late teens was the backdrop for the next photo: a young man in tweeds, hair swept back off the small elegant forehead. A shipboard picture followed, a nameless rouged Chinese woman on his arm.

A shot of a Shanghai restaurant in the early thirties portrayed Chen, smooth and well-dressed among a gay crowd of generals, Europeans, Muscovites, and mobsters. There was a smile, but now the eyes betrayed the haze of the drug, perhaps explaining the absence of photos in the years following. There was no record of the dissolution, the crimes, the lapses, the alleged collusion with the Japanese, or the final brutal chop of one hand by the other in the den, exceeding the order of his Hill Chief: only a snapshot of a haggard but composed refugee stepping off the gangplank of a freighter in Victoria Harbor after the war, left hand waving, right arm at his side, empty at the cuff.

His dual resurrection in Hong Kong, both in the Lin organization after joining his comprador family and as the secret Shan Chu, Hill Chief of the Sun Yee On, leading the fight against the rival Green Pang in the forties and fifties until their defeat, bespoke a brilliant, wily man. The only photographic token of this rise was recent, and innocuous: Chen in business suit toasting his boss Harry Lin in the New Asia dining room the night before his assassination.

One would have to look further than these photographs to fully understand Left-Hand Chen's late rush to power, through the instrument of the Lin business.

A noisy knock came. Chen found pale, freckled Nigel Mason towering in the doorway, monumentally hung over.

"Please come in," Chen said softly.

"Wouldn't have a bit of drink, would you, Chen? Anything will do, really."

"Sorry. Only plum wine."

"Have to do. Cheers."

As Chen poured from a decanter, the rumpled banking scion, lecher, and lush slouched back and forth, looking ridiculously over-sized and unkempt in the fastidious room.

"The Mafia fellow is arriving as planned?"

"This afternoon. I've sent Fook and several escorts to Kai Tak to pick him up."

"When's the meeting?"

"Night after next."

"Lovely. Cheers," he said, downing the plum wine. "Hope he beats the monsoon. Don't think we'll see a *dai foo,* do you, Chen?"

"Oh, dear. Let's hope not. Some rain would cure the drought, though."

"You're sure this gangster won't make any noise? Can't have any of our bank people seen with . . ."

"We've been tracking him all through Asia. He'll be on a short leash. I'm sure he has every intention of leaving Hong Kong in good health."

"Ouch!"

Mason had hit his head against a cage, sending a pair of tiny blue-flecked finches hopping with anger and beating against the bars.

"Damned tweeters."

Mason's insult to his beloved birds caused Chen to smile softly, his scorn of the crude round-eye cooled far beyond any need for display, their inferiority profound, implicit.

"Please," Chen said, guiding him to a seat.

"Bring the bottle over, would you, Chen old boy."

The two men sat in rattan chairs, Chen upright but comfortable, Mason leaning forward, elbows on knees, sloshing the plum wine from the decanter into a glass, striped tie dangling between his legs. Beyond, darkening clouds fulminated over the New Territories; gusts rose and fell like furnace blasts.

Nigel Mason took a couple of bolts of the sweet stuff, then sighed and sat back.

"It's more comfortable in some ways now, Chennie, isn't it?"

"In what regard, Nigel?"

"With Harry Lin gone."

"Perhaps, yes. We Chinese and British understand each other."

"It was the right thing to do, wasn't it? I mean, it had to stop somewhere. Sooner we get the rest of the Yanks out of Asia the better."

"Of course Harry Lin was Eurasian. He wasn't exactly a . . . Yank."

"Splitting hairs, aren't we? He was their boy for thirty years. Always promoted the American interest. I figured he was CIA. Was I right, old Chennie?" Nigel Mason leaned toward the ancient mandarin and grinned.

When Chen didn't answer, he went on: "Harry Lin just wanted to make money. He wasn't Chinese, and he rarely took the British side. So good riddance, I say."

But Mason had talked himself down a bit and became morose. He slumped, and looked at Chen with hangdog eyes.

"Still I never thought it would go that far."

"It was necessary."

"Does anyone know? Tell me truthfully."

"One man suspects it."

This brought Mason up. "Who?"

"An American named Terhune."

Mason reached for the bottle. "Where the bloody Christ is he?"

"In the Walled City. Addicted. And soon to die."

Chen had decided while walking his bird to issue the order to have Terhune killed. Unable to extract from him the whereabouts of those journals whose public disclosure could threaten his plans, he failed to see any reason to allow Terhune to live. Effectively neutralized, Terhune alive still haunted Chen; only his elimination would ease his concern.

"Wretched." Mason wiped his blotched forehead on the sleeve of his jacket. "When will the killing stop?"

Chen was gauging how much to convey; Mason was too much the Asia hand to withhold everything. Surely he'd heard about Su Lin's disappearance, and possibly the ransacking of the Lin Orphanage. But he couldn't know of Terhune or his journals. And what of Song Wei's defection from both the Lins and his own father? Did Mason even know after all these years that Chen was the head of the Sun Yee On?

Chen would go slowly.

"You've heard from Shanghai?" Mason asked.

"Indirectly."

"The plan proceeds?"

"Yes. But patience is necessary."

"The deal is as we discussed this summer?"

"Yes. The Shanghai faction has Russian backing to topple Mao. The Triads and the British will help from here. The Shanghai faction guarantees you the return of the banking privileges Mao has taken away, and the continuation of British commercial interests throughout the Far East for the coming decades, at least until Hong Kong's lease runs out in 1997."

"And you get the trade."

Chen nodded circumspectly. "With it we free Chinese can survive. We will reconquer the Mainland inside of a generation."

"The old British ploy, eh?" He flashed Chen a sotted grin. "We knock out Mao, the Mafia, and the Yanks in three punches."

"Many things must go right. The coup may not happen for some years, and even then it may fail. It won't be Lin Biao but his son, Lin Liguo, who will lead."

"Corruptible little bugger, I hear."

Left-Hand Chen didn't reply.

"There are twenty thousand Yank troops in Vietnam now. I'm told Johnson has authorized more. From what I hear the American streets are already awash in the white powder." He turned to Chen. "How many labs do you have in now up along the Mekong?"

"Twelve."

"What's that name again, Chennie? The bit you print on the packages?"

"Tiger and Globe."

"Ah, yes. Picturesque."

Mason's pretense of distaste and ignorance about opium Chen

found quaint. No Mason would admit to touching the stuff, though their fortunes, like that of the Empire itself, had been built upon it. But Chen knew that nobody would be happier than Whitehall if Asian opium production reached a thousand tons a year, and the xenophobic Mao—whose new policy was to route overseas Chinese funds out of the British banks and directly into Chinese-held ones—was overthrown.

"Don't get me wrong, Chen. I'm not advocating going back to the old days with the mud. But opium has paid the tab out here for a hundred and fifty years. Yes, sell it to the Yank soldiers. But we bank it. Not your overseas Chiu Chao boys in Bangkok and Saigon." Nigel Mason shook a bony, quivering finger over his head. "Chinese laundry handle clothes. British laundry handle money. Agreed?"

"Certainly, Nigel."

Mason stood up as a warm wind rippled the Mid-Levels hillside. "This is the hour, Chen."

"It is time to move with firmness," Chen agreed.

"What about Peter Lin?"

"Under my wing, I can assure you." If Chen was certain of anything it was that since the Sun Yee On initiation, Peter was as much Chen's as his father had been, safely bound by Triad law.

"Where's Song Wei? Your half-boy. He was a good lawyer, you know. But I don't trust him since he went Red on us."

"He's gone underground. Disappeared."

"Out of the picture?"

"Yes," Chen said, hoping this was true.

"And Su Lin?"

"She ran off, or was abducted. We don't know. Either way, we'll soon find her. She can't go far."

"What about the Yank?"

"Potter's in hospital. The stab wound is the least of his difficulties. He has some rather desperate venereal disease. A profligate boy. He'll be out today, I understand. But hobbled somewhat."

"We'll have his type out of the picture soon enough."

Nigel Mason raised the empty decanter in a toast. "To Tiger and Globe. And prosperity."

Chen smiled placidly up at the lurching banker. "To your health, Nigel."

Inside, Chen was immensely uneasy. There were things wrong.

He was old, for one; the souring of his plan to wrest the Lin empire with his son's death had wearied him. He had taken it out on Peter Lin, manipulating him mercilessly; but the business would still bear the Lin name: Chen Po-chi was still comprador. This was an insult to the ancestors.

Enraged at the sentimentalism of Harry Lin's orphanage, Chen had made his statement that very morning. Hadn't he been an orphan himself, and a bastard? Who was Harry Lin to immortalize himself in that manner?

Silently he inventoried the victories: the Corsicans out of the way; Su Lin's lover Cross chased back to America and she trapped somewhere in Hong Kong like a fly in a bottle; Doody and the Americans agreeing to allow the fields to continue; Termini coming to pay tribute and give them the distribution system they needed; Peter neutralized; and Mason and the British utterly dependent upon his moves, and upon the poppy as of old.

But he had failed.

Terhune would understand.

Chen, watching the scholar refuse to give him the journals that day, had admired him. He had sent Peter away so as not to see. There had been a moment during the beating when Chen had called off the Red Poles and, when Terhune had refused the pipe, injected him with 99 percent pure No. 4—an act Chen now regarded as an inexplicable sentimentalism when he could have killed him then and there.

Though tossed like a cur back to the dens and his drug, the brooding poet-scholar cast a dark shadow over Chen. Terhune knew far too much for a *gwailo;* he brushed the Chinese soul.

They were of a kind, he and Terhune: both Orientalists trained in England, both rooted in a China of long ago, both adepts, then victims of the *yen*. Their dreams were not dissimilar: the old Chinese system, the mandarin meritocracy, a Ming empire of scholarship and wisdom and art. Chen had dreamed of this restoration, and had imagined that opium would sponsor it. The Triads, reduced for too long to cheap criminality, would return to fulfill the lofty mission of the Hung League.

He had discussed it once with Terhune, many years ago in Winny Lin's garden. They had agreed it would be superior to the present degradations.

The memory brought Chen pain. It was the only time he had felt close to another person.

It was a doomed, quixotic idea; the tides of history ran against them both. Now there was only Mao and a group of warlords in Shanghai straining at the bit—corrupted, like Chiang Kai-shek, even before they began. And Hong Kong was nothing but a town full of avaricious white and yellow fools crawling over each other like vermin to make money.

As for himself, there were moments when he wondered if his single remaining hand should finish the job begun in the Shanghai den.

No, one must complete what one has started; this was the Han way. In forty-eight hours it would be done.

Nigel Mason was standing at the open doorway, his arms spread against the jambs, commanding the small veranda against the bucking early monsoon gusts as if it were the deck of his yacht.

Watching his gangly, freckled guest—guilty, sotted heir of two centuries of vast Asian white power—Chen thought how in another sense he and Mason were alike too, both rooted in a colonial China they understood better than the new postwar relativisms under which both were presently forced to operate.

Is it really true that I end my life closer to these colonial monsters than my own people?

This was the deepest humiliation.

"Chennie," Mason called. "I heard the damnedest rumor. I heard that Harry Lin is still alive. In Peking."

Chen rejoined Mason on the veranda. "Ridiculous. We were both there when he was shot."

"I got clipped myself."

"Whose interest would this rumor serve? It's patently absurd."

"Yes, absurd." Mason shrugged. "Who will be at the dinner?"

"Peter, Termini, myself. A few Lin people. Heads of the other four Chiu Chao families. Several others."

"I'm dying of curiosity, you know. Cosa Nostra and all that. Right here in Hong Kong. I've seen the movies, you know. Read about this chap Valachi."

"You shouldn't be seen there, Nigel."

Beyond, the sky was darkening rapidly. Mason stepped to the edge of the veranda, then turned and scowled. "Careful, Chennie. These Mafia are desperate chaps."

"Really, Nigel, you needn't worry. They've been all but crippled in Europe and the Crescent. We will make sure Termini understands his role. It will go well, I assure you."

A sudden rush of wind slammed the doors behind them. Lightning flashed, illuminating the cages of the startled songbirds, throwing sudden elongated prisonlike shadows on the wooden walls.

The thunderclap hit overhead. When it was over, Mason was left clutching his shoulders, his eyes wide. Chen stood smoking, his handless arm behind his back, as if nothing had happened.

"We'll have all of the trade in five years," Chen said firmly.

Nigel Mason looked at the tiny ancient mandarin with amazement. "Chen. You want to take over the bloody world, don't you?"

"No." Left-Hand Chen looked thoughtfully up at his birds. "I simply want to restore the order."

The clouds broke, the deluge began.

Mason was halfway down the stairs to his chauffeured Rolls, his coat over his head, already drenched, when he turned and looked back up at Chen. The little man, in silhouette, was imperturbably feeding his birds as if the sun were still out.

Mason turned and stumbled down the stairs to the waiting Rolls.

50

It was against uneasy intermittent squalls and winds—the Black Ball signal was up, signifying a tropical storm within twelve hours of Hong Kong, the sampans lashing down—that Fook, with two Lin bodyguards in the backseat, drew the cream Rolls up before the Kai Tak ingress and got out.

Inside the terminal, Fook found that the plane from Saigon was on approach, coming in behind a Pan Am originating in Boston. This sorted out, Fook hastened to the blind Hakka cigarette woman, who took fat coin for a pack of Players, then delivered a nod ensuring magic entrée to the broom closet in the wall.

The Lin guards rifled through Chinese comics at the newsstand.

Fook came out fifteen minutes later looking like some doll made of rubber. Mouth slack, eyes watery, he drifted like an abandoned sloop in a high wind, rather more sideways than forward, toward customs. The closet man had dealt him a deadly treat: White Dragon Pearl No. 4.

Only the urgency of this mission, impressed upon him by Chen; his need to make amends for having aided Su Lin's attempted escape; and an uncanny radar old users seem to employ under quantities of the drug that could mesmerize a neophyte, had kept Fook from remaining on the closet floor staring at his sock for the next several hours.

A tiny bombed wraith, Fook stood blearily among the passengers pouring from the gate. He had entirely forgotten who he had come to meet. But the two beefy bodyguards had joined him, one holding aloft, as is the custom, a piece of paper with the arrival's name upon it.

A middle-size, swarthy, slightly balding man headed for them smiling. Fook, transposed out of time and place behind the stiff message dealt him by White Dragon Pearl, took his heavy leather suitcase and dragged it toward the exit.

Moments later, the cream Rolls was roaring through the wind and rain toward town. Franco Termini Jr., seated in back between the two hoods, lit a cigar.

It was developing from the north, a winter monsoon storm, the winds around twenty-five knots. Circular isobars were plotted carefully but without undue alarm at the Royal Observatory. Still, small craft warnings were up, the White / Green / White night signal was readied, and local flights from Taiwan were canceled shortly after Termini's plane arrived.

The storm would bring mixed blessings: a degree of damage, but an end to the water shortage. This was a tolerable event as long as one didn't mention the word typhoon: the dark memory of Typhoon Wanda six months earlier still haunted the Colony.

Wanda had swept out of the Philippines, breaking the sea walls and battering buildings, capsizing freighters and reducing construction sites to rubble. High rises had slid down mountains; Nathan Road had turned into a forest of broken scaffolding like pick-up-sticks. Entire squatter villages had been washed away by mud or wind.

A tropical cyclone, known in its most intense degree as a typhoon, is generally preceded by calm, very hot weather. There was no reason to believe this was anything but a monsoon.

The vehicular ferry was still running. Fook wheeled the Rolls onto her. Termini didn't say much during the crossing but stood on deck. Fook took the opportunity to nod off for a few moments.

On Hong Kong side he drove Termini, as he had been instructed to do, to the New Asia, pulling up in front at the Hollywood Road entrance. Termini got out and went inside. A wind was whipping detritus down the street, and rain pounded the hood of the car. Some minutes later Termini emerged smiling and handed Fook a piece of paper instructing him in Chinese to take his passenger to the Hilton.

Fook drove the few short blocks, letting Termini off at the lower entrance. The Lin guards followed him inside.

Then Fook, watching to see that he wasn't followed, headed back toward the harbor on another mission.

It is a beneficent peculiarity of opiates that they arrest nausea in the acclimated user; so Fook, riding behind his No. 4, avoided the green trip to the pitching railing as the final ferry before the monsoon lurched and dipped back across the harbor to Kowloon.

Once on land, a rocketing ride down Jordan Road brought him alongside the bleak sunken expanse of the Walled City, shuddering under the winds and sheets of rain, cardboard roofing buckling or flying off, tin sheeting rat-a-tatting like drums from raindrops fat as grapes.

Fook passed the Carpenter Road entrance, then drove on a few dozen yards to the Hoklo Tsuen intersection where the users bought, hoping to smooth his fears and ease his mission with a score. But the presence of too many 14K Red Poles forced him to forswear shooting the ack-ack gun; he backed the limousine up to Carpenter Road again and packed it next to a noodle stall.

Fook opened the glove compartment and took out a tiny black snub-nosed revolver. He checked the chambers to ensure that it was loaded, then put it in the pocket of his coat.

He stepped out into the thirty-knot wind and rain. He tipped the noodle vendor to look after the Rolls while he was gone, then scurried toward the entrance of the Walled City.

The storm soaked and shook the rotting human termitary. No planes passed overhead now, as Kai Tak had been shut down, lending the subterranean shantytown an unnatural sense of expectancy. There was only the violent drumming and dripping of the rain on the tin sheeting, the whine of the wind, and the shifting and crumbling of things within.

Fook paused at the entrance and looked behind him, then dropped out of sight.

FIVE

The Milk
of Paradise

51

Billy Strange would never forget that muggy monsoon day when the knock came on the door of his little room at the Hong Kong YMCA—the one he and the GI's he counseled called the "American Embassy in Exile"— and suddenly there he was: the Orpheus kid, in all his strange glory—tall and lean, with that dark hair and pale haunted face with the surfing scar, wearing the same dirty white linen jacket Billy remembered from shipboard, sleeves too short, wrists sticking out. And those green gypsy eyes, clouded now, definitely under the weather. God! thought Billy.

And he'd found his Eurydice all right.

Billy had seen Su Lin at Consul Doody's Peak party that night before he had been so rudely ejected, but had never in his wildest dreams imagined this was the woman Jim Cross had sailed an ocean to find. When Su Lin, her eyes full of terror and pleading, asked if they could hide out there for a couple of days, Billy had little doubt their danger was real, she being who she was, and Cross in the state he was in.

Who could say no to Su Lin? He would recall how even in rain-drenched agitation her high quivering cheekbones and porcelain skin glowed, her sloe eyes giving off heat, some trace of Tartar power flashing in among the delicacy and art.

"Of course you can stay," he said, dealing himself a hand in events that would change everything for him too.

It's not a pretty sight, opium withdrawal: chills, fevers, agonized moanings. Cross's eyes looked rheumy, his pupils like two sesame seeds, and he kept shivering. His nose was running and he wiped it on the sleeve of his jacket. His teeth actually made a clicking, clattering noise as Billy fiddled about boiling up coffee on the hot plate and spreading smuggled PX peanut butter on Saltines.

Billy's lasting image of Cross would have him sitting on the edge of the bed in front of the hot plate, swathed in every blanket, sweater, and coat in the room, his teeth rattling, calling out, "More heat!" though it was steaming monsoon weather, the wind and rain abating as a dead, clamping stillness descended upon the Colony.

Billy Strange managed to get it out of Cross—who kept muttering something about journals, and a guy named Terhune—that he had seen Billy in a Kowloon bar riot and remembered his mention of the YMCA from the *Brazil Maru;* what with all the powers of Hong Kong after their heads, and with no better place to go, they had chanced he would be there at the YMCA.

It was not a bad refuge, a three-story white brick building a block up from the Kowloon Star Ferry pier, crawling with all manner of foreigners on the cheap. But Billy Strange was on thin ice himself. Fresh back from Hanoi, he was entering what he would later call his "early quixotic period" of opposition to the burgeoning war being run out of Saigon—though he would never view it as any less than an unqualified moral plague. He had spent the last few weeks counseling soldiers on R&R from Saigon about resistance, medical discharge, and AWOL options; and finishing a piece for a couple of papers stateside, a new thing starting up back home called a "free press." Billy knew he was a marked man, his safe days in Hong Kong numbered, and was already designing his exit.

When Cross arrived so suddenly that day with Su Lin he was carrying a canvas bag Billy assumed contained clothes. When it hit the floor with a deadening clunk, he changed his assumption to books. The next day Cross, feeling somewhat better, opened it and showed him small notebooks, bound in brocade, filled in a neat hand—the journals of this very Terhune whose name had become a mantra during Cross's sickness. How Cross had come into possession of them, or what they contained, Biilly didn't yet know; but Su Lin seemed to consider their contents significant too, and their author much in need of rescue from the Walled City.

As Cross came back to life, Billy Strange didn't need radar to see that he and Su Lin couldn't keep their hands off each other; so he retired to the cafeteria downstairs with his portable Smith Corona and did his work at a window facing the harbor clock tower, returning upstairs with food in cellophane for his fugitives. At night he slept on the floor.

Su Lin and Cross spent much of those brief days wrapped up in each other. Billy thought he'd never seen two people more in love. It made him happy, and not a little envious.

The South China weather was unseasonably hot, torpid, unmoving. It was the spring of 1964, and Billy, who would not return home for many years, read the U.S. papers with a certain melancholy. Cassius Clay was the new heavyweight champ and had abruptly changed his name to Ali, to the consternation of the sports fraternity. Kubrick's *Dr. Strangelove* was detonating in America's theaters. And even the Cantonese kids around the Y hummed "I Want to Hold Your Hand."

Finally late the second night, there was a chance for Cross and Billy to talk. Since the voyage across the Pacific, both their problems cut a little closer to the bone of mortality: Billy Strange had found his cause, and more trouble; and Jim Cross his girl, and plenty of trouble of his own.

They talked about opium; for it was here that politics—Billy's domain—and desire—Cross's, converged. Everything Su Lin and Cross had found out fit in with Billy's conjectures about the role of the trade in the war. The labs were going in along the Mekong to deliver No. 4 directly to the U.S. soldiers; the axis of the world trade was shifting East. Opiates in unimaginable amounts would flow into the United States for decades, altering the life of the nation, a pact of misguided expediency to keep juntas in power, Commies at bay, and Western banks fluid. Inevitably, Billy could see, this logic would embrace drugs from other parts of the world. The history and psychology of this Faustian contract, Cross said, was in Terhune's journals.

Billy was surprised to learn that the architect of this development was the Lin family syndicate, presently in the person of Chen Po-chi, with Su Lin's brother Peter as figurehead. As Billy got it from Su Lin, a leading Mafioso named Termini was in Hong Kong to strike a distribution deal, signaling the capitulation of the West as suppliers; the celebratory dinner was to take place at the New Asia the next day.

This is the knowledge the three of them shared that last damp, still night on Billy Strange's floor at the Hong Kong YMCA. The point on which they differed—and it was to color all that followed—was whether the American complicity was deliberate.

Billy had little doubt that the Americans were encouraging the trade. He had seen the opium-laden Civil Air Transport planes coming down from the Mekong, and heard the Berets brag. His tour of duty with *Time* had convinced him that official America was not to be trusted; he would no more go to the Americans for justice in this matter than offer his hand to a shark.

Su Lin, who had come to understand the magnitude and corruption of the traffic from within, had arrived at an Asian pessimism on the subject. Five generations of opium told her that the trade would always be—she had come around to Left-Hand Chen's view in this regard—and she and Cross shouldn't concern themselves with the meeting at the New Asia but try and escape Hong Kong immediately. She held out the thin thread of hope that her Maoist lawyer friend Song Wei could help them get out through China, an idea that struck Billy as improbable.

Then Cross forwarded what seemed to Billy the preposterous idea that if the U.S. Consulate knew the facts they would move against the trade and break up the East-West deal about to be forged, if only to stop the epidemic influx of heroin into the United States. In exchange for the tipoff about the New Asia meeting, they would provide Cross and Su Lin asylum and safe passage out. Cross proposed that he go directly to the American Consulate.

"Man, do you know who these guys *are?*" he howled. "Fletcher Doody. This is not a man of *character*. It's a spy post up there! Their hands are *filthy!*"

But nothing Billy or Su Lin could say would dissuade him. Billy could only attribute Cross's clearly suicidal idea to his brush with the drug, the zealous amends of the recently cured.

"You have become obsessed, Jim," Su Lin said. "Like Terhune."

But Cross had convinced himself that this was the only way out for all of them.

"We've come too far," he said feverishly. "We can't stay here. Sooner or later we'll be found out. And what about Terhune? Peter? Billy's involved now. We have to try, or we'll all go down."

He asked Billy to arrange a meeting with the American Consul-General. Regardless of the fact that Billy of all people was persona non grata with Consul Doody right now, he considered this scheme the height of madness, the ravings of an opiated fool, and refused.

But there was something in Cross, some stubborn American thing that wouldn't be stayed. Billy only hoped it would pass by morning.

Near midnight they heard on the radio that a warm mass of circulating air was centered about two hundred nautical miles south-southeast of Hong Kong, off the Philippines, and might later come this way. The number one Tropical Cyclone warning signal went up at the harbor, signifying a state of alert.

It was a routine signal, no reason for alarm; Cross and Su Lin's forebodings as they lay in each other's arms that night were of a different kind.

52

Su Lin remembered from childhood the howling winds that woke her early, and what they portended. She leaned over and kissed Cross, then rose and went to the window.

At the Star Ferry terminal the number three flag was up: Green / White / Green. Life proceeded normally below, but the posting, raised to warn of thirty-knot winds and sixty-knot gusts, brought the possibility of worse typhoon weather in Victoria Harbor within the day. Already the pitching whitecaps, the deep dipping of the junk sails, and the moan of the horns heralded the uneasy change.

"What time is it?"

Cross was sitting up on the Y bunk looking at her. She realized she was naked.

"Around nine."

The room was spare, yellow-white, the furniture a tiny green desk and a chair. Only Billy's typewriter and a vase of flowers he'd scrounged God knows where to celebrate their stay adorned the monastic room.

As she crossed the linoleum floor toward him, Cross said, "I have to go."

She dropped her eyes. She had hoped the night would change his mind, suspecting it wouldn't.

"Typhoon warnings are up," she said.

"Then I should go now."

"I'll go with you."

"No. You can't be seen. I'll come back."

This echoed horribly the conversation in San Francisco, the morning he had gone to Berkeley alone and the Chiu Chao had come with their guns and their needles.

Seeing her weeping, Cross reached up and held her.

"Last time," she said, "we complicated things and lost each other."

She sat beside him. He stroked her hair, looking past her to the window, caught in his own recollections of the empty vigil in the Vallejo flat.

"Will it matter?" she said. "Even if we could stop Chen and Termini, the trade will re-form under someone else. It's a cancer."

"I know."

"Then why . . ."

He put his hands to her lips. She closed her eyes and looked away.

She told him she'd left a note for her brother in his room in the villa telling him that Chen and Mason had murdered their father.

"What will he do?"

"I wish I knew. I fear for him."

"What about your Red Guard friend?"

"Billy said he'd help me try and contact him this morning."

A sheet of rain battered the panes. They fell silent, caressing each other studiedly, aware that their refuge was about to be broken forever.

"Did you think I'd come to Hong Kong?"

"I suppose not." She looked away. "But then we didn't know each other. They kept telling me about the Corsicans."

"Did you believe them?"

"No." But her eyes held the question.

"Somebody from here searched my place in Berkeley and took a notebook of mine. It had the name of a Corsican gangster in it."

"Why?"

"I'd brought him heroin."

She paled. "Then Chen . . ."

"No, listen." Cross told her quickly about Europe: Eva and the abortion, and El Jefe's blackmail forcing him to deliver the suitcase to the Corsicans in Paris.

"You think all this had nothing to do with why we met?"

"We met by accident," he said.

"You're sure?"

Cross fell silent, envisioning the man who looked like Gurdjieff in the car outside of Oak Knoll Hospital. Then he laughed.

"Accidents," he said. "Are there such things?" He thought of Terhune. "I *have* become more Asian."

She didn't know what he meant, but she held him hard.

"After all this. To lose each other again . . ." They kissed, then moved out of the embrace. "That's not what I meant to say," she said.

"Regrets?"

"No."

"If this was it?"

"It was perfect."

She sat on the edge of the bed watching him dress. "Would you have gone on to become a doctor if you hadn't met me?"

Cross thought of Dean Whiteman and his "humble human event." No, that had never been it. Rather it was this: Su Lin's love, and encounter with evil's living guise.

"No," he said. "I never would have made it."

She stood up and walked to the window again. "Why did you go to the drug?"

Cross looked into some distance she couldn't see. "It's a substitute for desire. Those who can't live, and those who can't die, take opium. It obliterates life while keeping the body alive. Opium is slowed suicide." He touched her hair, her lips. "Drugs are for the wounded, the dying. People in whom desire has gone dead."

Cross felt her body with his fingertips as if encoding it there. "Where shall we go afterwards?" he said.

"Someplace where nobody watches. Where we can live and breathe. I want to paint."

"Paris."

"Why Paris?"

"Billy's in touch with a group there against the war. Maybe we can help."

"And you can write."

"The refugee clinics will be busy. They'll need medical help," he said.

A gale wind shook the jambs. Glass shattered somewhere in the building, bringing them out of each other. They heard Billy coming back.

"You should go. The harbor shuts down in typhoons."

They took a final kiss by the window. Then a gust swirled the curtains up around them. The vase on the desk fell and cracked, strewing Billy's flowers.

53

That morning Plantation Road's best homes were awakened to the rude sounds of Chicago blues as performed by Muddy Waters. Servants and matrons peered out of their windows trying to locate the source of the howling hi-fi thump and mojo twang because of the winds.

Then they saw kites, dozens of them, their strings unowned, whirling fitfully through the uneasy air—box kites, bowed Malay kites, Chinese fish and bird kites, Japanese rice-paper kites—dipping, racing, and swirling before they caught in trees or shredded in mid-air or danced hopelessly off down the mountain.

Neighborhood wisdom suggested that this performance issued from the Lin villa; the same wisdom told them that the huge home with the shuttered windows behind the tall black gates was best left to its own affairs. But the Communist banker who lived several houses away called Chen Po-chi at home to inform him.

Peter Lin, author of the ruckus, stood unsteadily on the villa porch, unshaven and unraveled, breasting the thirty-knot blow whirling up the mountain. He held straight Scotch in a glass in one hand, and the string to the last of the kites he had brought from his room in the other: a long, ferocious dragon kite in many sections, like a caterpillar, that his father had once brought from Peking during better days for them both. Above him, the other kites whirled and went down, one after the other, ravaged by the winds.

The night had upended chairs, cracked tiles, and brought down hanging pots. A shattered bottle of Johnnie Walker lay strewn among the carnage on the porch floor.

"Candace!!!" Peter wailed in the direction of Repulse Bay, letting the dragon kite go.

It danced, leered, swooped. Peter took his Beretta from his pocket and shot several rounds into its head. Then it crashed into the trees lining Peel Rise, the dirt path down to Aberdeen, and hung there.

Peter looked dully out across the landscape, his partially shaved head from the Sun Yee On ceremony and his drunken eyes lending him the strange glaze of the adept: a blend of stillness and the promise of sudden violence, not unlike the weather clustering around the Peak.

There was nobody else in or around the villa. The Sikh was off, Amah had disappeared with Su Lin, and Fook had mysteriously disappeared after his airport run to pick up Franco Termini. And Su Lin was gone.

Peter was alone, and afraid.

The warm clouds formed by the outer cirrus edges of the cyclone crowded northwesterly above the coastline, dropping intermittent patches of rain. To sea, the random dots of vessels on the silvery waters had disappeared, chased to shore to lash down in the shelters against the impending uncertainty. The Royal Observatory had given the season's first tropical cyclone a name: Lulu. The hope was for a recurving cyclone, which would veer northward, missing Hong Kong, and disperse back out to sea. The odds were good this time of year.

The blues record came to an end, leaving the needle circling with a click. Clenching his fists, Peter Lin called the name of his lost Boston deb once more to the empty morning, then stumbled toward his mother's room.

The quiet room of rattan, teak, and mahogany into which sunlight never fell had been the scene of much turmoil, from the time of Su

Lin's return to the night she had disappeared, and Peter and Chen had found Alec Potter, erstwhile rapist, on the floor, blood leaking from his gut.

The official reading was that she had been abducted by Potter's attacker; alarms had gone out all over Hong Kong among both the police and the Chiu Chao underground. But Peter and Chen knew who the Jim was she reportedly called to that night. Chen had seemed uncharacteristically upset about the incident, lamenting its "bad timing."

But what had set off Peter's drunk was the note Su Lin had left in his bed, which he now took from his pocket, uncrumpled, and read again:

YOUR HILL CHIEF KILLED FATHER. MASON BEHIND CHEN. GET OUT. PLEASE. I LOVE YOU. I'M OKAY. SU.

Grimacing, Peter stuffed the paper back in his pocket and went back outside. Lulu was hiding behind a gray front; fresh, thick raindrops fell.

Circling the empty house, Peter came to the room where the photo hung of his father, dressed in his Heung Chu outfit. The image enraged him.

So Chen and Mason controlled you the whole time, then knocked you off. You abandoned Mother and let her die. Then you left me an inheritance with strings, and this unholy criminal empire. Bastard!

He took the Beretta out and aimed it at Harry Lin's forehead, as if to dispatch him a second time.

"Wait, Peter. Don't do that."

Nothing could have prepared Peter for the apparition emerging from the shadows. In his drunken stupor, Peter beheld the ghost of Harry Lin himself.

"Son," it said, "I know you have every right to be angry. But there were reasons. I think you know now what those were."

Peter buried his face in his hands, waiting for the hallucination to subside. The sensation of Harry Lin's hand upon his shoulder caused him to shudder, then sink to his knees.

"I was in a tough position, Peter. Not unlike the one you're in now. The stone was rolling down the hill. You see, I wanted to move the family out of the trade. But there was a mutiny, led by Chen."

Peter looked up at the ghost.

"So I staged my own death. To flush him out."

"No," Peter whispered.

"Mask and wig, Peter. We Eurasians are always playing it, aren't we?"

He gently took the pistol from Peter's hand.

"Hasty Pudding. *Mikado* at Harvard. Remember?"

Peter shut his eyes tightly and stared at the floor.

"I was sick of the violence. I'd ruined your mother. I couldn't face you or your sister any more. It was the only way. I've been in Peking—you probably heard the rumor—through an arrangement with our Communist banker friend down the street. Now I've come back, but only to warn you about this meeting today."

Peter Lin, weeping, pressed his fists to the floor, waiting for the visitation to depart.

"You've done well, son. You weren't prepared for this. But you must complete what I began and set things right. But let's have an end to the vengeance. It's an endless descent. Yes, Chen is the worm in the apple. Before he came we were all right, all of us. But don't shoot him or Mason. Empty your gun into the floor."

Peter found the pistol in his hand again. He fired it at the floor until there were no more bullets. The click relieved him. Peter looked up at his father penitently.

"Father!"

Peter wheeled frantically around.

The phone was ringing.

He stumbled into the living room and picked it up.

It was Chen, his Hill Chief, now in the guise of the solicitous family comprador.

"Is anything wrong, Peter?"

"Wrong?"

"There were calls about a disturbance up there."

Left-Hand Chen's smooth voice seemed far away. The vision of his father had snapped Peter sober. Coolly he answered, "No. Actually everything is fine, Chen. Thank you."

"Good. Termini was at Happy Valley all day yesterday. He won the double quinella. Lucky fellow. Now he is resting in his room at the Hilton."

"Very good." Peter laid the cold pistol barrel against his cheek.

The blues record scratched repetitively on the hi-fi. A sudden burst of rain attacked the porch.

"I'll see you at the New Asia then for the dinner."

"Typhoon warnings are up."

"We'll start early. Around three."

"Fine, Chen."

"We'll have swallow's nest."

"From father's collection?"

"Of course. We'll take the biggest one from the display case."

Peter fell silent.

"This is a great day for the Lin family. Your father would have been pleased."

"I'm sure."

When he had hung up, Peter ran through the villa calling out his father's name. No answer came.

54

Billy Strange liked to consider himself radical, but he would come with time to view Jim Cross as more so. Billy's was a revolt of the mind, of ideas. As Billy saw it, Cross's rebellion was one of desire; this is why he had taken to the pipe, whereas Billy never would. In Cross, Billy sensed the end of ideology. Around this bright California child of aerospace, medicine, and surf, bereft of political zeal, Billy—romanticizing Cross, perhaps—found the one thing American that was worth anything—that blind innocent dream of transcendence that lurks within the soul of the new world like the seed within the rotting fruit. Touching it, Billy felt renewed.

But he would many times afterward conjure the riddle of why Jim Cross flew into the face of the typhoon that morning, why he went to the American Consulate.

Perhaps it was an act of faith, as if to say, "Here. We're Americans. Whatever else we might do, certainly when it comes down to it we're decent, aren't we?" Kennedy's death was fresh; maybe Cross just needed to believe that there was still hope, that when the chips were down a moral decision would issue forth.

Maybe Cross had never been able to forgive himself for running away from his first trouble with the girl in the Canaries, and this was the gesture that would set it right, the evil he would take on, some war he could call his own; as if only by saving Su Lin—by his own conception of it, not hers—could he have her.

Or it could have been simply that Jim Cross was one of those who got caught between the seams, stranded in the fission of opposites, strung between his own youth and his maturity, the things he had been told growing up and the world he actually found. Something in him held on to the old vision and would not admit the new darkness cloaking the American spirit.

In any event, the times resisted an interloper, as Billy Strange himself was finding out. Desire had departed the warm arena of the flesh and now stood above a chessboard whose squares were countries and whose pieces were drugs, poised to reinvade the body in syringes and spansules, powders and pills, turning desire into its mockery: obsession.

That spring, the opium players were locked in final convulsive struggle for world domination. Heads of state openly plied the trade, which had become inextricably blended with issues of politics and money, as a new war—the one Chen Po-chi liked to call the Third Opium War—blossomed in Vietnam. Golden Triangle production was up to seven hundred tons a year; already the first GI junkies were coming out of combat and heading home with Tiger and Globe no. 4 sewn into their duffels. The Lin syndicate was hours away from virtual monopoly of the traffic, symbolized by the kowtow of the American Mafia, its resurrection utterly dependent upon Franco Termini's visit: the keeling of the final illicit obstacle.

Back in the States, drugs were being pushed hard onto the streets, the CIA's MKULTRA mind-control programs of the fifties culminating in potent new lab drugs spirited onto the campuses of Harvard and Berkeley for professors and their students to experiment with, synthesized by Sandoz and Hoffman in Basel. In Millbrook, Leary was in full swing, and "therapy" groups were opening in San Francisco, Los Angeles, and New York to push LSD-25, still legal. Pot, hash, mescaline, psylocybin, peyote, and cocaine rushed in behind opiates to be institutionalized. Billy and Cross's generation gleefully embraced the new drugs, consumerism with a twist to beat Chubby Checker's. Children drifted beyond their parents' command, and the tone of the country went into polar shift.

It is questionable whether any single encounter turns history's tides. Still Billy would wonder later what might have ensued had Fletcher Doody—the one man in a position to have arrested the secret alliance about to be written in the world of *yen*—been a different kind of man, or come round to seeing things another way that morning.

The number three signal remained up through midmorning. At the Consulate the radios were on in every room, and a phone line was kept open to the Royal Observatory. There was no reason yet to believe Typhoon Lulu would come close enough to Hong Kong to wreak its worst, or cause the next incremental signal, the number eight, to go up. In any event, typhoons move slowly, about twelve knots an hour, and it would be late afternoon before the major blow, if indeed it came.

When his secretary buzzed and told him there was a young man downstairs to see him, Doody had him sent to an attaché, as he routinely did with the amok, often drug-crazed Americans suddenly and inexplicably flooding U.S. consulates and embassies all over the world the last few years. Doody was in a meeting with his vice-consuls, speculating upon the distasteful prospect of Goldwater running against Johnson the following term. The destroyer *Maddox* was due through that day, as was the carrier *Ticonderoga*, both headed for the Gulf of Tonkin; there was concern over Lulu's effects upon these movements. A major U.S. trade mission, a pet project of Doody's, was hung up in Tokyo with Kai Tak's closing. Fresh spooks from Langley had commandeered another two rooms on the third floor in their seeming locustlike infestation of the Consulate with each escalation in Saigon, ruffling the other Consulate staff. And Doody was waiting for the Lin-Potter affair to run its anxious course.

"We going to a number eight?" he asked edgily.

"We're trying to find out, Consul."

"Still a number three," someone called in.

"Keep the line open to the Observatory."

"We've got an Air Force jet out of Subic entering the eye. It'll radio back in a few minutes, Consul."

The telex operator reported that the line to Washington kept cutting out.

Outside, it was dark and howling. The top of a tree flew past the window. The lights in the room dipped from a power surge. Nervous time, Doody thought, drumming his long fingers on the tabletop.

The word came that a number eight SW was going up.

"Look like a *dai foo,* Consul."

As if in affirmation, new gusts rattled the building.

Immediately the signals went up at fixed points through the city and along the waterfronts. The clearing of the streets began. The number eight signified that within twelve hours there were two chances out of five that the cyclone would come out of the southwest and pass nearby, blowing a sustained wind speed of thirty-four to sixty-three knots, and gusts exceeding a hundred knots.

Schools and law courts were closed. People away from home were told to return immediately or find a safe place and remain there until the danger had passed. Windows and doors were bolted and shuttered, and cars parked in sheltered areas.

The number eight assured a certain minimum of devastation: flying debris, flooding, landslides, windows breaking. The torrential rains, heavier afterwards, would do more damage than the winds. Only a number nine—increasing gale or storm, or a rare number ten—typhoon—was dreaded more.

The Consulate along with the rest of the Colony would receive radio reports from the Royal Observatory of wind direction, tide heights, the center of the typhoon, rainfall. But there was little else anyone could do except lie low and hope Lulu would recurve northwards and miss Hong Kong.

In the midst of this the attaché, whose name was Lewis, phoned again. "Sir. I think you'd better see this fellow."

"What fellow?"

"The American who came."

"Lewis, we may have a typhoon up here and you want me to see some crazy American. Handle him, would you, for Christ's sake?"

"He's muttering something about opium, sir. And the Lin family. And your name."

Doody's jaw tightened. "Send him up."

Consul Doody shortly found himself staring into the wild green eyes of a tall, gaunt, wind-blown young man. He greeted him without a handshake, ordered everyone else out of the room, then turned to him as if he were a messenger from hell.

"Well, what?"

Cross, in a less than coherent manner, began telling Consul Doody of a criminal opium syndicate that this very day was making a deal with the American Mafia here in Hong Kong, its target the United States, through the military in Vietnam. Lives were at stake, Cross asserted; they must act.

Doody acted suitably surprised. "This all sounds quite preposterous."

The two men remained standing across the desk, Doody appraising his visitor, Cross staring down at the circular eagle motif of the Seal of the United States affixed to the front of Doody's broad desk.

"Who are you, anyway?"

"My name is James Cross."

"And?"

Cross paused, then said, "I'm an American."

As if that were enough, Billy Strange would later lament. As if that were enough.

Doody said, "Even if all this were true, what do you propose we do about it?"

"They're meeting this afternoon at the New Asia restaurant. They must be stopped."

Doody began his storklike marking off of the carpet, passing back and forth before the flag.

"An American of Italian descent and some Chinese gentlemen are having dinner at one of the town's top restaurants. We're to walk in on them, in a Chinese city, and have them arrested on hearsay. Is that what you propose?"

Cross recalled what Terhune had asserted about the invisibility of the trade, that it evaded the rhetoric of "normal" discussion, that it always took on the ring of the fantastical. A desperate lassitude swept over him, and the first inkling that he was trapped. He thought of Su Lin back at the Y, and of Terhune and Billy, fearing already he had betrayed them.

"This involves American soldiers, Consul. American streets, American children. An epidemic. We will be the victims."

"Conspiracies." Consul Doody displayed a jaundiced glare. "What are you doing in Hong Kong?"

Cross answered guardedly, "Visiting a friend."

"How have you come to know of these alleged matters? Are you a smoker? Is that it? Is this gossip going around the dens?"

"No, Consul."

"Then what's your interest here? How do you know about it?"

"The friend I'm visiting is the Lin daughter."

Doody stiffened and turned away with suppressed excitement. So it's *him*. The one who stabbed Potter and took the Lin girl off. And he's come to *me*.

He wheeled and spoke with a touch of triumph. "All of Hong Kong wants your head, you know. Kidnapping. Attempted murder."

"We need your help, Consul. You're our one hope." Cross spread his hands.

This wasn't simple for Consul-General Doody. The fervid, strung-out American before him provided an uncomfortable moral presence; Cross's words took the Consul back to a bridge he thought he'd crossed the day Alec Potter had first come to see him. He fished for his pipe, as if by lighting it he could effectively burn that bridge once and for all, and remove the unwelcome ghosts haunting his office again.

As the gusts rattled the tall panes, Doody thought, Does he know anything? Maybe through Potter by way of Su Lin? Is this a prelude to blackmail? Is this man a wild animal? He looks like one of those addicts.

What does he know?

The winds and rain let up momentarily; the room grew silent, expectant. Cross said something about the Lin girl, and how she had been kidnapped back to Hong Kong by Chen and her brother Peter, and how she was American and should be assisted here. Doody let Cross go on for a while, then broke in peremptorily: "So what do you want?"

Cross answered quickly: "Guarantees for both our safety. Help get us both out of here and back to the States. Together."

"Is that it?"

"Stop the meeting at the New Asia." Then Cross added with an intensity that alarmed the consul, "There's another American. A scholar named Terhune. He's in the Walled City. We need to get him out of Hong Kong and back to Japan or he will die."

Doody grimaced and looked toward the ceiling. "Outrageous. Who are you people? What are you talking about?" He flapped his arms like some flustered shore bird. "And what if we're unable to provide these things?"

Cross looked into Consul Doody's wan, jumping eyes. "You'll have me. But Su Lin will escape. There are notebooks of Terhune's detailing your Consulate's complicity in the trade. I've left them with a journalist, with instructions to release to magazines and newspapers in New York, Washington, London, and Hong Kong if I don't come back."

"What the hell . . ." Doody tried to swallow, but couldn't. He glared once at Cross, drew up to his full, considerable height, then drooped like a doll, lowering his eyes and turning away.

"Strange," he whispered. "It's that goddamned Billy Strange, isn't it?"

Doody paced, hands behind his back.

Cross waited, expecting nothing. The journals were indeed with Billy. But for all Terhune's rhapsodic indictments, they contained nothing concrete on Doody or the American diplomatic corps. Cross's bluff was intended to force Doody's hand, disarm him.

Consul Doody was equally certain Cross had little of consequence; the only words ever spoken in his office on the subject of opium had been with Potter.

Unless Potter had sold him down the river.

This could, and would, be easily checked.

But these alleged journals could make mischief. Doody would be under a cloud, suddenly visible, forced to defend himself.

He was not the man for that. Certainly not now.

Fletcher Doody wasn't a bad man, nor by any reckoning a criminal. But inexorable events pushed hard upon him: the spooks and hustlers straggling into Southeast Asia from every corner of the globe for the new war, the deal making, Washington, Alec Potter, the career, the unremitting demands of his wife, the entire miserable fabric of an existence whose demands he was woefully unprepared to meet.

One call to Chen would kill the New Asia meeting, one chop of the hand. After all, he represented America. Washington would activate the crop conversion programs; he could even look good doing it. And it would get the plague of opium out of his office once and for all—and off America's streets.

Which end is my basket?

The metaphor was Doody's own, dating from a college incident that would haunt him to his death: Dartmouth vs. Princeton for the 1946 Ivy League championship. At the opening of the second half, Big Fletch Doody got the tipoff, raced down the court, and made a layup.

Swish.

It had been the other team's basket. Wrong Way Doody. Two points for Princeton: their margin of victory.

Doody had survived it; but one wrong basket in a lifetime was one too many.

He took the pipe from his mouth and looked at Cross. "I agree. We must do something immediately."

Doody stepped out from behind the desk and offered his hand. "We'll stop the meeting at the New Asia. And we'll get you home."

Dazedly Cross shook Doody's hand, finding it large and clammy. "Sit down."

Wearily Cross slumped into the chair in front of the desk with the State Department seal.

"Now. Where's Su Lin?"

Cross hesitated.

"How can we help her, man, if we don't know where she is?"

Still Cross refused to answer.

"They're shutting down the harbor," Doody said. "We can't move against these people unless you tell me. I have to assure the Hong Kong police she's safe."

A shuddering rocket of wind caused the large U.S. flag behind his desk to jiggle in its holder and the ice cubes in the wet bar to rattle. Outside it grew suddenly dark. Doody fiddled nervously with his pipe stem.

"She's at the YMCA," Cross said. "Kowloon side."

Doody nodded. "Good boy."

Cross watched the Consul get to his feet and walk toward the door of his office.

"I think there's someone else who should hear this."

Doody stepped into the foyer. Cross closed his eyes and waited, tired and hopeful, in the leather chair. Rushes of wind sang through the banyans on Upper Albert Road.

Su Lin, he thought. We'll be out of here.

Doody returned with a man, vaguely familiar. Cross struggled to fix his identity.

Behind them were four Marine guards.

"We've found her," Doody said to the man.

He was American, young, corseted around his middle, limping with the aid of a silver-tipped cane. His head was slightly tilted back, his expression pained, haughty.

Cross gripped the arms of his chair.

"There he is," Doody said, pointing at Cross.

"Bastard," Alec Potter hissed.

Cross looked over at Doody.

"We're shipping you home, fellah," Consul Doody said. "Just like I said."

"No!"

As Cross jumped up the Marines readied by the door.

"Hong Kong has agreed to drop charges if we'll deport you. We'll send you back to Oakland by merchant marine. No charge. Stateside you'll be let go."

Cross looked wildly around the room.

"You think I betrayed you," Doody said, his voice rising and thinning. "On the contrary. You should be thankful. You're an undesirable, traveling on a false passport. You attacked this man, nearly killing him. As if that weren't enough, you're an opium user. I'm saving you from years in a Hong Kong prison."

Cross realized that Chen and Peter Lin must know he was here.

They all knew.

"What about Su Lin?"

"We'll see to her."

Doody turned toward Alec Potter, who smiled smugly.

Cross went for him. But two bull-necked Marines with fish eyes blocked his way; the other two wrestled him down from behind. He was on his stomach on the floor, a knee in the small of his back, a rifle across his neck.

Rain hammered the windows. Cross, breathing the unpleasant odor of the carpet's synthetic nap, strained against his captors.

"It's for your own protection," Consul Doody said.

"Terhune and Billy were right!" Cross called up with what little air remained in his chest. "You're all players in the game!"

Watching Cross hauled roughly to his feet, Doody thought, What in Jesus's name does this vagabond know about the price of freedom? What does he know?

The Marines dragged Cross out of Doody's office and down the hall. At the landing at the top of the stairs they passed a group of crewcut vice-consuls and covert operative types gathered around a coffee machine. Passing by, Cross saw among them a small, pale figure that made his insides go weak.

The figure was dressed in an inexpensive suit and tie, his graying blond hair rather short. His eyes were vacuous, and a soft empty smile was affixed to his face. Seeing Cross, he raised his coffee cup in salute and said softly, "Hippocrates."

Cross struggled vainly against the arms owning him.

"*Ilya!*" he cried, his voice echoing down the empty stairwell.

"Super, Consul," said Alec Potter jauntily when Doody had closed the door. "Let's get her."

"I've already called Commissioner Hughes," Doody said glumly. "And get screwed, would you?"

Potter's expression fell.

Consul Doody was shaking. "You're through, Potter. I have half a mind to have you arrested too."

"But, Consul . . ."

Doody wheeled and with a rage Alec Potter hadn't known was in the man, said, "Get the hell back to Chiengmai. Get out of my sight!"

Potter, seeing that no response would make a difference, silently limped from the room.

Fletcher Doody slammed the door after him, then walked to the tall window facing Albert Road. He stood for a while, his fists against the dark panes of security glass, his face screwed up in bitter pain.

Then he walked to the desk and picked up the phone. He needed to talk to someone.

"Joyce," he whispered, starting to dial.

But it occurred to him there was no solace there. He put the phone back down.

In truth, there was nobody to call. Nobody at all.

Fletcher Doody looked up at the patterned quadrangle of cloth that had hung over him practically all the years of his life, ever since grade school, blessing his days.

I pledge allegiance . . .

His arm twitched instinctively toward the drilled gesture: hand to heart. Then he turned away sobbing, squeezing his fists as if they were sponges. "Ah, God . . ."

A vicious gale wind buffeted the stucco Garden Road enclave, shaking the beams. A whine of anguish swept through the trees outside on Lower Albert Road. Then the power cut out. The room went black.

"Someone! Help me!"

Consul Doody wandered in the dark alone, his hands outstretched.

55

Royal Police Commissioner Roderick Hughes had received the American Consulate's call about the Lin girl close to noon, just after the number eight had gone up. Haunted by his earlier failure to turn up even a credible suspect in the murder of Harry Lin, his office still under the cloud of his predecessor's scandalous amassing of obscene wealth from opium tribute, Hughes was desperate to make good on this. He insisted, in the face of his staff's protestations, on attempting to cross Victoria Harbor in a police boat. It was his first typhoon.

Twenty yards out from the Macao Ferry pier, the boat was picked up by a swell and washed back against the wharf, splintering on the pilings. Commissioner Hughes, ignominiously fished out of the lashing waters by his Chinese assistants, retired to his home Mid-Levels to run the operation from there.

Drenched and chastened, a cup of tea before him, he tried to get hold of the Assistant Commissioner, but he had gone to his daughter's for a typhoon party. Finally, needing someone Kowloon side, he rang up Detective Chief Superintendent Gordon Smythe, Tsimshatsui District, in his flat off Prince Edward Road, and gave him the instructions.

Then Commissioner Hughes, veteran of many a campaign but never retired from the field so abruptly or unceremoniously, put on a robe and stationed himself by the window to observe this phenomenon with a little more respect.

In the northern hemisphere, the winds of a tropical cyclone spiral inward toward the center in a counterclockwise direction; in the southern, the rotation is clockwise. Tropical cyclones do not form on the equator, where the earth has no vertical component of rotation.

The conditions are precise. There must be a warm sea, then rain must develop over a large area, and the air at low levels must converge on a large scale. This air is deflected by the rotation of the earth and spirals inward. If the air, rising up in the warm moist core, moves away from the region at the top of the circulation, while at the same time at the top there is an anticyclone, or divergent flow, there will be a tropical cyclone—a rotating mass of warm humid air between two hundred and a thousand miles in diameter, known in its fiercest aspect as a typhoon.

In Asia, five or six cyclones a year develop east of the Philippines and come rushing west-northwesterly: wide bands of thick clouds extending to great heights, with areas of torrential rains and violent winds reaching two hundred knots blowing in a tight circle around the eye.

While a typhoon moves rather slowly—eight to twelve knots around Hong Kong—and can be observed with some accuracy, it is impossible to do anything to alter its destiny; it sweeps across the South China Sea, wreaking death and devastation as it goes, reducing human action to futility.

The eye of a tropical cyclone is a region of light winds and lightly clouded sky, usually circular or elliptical in shape and ranging from a few miles to over eighty miles in diameter. Winds diminish rapidly with distance from the wall of the eye.

About every ten years the eye of a typhoon passes over Hong Kong. When this happens, a lull may occur, lasting for a few minutes or even some hours. This will be followed by a return of hurricane-force winds from a totally different direction. Places that were well sheltered earlier now become dangerously exposed.

The babbling klatch of foreigners thrown together in the YMCA cafeteria up from the Kowloon Star Ferry terminal to savor the havoc out the window turned en masse when a dozen white-gloved, blue-slickered Royal Hong Kong Police rushed into the building. The coppers paused at the front desk long enough to allow bulbous, beery Detective Chief Superintendent Gordon Smythe, Tsimshatsui District, to inquire of the Indonesian Christian couple running the place about a certain room, then stormed upstairs.

The second floor resounded with rude knocks upon a narrow yellow door. They were greeted by Billy Strange, in shorts and undershirt, a sheet of typewriter paper in his hand.

"Where is she, Billy?" growled Detective Smythe. "And I mean it."

Billy, blinking behind his rimless glasses, looked defiantly into Detective Smythe's girth. "What the hell are you talking about? And what are you doing in my room?"

Police poured into every corner of the room, a brief maneuver considering its size—tiny open closet, desk, and bunk bed.

"She's not here, sir," reported a venal-eyed Sergeant Lam.

"The Lin girl, Billy. We know she's here."

"Never heard of her. And what ever happened to privacy, Smythe?" Billy was hopping mad. "I pay good money for this room, you know."

"It's two dollars a night you pay. And I've got cause."

As the weather roared and thrashed outside, the police rummaged through Billy's things, looking for something else as well: Terhune's alleged journals, on the firm orders of Consul Doody.

"Get out of there, would you?" Billy squawked, rushing to his satchel. "She's not in there, is she? Whoever she is."

"Come on, Billy. Cough her up," Detective Smythe said. "If not, in you go."

"What for?"

"Harboring a fugitive. Or how's about this AWOL counseling's been going on here, Billy, hm? The Yanks don't like it one bit."

While Detective Smythe went on in this vein, Sergeant Lam slipped a plastic bag full of white powder out of his pocket, stuffed it into the springs of Billy Strange's mattress, then quickly removed it.

"Well, look at that, will you?" said Smythe.

Billy wheeled.

"White Dragon Pearl, sir," said Sergeant Lam, holding the bag up.

"Oh, pity."

"Fucking plant! I'll sue!" howled Billy as two policemen held him. Chief Detective Smythe turned expectantly to Sergeant Lam.

"No sign of the journals, sir," Lam muttered out of Billy's hearing.

Smythe became stony. He turned to Billy and squeezed his arm as if testing a melon. Billy grimaced in pain.

"I want to speak to my Consul!"

Smythe hissed, "Your Consul's just what's the reason we're roundin' you up."

Before they hauled Billy off to Tsimshatsui Station, Detective Smythe said peremptorily to Sergeant Lam, "Search the building for the girl. If you don't find her, put out a bulletin to arrest her on sight. And don't come back without those journals or it'll be all our heads."

A splintering banister in a tenement doorway in Western offered Su Lin rough anchor against forty-knot winds circling up deserted Man Wa Lane, carrying civilization's detritus: an armchair, a cat, bales of wire, a bicycle. Whipped by wind, her clothing torn, tears mingling with the sheeting rain, she was able to move only a few feet between gusts. She could still see back to the harbor, the warning signals aloft: double upside-down triangles of the number eight SE, and the colored circles: White / White / Green. A wave exploded against the wharf, feathering spray high into the air, the water flooding the dockside streets.

When Cross hadn't returned or called, she knew it had gone wrong. Watching her come apart, Billy Strange had finally insisted she flee while he stashed Terhune's journals safely. A renegade *walla walla* had brought her across just after the number eight had gone up. It had taken her an hour to make it these few hundred yards from the harbor.

Occasionally she saw homeless people the Emergency Service vehicles had failed to round up huddled in doorways. In the last gust, a woman already dead had rolled past, her rags unraveling, coming to rest in the middle of the road in front of her, limbs splayed, milky eyes cast upward.

Eerily, the wind abated as suddenly as it had come up. She began to pick her way up Man Wa Lane among the refuse, falling on slicks, scrambling to the next shelter. She reached Bonham Strand and worked her way onward, foot by foot. The collapsed metal ribbing of an advertising sign drew blood from her calves as she contorted and climbed through it. A strap on her shoe had broken; she gave up and cast both shoes away.

A patrolling Emergency Service vehicle sent her ducking under the overhang of a looted rice store, its windows knocked out, the casks on their sides. If she were seen she would be rounded up; the streets were being swept of all life by nature and man.

Hong Kong, brightest and most bustling of earth's cities, had become a scene of lunar desolation: dark, wind-whipped, deathful. As a new wind came up, sweeping before it man-made objects like a broom, Hong Kong's impermanence revealed itself.

The streets had begun to flood, a convergence of tidal waters breaking over the sea walls below and muddy effluences from the mountain above. She saw a huge ancient tree, ripped from cement, tilted against a building. Railings and signs strewed Jervois Street. Broken neon displays hung precariously from the merchants' buildings, exposed wires crackling.

And Jim Cross was gone again, just when she'd found him.

"Cross!" she shrieked angrily to the suffocating wind.

On Queen's Road a flood drain had broken. Human feces bubbled up and poured into the streets like lava. Ahead, the Central Market's corrugated tin sidings were being stripped by wind, laying bare the metal framework. The market's abandoned ceramic cleaning basins had flooded, sending mammal entrails swirling into the streets. Hooves, tails, heads—and the vermin they attracted—skidded down the alleys and lanes.

A drenched mongrel stood frozen at the foot of Cat Street, keening. Su Lin saw a whorl of wind actually pick it up, then set it back down. She called to it, but it took off howling, chased by a sharp-edged piece of tin sheeting spinning in the wind, shearing whatever it touched.

The path steepened. Where Hollywood Road met Ladder Street she came to Man Mo, a temple dedicated to Man, god of intelligentsia, and Mo, god of war. Derelicts huddled beneath Taoist statues. Within, joss and candles burned; robed silhouettes floated like wraiths.

A wizened priest opened the doors and raised his arms in welcome. From a radio somewhere she heard a British babble detailing worsening conditions. The center of the typhoon was some two hours away from Hong Kong; the chances were two out of five the Royal Observatory would post the number nine, signifying the main force of the cyclone passing over Hong Kong.

". . . advised not to leave your house under any circumstances. Tidal waves in Tai Po Harbor, in Aberdeen, developing in Victoria Harbor. All ships . . ."

She turned and looked down toward the harbor. Hong Kong was in shambles. Above her, Mid-Levels, was Chen's house. To her left, two blocks down Hollywood Road, was the New Asia.

Hollywood Road was piled with scaffolding and rubble from a collapsed construction. Rainwater coursed through the wreckage. She studied the street, trying to imagine a way through.

The priest had stepped out into the rain. He beckoned, offering the warm orange esthetic refuge of Chinese religion. He seemed to be calling her name.

"Su Lin . . ."

She turned away sobbing, and began to pick her way barefoot through the wood and metal toward the New Asia. The priest's voice called after her—ancient, somber, rich with injunction.

The bamboo struts were tangled like toothpicks. A refrigerator skidded along the street, actually propelled by the wind, clearing a path for her. A flying shard of metal nicked her arm.

A half block from the restaurant she saw the limousines and knew the guests had arrived before the streets were cleared. Lights were on in the entrance.

So the meal proceeded: none would leave for hours in this weather. She fought on toward the restaurant, the only place she could think to go. Within, she had to believe, lay answers.

As she neared the intersection, a torrent of muddy water poured down from the mountain, carrying trees, plants, garbage. A gum tree broke from the current, propelled itself end over end toward the intersection, then snagged on a stoop. It shot into the air, bounced off a building, and hit Su Lin in the back, knocking her into the doorway of an antique shop across the street from the New Asia. Pain roared through her head.

The base of the tree hit the wrought-iron porch above with enough force to cause it to collapse. It crashed into the street, potted plants and buckets and urns exploding on the pavement. The porch missed Su Lin—it would have killed her—but the metal railing came to settle upon her legs, pinning them outside, the rest of her in the entryway.

Wind screamed in fury. Pain shot from her legs up through her belly and chest. She tried to move but could only raise her head enough to see the dragon pillars at the New Asia entrance. Within, the lights had gone out.

She struggled up, pushing against the railing. Then the pain overcame her. Calling Cross's name, she blacked out.

56

It was a gray 2,300-ton oiler—Liberian-registered, American-crewed—in military use. Cross sat belowdecks in a small messroom, his right wrist manacled to a table bolted to the floor. Through a low porthole he watched the furious seas of Victoria Harbor off North Point; he had never seen or imagined such natural tumult.

A pair of U.S. Marines had been assigned to watch him until the tanker sailed, which looked, considering the weather, to be some days hence. For the first hours his guards had sat on chairs turned backwards, smoking and staring into space, speaking to each other occasionally: "Storm's a real fucker." They glowered at Cross, then went back to staring. They wouldn't give him a cigarette or the time of day, except once the taller one said, "What are you? A dope fiend? A draft dodger?"

"A Russian spy," Cross said.

But as the storm worsened, the young Marines paled with nausea, and fear changed the way they sat; the banter thinned, and with it the hostility. The smaller one offered Cross a cigarette.

Cross was too livid to be ill. His rage turned inward as he contemplated his own foolishness at having believed the Consul, and the consequences he'd unleashed for all of them—Su Lin, Billy, Terhune, himself.

The Marines talked about a guy they both knew who'd gone over the wall, seduced by a journalist in a Kowloon bar who promised to fly him to Sweden.

"Fuckin' Benedict Arnold," the tall one said. "Gutless bastard. Like this guy." He jerked his thumb at Cross.

But the other one didn't say anything.

The oil tanker bucked with the storm. The bridge seemed to be having some difficulty keeping it from swinging broadside; Cross heard the order piped down to remoor it, a sticky feat in these winds and waters. The concern was evidently that a strong swell would push it too close to the sea wall; the ship had been the last one into port the night before and hadn't anchored well.

One of the Marines claimed this storm was worse than Gulf hurricanes in Louisiana, where he was from. Hell, this isn't even a typhoon yet, said the other.

Then, rising on a heavy swell, the tanker's portside actually nudged the sea wall; the boat gave a sickening little hitch. Cross and the Marines fell off their chairs. Murky water covered the porthole.

The short Marine cried out in genuine terror. The three of them tried to scramble up but fell the other way as the tanker righted itself. The water receded from the porthole and there was a patch of fog outside. The tall Marine rushed off vomiting; the other's eyes had grown wide. Water spilled in through the door.

"Let's get up on deck!" Cross yelled. "We'll drown down here!"

Cross's lone guard surveyed him suspiciously, deciding whether he would be held accountable for leaving him there to drown. Finally he uncuffed Cross and led him at rifle point to the stairs. They passed the other guard on his knees in the latrine vomiting.

"Evacuate! Evacuate!" came the order.

They stood at the top of the stairs gripping the handholds bolted to the bulwarks. The decks were awash. Behind the window of the rain-lashed bridge a yellow-slickered captain gesticulated. At another hatch Cross saw the fearful eyes of a crewman essaying a run across the deck to a lifeboat.

"Evacuate!"

But it was too late. The oiler was parallel to the sea wall, rocking like a cradle with each swell. The gale winds hummed in ferocious crescendo.

"Man overboard!" came the lonely call. But the crewman who had bolted for the boats was gone.

Cross and his guard hung in the stairwell, not wanting to go below, less willing to try the deck. They awaited the next swell, hoping the oiler could withstand the hammering against the sea wall. Cross had seen photos of capsized freighters and tankers during Typhoon Wanda the September before, and knew they could go over.

"Stay put," said the Marine, his eyes jumping—as if their roles as prisoner and guard meant anything anymore. He was as afraid as Cross, flattened against the bulwark by the gale wind singing across the deck.

Then Cross looked out to sea; what he saw made his heart stop. A dark shadow of a swell loomed, hissing as it closed upon them. Cross knew surf: it was a tidal wave. The tanker seemed to ease itself around to meet it broadside.

Screams went up as it hit. The upper part of the wave broke across the decks; its underside lifted the tanker, then set it against the sea wall with a shuddering crunch.

Cross gripped the steel handholds; the rest of his body tried to fly away from his arms. The ship lurched, then bobbed away from the wall, tipping in the other direction as the flood of water passed on to shore.

Cross slumped to his knees, still clinging to the bulwark as the tanker listed, righted itself partway, then hung crippled in the water.

The Marine had fallen halfway down the stairs and sat studying blood on his hands from a head wound. Water rushed down the hatch over him.

"Grab something!" Cross yelled.

The undertow of the receding waters bent them sickeningly down again, then dipped them the other way. When it had passed, Cross looked back out into the harbor and saw the next swell gathering on the close horizon.

It came fast, clearing everything before it. At the first push of water, the oiler abruptly tilted and rammed its rear deck into the wall. Its bow broke water like a rearing horse, spilling sea down its deck backwards. The water rushed on, and the tanker's aft end began to

submerge with horrifying speed. The Marine had disappeared belowdecks.

Cross clung until he saw the sea rushing up below him, a slurping
maw forming along the edge of the tipping tanker, then readied to
jump free as soon as the last of the swell had passed to shore: a
hopeless maneuver, but he couldn't stay aboard.

He took a flat dive, facing forward. As he broke the surface he
felt the hollow behind him drag at his legs. Hearing the wave thunder over the sea wall, he knew its rip would join the sinking tanker's
waters in an inescapable vortex. The sea wall and adjacent wharf
were a dozen yards away, unswimmable.

Water filled his mouth. Cross enacted the futile last gestures of
life. A vision of Su Lin appeared and came close. He embraced her,
feeling warm, then yielded to go down.

"Grab it!" a voice called through the darkness.

Cross's forehead bumped the white brightness of a life buoy.

Coughing water, he fumbled to hook his arm around the ring. He
saw in the ricocheting lights of the upending oiler a young Chinese
lashed to the wharf next to the sea wall.

"Hurry!" he shouted.

Cross got both arms through and hugged the ring to his cheek.
But as the ebb of the tidal wave joined the dying tanker's whirl-
pool, sucking out his insides, Cross knew the buoy would simply go
down with him.

As the maelstrom drew him in, a contesting pull arrested him at
its rim. He realized the buoy was attached to a rope attached to the
Chinese, binding him to the sea wall.

The screams of the tanker's crew broke the air. Cross saw dark
human forms drawn helplessly under. Then the tidal bore receded,
sweeping back out into Victoria Harbor to re-form. Cross felt the
rope hauling him in.

"Hold on!" called his rescuer. Spitting seawater, Cross flailed
shoreward. The tides lifted him right onto the wharf, depositing him
at the feet of the Chinese.

After he had untied himself the Chinese attempted to lift Cross to
his feet; but it was a few moments before Cross, convulsed from
coughing up water, could operate his legs.

"You must get up!" commanded the voice in British English.
"We need to run before the next one!"

He held out his hand. Cross took it. Together they sloshed up the wharf and across the street.

A brass banister on the wide steps of a maritime building offered the only stationary object in sight; they sat down and clung to it.

The next wave thundered toward shore. Cross saw the broken foremast of the capsized oiler bobbing piteously against the sea wall. The wave took the street and slithered toward them.

The Chinese lost his grip on the banister and began slipping helplessly down the water-slicked stairs. Cross removed a hand from the railing and grabbed his collar, arresting his slide. Now it was the Chinese who held on to Cross as the water coursed up and over them.

Sputtering, they clung to the banister until the ebb swept out, as strong as the wave. It left them staring madly at each other.

"You all right?" Cross asked.

The young Chinese nodded.

They untangled their limbs and scrambled inland another block, beyond the water's reach. A deserted tailor shop's entry offered shelter from the winds. They slumped against the storm-shuttered windows.

Cross looked at his mysterious savior. He was lean, fair, with wide-set eyes.

"Who are you?"

The Chinese smiled.

Cross saw now that he wore a Mao jacket.

"You're Song Wei."

The Chinese put out his hand. "And you are Jim Cross."

57

"**F**ish Boy! Stop loafing! Clean mullet!"

Fish Boy peered out from behind rice sacks, munching *dim sum* from the *yum cha* tray left over from the Sunday meal before the number eight went up. Seeing Chef Wen cross the kitchen brandishing his wood-handled cleaver, Fish Boy scuttled over to the barrels of crab, pomfret, mullet, and eel, his clop-clops skidding on the tiles.

"Fowl Boy! Fry goose blood!"

The New Asia kitchen was a nest of solemn, irritable activity as Chef Wen, the Lin diva, flayed his aproned team among abundant comestibles, rich sauces and flavorings, fresh sea catch, and steaming vats and sizzling woks in the great kitchen. Returning to his perch, a rattan stool near the double doors, Chef Wen fished a Marlboro from his Louis Vuitton bag and sipped Johnnie Walker Red Label and soda water from a teacup.

"Don't burn! Too much sauce!"

Sunken caldrons in metal holders over fires kept a palette of Chiu Chao sauces steaming. Overhead on bamboo poles hung chickens, goose, crab, sausages, pig. Wooden and tin containers, spice and herb shelves, and serving utensils clustered along the walls. Beneath the counters were square tins, bottles, and jars containing cooking esoterica.

Chef Wen was in a fevered snit. He whom the *Morning Post* had just this week voted one of Hong Kong's top five chefs, while the New Asia itself had dropped half a star, considered himself in no way obliged by his vast salary to prepare a special banquet in a deserted restaurant in a typhoon. It was a humiliation not to be repeated; this would be his swan song at the New Asia.

It was no longer clear who ran the place, Left-Hand Chen or the Lin son, the half-devil lawyer who poured soy sauce on his rice and asked him to fix hamburgers. Now they wanted to break the glass case and remove the thousand-dollar swallow's nest that Harry Lin himself had procured at great peril—by buying the mountain in Thailand on which it rested—only to waste upon another devil, an oily-mouthed *mei li chien,* American, who had revealed his culinary low breeding on a tour of Chef Wen's kitchen by sticking his finger in the brown sauce, then licking the finger.

Left-Hand Chen had impressed upon him that this was an important taipan from New York who had to leave as soon as the weather cleared, hence the banquet in the midst of the *dai foo.* Only Market Boy's early trip to Central Market before its shredding by the storm had assured a meal at all.

Chef Wen peered through the crack in the swinging doors. A small room had been partitioned off for the meal, the rest of the New Asia unoccupied and dimmed; a sad echo, Chef Wen thought, of the infamous grand banquet the summer before when Harry Lin had been killed by the Green Pang—and Chef Wen had made his reputation on the meal.

There were some dozen guests chatting and drinking. Left-Hand Chen stood with his guest of honor and three other *gwailo;* three corresponding Lin bodyguards flanked them. The heads of the other four ranking Hong Kong Chiu Chao families talked with Chef Wen's cousin, called by his family the "other cook": Yuk, the legendary master *yen* chemist, back from his special project for the Lins in Southeast Asia. And there was Peter Lin, who didn't even speak Cantonese, let alone Swatownese or Mandarin.

Chef Wen brightened when he spotted the British banker Mason and the American Consul Doody; he always liked to impress the taipans. At least his meal would pass the lips of the right people; perhaps they would follow him to the new restaurant.

Chef Wen turned back to the kitchen and sought out Noodle Boy, his hands deep in dough. The guest was said to have come from a place where the noodle was appreciated, so they would offer the wide flat noodle, the narrow noodle, the clear noodle, the opaque noodle, and a half dozen others. But first Noodle Boy would dazzle the guests with his conjuration of the *lie mien,* the very best vermicelli from Shantung. *Then we'll see the round eyes of the New York devil pop from his head. A noodle expert? Lap sap!*

A gale wind shrieked, rattling the storm shutters. The sound of crashing in the streets sped the grim chopping of the knives. The light bulbs rocked and flickered. Chef Wen glanced toward the corner where flashlights, oil lamps, and butane tanks were piled to rescue the dinner in case of a blackout.

The request for the bird's-nest soup haunted the kitchen. It was a bad omen; none of the cooks felt good about it. There was an element of profanation in breaking into the swallows'-nest cases for a round-eye. Chef Wen's astrologer had told him it shouldn't be done, and would bring further bad joss upon the Lin establishment.

As if bearing this out, the power surged, dimmed, and went out. Vegetable Boy groped on his knees for flashlights. Chef Wen swore and picked his way around the darkened kitchen shouting orders. As he cuffed Pork Boy on the side of the head, the lights suddenly came back on. Chef Wen stared bemusedly at his hand, then up at the lights.

Endlessly superstitious, he decided not to hit Pork Boy anymore.

Instead, he cuffed Tea Boy.

The venetian blinds of the Lin offices at the back of the restaurant were slightly open, allowing little Fook, his face flat against the glass, a partial view from the alley to the dim, empty room.

Then lights came on; Chen entered from the hall.

Fook dropped to his knees so that only the corner of his head remained in the window. He watched Chen Po-chi grind a burning Lucky Strike into an ashtray, then flip the combination dials of the wall safe and open it.

Chen took from the safe a tiny silver derringer and stuck it up the sleeve of his handless arm, the barrel facing down, securing it in some manner of holster or sling. He turned off the light.

Just as Fook was about to make off, the light came back on. A balding compact European Fook had never seen entered the room holding a drink. He was voluble and friendly toward Chen, who was more reserved. Fook was unable to read their lips, but his eyes widened when the man slapped Chen on the back. Nobody, white or yellow, ever displayed such intimacy with Left-Hand Chen.

As Chen and the *gwailo* neared the window, Fook slipped away. He began to work his way up the steep lane toward the cream Rolls, stranded on the storm-lashed street above, a tire blown. A silhouetted head, then a hand, moved slightly in the rear window.

A cyclone gust sang down the alley, carrying a flying orange crate; it hit Fook in the forehead. He sank to his knees grunting. Blood broke from his scalp. A flash of muddy water from the Peak wilds rushed down the stone steps, spinning Fook downhill and depositing him again before the New Asia's back entrance. He remained still for a moment, hat low over his eyes, browned with mud, blood coursing down his face.

Then the torrent picked him up again. He waved his arms to no avail as the furious waters carried him down.

Cross and Song Wei huddled in the cab of a khaki truck behind the Bank of China in Central, watching treetops bend to the ground before the hundred-knot winds screaming up from the harbor. A tiny truck radio spat static-laden bulletins from the Royal Observatory: the area was being laid waste; the eye of the cyclone was an hour southeast of Hong Kong, and might pass directly over or veer north; wind and rain were expected to worsen. A litany of tragedies was intoned with melancholy precision, including the news of the capsized Liberian oiler at North Point. They could see the Star Ferry terminal, and the number nine posting: Green / Green / Green.

Song Wei had borrowed the truck from Red Guards at the New China News Agency on Sharp Street in Causeway Bay and illegally worked it through the tumult to Queens Road Central, behind the Bank of China, where felled power lines had stranded them.

Cross considered his unlikely companion, who now offered a section of a mandarin orange he had produced from the pocket of his Mao jacket.

"A fellow named Strange," Song Wei said, "contacted me this morning about arranging an escape through China for Su Lin and you. When he told me you'd gone to the Consulate I thought I'd better go over there and wait outside. I was only a couple of blocks away. I expected you'd have trouble. When the Marines came out with you in tow, I followed them."

Cross looked at him in confusion. "Why?"

"Why?" Song Wei looked puzzled.

"Where does Mao say to save *me*?"

Song Wei smiled and shook his head. "You misunderstand."

"Is it because you love Su Lin?"

Song Wei looked at Cross. "If you like."

The gust heightened, shaking the truck. A window blew out in the Bank of China, raining glass down around the truck.

"But I need you too, Cross. You're part of our plan."

"What plan?"

"Let's just say the Lin-Termini alliance is not in China's best interest."

"Or anyone's."

The winds softened to a steady whine. Cross saw a wicker bird-cage hop down the sidewalk.

"Where is she?"

"I don't know. Billy Strange said she might try and cross the harbor to the New Asia. But that was before the number eight."

"Thanks," Cross said. He extended his hand.

"Where are you going?"

Cross had grabbed the handle of the door. "To the New Asia."

"No. You'll never make it." Song Wei reached over. But seeing Cross's determination, he simply added, "At least wait until the wind dies down."

Cross fished in his shirt pocket for a cigarette, but the pack was soggy from the dunking in Victoria Harbor.

"Can you get us out through China?"

Song Wei seemed to sadden at the question. He stared silently out at the storm for some time. "There is a prisoner China wants back," he said. "There might be an exchange arranged through Peking and the British Consulate. You and Su Lin would be taken into China, secretly."

"Then where?"

"Wherever you want."

"Paris," Cross whispered.

"Pardon?"

Cross didn't reply.

"But perhaps you care more about the struggle against criminal elements than your life. Or hers."

Cross looked at Song Wei. "I just want to find Su Lin. And be with her."

The gusts eased. Song Wei rolled down the window and peered out.

"Let's see if we can get to Ice House Road before the next blow."

Cross looked at him and grinned. "Let's go."

58

"To Tiger and Globe," Franco Termini Jr. said volubly, raising his Campari. "Salud, Lefty."

Left-Hand Chen squeamishly toasted his Tsingtao at the door of the New Asia's rear offices. When Termini put down his drink and offered his opened arms, Chen looked appalled. Termini, disguising his own humiliation, enveloped Chen in an oily, expansive hug.

This unfortunate display over, Termini picked up the briefcase Chen had given him and draped his arm around the little man's shoulders. Cringing, Chen walked with him back to the banquet room to rejoin the guests.

The scene presenting itself was bizarre, yet in Hong Kong's very nature. It would never have come to pass in New York or London that a Consul-General would dine in a restaurant with a Mafia don, or the head of a major British bank eat openly with a Triad Hill Chief, let alone an Asian heroin chemist. But this was Hong Kong, illicit from the day of its founding. This meeting to "divvy up the world," in Mason's words, was a moment outside of time, a concordat sanctified by staggering monies, marking the rare convergence of visible and invisible, exoteric and esoteric, legitimate and illegitimate. None should have been there; none could stay away.

An outsider would have perceived a midafternoon gathering of well-dressed Europeans and Asians having drinks and a meal, indistinguishable from any private business affair. There were no decorations or extraneous festivities. The subject was never, ever mentioned. Typhoon Lulu, ravening beyond the storm shutters, lent a fateful timbre to the unholy summit—the cool sociability, like the still eye of a typhoon, serving to emphasize its thunderous import.

For some of them, the ghost of Harry Lin haunted the room. Behind the lone round dinner table was an empty space where the dais had stood the summer before. Peter Lin kept looking up, envisioning his father there. So did Mason, who had come earlier in the day to see Chen and, stranded by the typhoon, allowed curiosity to overrule judgment and joined the guests. In fact there was an awkward moment when Peter, Mason, and Consul Doody caught each other looking toward that very spot where ten months earlier Harry Lin had raised his final glass to the serenade of orphans.

Kuan Yin, Goddess of Mercy, ivory eyes downcast, stood silently in the corner against silk brocade wallpaper. Tall dragon-brushed partitions shrouded the New Asia's deserted rooms beyond. The Lin bodyguards, all Red Pole 49s of the Sun Yee On, hovered against the wall, eyeing, on Chen's orders, a pair of beefy, noisily dressed Italians Termini had trailed in from Saigon. The other four ranking Hong Kong Chiu Chao families, sullen at the Lin coup structured behind their backs but not about to refuse Chen's invitation, as they too stood to benefit from the new arrangement, talked quietly with Yuk the Cook, the master chemist back from Ban Houei Sai. Bessie the bookkeeper was there, as was a vaguely military man from Bangkok, a Thai-Chinese.

Consul Doody's surprise appearance disconcerted Mason and Chen, raising the fear that he suspected the arrangement with the Shanghai faction. But it was simply that Doody, intending to send Alec Potter in his stead as his surrogate and spy before the morning's travesties at the Consulate, had no choice now but to come personally. Of course that meant Joyce too, who stood by Kuan Yin, fingering a string of Mikimoto pearls like prayer beads, sourly studying the waiters.

Franco Termini Jr. was enlisting Chen to translate to the other Chiu Chao heads something about the parallels between Sicilian and Chinese fraternal social organizations. Chen, eager to deflect this inept sociology, quickly presented Peter Lin.

As they shook hands, Peter and Termini both recalled the Havana weekend, the gambling at Hialeah, and Peter's debt. But this lingering business was best left unspoken in the heady new landscape. Chen, watching his disciple, noticed the brittleness in Peter's smile, the tension pouring off him like heat from a turbine.

"Your family goes way back," Franco Termini Jr. said to Peter Lin. "Like mine. I saw the photo in the office. The first, the one with the pigtail."

"My great-great-grandfather," Peter said quietly. "The comprador."

"Ah. Almost like the word in Italian," Termini said soberly. "Our peoples understand tradition."

A great crash outside was followed by the ebbing of the lights. Peter tightened.

"Hell, we have worse hurricanes in Florida." Termini laughed and nudged Peter. "Ever see *Key Largo* with Bogart and Bacall? That's Florida."

But it was swagger; Termini had never been in a blow like this in his life.

The radio had gone out, and with it the Royal Observatory's steady reports. This was just as well by Chen, as they tended to create alarm. When the lights suddenly came back up, the guests applauded in good cheer.

Chen was pleased too with the turnout of official people. It sanctioned the arrangement, locked in the players on all sides, and enforced silence later on. Also this bringing together of open and secret worlds was to him a philosophic triumph, a yoking of yin and yang, a rejection of the false, puritanical Communist doctrine pitting "honesty" against "corruption" that his very own illegitimate son Song Wei sought to purvey.

As Chen turned toward the kitchen to signal Chef Wen to proceed with the meal, Fletcher Doody slipped off to the telephone in the rear hall. Dialing Police Commissioner Hughes's home number, his hands shook.

No, Hughes told him, the girl hadn't been found but had fled the

YMCA. Billy Strange was in custody but wouldn't admit to anything.

And the journals? Doody blotted his sweating forehead with a handkerchief, waiting for Commissioner Hughes to come back to the phone.

"Sorry, Consul. No sign of them at all. Billy Strange denies they exist."

"Yes, use every persuasive technique on him," Doody told the Commissioner.

As Doody hung up, the hall lights failed. He groped his way back to the banquet room to find it darkened as well, the waiters lighting oil lamps.

A pall swept the guests taking their places at the round table. Doody's wife made an unfunny reference to the fact that it must have been this way before Edison invented the electric light, and people still ate then, didn't they?

The building shook. The keening winds seemed to penetrate the very walls. Hong Kong, like a strung wire, was stretched taut. To the melancholy Doody, surveying the guests gathered around the circular table in the flickering light, it looked like the Last Supper, and filled him with clammy dread.

The rain drummed on the dented metal roof of the stranded Lin Rolls-Royce like the hooves of a thousand horses. It was atilt, the rear tire on the sidewalk, the front one flat. On the backseat reclined the shaggy, sweating, straining figure of Jack Terhune, coming hard off the Milk of Paradise.

"Fook?" Terhune muttered, his yellow eyes half shut. *"Fook!"*

The car radio had been on for the news reports, but the battery was almost gone; intermittently it squeezed a word or two from the Royal Observatory before crackling out:

"Number nine signal . . . drownings at Shek O . . . oiler capsized at North Point. . . . The eye may pass over Hong Kong."

A soaked yellow mutt Fook had let in from the street curled in the front passenger's seat whimpering into the rich leather.

Great yawns rocked Terhune's body, seeming to stretch his mouth beyond its limits, as if he sought to escape his own skin. His fists curled, the nails drawing blood from his palms. He looked fearfully up and said in a shredded, ghostly voice, "Opium! Fook! For God's sake get me opium!"

A violent shudder rose and passed through him, from his feet to his head. Terhune whitened and stiffened, his eyes rolling back in convulsion.

The cur, sensing some organic event of import, slithered into the backseat and began licking Terhune's face.

The old opiaste opened one eye. Wincing, he turned away, then eased into twitching sleep.

Alec Potter sat alone in his robe on the broad Hotel Mandarin bed-spread. The silk curtains were closed, the double-paned windows bolted against Lulu. A wide mirror framed in ornate black cherry-wood hung above a bureau across from him, giving him his image. His Walther PPK/S .380 semiautomatic sat on the bed, a seven-shot clip beside it.

The face in the mirror was still boyish, smart, but for a ring of blisters around one side of the mouth. Opening his robe, Potter ex-amined in reflection the broad scar from Cross's slash, a dark tattoo of his failure with Su Lin. Looking further down, a moan broke from his lips.

The doctors at Matilda Hospital had neither name nor cure, only "a virulent Southeast Asian strain"—no more help than the snake medicine. Slow, they said—as if that were a blessing: just sores, dripping.

Potter curled his fingers around the cross-hatched Bakelite grip he hadn't held since the day in Old So's teahouse shed in Chiengmai the spring before. He rested the cold dark blue steel against his cheek.

The typhoon raised a fevered baying like endlessly pained hounds. The winds and waters beyond seemed bent upon cleansing the southern Asian earth of some stain. The windows shook as if by im-prisoned fists. Without hatred or vengeance, only a leaden self-pity, he jammed the seven-shot clip into the butt handle. Alec Potter, his dreams of Asian grandeur shattered, watched his reflection raise the Walther to his temple.

His hand shook badly; the pistol wobbled. He lowered it, flipped off the safety catch, raised it once more. Muttering Su Lin's name to the mirror, he squeezed.

A window imploded from the storm, crashing inward, spewing glass across the room, sucking the curtain out. The mirror shattered. Light and pulsing pain whitened into a void. Then a sliver of consciousness reappeared, something still alive.

I even fucked this up was his last thought before nothing.

The oil lamps lent an uncharacteristically intimate, subterranean atmosphere to the New Asia dinner, more like a European restaurant. Chinese eateries are traditionally boisterous, brightly lit. The hushed, glowing scene etched character into the faces and hands of the disparate guests, spreading an unease they attempted to alleviate with extra jollity as they sipped the astringent Chiu Chao prelude—three thimble cups of Iron Buddha tea.

Peter Lin poured another San Miguel into a glass with ice, wondering if his head was going to explode. He felt himself at this moment to be the personal embodiment of all that was contradictory in the situation: East and West, good and evil, legitimate and illegitimate, father and son, sister and brother—a lightning rod for the terrible storm raging outside. In the coming hours he would either be driven under or raised up; things would no longer be the same. The typhoon would level and reveal them all.

A metal cart had been rolled out from the kitchen, a mound of white dough upon it. It faced Termini, but all turned to watch. Noodle Boy, a dour pock-faced man of forty, picked up the dough and began to work it. Twenty-five years, ten in Shanghai, stood behind this performance. He elongated the wad into a taffylike cable, whirled it in the air, turned it upon itself, stretched it once again. Deft fingers conjured a figure eight, a knotted coathanger, an undulating snake. Magically, the thick strand of dough divided itself in two.

"Fabulous!" oozed Joyce Doody.

Peter Lin watched the watchers of the noodle become transfixed like children. Since that morning he had seen his father in a vision; been told by Police Commissioner Hughes his sister had been found; then learned that she hadn't. Reality, like the dough dancing in the yellow half light, seemed to unravel into a thousand ribbons.

Noodle Boy elaborated, ever faster. The guests, for a moment innocent before the conjurer's whirl, saw the paste transform with each turning into thinner strands.

Everything is going to be all right, Peter Lin thought. There is a harmony, an order here.

Noodle Boy suddenly flourished a dowel in the air and draped the hundreds of tiny vermicelli noodle strands upon it. He held it forward and bowed slightly.

Joyce Doody applauded loudly, already wondering how she could secure this man for her next Peak party.

Ceremoniously, Noodle Boy removed a single strand from the dowel and presented it to Franco Termini Jr.

Termini held the noodle up to the guests and smiled broadly, then smacked his fingers with his lips.

"That," he said, "was impressive."

He reached into his pocket, took out an American twenty, creased it lengthwise between his first and second fingers, and thrust it forward. Noodle Boy looked at Chen, who signaled him to go ahead and take it.

Peter Lin looked at Chen too. *Yes, the Hill Chief is uneasy, and not because of the weather.* Seeing Chen glance his way, Peter thought, He knows I know. He worries.

"Western people learned of the noodle from us," Bessie the bookkeeper said to Termini with prim erudition.

"Marco Polo," Termini answered graciously. "That goes to show you. Our people go way back."

Steaming platters of food from Chef Wen's kitchen overflowed the round table. The guests, entranced by the noodle display and secure with the appearance of food, seemed bent upon banishing the typhoon from their thoughts. Chopsticks and spoons flicked food from the rotating center onto the plates.

"How do you use these things?" one Italian whispered to the other, struggling with the ivory implements. A waiter brought a fork. Yuk the Cook made a complimentary reference to a sauce in Swatownese.

A piece of ceiling gave way somewhere in the darkened restaurant behind the partitions. The Lin guards ran to the area. Chef Wen peered worriedly from the kitchen. Plaster rained down, spreading dust into the light.

Termini leaned over to Chen. "Lefty. You're sure this building's *safe?*"

"It's old, but well built."

The heavy dripping of rain into buckets behind the partitions thinned the conversation. A leaden silence descended upon the eaters.

Consul Doody, to alleviate the gloom, proposed a toast: "To the future of Asia."

"And the United States," said Bessie, who seemed to have drunk too much and was overstepping.

Joyce Doody, irrelevantly, said, "To England."

Nigel Mason smiled wanly and clinked his Watney's.

Left-Hand Chen looked at Peter, sitting like a coiled spring next to Mason. Yes, something had changed. Chen had thought that after the Triad meeting he had Peter; but he saw now that he didn't. Worse, Chen thought with a certain melancholy, Peter wants to have me.

Somewhere within Peter, Chen observed, his sister held sway.

One can never account for everything, after all. Chen realized again his own failure. Mason had been right; he had indeed wanted to control the world. As Terhune had admonished the day he had arrived in Hong Kong, Chen had not rested in the Tao. The Arrangement of the Inner World grew dim, indiscernible; a restive Dragon Current stirred.

And there's nothing, Chen thought, I can do about it.

Still, Peter by his turn mustn't interfere now but allow the plan to proceed, for good or ill. Considering his shaven-headed disciple, eyes glimmering with obscure zeal, Chen thought, Harry Lin should have educated him in England, not America. Still, Eurasians are cut off from grace. Certainly he intends to kill me. Or someone.

Furious wounded howls rose outside as the storm passed directly overhead. "A number ten, I'd say," Mason muttered nervously. "Shame we can't get the radio."

The guests looked around the room with rising panic. A spoon clattered to the floor. Then somewhere in the darkened restaurant an entire section of ceiling exploded downwards.

Termini ripped his napkin from his shirt and pushed back his chair. Chen saw Peter's hand go to his pocket.

Chen jumped up.

Suddenly all the lights came back on.

Chen and Peter stared at each other, frozen in the bright fluorescence.

"Well, how about that?" said Termini.

With disconcerting suddenness, the storm abated. The guests stood looking about, bewildered.

After some moments of tense silence Consul Doody said, "Lulu must have gone home."

"Probably recurved," Mason added, blinking in the light. "Lucky for us, what?"

Peter dropped his hand to his side. Chen turned to the guests. "Shall we take a look?"

Mason grabbed a flashlight. The others fell into step behind him, making their way single file through the dust-darkened interior, sidestepping rubble. They moved gingerly among the tables and inlaid columns like captives exiting a cave after a long time, filing in procession toward the exit.

Mason reached the dragon-scrolled double front doors first, and cautiously pushed them open.

Outside it was curiously silent. The sky was pale, lightly clouded. Somewhere far away a dog barked.

59

There was an unearthly stillness in the air. A plane droned overhead. Cross, looking up, saw a bird circling unevenly.

"It's over," he said to Song Wei.

Water coursed down the vertical streets. Moans of the injured arose from different quarters. Above, fearful heads appeared on the balconies and in the windows. A dead yellow cat washed up in front of Cross, a rat still between its teeth. Song Wei listened intently to a Chinese voice speaking from a radio in the store.

"No," he said. "We're in the eye."

He stood beside Cross, peering out along Hollywood Road. They were half a block from the New Asia, across from it, sheltered in the entry of a wicker store. "When the eye passes, the winds hit hard. Maybe two hundred knots, from another direction."

"When?"

"No way to tell. The eye could be a few miles wide, or eighty."

Cross stepped into the street. Song Wei pulled him back. "Look," he said.

Nigel Mason was standing in front of the New Asia blinking, a flashlight in his hand. Behind him were the others, looking up at the pale sky.

"They think it's over," Song Wei said. "They don't know they're in the eye."

"Su Lin's not with them," Cross murmured.

Then Song Wei saw Left-Hand Chen and his eyes narrowed. "Unless it's some trick."

The diners milled dazedly in front of the New Asia, looking up and down the ruined streets like survivors of a bombing. Their quiet voices echoed off the buildings in the unsettling silence.

Cross whispered, " 'On the day the emperor is crowned, Or the three officers of state installed . . .' "

Song Wei stared at him.

"Terhune *knew*." Recognition lit Cross's face. "Chen. Then Mason, Termini."

The light above was pale, numinous. Calm had descended over the street.

"Who is the third?" Cross muttered.

"Lin Biao," Song Wei whispered angrily. "The Shanghai faction."

"Go back, Peter!"

Her voice came from beyond them, in the direction of Man Mo Temple. Cross struggled against Song Wei's restraining hand.

"It's her," he whispered, his heart speeding.

Peter Lin had turned toward the calling voice.

"Su! Where are you?"

Chen moved in front of Peter, gesturing furiously with his lone hand. "Peter!" he ordered. "Stay here!"

Cross watched Peter face Chen in confusion, then looked past him toward his sister's voice.

Chen raised his left hand, displaying the sign of the Hill Chief: fist in the center of the chest, thumb out, little finger out.

Peter hesitated. Su Lin called again.

"Obey!" Chen commanded.

Peter took a step back. His Beretta came out of his pocket. Bracing himself against an inlaid pillar of the restaurant, he leveled it at Chen's chest.

"Chen!" he shouted in anguish. "I know who you are!"

"Don't, Peter!" Su Lin cried out.

In the doorway of the wicker shop Song Wei held Cross back.

Nigel Mason rushed forward and grabbed Peter's arm. "Wait!"

Peter spun away from Chen. "For my father!" he cried.

He raised his pistol with both hands and aimed it at Nigel Mason's forehead, precisely where Harry Lin had been shot.

The sound exploded off the buildings. Mason slumped soundlessly to the ground.

Weeping, Peter threw the gun away. He dropped to his knees and covered his face with his hands.

Chen's left arm rose and stiffened. His right one crossed to aid it. He brought his aim to the side of Peter's head.

Now it was Cross who restrained Song Wei in the entryway where they hid.

Fire emerged from Chen's sleeve. Peter Lin pitched forward, then rolled onto his side and lay still.

Joyce Doody began to shriek. Her husband dragged her back inside the restaurant.

"Su Lin!" Cross yelled now.

"What the hell . . ." Franco Termini looked frantically up and down the deserted street.

Each faction—Termini's aides, the Lin guards, the other four Chiu Chao—eyed the other, poised, ready to engage.

Chef Wen appeared at the restaurant entrance. Clutching his apron like a skirt, he took off running toward Man Mo Temple.

Cross called Su Lin's name again. No answer came.

Left-Hand Chen turned and saw Cross and Song Wei in the doorway. His face tightened in rage.

Cross stepped out into the street and began to make his way through the wreckage toward Su Lin's voice. Song Wei hesitated, then followed.

A sudden new wind stirred the strewn street, bending the trees.

"It's the eye!" Chen called to the others. "Get back inside!"

When they had all been herded through the doors of the New Asia, Chen turned back into the mounting wind. Seeing Song Wei across the street, making his way past with Cross, he grimly called, "Faithless son!"

"Murderer! I denounce you!"

A renegade wind howled between them.

"Mao will betray you!"

"It is you who have betrayed us all!"

Chen stepped into the rising wind and raised his arm. Cross tried to pull Song Wei out of Chen's range but Song Wei shook him off.

Cross watched Left-Hand Chen's eyes narrow as he brought his stiff arm level with Song Wei's heart. Song Wei stared furiously at his father, holding his ground.

Chen began to tremble, his face contort.

Then he let the pistol fall from his sleeve to the ground.

The wall of the eye hit: a booming, baffling thunderclap wind, from the west this time, sucking the air from the street, then releasing it back in as destruction. Cross and Song Wei were thrown hard against a building. Objects whirled through the air up Hollywood Road from Man Mo and the Central Market. Things piled against one side of the street now were picked up and tossed back to the other. The New Asia entrance collapsed, bringing down the green pagoda roofs and the carved dragon pillars, sealing off the diners who had fled back inside.

Then Cross saw the horror: the small mandarin head of Chen Po-chi, still fixed in an expression of rage, rose from its body and spun through the air on a corrugated tin siding from the Central Market, as if on a platter, eastward down Hollywood Road, before finally separating itself, hitting the ground, then dancing along in the direction of Ice House Street.

The headless body stood stiffly in the street in front of the New Asia—empty right sleeve still extended, blood shooting from the neck—then finally fell sideways, blown over by the wind.

Song Wei, his eyes wide, whispered some words in Chinese that seemed to Cross to contain no remorse.

The rain came in wide walls, flooding the lanes. The wind screamed. Cross clung to a pillar, calling Su Lin's name, but his voice carried no further than his lips, and no answer came back.

With the first lull, Cross groped through the rubble toward the place where he had heard Su Lin's voice. At the corner, across from the restaurant, he thought he saw her arm extending from a doorway. He worked his way toward it and knelt down to the flooded pavement. The hand gripped his ankle, tripping him. He lay staring into the bloodshot expiring eyes of a Lin Red Pole 49, caught out in the holocaust, a knife raised in his free hand. Cross evaded the lunge. The Red Pole's face dropped in the water. Cross pried his ankle free from the frozen fist and got back to his feet.

He stood at the empty, ruined intersection calling for her, prevented from going further by a muddy torrent coursing toward the harbor. A new wind began its low song.

Then he heard her answer from a doorway across the flooded lane.

He waded into the waters, bucking the current. The flood knocked him off his feet and swept him down half a block, finally bringing him close enough to a building on the other side to grab hold. He worked his way brick by brick back up to the intersection.

He staggered to the doorway where she lay semiconscious, still pinned beneath the railing that had fallen upon her legs.

"Is it you?" she whispered.

He worked the metal around until her legs were free.

"Try them," he said.

She moved her legs around until she was sure they still worked. "Peter?" she asked.

He shook his head.

A wind rose again, and more rain. They clung to each other, exhausted, unable to speak.

Finally the blow passed. Then the rain softened and the street became fordable.

A mother with an infant on her back appeared. An old man wandered past picking through refuse.

"Look," Su Lin said.

The trickling remains of the flooding had delivered at her feet a soggy, compacted clump of twigs.

"Father's thousand-dollar swallow's nest," she said.

Cross reached down to pick it up.

"No. Leave it."

They watched it bob off on the waters.

At the top of Ice House Street, amid the typhoon's ruin, Jack Terhune stood pale and ravaged. At his feet was the head of Chen Po-chi.

"So, mandarin," Terhune said softly. "The *yen* sees fit to expel us both."

He looked up. Cross and Su Lin were making their way toward him.

"American!" Terhune called out to Cross, raising his arm in salute.

Epilogue

That spring the opium dealers came to Chiengmai to buy. Talk was spirited, business brisk.

Alec Potter wasn't seen around the hotels, though he was in town; his father had gone to Hong Kong a few weeks before to pick up what remained of him. Alec would never be able to tell him what had happened or why—his speech was slurred, his memory erased—but Eliot Potter was inclined to trace it back to that incident a year ago, the *gong sou* meeting at Old So's. Now Alec sat on the museum steps most of the time, the light gone from his eyes, a brush in his hand, cleaning Sung shards smuggled from a new dig near the border. One Sunday he even came to church for the first time since he'd gone off to Harvard.

Up at the Erawan Hotel bar, a few cocky Green Berets and Company boys in from Saigon were drinking next to the new Chiu Chao bosses from Hong Kong and getting a kick out of old Perigord Trench, Peg the local Brit, who was giving soused oracular pronouncements to anyone who would listen.

"You Yanks will fall, I tell you. You could have had it. But you made a dirty deal with the mud. Just like we did before you. The *yen,* gents. The bloody Milk of Paradise. Lady Morphia. Mark my words. She'll lay you low."

Finally the Berets tired of this and one of them shoved Peg off his stool onto the floor. But as they stalked out, Peg's dire, boozy prophecy followed them into the hot, dusty street like some cloying fever they couldn't quite shake.

Billy Strange got a letter in Stockholm that June that left him so excited he could hardly sleep. At dawn he hitched down to the Malmö ferry and got a ride at the Copenhagen youth hostel with a couple of Danes going all the way to Paris.

On a clear morning they came in at the Gare de l'Est on the train from Moscow. The three of them exchanged ecstatic hugs on the platform until their breath was gone.

Cross had gained back some pounds, and Su Lin looked radiant. Billy had a hotel for them, but Cross seemed to have his heart fixed upon one on Rue Git le Coeur where he had stayed before.

Billy stayed on a few days; it seemed they'd never run out of things to talk about. Of course Billy wanted to know how they'd gotten out of Hong Kong. Peking and the British Embassy had arranged it. Whitehall provided false documentation; a Chinese prisoner was exchanged. It was all done quietly, without the knowledge of the Americans. They were taken to the Shum Chun border and put on a train to Canton. From there they were routed north to Peking, then across the border to the Trans-Siberian Railway and on through Moscow to Paris, haven of exiles, and the city where Cross's adventures had begun a year earlier.

Billy learned that Terhune, attempting to get free of the drug again, had returned to Kyoto. Song Wei had apparently gone underground after playing his role in Cross and Su Lin's escape.

As for little Fook, his body was never found. Billy proposed the oddly comforting idea that he might still be alive in the Walled City, chasing the dragon. They toasted to that.

Then it was Billy's turn to explain his own Hong Kong exit, and the narrow fresh scar on his lip. He told them how after some unfriendly persuasion at the Tsimshatsui Station he was let go, as there were no charges; they gave him twenty-four hours to clear out, which was just what Billy had in mind. He was aboard the first plane to leave Kai Tak after Typhoon Lulu.

When Su Lin asked about Terhune's journals, Billy materialized them out of his rucksack; he'd providently mailed them to himself in Stockholm that typhoon day before the cops came to the YMCA. He offered them to Su Lin to give back to Terhune, but it seemed Terhune didn't want them anymore. The old scholar was loudly declaring opium a closed book, a riddle that no longer ruled him, and she was to do with them what she wished. Billy kept the journals.

Then they told Billy the news: Su Lin was pregnant.

Before he left Paris, Billy got them in touch with some people in the Movement.

Early the next year Su Lin and Cross had a child; they named her May. Cross was back at the clinic at Neuilly with Vietnamese orphans, who were flooding in. That fall Su Lin had a small show of watercolors in a gallery on Rue de Seine.

In the years that followed, Cross, Su Lin, Billy and those of like mind worked from Europe, editing newsletters, lobbying Washington, counseling draft resisters and defectors, trying to get information out and bring pressure to bear. It was hard. American intelligence was at the height of its power and held all the cards. Privately they tried to disseminate facts about the politics of opium; but as Terhune had learned long ago, the subject possessed a disconcerting invisibility. Nobody wanted to know. Only they, it seemed at times, knew what the coming decades had in store.

The "Lin Snafu," as the New Asia incident came to be known in the Crown Colony's back rooms, had actually brought Peking, Hong Kong, London, and Washington closer. The drug trade quickly reorganized itself under the banner of the four remaining Chiu Chao families, supported tacitly by the Hong Kong Crown Bank and the laissez-faire cooperation of the Americans. Peking, wary of growing North Vietnamese power and in need of money, worked out an interim arrangement with both London and Washington. Franco Termini's deal with Chen Po-chi stood; the Mafia worked its way back into the trade, diversifying into other drugs as well, joining the Queen of Drugs to its jacks and spades: cocaine, hashish, marijuana.

By the end of the decade there were twenty-two heroin labs along the Mekong. Even as U.S. troops came home addicted, the Golden Crescent fields were being resurrected; opiate production spiraled to two thousand tons, an estimated $600 billion a year at street level, as the desperate rationale of anti-Communism drove America on into its night, embedding the drug economy deep in the nation's flesh.

In 1967 Cross came across an obituary for John Quincy Adams Terhune—expatriate Chinese scholar, teacher, and poet—in an Asian affairs quarterly. Apparently he had died in a high-class Hong Kong den, having returned to the drug at the end. Though saddened by the news, Cross was pleased to note that Terhune had lived to see his position as a Sinologue secure at last. In 1966 the government of China had invited Terhune to come for a state visit, and personally escorted him to the town of Hang-Chou, where he reportedly wept publicly. Upon his death the Boston Museum purchased his papers— everything but the journals, of course—for their collection of Orientalia. Included were love poems, written later in life, to a woman whose identity was not known, only her initials: W. L.

A rumor continued to circulate about Harry Lin, that he was still alive in China. Just in case, Su Lin sent him a seventy-fifth birthday card to Peking in care of the Hong Kong Trade Mission.

Tony Cohan was born in New York and grew up in California. He has lived in Europe, North Africa, and Japan. He is also a musician, a composer, and a lyricist whose work can be heard on numerous albums and in films. He presently lives in California with his wife, Masako, a painter.

fiction, Hardback

11